ONCE BITTEN, TWICE SPY

ONCE BITTEN, TWICE SPY

A SOLARPUNK FANTASY

SKYLAR ANTHONY

ISBN: 979-8-218-82715-1 (Paperback)

The story, all names, characters, and incidents portrayed in this production are fictitious. No identification with actual persons (living or deceased), places, buildings, and products is intended or should be inferred.

Cover design by Skylar and Wynn Anthony.

First edition 2025

DEDICATION

For my wife, who never gave up on me.
For my kids, who are a constant inspiration.
For my friends, who knew I could do it.
For the writers and raconteurs, who helped along the way.
For you, for giving me a chance.

A WARNING ON CONTENT

Once Bitten, Twice Spy is a high-intensity romp full of deadly criminals, fatal traps, and general mayhem. The story has multiple scenes of sci-fi fantasy action, complete with physical and magical brutality, weapon use, lipstick-shaped gun violence, dismemberment, homicidal house plants, bombing, medical trauma references, torture, murder, and attempted murder. The narrative includes triggers for various phobias, including blood, needles, snakes, spiders, and taking a book from a library without checking it out first.

The novel also deals with several serious issues, including references to off-page physical and emotional abuse, child abuse, and bullying, as well as cult recovery, anxiety, depression, hallucinations, CPTSD, hospitalization, and death.

If you're a fan of such things, buckle up for the heist of your life. Welcome to the planet of Vale!

PART 1

THE LORATHAR JOB

i dreamt I walked for days
through fields of lorathar
white petals cover all
turned pink in morning's glow

as pale as my skin's blanch
at winds that push me back
a memory tidal wave
an avalanche of snow

the scent is cloying sweet
it buries me in Past
my vision's covered now
i cannot breathe below
　　　　　　—*The Journal of Taylor Grey*

CASTLE CORVANE

It would be easy to believe the charm of Vale in the evening. The sinister beauty pulls at the edges of my resolve, tempting me to skip this craziness and grab a tea from one of the shops lining the verdant greenways. Bulbous living pods grow out of the nearby buildings like mushrooms from a tree, proclaiming that all is perfect here. They cast an alluring glow on the surroundings, lost on me as I creep in the darkness. I avoid the intricately woven lamps that illuminate the greenway, keeping to the shadows I call home.

My comm buzzes in my pocket. Slowing, I check for listening pointed ears, but there aren't many elves on the lush path this time of night. The screen flashes Kairo's name. "What?" I hiss in Hitari, the rare native tongue of my bat-winged fence. Call me paranoid for using a language few off Kairo's reclusive homeworld speak, but I can't be too careful. Not with what I'm planning.

I slide into the dark hollow of a tree as the voice of my surrogate older brother comes over my comm unit. *"Hey kid. Can you see the house?"*

"Not there yet. What do you need?" The hairs on my neck stand on end as I watch sleek stryders hover over the grassy street between the towering vine-covered buildings, my nerves awash in a comfortable, familiar sort of paranoia.

"Just checking on you. You really want to do this?"

I chuff out an annoyed laugh. "Kai, I don't have time for your mother-hen shit right now. I'm fine. I know it's risky—"

"Risky? Taylor, this is Ryland Corvane we're talking about. No one fucks

with Corvane. He's the biggest smuggler in three systems, and a vindictive bastard at that. And you're about to break into his house."

I groan, banging the back of my head against the tree. "This was your idea, Kai."

I can hear the Hitari ruffling his large, leathery wings in annoyance. *"No, you asked if I knew where you could score big quick. I said no."* There's a pause before he adds begrudgingly, *"I mean, sure. I mentioned the rumor-mill was wild about Corvane trying to move some high-value shit off-world, but I didn't think you were actually crazy enough to steal from the man. After what happened—"*

My annoyance flares in time with my cheeks. "After what happened, I need off this planet. They'll *know* I'm here, Kai. They'll fucking know!"

There's a long pause on the line before he asks in a quieter tone, *"Did you at least wear your glamour bracelet?"*

I step away from the tree, starting to move. "The glamour you've enchanted into it can't move as fast as I can. It keeps blurring. If you'd come with me—"

Kairo grumbles, "I'm a fence. That's not how it works. If word gets out that I'm running my own jobs, my vendors will dry up fast."

"Well then, fix the bracelet." He curses, but I override him. "Look, Kairo, I've got this. It's a simple in and out. I know the risk, but with what your buyer is paying, I'll finally be able to afford the documentation to—"

"*...run off and leave me.*" I think he means it as a joke, but I don't miss the bitter edge. Which is pretty rich, given he's the one who connected me with the buyer. What'd he think I'd do with a score this big? Getting travel documentation is difficult—and expensive—when you've never officially existed.

I sigh internally. He means well, but I need to do this. And he knows it. A few months ago, I screwed up on a job. Did the one thing I swore I'd never do.

I got caught. On camera.

Sure, I saved that guard's life, but at what cost? That's Kairo's point, because he knows who's after me. If something were to go wrong... if I drew the Initiative's attention...

The thought ramps up my paranoia. I can almost feel the press of the needle on my neck. The phantom scent of lorathar blossom almost overwhelms me, but I'm at least mostly certain it's in my head.

Softening my tone to keep the fear out of my voice, I reply, "Look, I promise I'll be careful. I'll message you after it's done. And then I'll stop by tomorrow and drop it off. Okay?" Glancing down the street, I add, "Look, I've got to go, or I'll miss my window. Love you."

"*Love you,*" he grumbles before clicking off.

I move faster, and a couple of green-skinned elvish ladies turn in my direction. They're at least a century and a half old, their mostly silver hair billowing in the evening breeze. One lady's dark plum-colored eyes meet mine, widening as she notices my slightly peaked ears standing out so incongruously from my red hair and pale human skin. With some rushed comments to her pointy-eared companion, they hurry to the other side of the grassy street.

Fuck. Maybe Kairo was right about the glamour bracelet. Enchanted with Kairo's rare Hitari light magic, it hides my pointed ears and other features that mark me as genetically enhanced—something that elves, with all their love for "natural balance," cannot stand and would definitely remember later.

You know, if being questioned about a break-in or something.

Maybe I should get it. I could come another day when I'm—

A large, old house filters into view.

As promised, the compound is creepy as hell. Tall spires loom like dead oaks in the darkness beyond the overgrown dwarven-made stone wall. Small, wide shadows move along the top, their strange insectoid shapes hard to make out in the mist and low light. Wind rustles like the whisper of ghosts, and I can barely hear the clicking of the guards' beetle feet on the stones.

Well, shit. Ryland Corvane increased his protection.

More dwarven guards stand at street level, never straying far from the small gate. The dwarves' burgundy exoskeletons are thrown into strange hues by garish neon strips lining the gate to Corvane's compound. It's the notorious smuggler's "human touch" to the vintage elvish décor, as out of place here as he is. The guards' small, scaly mouths are fixed in thin, firm lines as their large compound eyes survey the narrow street, blaster rifles at the ready.

I quickly count. Four dwarves on the roof. Two by the gate. Twice as many that I can't see. That's... a lot. Maybe those rumors were true. If he's moving it, I'll have to do this tonight. Because one thing isn't just rumor: Corvane owns some of the rarest items in the quadrant.

One of which I'm here to steal.

Staying in darkness, I slip across to the neighboring apartment building. Once out of the sight of the guards, I prepare myself and leap up to the second-story balcony some twenty feet above me. Scrambling over the magically wrought wooden railing, I dart silently inside the vacant loft.

The interior is characteristically elvish, with vines, trees, and other touches of vegetation throughout. However, without elves' magic to keep it in check, the plant life has gotten out of control, covering even the floors and counters. And beneath it all, the potent scent of lorathar blossom, the sweet stench of it—and the rush of terror it brings—almost debilitates me. With a huge, shaky breath, I push away memories of black claws and loaded needles to run forward. I sprint across the abandoned great room, swatting away vines to clear a small creek. I'm almost to the window when… WHAM!

My feet go out from under me, my chin colliding with the wooden floor. Everything rings and blurs for a moment. What the hell happened to—

I groan. A long root is twisted around my ankle. The tendril, which is slowly winding up my leg, is coming from a large potted plant near the center of the room. Rummaging in my belt for my blaster, I duck as a second root swipes at my head. A freaking Gruundlith security plant?! Damn elves fucking everything up when they aren't even here!

"Okay, there's no time for overambitious houseplants right now."

I blast the root at my ankle, severing it just as another smacks me upside the head. "Gods, I hate these things." I grunt, trying to kick off more roots twirling around my ankles. With my free hand, I bat away two others, reaching for my belt pack as I fire wildly at anything that gets too close. Fingers fumbling blindly over various shapes, I finally pull out a small vial and toss it at the enchanted plant. With a tinkling of glass, the vial shatters in a splattering of greenish liquid. After a few final tense moments, the vines slowly disintegrate. I kick away dust and splinters of browned vines, muttering to myself.

Elves and their nature magic. Like Vale itself, it's equal parts beautiful and deadly. Thankfully, the chemical compound in that vial is one of the few things that can actually kill an enchanted security plant—something I discovered after weeks of fiddling around with human-made fertilizer that was banned because it wreaks havoc with elvish enchantments.

At least it wasn't an entire grid of them. Those things are almost insurmountable.

Cursing the delay, I hurry to the window and look over at Corvane's villa. The wall's forty feet away. Only a dwarf could make that leap.

I tense at the faint rippling of the air above the wall, a reminder of my insanity. The anti-flying enchantment prevents infiltration from above, keeping out Hitari and other winged races. A three-foot gap above the ledge is the wall's only weak point. It's barely wide enough for a dwarven guard to shoot someone on the street.

To get inside, I need to fly horizontally across the gap and not touch the enchanted air above or the magicked vines on the wall below. And I'll need to do it all in about fifteen seconds if I want to stay out of sight.

This is going to be tight.

I pause, watching the guards, the twitching, half-dead plant, and my watch. The longer I wait, the farther the gap seems to grow. "Okay. Maybe I really am crazy," I mutter as I pull the ski mask over my head, hiding my red curls. I give a distracted look around the street, convinced there'll be another elf with a vidcorder filming me again.

Shots of that security guard falling from a tenth-floor window, of him landing on a cushion of air five feet off the ground and the blurry human girl with her hand raised and blood running from her nose, have been circulating on the darknet for weeks, even after all traces of the vid were mysteriously wiped everywhere else. The vid's disappearance, as much as anything, is proof they saw it. That they know.

After an interminable thirty seconds, the guard change happens, leaving a momentary gap in defenses. With a running start, I leap across the space, laying myself flat as an arrow. The wind whips as I soar, my enhanced strength taking me half the way. Now it's time for the one thing that makes me truly unique. That made me a viral obsession, a debunked net rumor, and an abomination that certain parties would pay anything to possess.

It's time for magic.

With a burst of air, I push my body up and forward. I skim across the cushion of air, landing with a roll on the parapet. Not stopping, I leap over the side and into the courtyard twenty-five feet below.

My breath comes in ragged gasps that I try to silence. Light shines from above, roving across the courtyard. I dive under a bench, pulling myself tight underneath the wooden seat. After a second, the light goes off, and the clicking footsteps of the Zeridian guard continue their rhythmic pace.

I made it. I can't believe I actually fucking made it! While I'm comfortable using magic, I've only managed that harebrained stunt a handful of times.

Staying in the shadows, I race along the edge of the courtyard to a large door on one side. From my pocket, I pull out the item that's key (pun intended) to this entire operation: Liam Goran's security card, magically lifted from the control engineer's pocket while flirting with the jackass at the local bar.

The door beeps and then opens as I press Goran's ID to the panel, allowing me entry to the impenetrable manor.

It takes a good four minutes to make my way to Corvane's office, winding through wood-lined corridors and slipping along long-forgotten passageways that took weeks of research to uncover. The tight, labyrinthine design is quintessentially Valen, and it takes too fucking long to navigate. The extra guards don't help either.

Finally, I locate the room I've been mapping out using hearsay and dubious schematics. Ryland Corvane's private study.

Unlike the rest of the house, the office is full-on Union chic. It's like Corvane transported the whole thing up en masse from one of the Union's human-populated planets. Maybe he did. The aesthetic is exactly what you'd expect from a man like Corvane. Books, antiques, and other odd items give the only decoration in the sparse, almost sterile room, but no concept ties the trinkets together. There's no sense of taste or preference beyond what is expensive.

Hidden cove lighting gives a soft blue hue to each over-polished metal shelf or counter. Large screens counterbalance the collectibles, with the shelves oriented just so. It's obvious what these objects are to Corvane. They're trophies. Valuable ones. He's quite a collector.

Resting on the corner of Corvane's glossy black desk is an ornate wooden lamp, emitting an eerie, otherworldly glow. The desk's sharp Union lines and harsh crimson edge lighting contrast uncomfortably with the yellow-green hue of the elf-made lamp. I almost get lost in the interwoven branches that surround the lamp's shining dwarven crystal housing a luminescent yellow liquid, the source for the strange light.

From my research, I knew what to expect, but I'm still breathless. The elves' Valen Republic and the dwarven Kingdom of Zeridia may have a tenuous peace, but enchanted dwarven crystal has been illegal in the Republic for a millennium. Any combination of elvish and dwarven craftsmanship in a single item is priceless for collectors. But this artifact is… *more*. I doubt Corvane even realizes the true extent of what he has here.

My grin widens at the soft chartreuse hue. This is it. My shot off this fucking planet. This haul will buy fake papers to ditch the Initiative for good—and these awful memories.

The relic is surprisingly heavy. The luminescent liquid sloshes inside as I pick it up, sending shadows dancing around the room in waves. It reminds me of a powerseed, the unique biotech power source that forces the Zeridians and the human Union of Independent Planets to play nice with the Valen Republic. But this isn't tech.

It's special.

The doors open with a whoosh. In walks Ryland Corvane, two bug-like Zeridian guards lurking behind his shoulders. The burly, slightly pudgy man is swaying, clearly returning from some fancy party. He barely fits into his Union-style suit, and he seems ready to be rid of it. The collar and tie are already undone, the skin bulge of his biotech interface peeking through on his neck.

His eyes widen as they land on me, before he masks his surprise. "Well, this is unexpected." Seeming almost bored, he pulls a blaster from his jacket and motions for me to pull off my mask.

Shit. Kairo was right, damn him. I should have brought the bracelet. Shit. Shit. Shit.

Slowly, I peel the ski mask off my head, freeing my distinctive fiery locks. Putting on my best unimpressed smirk, I sigh, "I'm not surprised you don't expect to find women in your home, Corvane."

The two guards extend their stingers, the thick, eighteen-inch spikes glistening with paralytic neurotoxin (okay, maybe the glistening part is my imagination). "Cute," Corvane sneers.

"Thanks. Not interested."

He chuckles. "That's too bad. Now, tell me about yourself. But first, put the item on the table."

"What? This?" I swing the lamp about, sending spirals of light across Corvane's collection.

The smuggler's eyes widen, hand outstretched but unable to grab it from his distance. "Do you know what that's worth?" The guards move a step closer, nearly flanking Corvane but leaving him in the lead. I'm close enough now to see the intricate carvings on their exoskeletons blending with the range of scratches and dents on their large chests.

"No." I cock my head as if considering. "But could you tell me? I worry my fence is screwing me on this deal. I bet it commands a steeper price than I'm getting for it."

"Oh, trust me. You're screwed already. Because the only one commanding anything here is me. Commanding your death." Corvane grins again, and it's anything but pleasant.

I grin back, because I got him to say, "Command."

"If it's so valuable, I'm surprised you're selling it. The value of this collection is…" I whistle. "If I had more time, I'd steal more, honestly." Taunting this prick is my favorite part of this backup plan.

Corvane scowls, stepping forward slightly. "You arrogant bitch. You think you can steal from *me*? Do you have any idea who I am? I'm Ryland Fucking Corvane."

The two guards raise their blasters. I grin wider, holding up the bag in front of me like a shield. "Go ahead. Try it."

"No, you fools!" Corvane cries. "Don't shoot!"

Bingo.

Corvane doesn't notice me mirroring his movements. It looks like I'm trying to get away from Corvane and the Zeridian guards, but really, I'm inching closer to the rear wall. Closer to my exit. When I feel the hard surface at my back, I grin again.

"You know, it gets old, pretending to listen to comments from ignorant blowhards like you."

Corvane lunges toward me. I shove against his legs with a wind burst, sending him careening into his guards and toppling the three of them. Pulling out my comm, I press a button and the speaker blasts, *"Ryland Corvane. Command. Open chute."*

Homophones for the win.

Recognizing the audio command, the system opens a hidden access hatch as shots fire wildly in the dark. "I said, don't shoot!" Corvane hollers.

Having no such compunction, I pull out my blaster and send a couple of shots in their direction, trying to keep them back as I head to the trash chute. Thank the gods for Valen design.

The trio tumbles back before a Zeridian sends a chunk of rock hurtling from the stone floor, missing my head by inches. There's a scrabbling, and I can sense a broad figure lurching toward me. Without glancing back, I leap through the narrow hatch headfirst, lamp clutched to my chest as my world becomes the dark abyss of the passage.

2

THE KURO ONI

It's admittedly a little early when I burst through the doors of "Galactic Pages, Rare Finds, & Tech Emporium," but I could barely sleep from the excitement—and the vague fear that Corvane's goons could arrive at any minute. But even for the early hour, Kairo's bookshop is surprisingly empty for a Saturday. The door jingles as I head inside, the familiar homey tinkling the only sound to greet me.

I adjust the large bag on my back and frown. Normally, I'm accosted by Kairo by this point, along with a flood of questions from Frank, part of his halfling staff. Instead, I'm just greeted by the familiar scents of aged paper, wood polish, incense, and old grease. "Kairo!" I call as the door closes. Absentmindedly, I adjust the glamour bracelet. After last night, I'm never leaving without this fucking thing.

It's hard to see in the dense space. Wooden shelves line every surface, proudly displaying old leather-bound tomes, delicate relics, and intricately designed elvish wood art. When Kairo bought the store from a retiring elvish couple, it was a convenient cover to hide his profits and launder money. But now he loves this place.

"Kai?" I sneak along the aisles of books, searching for him amidst the faded blues, greens, and browns of leather covers, hand reaching for my blaster.

"I wouldn't." The cold press of a blaster is the only sign someone is behind me. I raise my arms as a hand reaches to my waist, removing my weapon. A second later, they press some sort of device to my wristband, and I can feel my ears shimmering into view.

"It's her," the voice in my ear says. They tug on my backpack, but I grip the strap, refusing to let go. The relic inside is my ticket off this gods-forsaken rock. This score will cover the forged documents to make me a Union citizen, fund the interstellar flight, and set me up somewhere far from Vale and the Initiative.

"Let go of the artifact, Taylor," the unfamiliar voice hisses, the blaster barrel digging harder into my temple. With one last yank, they pull it from me. I spin, trying to catch them off guard, but they're too quick, whoever they are. A second later, they're out of my grasp, moving faster than I've ever seen.

When I look up, it's clear why. The sleek cat-like Pardusian female cocks her head, her furry, triangular ear flicking distractedly as she points her blaster rifle at me. Beneath the black fur of her shoulder gleams the white skin of a strange brand, a thin C or crescent I don't recognize. Where the hell did she come from?

As if conjured, shapes shimmer into existence throughout the shop. Kairo's light magic. I'd say it was his idea of a prank, except the group is a strange mix of races I've rarely seen before, from a reptilian Caldrake to a couple more feline Pardusians to a crystalline-looking dude who is nearly as tall as an elf and twice as wide. They all have the same sinister brand (the crystal dude's is engraved directly onto his chest). One of the Pardusians, a male with brindle-patterned fur, pulls Kairo into view, a blaster pointed at his head.

Okay, so *not* a prank. Some of Corvane's goons? But how'd they even know about my bracelet, let alone bypass the enchantment?

Despite the situation, my friend and mentor looks unfazed. Kairo's tall, broad-shouldered form and leathery bat-like wings dwarf his feline captor, but he doesn't seem to have fought back—they both seem unharmed. The only signs of irritation are his muscular arms straining against a short-sleeved black t-shirt, snake tattoo dancing as it spirals up his flexing arm and disappears beneath the shirt. Long black hair flops between a pair of short black horns sticking out in four-inch spikes from his temples, and he winks at me.

"Hey kid. We have some guests."

"I can see that. Who—"

"Well, well, well," a voice booms. "Kairo, my boy. It's been a long time."

"What are you doing here, Dad?" Kairo's tone is glacial, his jovial aloofness gone in a second.

"What am I doing here?" the voice echoes from the shelves. "Can't a father come visit his son?"

I gape, frozen in place. Kairo's *father*?! As rare as it is to encounter even one Hitari, I never expected to meet Kairo's father. From the look on Kairo's face, it doesn't seem like I've missed much.

The man looms into view. He's large, like Kairo, with similar keen dark eyes set against hair that's pepper-gray instead of black. Rather than Kairo's fondness for elvish tunics, his broad chest presses against a tight cambric shirt and Union-style suit jacket. The strange half-familiarity unnerves me, like looking through a funhouse mirror.

Kairo scowls at the grinning man. "Don't give me that 'father' shit. You lost the right to use that term long ago. Why are you here?"

Kairo's father's wings billow, knocking over books as he glares into his son's face. A moment later, he retreats, straightening his suit jacket. "Fate, my boy. Fate draws us together again. As I told you it would."

"Fuck fate," Kairo growls. "What do you want?"

"I have a job."

"Great!" Kairo exclaims in false cheer. "Now you aren't a deadbeat dad anymore! Just an asshole. Give Taylor her bag back and get out."

The elder Hitari looks at me apologetically. "He was like this as a boy, too. Always so temperamental."

"Are you seriously going to—"

Kairo's dad holds up a finger, silencing his son. "I have a job. I need someone. Someone good." He glances at me. "And Hikario has blessed you with exactly what I need."

Kairo lurches forward, his captor struggling to hold him in place. "You listen to me, Akio—"

"NEVER—" Kairo's father begins, then pauses. He pulls out a thin blade, the same crescent eclipse gleaming from the handle.

The Pardusian goons press their blaster barrels even harder into our heads. Kairo doesn't even flinch, but his eyes are shuttered as Akio runs the blade slowly along his son's cheek. The tiniest trickle of blood wells at the thin line he traces.

In a voice barely above a whisper, he continues, "You know better than to use that name, boy. Do I need to remind you? Because if I do, it won't be you I use for the lesson. It'll be her."

"Fine," Kairo sighs. I don't know if I am more unnerved by Akio's easy violence or Kairo's sheer lack of concern over it. "But I'll ask again, Mr. Kuro Oni, *sir*. Why are you here? The Eclipse Consortium has an army of talented thieves on call."

Fuck. Kairo's dad is the Kuro Oni? The mysterious and deadly leader of the Eclipse Consortium? His dad's practically the bogeyman, even amongst thieves, and he's giving me shit for stealing from Corvane?! How could he not tell me this? The Eclipse Consortium is one of the most dangerous bands of mercenaries and criminals-for-hire in the galaxy. They have massive interstellar reach with active operations in over fifteen systems. Have a leader to assassinate? An enemy to bring down? A heist involving a lot of bodies? The Eclipse Consortium is your first choice. Makes Corvane seem a small-time hood. And he's Kairo's *dad*?

And then I get it. The C-shaped brand. It's a crescent. An eclipse.

Akio sighs heavily. "We do. Several, in fact. But despite your selfish desire to take everything personally, this isn't about you."

His slightly feral grin widens as he looks to me. "You've garnered a lot of attention, Taylor, after that jewelry heist. I would fault you for getting caught on camera, but then if that hadn't happened, I wouldn't know you exist. So, as you can see, Hikario's guiding light has drawn us together. And then you stole from *Corvane*? The man's a fool, and a thorn in my side, but bypassing his security alive? Very impressive."

"Thanks?" I reply, bemused.

The Kuro Oni's grin is unwavering. "Allow me to introduce myself, since my son is being so rude not to do so. My name is Akio Ryūkishi, as you now know, thanks to my son's loose tongue. But you will call me the Kuro Oni." His eyes crinkle in menacing amusement at the instinctive fear I feel on my face.

Summoning that inner smartass that gets both into and out of trouble, I manage "You know, no offense, but I'm gonna pass. I don't work for terrorists."

"I'm not a terrorist!" Akio gasps in mock insult. "I mean, I have no issue working for terrorists. I do it all the time. No, I need something only you can retrieve. Do that, and I'll return this." He motions to the relic, the product of the last two years of research—and my best chance off Vale. "Plus documentation to go anywhere in the galaxy. And given I don't see one of these on your neck, I imagine that would be valuable to you." He taps the white, circular bulge of skin covering his biotech interface. "Or I can make you enemy number one wherever you go. It's your choice, really."

Trying to push down the rising panic, I plead, "I don't know what you think you know about me, but—"

"I know everything about you, Taylor Grey," the Kuro Oni breathes. "Genetically enhanced. Daughter of Dr. Audrey Grey, a top scientist for the Lorathar Initiative until her death eleven years ago. Now a notorious thief, viral internet sensation, and, if my sources are correct, my son's chief money maker."

Blood drains from my face, fingers tingling and stomach clenching. "How do you know all this?" But I know the answer. That damn video. But even so, how'd he learn about my mom, about the organization she worked for? If the Kuro Oni knows who I am…

I need to get the hell off Vale.

"I know many things. Maybe I'll tell you some if you finish this job for me."

Bastard. He knows the right carrot to dangle.

"Oh, and one more thing." The Kuro Oni grins like a kid with a secret. "The target. It's a secure laboratory in Aelfswelth Forest. One you might be familiar with." My eyes widen, the walls feeling too close, everything too tight. I haven't been to the laboratory since my mom died. If the target is The Initiative… "Perhaps it's making sense now why I chose you for this?"

Kairo's wings flare, and there's a coinciding flash of light. "Absolutely the fuck not."

I swallow the boulder in my throat, then hold up a hand, cutting Kairo off. If it gets me off Vale, gets me the documents I need? Maybe the only way forward is back. "What's the job?"

"Just a crate of powerseeds."

Kairo stares at his father in confusion. "Why?"

Powerseeds are proprietary elvish biotech and the most efficient power source in the galaxy. Only the Valen can produce it, with antitheft enchantments to prevent rogue elves from duplicating it. This makes powerseeds extremely valuable. Still, they aren't difficult to get legally, and stealing a crate of them would hardly be earth-shattering.

The Kuro Oni laughs. "These seeds are… special. Next generation, you see. And because they're still in development, the usual magical copy protections aren't in place yet."

I push past the lingering panic. The take. Remember the take. Face this, and I'm gone for good. He said he could get me enough money to buy passage anywhere I wanted.

This is my last chance. And I'm running out of time.

"The seeds are… uh, it's what my mom and Dr. Lirael were working on. More than next-gen. They're next-gen after next-gen, from what little I remember. And if there's no copy protection…" The realization focuses me, helps override the dread. "You'd need a Valen's help with the magic, but in theory… you could duplicate them."

The Kuro Oni nods. Powerseeds are the key to all elvish tech (and power sources for tech throughout the galaxy). Their manufacture is one of the most closely guarded industrial secrets ever. If someone else could reverse engineer seeds? I couldn't imagine the impact.

"That's insane," Kairo gasps. "You're… do you know the heat that would bring?"

"Hikario rewards the bold," the Kuro Oni says airily. "Though, speaking of that. I'll be honest. This will be difficult. The place is heavily guarded."

"Doesn't matter," Kairo grunts, crossing his arms. "She's not doing it."

Doesn't he understand? Even now, after all this? They know. I've got to get out. There's no time to play it safe. Keeping my eyes on the Kuro Oni and not his son, I say, "I'll do it."

Kairo makes some sort of noise that I ignore.

"But I'm not killing anyone."

The Eclipse Consortium may have a certain… reputation, but I'm not like them. I may blame the Initiative for what happened to my mom, but I'm a thief. Not a killer. I refuse to be.

Akio waves this off. "Deal with it how you like. There's also a Gruundlith defense grid, biometric access points, and probably some nasty surprises to boot. But I'm sure you'll do fine."

I remain silent, but repress my concern about the Gruundlith grid. I'm gonna need more VerdantBoost.

"Now, to get the seeds, you'll need a Valen biometric key," Akio continues. "It's a small vial with an elvish biosensor on it. Certain parts of the facility, including the vault itself, respond only to the unique energy signature of the new enhanced seeds. You'll need the key to access the secure parts of the facility."

Kairo shoves off the Pardusian guard, walking over to lean against a bookshelf, which creaks at his weight. "How do we get that?"

"There's a party in a week. The Liraels host it once a year to gain support from affluent government officials. Luckily, you're invited. You may want to wear a disguise. Or at least cover the hair and ears." He chuckles darkly at the flush on my neck at his words. "I'll message you the details. Now, don't forget. We need a full crate. And their records."

I gape at him. "How the hell am I—"

Akio checks his nails. "I'm sure you'll figure something out."

"Taylor," Kairo says in a low tone. "You can't—"

I turn to the man who kept me alive and hidden for years. I see the panic there that I'm trying so hard to hide within myself. "I don't think he's really giving us a choice, Kai."

His father gives a smile that sends ice down my spine. "Get me my seeds, and you'll get what's coming to you. I'll enjoy collaborating with the two of you. Kairo, you'll handle the transfer, yes?"

Kairo frowns, but nods.

"Excellent. Now, I need this done soon. Is that understood? Don't make me wait."

Without even a word of farewell to his son, the Kuro Oni shuffles his shoulders, glamouring his wings away as he heads to the door.

3

A WALK IN THE PARK

Children laugh and bedraggled parents shout in the cultivated grove, a perfect backdrop for my nerves. I sit in the corner of the park on a bench made from a magically flattened tree root, the scratching of my pen filling the air as I write in my black notebook. The words come in bursts, more pressure valve than poetry. But the journal's not working today.

So I stop writing. And watch.

I survey the sea of youth for a bit, zeroing in on the few breaks in the tide of green-skinned Valen. There are a few tan and brown-skinned humans, a couple of golden-furred Pardusian pups, and even one small, skittering Zeridian playing by themselves in a corner.

I notice one dark-skinned human girl by a small sliding bush, black braids pressed against the ladder branches. A Valen boy is towering over her, and while I can't hear what he's saying, I can guess from the tears in the girl's eyes.

I move to stand and intervene when two human boys come to her aid, both as tall as the Valen and twice as wide. One is pale, with long blond hair that gets into his eyes, while the other has dark skin like the girl and shorn black hair. The blond kid yanks the Valen boy away from the girl, and I sag in relief.

Then I hear the Valen snarl.

I'm rooted to the spot as if a tree grew over and bound me here. This is bad. The Valen crouches, hands extended at his sides. The human boys don't notice the glint of black claws, too busy pressing the advantage they foolishly think they have.

"Get back," I try, but I can barely hear myself over the din of children.

Quicker than I can track it, the Valen swipes, and the blond boy screams.

The park erupts, parents rushing over to break up the fight. The Valen boy's parents carry him bodily from the park as he growls and swipes.

"Here," one of the Valen males says to the human boy's parents. "I can heal him. Let me—"

"Stay the fuck back!" the boy's father snaps. "Your kind has done enough."

"My kind?" the man huffs indignantly. "Now, see here, you—"

I turn back to my notebook, tuning out the argument as things devolve further.

I'm frozen, awash in thoughts that blur the then and now. I remember Phina grabbing me roughly by the arm, extending her talons so they dig deep into my skin. I feel the warm trickle of blood running down my elbows, pooling in the grass.

The elf girl's words echo from years past, as real as if she were standing next to me. "*Leave us alone, you geneblight freak. We're never going to play with you, even if you weren't a sniveling little trashblood geneblight. Got it?*"

Phina always got away with it. When someone would come, she'd retract her claws, and then roughly heal the wounds in a spike of pain. Plaster that damn pointy girlish grin and the adults would believe her.

Or they knew and didn't care. They called me geneblight, too.

It's why I need to go. My kind isn't welcome here.

"What the hell did I miss?" Kairo asks from behind me, surveying the bedlam. I turn to find him carrying two cups of coffee and a brown paper bag, eyes wide at the scene. I'm not surprised he found me here. There are other parks closer to my apartment, but this one, near Kairo's shop, still feels like home.

"Just the typical Valen bullshit." I set the notebook down and reach for a coffee. "Some elf kid got pushed and went feral. Slashed a human boy in the face."

Kairo comes over to the bench and picks up the journal. Moving it to the side without comment, he sits next to me and watches the lingering commotion. After some bickering, it appears the father finally let the Valen close the boy's wounds. "Shit," Kairo mutters. "Don't fuck with the Valen."

I shudder. It's a lesson I learned early. And have the scars to prove it.

Slipping into Hitari, I say quietly, "That's why I have to leave, Kai. It's why I have to do this." Feeling jittery, I stand and begin a lap around the outer edge of the park, weaving between trees and parting a path through the long grass.

Kairo falls in step with me. The din lessens with the fleeing crowd of parents. "Do you, though?" he replies, also in Hitari. With his kind incredibly rare off their homeworld of Kagēkami, few speak the ancestral language. It makes it the perfect cover. "We can figure something else out. I can try to improve the glamour bracelets, or maybe it's time to actually have a genetic retyping procedure and be done with it."

"People die from those procedures, Kai," I sigh. "And I like my face. I don't want a new one."

Kairo picks up a stray stick and chucks it. "I know. It's just… I worked so hard to keep you away from people like my father. You don't understand how dangerous he is, Taylor. He—"

"I know, Kai."

"No, you really don't." His voice is barely above a whisper. There's a faint shimmering in the air, his wings flickering briefly into view before they vanish again.

I move past his large, invisible wing to put a hand on one heaving shoulder, forcing him to a stop. He stares at a hedge of bushes as if his glare could somehow set fire to it. His breaths come in quick, low gasps as if each one is a struggle.

"It's fine," I say. "I'm fine. You're fine. We have a plan. We get it done and then we're out." Maybe if I say it enough, I can will it true.

"I hate him."

"I know," I say, rubbing a rippling shoulder. "And if there's another option—"

"No," he says, shaking his head. "You made the right call. He didn't really give us a choice. I'm just worried about you. You spent most of your life hiding from these people. The Initiative may not know you're still alive, but if they do—"

"They'll want their prized lab rat back," I say, running a hand through a nearby bush. "I'm aware. Don't you think I know that?"

Kairo grabs my arm and slowly turns me to him. Holding my hand as if he could somehow will sense into me by sheer touch, he says, "What if someone recognizes you at this party? Or at the lab? You could be running right into their clutches again. Will you be alright returning to that hellhole?"

I raise a single shoulder. "I'll be fine."

Kairo scowls. "Don't give me that brave-girl shit. Serious answer. I still remember you waking up screaming the first year."

I don't reply right away. "It wasn't just the first year. I learned to be quieter so I wouldn't wake you."

"Taylor—"

"I'll be okay. It'll be... I know it will be hard. But I know how to keep hidden, and I've faced worse things than my own fucking memories. I'll be fine—if you can find a solution to your glamour bracelets. They can't respond as fast as you can. If you're not there, I need the glamour to move faster."

"I told you: an enchanted object can only hold so much power without a strongly magical source to preserve the enchantment. And I don't think you have the funds for an arcane crystal. If you want it to work for longer than a few minutes, it's a tradeoff of speed and light resistance. I have something for you that can move a small glamour as quickly as you do, but it'll only work in low light. Otherwise, they'll see through it. Here."

He hands me the paper bag, and I look inside, noting the distinct glint of lab-grown jewels. "A mask?"

"I spent the last four days working on it. The party's a masquerade." Kairo grins for a moment, but then it falls. "Look Taylor. I know you'll get it done. Just be careful, don't interact with those idiots, and... don't show off too much, okay? The last thing I want is you on my dad's radar. If he's involved, there's some nasty shit going on. And he won't want it to be only one time. Particularly if you're *too* good."

"So, survive, but otherwise half-ass it."

"Look at that butt." He motions to my backside, which the tan pants I'm wearing are trying and failing to accentuate. "Everything you do is only *half*-assed."

"Bastard!" I say, hitting him in his too-muscular shoulder. "Well, disparaging remarks about my ass aside, I promise to be careful and not do anything *too* stupid."

Kairo scowls, but then starts walking again, weeds crunching under his feet. "I'll believe that when I see it. Don't risk everything for one score, even if it seems like it's the last one."

"It *is* the last one," I insist, putting an arm around Kairo's middle as we finish the stroll.

That coaxes a begrudging smile. "Don't forget it. We get this done, and then you're out. And I'm out too."

"You sure?" I ask dubiously, motioning to the bookstore out of sight down the greenway. Kairo talked about getting out, but no score's been big enough.

"Yeah," he says, as if reading my mind. "I fought too hard to get out. My dad won't fuck this up now. If he's sniffing around on Vale, that's it. He and his 'destiny' can go to hell. Time to take the shop legit. No more fencing or money laundering. Give Frank and Emma a safer place to work."

I think of Kairo's twin halfling employees and smile.

Kairo hesitates before adding, "And hell, maybe you can too, wherever you end up. Go to college somewhere. Learn a skill. Do whatever things a normal twenty-two-year-old human girl does."

"Yeah," I say, because I can't think of any other reply. "And what exactly is that? Honestly, I've got no clue what normal human girls do."

That finally coaxes a smile out of Kairo. "I can see your point," he admits. "But maybe find something with a longer life expectancy?"

I don't respond. I should say yes, but the idea of quitting squirms inside of me. Pushing that aside, I grin. "So… one more score?"

He nods as we reach the end of the park loop. "One more score." He motions toward his bookstore. "Want to come check out my latest batch? I got this Zeridian romance that seems right up your alley. Very steamy. It's two male military officers from rival clans that—"

"Not today." I hold up my journal as an explanation. "Need to clear my head first."

Kairo's smile softens. "Suit yourself. Catch you later."

I watch Kairo leave before turning back to the journal. All the emotions roil again, clogged in my distracted brain.

In jagged writing, I scrawl across the page, "FUCK NORMAL." I close the notebook with a small smile and survey the joyful chaos of the park, finding peace in the noise.

4

MEET NOT-SO-CUTE

If there's one thing I can rely on in this business, it's that men are fucking creeps.

I do a sweep of Dr. Thalion Lirael's extensive, half-lit garden, the masked partygoers eyeing me like a piece of meat. If they knew I was enhanced, the Valen at this kitschy masquerade wouldn't be so eager. But with a blond wig, Kairo's jewel-encrusted mask, and a carefully chosen silver dress that shows off quite a bit of leg… even the elvish men are looking a little thirsty.

Let's hope the same goes for my mark.

By the way, where the hell is he? Despite the round paper lanterns hanging strategically from various walls and branches, it's hard to see anyone. Small clusters of candles flicker sporadically in various corners, giving everyone ghoulishly up-lit shadows.

Finally, I spot Eilrach Feylon standing with a couple of other tall Valen sipping ice wine. A spike of fear twists and squirms. Besides Dr. Lirael, Eilrach seems the sole Lorathar Initiative representative here. The Initiative is a secret operation dedicated to furthering some dubiously legal scientific advancements, particularly ones that would violate the Valen Republic's strict environmental ethics laws. So schmoozing is required.

That's apparently Eilrach's job at the Initiative, and one that he does well. Eilrach grew up at the lab like I did, but from what I remember (and what little I could dig up), he doesn't have his scientist father's gifting. Instead, he seems to be one of the few semi-public faces in the covert organization.

Eilrach turns finally, revealing his face. His elegant mask is white and… vaguely fluffy? It looks to be covered in a sort of white plumage, or… no. It's lorathar blossom.

Panic sweeps over me again. What the hell am I doing? I need to get out of here. Am I crazy? They'll see me. Recognize me.

Pain sears across my skin as… no. It's not there. It's your imagination, Taylor. It's been eleven years. You're fine. There are no claws digging in, no hand around my neck. I'm fine. I'm a fucking badass, and they can't hurt me.

They'll never hurt me again.

With a flip of my fake blond hair, I slip back into character: the spoiled political debutante. I don't want to know how the Kuro Oni arranged for me to pose as the daughter of some politician from the Union of Independent Planets—or what they did with the real Sarah Ableton. As long as I act slightly tipsy and sway my hips enough that even my too-muscular, not curvy enough frame draws men's eyes, I'll be fine.

Proving my point, Eilrach looks up across the mass of Valen, humans, and others in attendance. His dark brown eyes meet mine, and they narrow hungrily behind the mask. A smirk plays on his green lips, revealing a hint of pointed teeth. I freeze like a sage hare staring down a silberwolf. But there's no flash of recognition. The predatory look is horny, not sadistic.

Gods, now I can't tell if I'm scared or just nauseous.

Suppressing both emotions, I walk up to the tall Valen and smile, drawing on my best York twang. "Excuse me." I adjust my silver mask in a way that makes me seem self-conscious. "Where can I find a beer? Or a whiskey? No offense, but this cold wine stuff they serve here is disgusting."

Eilrach smiles without humor, the sharp lines of his elvish face twitching slightly under the floral mask. "Val'Gruunthar ice wine is a delicacy," he chastises, as if at twenty-seven (young for a Valen), he's some connoisseur of finery. "This particular blend has been carefully cultivated with Gruundlith magic for centuries. But…" He shrugs with a familiar condescending laugh that's like claws along my spine. "I know in the human Union you don't serve your wine with ice. In fact, you often serve it at room temperature." He shudders in mock horror.

"So, if you'd prefer, I do have some thundral." He holds out a flask of the smoky liquor, and I feign a sip.

"That's better," I say, handing it back to him. "My hero." I place my palm on his chest, smiling coyly up at him. He stares imperiously down at me from his six-and-a-half-foot height, his cocky grin widening further at my attention. The distraction is all I need. Keeping my hand on his chest for another moment, I reach a hand in and lift the access key from his jacket pocket. Dropping the thin cylindrical device, I pull away, running the hand up to his neck. With a tendril of magic, I catch it on a puff of air. He gives me a wide smile as the biotech key disappears into my small clutch, hidden from sight by our bodies.

That's half of Phase One done.

For a moment, Eilrach frowns, lines creasing his brows. "Have we—"

I reach my hand up to his face, touching my knuckles to his cheek, and his words trail off. The thought of touching him makes my skin crawl, but I push past the urge to pull away. "You know," I say. "You're pretty cute." I trace the back of my hand gingerly across his face, and a strategically sharpened edge of my ring snags his cheek, drawing a thin line of blood.

"Oh, fuck," he says, hunching over.

"Oh my gods," I exclaim. "Let me get you a napkin or—"

"No, thank you," Eilrach says, waving me off, his other hand to his bloody cheek. "You've done enough."

"I'm sorry!" Waving as he walks off, my shoulders finally relax. That was surprisingly satisfying. Suppressing a grin, I cork a small vial of blood magicked from his wound. DNA scanners aren't super accurate (I've fooled them with family members before), so I don't need much.

"You know, I've come to several of Dr. Lirael's parties, and I don't believe I've seen you before."

The silky, polite voice with a distinct tilt sends my heart racing. I turn, suppressing my instinctive dread. Though I know what to expect, this guy is still somehow nothing like what I expected. Sure, I knew he was a Valen male (the accent was a dead giveaway), but he's still the most remarkable male I've ever laid eyes on.

Whoever he is (and I can't believe I'm saying this about a damn *Valen*), this guy is nothing short of gorgeous. He's extremely tall even for an elf, over seven feet, with angular features and a well-trimmed

Union-style suit that hints at the curves of broad shoulders and long, powerful arms. His green elvish skin is on the lighter side, marking him as a city dweller. The soft sage color of his pointed ears stands out against his expertly tousled forest-green hair. He's wearing an intricate mask, no doubt magically grown from eldertree branches. The distinctive silvery bark draws attention to his brilliant amethyst eyes, which are assessing and slightly amused.

It's their crinkling—plus the upturned corner of his perfectly sculpted mouth—that clues me in that I should have responded seconds ago.

"Yeah, normally it's my dad that comes to these things."

The violet-eyed Valen smirks, appearing amused by something. Condescending elvish assholes. "Would you like to dance?"

I do a quick sweep of the space before turning back to him, frowning as one of his thin green eyebrows raises. "No one else is dancing."

He winks conspiratorially. "There's music. Just because everyone else is lame, that doesn't mean we need to be."

Unsure what else to do, I hold out a hand as if I actually want this elf to touch me. After brief consideration, he grins, dimples forming in his tea-green cheeks.

Fuck, the impact of that smile. His long, thick fingers engulf my proffered hand, and my skin's somehow hot and clammy at once. Don't be weird. Don't be weird.

No, Taylor, you moron. This is a Valen elf. There are claws hidden beneath those manicured nails and a carnivore's teeth behind that smile.

The Valen are predators.

With a hand on the small of my back, he asks, "And what's your name?"

"Sarah Ableton." That's my name for the evening, right? He pulls my body to his, and my brain scrambles. Yes. That's the right name. "And you are?"

"…finally not bored," the Valen says with a wink.

My stomach flops as he spins me, the grass crunching lightly under me.

"So, what's a young human woman like yourself doing at a party like this, Sarah Ableton?"

It didn't escape my notice that he never gave his name.

I grin sheepishly. "My dad's an assistant ambassador from Planet York. Normally he attends these things, but he couldn't make it. I don't really know anyone here," I admit, leaning in as if confessing a scandalous secret. "Still, it's a party with free booze. So, naturally, I'm there. Even if it's this cold wine… stuff."

The Valen leans in as well, his voice dropping low enough to send shivers up my spine. "Does this… supposed father know you're pickpocketing?"

I swallow a lump before speaking. "I don't know what you mean." Was my voice even? I can't tell if my voice was even.

The Valen moves closer. Too close. Heat radiates off him, my skin tingling at his nearness.

His grin is predatory. "You had that guy eating out of your hand so well, he didn't even notice. I thought you were making a pass at first. Bet he did too. But then I saw you lift this."

He holds up the key, his frosty smile freezing my insides. "Nice lift. Now spare me the protests of innocence and tell me who the fuck you are."

My heart is pulsing in my throat, but I keep my voice flat. "You first."

He cocks his head before reaching out a hand to cup my cheek. I stiffen, breath shaky as I feel a sharp bite of his claw under my chin, pressing against my throat. Lights pulse and streak across the floor as the music heightens, and his thumb placement, the subtle threat, goes unnoticed in the party's fury.

"Give me a reason not to." His eyes rove over me, searching. Hungry.

The tiniest prickle of pain sparks as his nail bites in. My mind blurs, but I push it back. Push the instinctive dread back.

Don't think of Phina now. Keep your wits. You've got this.

"I… I don't want any trouble. Let's not make a scene, okay? That wouldn't be good for anyone."

He gets it. Mutually assured destruction. Raising a single eyebrow, he slowly lets his thumb drop. A single dimple makes an appearance as the corner of his mouth lifts, his hair glinting in the light like some angelic warrior. My stomach twists as he raises his hand to my mask, lifting it slightly.

My panic doubles impossibly at the sight of his sudden glare. Shit!

The bright lights must be messing with the enchantment on the mask. At the sight of my enhanced ears, his body goes rigid.

He grabs my arm for a moment, those purple eyes electric with fury. Then the look's gone. He lets my wrist go with a bit of a push. Stepping closer to loom over me, he whispers into my ear, "I'll ask you again. Who are you? Why are you here?" With his… all of him so close to me, he doesn't notice the hand reaching into my purse.

His eyes widen at the pressure in his gut, then drop. When he looks back, there's a confused, almost amused look on his face. "Lipstick?"

"Blaster. It was a birthday gift." The best thing Kairo's ever given me, to be honest.

"You're bluffing."

I adjust a small circular knob on the tiny tube and then depress the end. He grunts; the lowest stun setting equals a good punch in the gut. No visible marks, but painful.

The Valen laughs a low, dark chuckle, and it's the scariest thing he's done so far. "You snuck a blaster into a party crawling with top security teams from every political delegation in the quadrant? That's gutsy. Or stupid."

"My specialty."

The Valen scoffs. "Clearly."

I hold out a bored hand. "Key?"

The Valen shakes his head, not moving.

"Don't make me stun you harder. I will, guards be damned." Glowering, he hands over the strange device, which I stuff into my bra, not trusting my handbag. "Now walk away. You stay out of my hair, and I'll stay out of yours. Got it?"

"Fine," the Valen spits out. "But know this. I will find you. And if you go anywhere near those seeds… I'll kill you. And if you hurt anyone—"

"You'll kill me. I get it."

The Valen chuckles again as he steps away, that cool grin returning. "Have a good evening, Ms. Ableton. Thanks for the dance."

I watch him disappear into the crowd, unsure whether I should be nervous or turned on. But I am sure of one thing.

He's going to be a problem.

5

ATTACK OF THE KILLER FLOWERS

I hate to admit it, but I can see why Aelfswelth Forest is so protected. Thirty minutes outside Vaeloria City, it's home to the silver-barked eldertrees. The trees, considered sacred to the elves, loom hundreds of feet above everything, timeless sentinels of immense beauty. Dappled rays cast patterns from the canopy as I near the secret home of the Lorathar Initiative. Roots glimmer in a soft, enchanting light that shines in harmony with the sporadic pockets of glowfruit littering the low brush. With the unspoiled beauty of this place, I can see why the ancient Valen believed the forest contained mystic power.

It's something I couldn't appreciate as a kid. Though I lived in the forest for the first eleven years of my life, they rarely let me outside the lab. Even as an adult, it lies beyond the multicultural district that non-elves are permitted to travel. I barely got a short-term pass for my "art project."

So, it's no wonder that finding the lab took two weeks. I escaped with my mom over ten years ago, running through the forest late at night. Thanks to the intricate camouflage enchantments and dense foliage magicked to hide the place from prying eyes, it's surprising I found it at all.

Seated on a branch in one of the massive eldertrees, I survey the compound through my specs. A line of starflowers and aelan plants marks the boundary, the hardy low-growing shrubs and distinctive radial blooms not quite blending in with the rest of the forest floor—at least if you're looking for them. The large, curving bulge of the lab is near-invisible amidst the surrounding forest.

When I told Kairo about my infiltration plan, he called it "the dumbest, most brilliant idea you've had yet."

I'm wondering which part of that statement was truer. I try to visualize the path I've laid out from murky memories and days of recon, mumbling the steps to myself. "Grid. Guards. Garden. Guards. Lab. Seeds. Data." With a deep breath, I repeat, "Grid. Guards. Garden—"

"You know, you're not supposed to climb these trees." I jump and feel the bark of the thick branch sliding under me as I slip. Out of nowhere, a firm hand grabs me by the upper arm. "Watch it! Fuck's sake." Once I'm seated again on the branch, he grunts, "I should have let you fall."

I turn and gape at the Valen from the party, still hot as sin in a white button-down, the top two buttons undone, sleeves rolled up to his elbows. It's been almost two weeks since we met. Why's he showing up now?

Mustering annoyance from beneath the shock, I say, "What the hell are you doing here?"

"Last I remember, I was asking *you* that." Underneath the bored tone, I can still sense his simmering anger.

Oh, he's definitely still pissed about me one-upping him.

"You know, I've got a lot to do today. And treetop convos with assholes who threaten to kill me isn't one of them. Why don't you kindly fuck off?"

His scoff turns into a bit of a laugh, his grin going keen and toothy. "You've got quite a mouth on you."

I smirk right back. "You have no idea. And you'll never find out either. Now, who the hell are you?"

He shrugs, leaning against the trunk of the eldertree. "Again, I asked you the same question, *Sarah*."

I groan. "Why are you even here? I'm the one who has the key. Find another job to work." The last thing I need is another thief horning in on something I've already cased.

The Valen shoves off the trunk, invading my space. His breaths caress my cheek. "You don't know what you're fucking with here."

"I know exactly what I'm fucking with."

A biting laugh escapes his lips. "I doubt that." The scent of earth and mint and elderwood overwhelms as his gaze captures me, mouth inches from mine.

My heart races. My skin heats at his closeness, like the ghost of his touch.

Then the harshness melts, gold glinting in his violet eyes. "Or maybe you do—"

I lean back, heaving a deep breath as I turn my gaze back on the compound. Why do my thoughts scramble around him?

With a tiny head shake, the Valen leans back, and that familiar dimpled grin returns. It's a mask as real as the one he wore to Dr. Lirael's party, something that he wears as elegantly as that suit. A beautiful, powerful lie. "Look," he says in a calmer tone. "I think we got off on the wrong foot. Hi. My name is Eiran Valtir. And yours is—"

"Sarah?"

"Don't even."

I sigh. Fine. "Taylor Grey. I'd say I was pleased to meet you, but…"

"But why lie, right?" Eiran supplies. His glinting grin is not quite as fierce as before.

"Exactly," I say, tossing my curls over my shoulder in dramatic fashion. "Now, who do you work for?"

Eiran frowns. "Who says I work for anyone?"

I scoff. "You don't strike me as an independent contractor. Too stuffy and refined. So who is it?" If he works for the Eclipse Consortium, I swear…

He extends a single retractable black claw as if to inspect it. "I work for the SRF."

Even the forest seems to quiet. "Valen intelligence?" Fuck, fuck, fuckity, fuck.

Eiran points a claw at me, and it's as if I can feel it scraping against my skin. "That's the one."

"But why—" Chill, Taylor. Chill the fuck out.

"…am I here? Why are *you* here? The Kuro Oni's on Vale. First time in years. Any connection?"

"I don't work for the Eclipse Consortium," I say flatly.

Eiran surveys me, his gaze an x-ray. "That I believe, because you *do* strike me as an independent contractor. No wonder you could lift that badge so easily. It's your playbook, right? Smile, distract, and then slip the knife in while we're too busy looking at your mouth."

I falter at that for a moment.

"I don't think it was my mouth you were looking at. And if you're easily distracted, don't blame me." I slide away from him, further down the branch. I need to get out of here, away from him. Do this another day.

"That's the thing, isn't it?" he says, following me along the branch. "Touching me like that? It threw me off my game. That doesn't happen often."

"Which part? Getting bested by a woman or touched by one?"

With no warning, he waves a hand, and the branches of the tree wind around me like snakes, moving too fast to dodge.

Dammit. That entire exchange was a distraction. His little smirk is smug. Gods why is he so annoyingly attractive?

"Those seeds are a matter of national security. They shouldn't exist at all, so I obviously can't let them fall into the hands of the Eclipse Consortium. You understand, I'm sure."

"Eiran. Don't—"

His smirk widens, his dimples making another appearance. "Key?"

I give a derisive chuckle. "Like I keep it on me when I'm scouting."

Eiran leans in, his breath against my earlobe raising the hairs on my neck. "You've been here for days scouting. I know for a fact that it's your infiltration day. Now, give me the key."

I try to back away, but the branches hold me in place. "Fuck off."

His grin disappears behind a mask of calm. He raises a hand to my throat, claws extended. He growls, baring his pointed teeth. "Key?"

My heart is in my throat. This place is too hot. I'm confined. Held down. Captured. Claws at my neck. A needle. A cheerful voice. *"Ready to play a game, my Starflower?"*

The claws disappear suddenly, Eiran's hand softer around my throat. "Taylor," he says, searchingly. "I just need the key."

My breath still coming in ragged gulps, I don't respond.

Eiran drops his hands, raising them as his eyes rove over my face. He's reading too much. "Taylor, you're safe. I won't hurt you, but this is serious. Where's the key?"

"Go to hell," I manage.

His stony look returns, and the branches tighten further, stealing my breath. "Don't make me break my word, Taylor. The key."

In a shaky voice, I say, "Left pant pocket."

Eiran loosens the branches slightly. Air rushes into my lungs as my wooden prison makes a space for him to grab the long cylinder from my pants. He taps the cylinder on my nose and then climbs down the tree. I watch him in fury as he lowers himself thirty feet to the forest floor. When he nears the bottom, I send a burst of air, slamming him hard against the tree.

He collapses in a heap. With a surge of my enhanced strength, I send splinters of wood flying before leaping off the branch, landing in a crouch. "Sorry," I say to his knocked-out form, reaching down to pull the key from his hand and slipping it into a pocket. "At least I waited until you were out of the tree."

Giving one last glance to Eiran, I run toward the compound, eyeing the shrubs and small plants that surround it warily. Like the lab itself, you can't see it at first. But when you look past the low ferns, clover, and other undergrowth, you begin to see the pattern. In a regular, grid-like shape across the expanse, large thorny bushes have been planted at regular intervals.

A Gruundlith security grid.

Nearing the clearing, I hide behind a tree and don a large landscaping sprayer. The bioplastic tank sloshes with green VerdantBoost enhancer—the same solution I used to kill the Gruundlith plant just weeks ago. I throw the black padded straps over my shoulder, grasping the connected sprayer nozzle in my hands.

The Union-sourced enhancer solution, designed to help plants grow, inadvertently kills anything touched by elvish magic. It's perfect for my needs, but it's been near-impossible to get ever since the "buy local" movement got the substance banned. I was lucky to source it in this quantity. Hopefully, this idea will work.

Arm digging into the silver bark of the eldertree's trunk, I focus my specs on the one place where the lab's camouflage illusion breaks: the security checkpoint. I know from past recons that two elvish guards man it continually, rotating their shifts so they never change at the same time. Despite the tight security of the space—or perhaps because of it—the guards seem a little bored.

Perhaps that's why neither of them sees the small knockout grenade floating above their heads. With effort, I use magic to pull the pin and let the grenade drop. The small booth fills with smoke, and the guards drop.

There's a faint ringing in my ears, and I shake my head to clear it.

It's hard to control magic from that far away, but I couldn't have the guards sounding the alarm on me. This'll be hard enough without them coming at me, too. Entering the clearing in a crouch, I eye the closest bushes like they're stalking predators. After a breath to steel myself, I step into the Gruundlith grid.

Instantly, a nearby bush lurches toward me, a thorny branch reaching out like claws to grab me. Reacting instinctively, I point the nozzle at the branch and spray it with a burst of solution from my backpack. The branchy arm continues its progress for another moment before the leaves slowly brown, the branch wilting and falling, hardened and dead, to the forest floor.

Two steps later, and three more branches are reaching for me. I blast them in rapid succession with the sprayer before ducking to evade a swinging clothesline from the branch of a tree. The bark scrapes across my brow, searing pain distracting me momentarily. I can feel the warm trickle of blood, and my eyes sting slightly as it gets in them.

There's barely time to wipe it away before the branch returns for my feet. I leap forward, using my enhanced strength to send me twenty feet ahead. Tucking my head, I land in a roll to evade a swipe from two thorny flower bushes I kill with two more sprays.

There's rustling and stomping behind me. "Shit!" I hiss. Eiran's following, doing his own battle with the shrubbery.

I don't have time for this. Fuck.

I keep spraying branches and other attacking fauna as they come, heading through the gauntlet of plant life. Thrashing and swishing rumble behind me as the plants try and fail to catch me.

The path is close now, and two large quithra trees stand as guards. Although shorter than the three-hundred-foot eldertrees around it, the trees are still large in their own right, with broad leaves, thick brown bark, and sturdy branches perfect for gouging your eyes out.

I grip the sprayer tighter as I run, hitting errant branches as they come and checking the trees for movement. The left one lurches forward, and I jump and roll as it pounds the ground like a giant mace.

A huge divot mars where I just was. I calculate the time as it prepares to pound me again. Now, it's the right-side tree that pulverizes the ground where I'm standing, my evading leap taking me farther back the other way.

Alright. I have a better feel for the timing now.

Two more swings, then I'm lined up. The left tree pummels toward me again. I jump backward, eyes closed against the onslaught as the smaller branches scrape into my shoulders, neck, and face. With a calculated aim, I spray the branches of the tree, opening a space on the trunk for me to jump onto.

As I leap, a nearby vine tries to grab at my feet and throws off my jump. A burning, mind-numbing streak of pain wrenches up my leg as I land precariously amongst the grabbing branches of the tree. I have only a moment to recover before the tree rears back up. At the last possible moment, I jump. The combined momentum hurtles me up and forward.

With a thump, I land amidst the knocked-out guards at the checkpoint. Limping, I grab one of the heavy Valen and move them over to the biometric access point, scanning his fingerprint before struggling to hold open one eye toward the camera. It takes three tries, but finally, the door swishes open. I step through, leaving the sprayer next to the guards out cold on the floor of the checkpoint.

At a scraping footstep behind me, I whirl. Eiran walks through the door behind me, his shirt in tatters and a dark red cut above his right eyebrow.

"Well, Miss Grey. That wasn't very nice at all."

6

A CHASE DOWN MEMORY LANE

Eiran seems worse for wear after facing the grid, though still annoyingly gorgeous. Leaves and sticks litter his hair. His white button-up shirt is torn in several places, and there are red-brown specks—bloodstains?—on his khaki slacks. I can't tell if the forehead scrape was the grid or my knocking him into the tree, but either way he looks pissed.

I doubt I look much better. Given how dirty I feel, my normally freckly appearance is probably now one giant freckle. Why does that idea make me self-conscious? Why is his presence more relief than an annoyance?

"Now, Miss Grey, we're going to have a conversation." He stalks forward, fangs and claws bared. The doors swish closed behind him, plunging the small, empty guardhouse into silence.

Despite myself, I take an instinctive step back, pressing against the cold steel wall. The gash on my leg flares, making me wince.

Eiran's eyes sharpen. "Are you… shit." He kneels quickly, trying to examine the bleeding wound. "I saw you land weird on that tree, but… damn it. Drop your pants," he says. "I need to look at it."

"Like hell," I scoff.

Why won't this asshole leave? If I can get him off my ass, I can wrap the leg, sneak past the cameras, and then get this done. I can. I have to.

"I'm sure as hell not leaving you here to get us killed or shot," Eiran growls. "Drop. Your. Pants."

I laugh dryly, trying for as much bravado as I can manage. "Is that your usual pickup line?" When his expression doesn't change, I say. "Look, I'm not your problem. Let me go. You can go your way and I'll go mine and—"

Eiran puts a hand to my cheek for a moment, and my words die in my throat. "Show me your wound, Miss Grey. Let me help."

Crap. Am I really considering this?

Well, getting through this alone with an injured leg might be too big a task even for me. If I had help… at least for now…

"Why?" I ask. "Why help me?"

His cocky, dimpled grin reappears. "Because you're going to give me the key."

I groan. "Should've seen that one coming." Not having much choice if I want his help, I reach into my pocket and hand him the key.

Eiran quickly spirits it away, and then says, "Now, if you would be so kind as to drop your pants."

Damn, why'd it have to be the hip? "Umm… okay." I try to tell myself that I'm an adult and this is no big deal. It's clinical, like at a doctor's office. Still, I somehow feel fifteen again as I lower my tactical pants, transported back to the servant's quarters of that porter… What was his name?

Eiran's hand on my thigh stops my racing thoughts, frying my brain.

"Shit," he says again, lifting a hand to examine the wound. I don't know if I should feel insulted that he isn't gaping in awe at my bared flesh, but his eyes are glued on the gash in my leg, his emerald eyebrows in a sharp V. "You should be in a lot more pain. Why… hell, that was a quithra tree. The sap is a paralytic."

"That must be why I can't move my foot," I mutter. "I've got some salve in my pack. Ten minutes and I'll be fine."

"We rarely get quithra trees this far north," he says absently, and the distraction technique works despite myself. "They're all over where I grew up. My brother mixed some sap into a glowfruit bowl once. I couldn't talk for a week."

Eiran extends a single black claw, and I freeze. "Can you feel this?" he asks, placing the sharp tip against my knee.

I swallow and shake my head no.

He moves the nail upward, tracing its razor-like point in a whisper against the lines of my leg. "Here?"

I shake it again.

He slides the tip above the wound, high on my hip, and a faint bite nips my flesh. I nod, and he retracts the talon with a shaky breath.

"Okay, hold on a second. No time for field mending, but I can give you movement and stop the bleeding." He looks at me, waiting for permission.

I want to tell him no. He can go to hell. I don't even like letting elves *touch me*, much less use their magic on me. But we're out of time. I nod in consent, and he wraps one long-fingered hand around my leg, just below the wound.

He concentrates on the gash, and I brace myself for the pain I always felt when—

Wait. The skin tickles as he coaxes it to knit itself back together. The buzzing sensation branches out from his touch. It still hurts, but my mobility has returned.

"Get dressed," he sighs, stepping back. "We've spent too long here already."

"Okay," I say. Hesitating, I add, "And thanks."

"No problem. Now get out of here before I change my mind."

I laugh. "Like hell."

He glowers. "I just healed—" Catching himself before he yells, he says instead, "You have no idea how serious this is. You have no clue who you're dealing with. What they'll do with that tech."

"I don't care," I say, though my gut twists.

"I'm not letting you get those seeds."

I cross my arms. "We'll see about that."

Eiran's mouth tugs in what might be a faint grin as he raises a blaster at me. "We sure will."

I stand, not bothering to raise my own blaster in response. "You won't get ten feet in there without me. Unless you know where the cameras are." I nod toward a very familiar garden.

"I've done extensive recon of this place, and I've confirmed there are no cameras in the garden space."

I shrug. "Well then, they must be hidden, because I can assure you they're there."

Eiran motions me toward the door with the blaster. "If this is some sort of trick—"

"—you'll kill me. I get it. Gods, you're boringly redundant. You know that?"

I don't catch whatever retort he makes as I'm hit with the pungent scent of lorathar blossom. There's a wide central clearing full of them beyond these lush trees. You can't see it from here, but I know it's there.

Scientists would tend various plant troughs or take breaks on the benches, while kids would run, play, and hide between the trees. And I'd sit. Alone in the lorathar. Until they got bored and found me.

"Cameras?" he prompts in my ear.

I nod, struggling to speak amidst the rush of memories.

He lowers the blaster and steps around me, heading for a clearing between the trees. "Where?"

Snapping out of my momentary distraction, I grab his arm and pull him to the narrower, darker area on the left. "This way."

Eiran pulls back, tugging me to a stop behind one of the enormous trunks. "How do you know there are cameras?"

I don't say the truth: that I heard the guards talking about it. They saw what the kids did to me. And didn't care. They watched Eilrach and the other kids corner me in this very garden. They'd call me "geneblight" and "trashblood." Poke and prod like I was diseased. One girl, Phina, liked to grab me by the arm or shoulder, dig her pointed claws so deep they left tracks in my bones. And then she'd "heal" me to hide the evidence. Pain wrapped up in silence—gift-wrapped and shoved down my throat.

Not that it mattered. The adults knew. And they didn't give a shit.

"Grey!" Eiran hisses, shaking me roughly. I squeeze my eyes shut, trying to return to the now. Coming to this place was a stupid, stupid idea. But I need to get the powerseeds. "You're shaking. You alright?" His eyes narrow in… is that worry? Surely not.

My breathing comes in gasps that I try to rein back under control. "Sorry," I gasp. "I just… hold on a minute. This'll take a beat."

I trace along each tree with my magic, feeling for cameras. The process is slow going, but to Eiran's credit, he waits patiently. It takes another five minutes, but eventually I locate all of them and quickly put together a plan. With a little push here and there, I create a small trail of blind spots.

Glancing up at Eiran, I grin. "Follow me."

Surprisingly, he does so without complaint. I trace my hidden path along the walled edge of the bright courtyard. Honestly, I am amazed that a covert base could still be so… elvish. Something else I never really appreciated as a kid.

My stomach curdles as another wash of memories swarms me. My mother murmuring to someone on the comm about second thoughts. Of her sneaking me out in the middle of the night, half asleep. Of waking up to find my mother gone—

Eiran coughs, and I push the thoughts away, gritting my teeth in resolve. "Alright, let's find this damn thing."

As I near the door to the interior checkpoint, I notice a mossy green pad surrounded by wood, the face lit by a faint bioluminescent glow. A biotech lock. I motion to Eiran to handle it, and he frowns. I motion to my bulge-free neck, showing him I don't have a biotech interface, the device that allows non-Elves to use the Valen's Gruundlith-based tech. I don't mention that I have a pair of biotech goggles in my bag. While it works, the tech is clunky, designed for younger or temporary users who don't have a biotech implant.

Eiran reaches out and touches the soft pad, typing in the air on a holographic keypad I can't see. The doors swish open, and before the three guards inside can react, I lob a smoke bomb into the space. While the guards are disoriented, Eiran and I bring them down with stunning blaster shots. Grinning, I run to the door leading into the lab itself… and grind to a halt.

Eiran chuckles. "Well, I guess it's a good thing I came. Otherwise, you'd be fucked right now." He nods at the lock.

That damn grin is back, and it's fucking annoying. It and the accompanying dimple. "Looks like you wouldn't be getting in at any rate. Even if you had the key. Not without help."

I eye the Gruundlith lock. The tech is brilliant in its simplicity. The biometric scanner is hidden behind an interwoven wall of thick branches. With a simple touch of Gruundlith, an elf could easily bypass it. But any non-Valen would be out of luck. Unless…

I thumb my bag, where my remaining vials of VerdantBoost are stored. Maybe he didn't see me in the grid. Why give away that particular secret when there's a "big, strong elf" here with me?

"Do you know the layout of the base? Because I do." My words wipe the stupid grin off his stupid face. "I know the cameras and guards and shortcuts and the hiding spots. Without me? I give you about thirty seconds before you're caught."

Eiran's scowl is craterous. "Okay, how do you know—"

"I just do." I cross my arms, glaring back at him. Hopefully, after proving myself with the cameras, he believes me.

After a long pause, Eiran sighs. "I'll make you a deal. You help get me to the seeds, and I won't arrest you. Can't keep the seeds, but you stay out of jail. And if you find anything worth selling that *doesn't* give away state secrets, maybe I'll let you steal that instead. Call it… compensation."

I survey him for a moment. "Fine. Deal."

Eiran gives a tiny laugh. "You'll steal it from me as soon as you can, huh?"

I give him a wide, innocent look. "Me? Never."

He shakes his head before moving past me to press the key to the biotech sensor. I reach to hand him the vial of blood, but he holds up his own small container. "Always be prepared," he winks, and something about it makes my stomach do a flip.

Stupid, stupid, stupid.

The door beeps, and Eiran and I walk through together.

The déjà vu is swift and overpowering. Suddenly, I'm nine again, running through the corridors, chasing after Seraphina Lirael and the older kids, trying to avoid the wrath of the scientists who work here.

The place glows with daylight, the interior lights perfectly matching the sky outside. Too clean and sterile, the elves still bring elements of nature where possible. Pockets of plant life lurk in strategic spaces, with natural surfaces like wood and stone here and there, and a subtle woodsy smell masking the scent of chemicals and metal.

Eiran grabs me and pulls me down as one of the doctors walks by. He swiftly puts a hand behind my head, softening the blow as a long counter blocks us from view. His body is draped on me, my knees on either side of his waist as he supports himself with one hand. The other remains behind my neck. Each finger is a brand.

"You okay?" he mouths.

There's something large in my throat, and I swallow it down. Shit. My own brain delivering a double entendre, and now I'm wondering how large…

We've got to move. "This way."

He lifts, mercifully allowing me to crawl out from under him. Standing somewhat shakily, I lurch to the right and crouch-run to a closet hidden seamlessly in a nearby wall. I touch the near-invisible access button and slip inside before it even opens, grabbing Eiran as I go.

This was a favorite crawl space when I was little. I'd hide for hours. One of the few places I felt safe… until I overheard two Initiative heads arguing about whether allowing an "abomination" to live posed a bigger threat than pissing off my mom, the human geneticist vital to their program. Eventually, the director said if I ever became a problem, he'd "handle it."

That's when it clicked. I wasn't a person to them. I was an experiment. And at any time they could declare me a failed prototype. Something to be shut down.

It was a hell of a thing to realize at eight.

As Eiran crawls in behind me, I quickly realize we are *a lot* bigger than when I would hide from Phina and her minions. Eiran can barely fit, and he's forced to sink to his knees, his head pressed to my chest as he crunches inside the tight space.

I can feel his breath against my breasts as he tries to keep space between his face and my cleavage. "Umm… what's your plan now?" he asks quietly. It's a valid question.

I swallow. "Can you… um… turn around and check if the coast is clear? There's a small vent you can open."

"How do you—"

"Maybe we'll discuss this later, yeah?" I say, my cheeks heating. I can feel his quick breaths on my neck this time, sending tendrils down my spine into the core of me.

"Oh," he says. He looks up into my eyes, and then lower to my lips. "Y-yeah." After some finagling, Erian manages to turn around, his bulk pressing me into the back wall of the empty storage closet. The vent makes a quiet flick. "Okay. There's one worker at the other end of the lab. But they're heads-down at a microscope. The row of equipment on the right should hide us if we stay low and keep quiet."

"Great," I say. "It's that hallway at the end."

Eiran glances over his shoulder, the streaking light from the grate highlighting his raised eyebrow. I don't dare tell him I grew up here. He suspects me enough without adding that little detail into the mix. At my silence, he then leads the way back into the lab.

We quickly cross the first spacious lab area. I take the lead, navigating through a warren of winding corridors and half-abandoned service tunnels. Memories of my time here keep returning in waves. I'm shaking, though it's not cold, and there's a loud buzzing in my ears. I blink twice, trying to clear my head a bit.

It's fine. You're fine. It can't hurt you. It's just the past.

As if I believe that.

I feel Eiran's warm hand on my shoulder. "Are you alright?"

I should shake him off. It's just a job, and he's a Valen. I should tell him to go to hell, to shut up and focus. But I don't. "No. But I will be. Let's go."

I walk off, allowing his hand to slide slowly off my shoulder, the spot going cold from the loss of his touch. Refocusing on the job, I hurry through, navigating blind spots and hidden passageways with practiced ease.

It's amazing how small everything is, but otherwise unchanged in the intervening years. It's like time has placed a bubble around the lab, shrinking the place without the outsized presence of my mother to fill it. I see her everywhere, in spots where she taught me the periodic table or told me a bad joke about an Aztlanian merman and a dolphin. Her imprint is everywhere, and yet she… is not.

We reach the rear lobby, a short semicircular space with a door at the end, steel furniture and machines glinting beyond the large glass window. Eiran presses the key to the door scanner and then applies more blood to the DNA sensor. There's a loud buzzing sound, and the door remains stubbornly closed.

We're locked out.

7

TOPPING

"Damn it!" Eiran grunts, slamming the door in frustration. "Eilrach doesn't have lab access. What do we do now?" Running his finger along the glass, he shakes his head. "Window's too thick to break. I don't—"

"Move out of the way," I say, pushing him aside.

"There's nothing you can—"

Ignoring him, I yank the key from his hand and scan it again.

I hesitate for a moment. The needle isn't glistening, Taylor. It's in your head.

With a breath, I press my thumb to the DNA scanner, the prick sending a wash of memories roiling in the back of my head. I barely push them down when the door beeps, sliding open. Eiran gapes. "How in the hell—"

My voice distant even to my own ears, I mutter, "DNA scanners. So unreliable."

Guess they can still be faked out by familial matches. Some things never change.

Ignoring whatever Eiran mutters back, I walk into my mother's former office. The white machines along the walls hum faintly, but a single cold beam slices through the shadows, spotlighting the steel medical table. Long vines creep toward it like skeletal fingers, drawn to the only light.

The room's a broken mirror into the past, and the cracked edges don't quite line up. Most things are the same—same walls, same low machine humming, same goddamn table in the center lit like an altar.

But the details are wrong. The smell's too clean. The lighting's colder. None of the sinister tools of Mom's trade are here. It's like seeing a friend after many years, the familiar planes of their face hidden under the lines of distance and time.

I wrench my eyes from the table. I'm underwater. Dark and drowning in memories.

That's where she used to sit me. Where we would play "the game," as she called it. My legs would dangle off the edge while she made cooing noises and prepped the needle. Or the gun I always called an ingestor. Because I was too little to say injector.

Too little to realize her "game" was anything but.

She always promised it wouldn't hurt. Said it would be quick. Smiled, saying it was all part of her oh-so-important *work.*

I could always find her hunched over those machines, her long red hair, dark in the half-light, hanging down her back like a bloody curtain. Her fingers would twirl in the air, pressing invisible buttons on her biotech interface. Like she was communing with spirits. I'd run to her, crying about whatever horrid thing Phina did that day, and she'd call me her *starflower* and brush my hair behind my ear. Tell me elf girls don't matter. That I was special. That I was older. Smarter.

Then she'd lock the door.

Out came Dr. Puff. My stuffed silberwolf. Her favorite prop. She'd tell me to move him with my mind, whisper sweet encouragements like it was all a game, like it was fun. Most days, I couldn't do it. She'd get quiet. Cold.

But then finally… I did it. Lifted him clear off the cart. My nose bled. I felt dizzy. And she cried like it was the best day of her life. Called me amazing.

Then she wiped her eyes, cleared her throat, and said, "Let's try that again."

Like I was a machine finally doing what I was built for.

I can't look at the table anymore. My hands are shaking.

I remind myself to breathe. We're not doing this today. I'm an adult. I'm safe. I'm a badass. I won't let the past win today.

Repressing my shaking, I point to a row of secure lockers. "The seeds should be in there."

Eiran raises his blaster again and motions with it. "Over there. On the other side of the room."

Rolling my eyes, I walk over to a nearby terminal. Next to it is a biometric access point, just a small needle to draw a drop of blood. My hands tremble as I reach for it.

It's the past. Just the past. I need to be brave. Momma always said big girls are brave.

I press a finger to the scanner and try to push down the roaring emotions that always threaten at the needle prick. The scanner beeps, giving me access to my mom's account, which must still be active.

I glance at Eiran, who's busy throwing seeds into a duffel, and then quietly don my biotech glove and goggles. A quick perusal shows that most of her research has been removed, probably stored elsewhere on the server for others to access. I have only seconds, but I skim through. Is there anything that's worth keeping? Anything valuable to Akio… or me? Ugh. Nothing.

I don't have time for this. I reach to close the account—

Wait! There's a simple text file marked "Log Transcript Backup." I open it and discover a huge text file filled with what appear to be transcripts of my mom's personal video log. Using some backdoor hacks that I've picked up, I dump the file into one of my encrypted cloud storage accounts and close things down.

"How do you know this place?" Eiran turns as he asks, eyebrow raised in question. His gun is half raised as his attention is torn between me and the seeds.

"The truth is…" I pause, stunned.

There's Dr. Puff, sitting by one of the various machines.

My hands tremble violently as I stare, utterly transfixed.

The stuffed silberwolf's once bright pink synthetic fur is matted and faded from years of collecting dust in the corner. Forlorn and forgotten.

I walk over and pick up the small stuffed animal, ignoring Eiran's suspicious look. Dr. Puff is as soft as I remember. It's strange. He's here, but Mom isn't.

"How'd you get past that door, Grey?" Eiran's tone rolls and grows like a billowing storm cloud. His focus is all on me now. "What the hell is going on?"

I hold up Dr. Puff, refusing to rise to his anger. He might as well know the truth. What could it hurt at this point?

"I grew up here. I left when I was eleven. Haven't been back since."

His face slides into that stony smile. "And you what? Forgot to mention that?"

"Would you have helped me if you had known?"

Eiran scoffs, shaking his head. "Yeah, I guess not. Just another convenient omission. Sort of like how you say you're not working for the Kuro Oni, only we caught him on camera a block from the bookshop?"

"I… I… It's complicated."

"It always is," Eiran says, disgusted. "You try to play it off like you're some poor thief working a job. But you're connected to one of the galaxy's most dangerous mercenaries and grew up in *a compound for a group of fringe fanatics*! How am I supposed to trust you? I knew… I knew I should have arrested you when I had the chance. But I thought… hell, I don't know what I thought. I bought your act. Your lies. Again."

I'm all over the place. Hurt. Defensive. And more than a little pissed off. "You want to talk about trust? When you're trying to write the Initiative off as some fringe group? Don't give me that crap. They're *scientists*, Eiran. Working for a government-funded operation. Is what they're doing illegal and immoral? Sure. But from my experience, that's pretty standard for the Valen—"

"I've been investigating this group for six months, Miss Grey. Trust me. They're not associated with the Valen Republic. Now, I'm going to destroy the rest of these seeds, and then you're going to tell me everything you know. We can do this however you want, but you're coming with me." He prowls toward me with blaster raised. We circle each other slowly as he tries to box me in.

Fucking Valen. The reminder of who—what—he is calms me. Clears my head. "Well, I'm leaving with those seeds."

Eiran's eyes glimmer in the harsh lab light. "That would not be a good idea."

I shrug. "Gutsy and stupid. My specialty, remember?"

Eiran aims the blaster, but a flick of my magic sends it flying. Without hesitation, he lunges.

Shit, he's fast. I barely dodge out of the way, smacking him lightly on the side. It's enough to make him grunt. If I used full strength, it would probably shatter some ribs.

"Fuck," he mutters, rubbing his side as we circle again.

"Oh, sorry." I give him a saccharine smile. "Did that hurt?"

He grins, his sharp teeth peeking over his lips. "Actually? Not that much, given you're an Enhanced. Are you pulling your punches?"

The question takes me off guard. He bolts forward again, capitalizing on my distraction. I try to juke out of the way, but he grabs my shoulder and sweeps my leg to bring me down to the tile floor. Like before, he places a hand against the back of my neck, softening my fall. Despite that, my ears ring. Disoriented, Eiran is on top of me. Before I can even register what's happening, his forearm is at my throat, pressing down.

He's so close. My legs wrap around his lower back, squeezing. He grimaces but keeps pushing. The heat of him envelops me.

I could break his arm or a couple of ribs, but someone will be here any minute. And I'm not leaving him incapacitated in the Initiative's hands.

Eiran leans in further, pushing my head back and applying a bit more of his weight to my windpipe. He leans forward, pressing the advantage, wanting me to submit. His cheek brushes against mine, faint stubble scratching. I lean my head up… and lick his earlobe.

He freezes in shock. With a rocking surge of my enhanced strength mixed with a gust of magic, I fling him ten feet behind me, where he crashes into a couple of spindly chairs. I leap to my feet, running to the door before he can disentangle from the mess.

With an outstretched arm, I grab the bag of enhanced powerseeds I send flying toward me through the air. I reach the door as Eiran finally rights himself. I flick a mental hand at the "Fire Emergency" button. His eyes widen as the steel door slams behind me, locking him in while an alarm blares through the compound.

As white gas flows from the ceiling, I say, "The door'll open in a minute. Better hold your breath." He glares at me, slamming a fist on the door as he takes and holds a deep breath. I wave at him, and he cocks his head. The corner of his mouth is fighting against his scowl. He bows slightly, as if to say, "You win this round." I wink back.

Knowing I have only moments, I check the bag of powerseeds. Each seed is about a foot and a half long and pill-shaped, with a clear center section glowing with yellow-green light, standing out from the dark gray metal of each end. Hoping that's enough, I zip the duffel and run out the door. With only the tiniest of glances back, I head down the hallway toward the exit.

I said I wouldn't leave him incapacitated. I didn't say I wouldn't leave him.

It's stupid to feel guilty, but I do. He helped me, gave me a shot when he didn't need to. There's something… incredibly attractive about him taking care of me. But in the end, he wouldn't have let me sell these seeds. And I need that money, because I learned one thing coming back here. I need to get the hell away from the Initiative and these damn memories. Eiran'll find another way out.

He won't be foolish enough to chase me… right? Not with a wall of guards on my heels. Putting the question out of my mind, I grab the discarded water pack and grip the nozzle, ready to face the death garden once again.

My mind is already on my impending payday, and the promise of freedom it offers. And the little part of me that sinks at leaving Eiran behind that glass? Well, I'll bury it in the same basement where I shove memories of Mom, Phina, and all the other useless shit.

8

LENDING A HAND

Well, that went to hell faster than normal. Eiran is going to be pissed. That gives me a bit of pleasure, I won't lie, but I'll need to lie low for a while. The stryder I've hired zooms back into the city, the Valen transport skimming unobtrusively above the grass. Watching the undisturbed fields fly by, I pull out my comm and message Kairo.

Taylor: "got it. meet at the park in fifteen. watch ur ass. will explain later."
Kairo: "Okay."

I frown at the comm. Something about the reply feels off, but I can't explain what it is.

Taylor: "u alright?"
Kairo: "Yeah. It's been a long day. I'll see you shortly."

With a sigh, I tell my driver the location of the park. He nods, rumbling down the smooth stone street toward Kairo and an end to this hellscape of a day. And Kairo says *his day* was long.

Twelve minutes later, I'm exiting the bulbous stryder. As I'm wiring the driver extra for his silence, I finally realize what was off about Kairo's message. He was writing in full sentences. Even used the full spelling of "okay" rather than just the letter "K." With the hairs on my neck prickling, I turn and scan the deserted, gloomy park for Kairo. I see the shape of wings in the gloom and sigh in relief.

"Man, Kai, I can't tell you what—"

The figure looms closer, and I can make out the face and the faint hint of silvery gray amidst the black hair. It's not Kairo. It's Akio, his father.

The Kuro Oni smiles as he approaches, his wings spreading like arms opening for an embrace. "Taylor, my child! Do you have something for me?"

I take a step back. "Where's Kairo?"

Akio grins wider. "Why do you need him? You have what I need. Hand it over, and I'll give you the artifact. Let's get this over with."

I narrow my eyes at him. "You'd cut your own son out of this? Do you really hate him that much?"

Akio's lips tighten, and in a strange tone, he mutters, "This is not his path. Now, step forward and I'll give you what you're due."

"Is that supposed to be code? 'What you're due?' Like I haven't noticed that you don't seem to have my lamp. What's going on?"

The Kuro Oni sighs, and out of nowhere several burly guards materialize from where Akio's glamour hid them—all holding blasters. "I want you to know that I tried to argue for your life. You would've been a great asset to the Consortium. But the client was very insistent."

That's when I see it. Another set of wings approaching behind Akio. My first crazy thought: Kairo's come after all. But the wings are… wrong. The shape—

A single bright red eye cuts through the darkness, its artificial light sending an eerie glow onto everything. A massive figure steps forward from the shadows, a misshapen silhouette in Vaeloria's evening glow.

Dread billows in my gut at the *shunk-clank, shunk-clank, shunk-clank* of the footsteps, slow and relentless.

On the tips of the Hitari wings, where normally a long sharp claw sits, instead are grafted two large blasters, laser sights shining, sending red lines slicing in slow, wide arcs. The shoulders and torso of the figure seem misshapen and unbalanced.

Oh gods.

Half of the strange figure—a male, I think—is covered in a Zeridian exoskeleton. His chest and entire left arm have hewn remains grafted on in pinching strands of pinkish flesh. On the left forearm, where a Zeridian stinger would normally be, a metal spike hangs extended, a silent threat. The right arm and half of his face are covered in mech. His red electronic eye still glows menacingly in the darkness, putting his features in evil relief.

The cyborg gives a passing glance at Akio, and from his pointed ears, light brown skin, and lack of horns, I get confirmation of what I suspected: he's human. An Enhanced. Or at least he used to be. Who could have done this to him, created this mishmash of human and alien and mech?

"That's enough," he says to Akio in a cold, commanding voice that scrapes across my ears like chains on gravel.

With my heart beating in my throat now, I glance over my shoulder.

Before I can move, the figure adds, "Don't run." The blasters on his wings swivel, focusing on me. "You won't make it three feet." He cocks his head, red eye x-raying me (maybe literally).

"Did you know you can intercept calls and messages to a person's comm, only letting through the ones you want?" the Kuro Oni says mildly.

I don't bother responding. I glance around the small expanse of the park, trying to plan. There must be a way to escape.

The cyborg sneers. "That bat's not coming for you. No one knows you're here besides that stryder driver, and I can deal with him. Now tell me. Where are the seeds?"

"Go to hell," I spit, moving to put a couple of trees between the cyborg and me.

"I've already been there," the cyborg says, maneuvering around the trees with ease and always keeping his path and line-of-sight to me clear. How the hell do I shake this guy? "Now, answer the question. Where are my seeds? In the bag?"

I try not to react, but I can't help tightening my grip on the bag. His one human eye narrows, clearly noticing the motion. "I… I give you the seeds, and you give me the lamp. Right?" This is why I never meet clients. Scary assholes like this. The cyborg's grin sharpens; his non-answer is an answer enough for me. "Who the hell are you?"

"This is—" the Kuro Oni begins.

The cyborg holds up a hand. "You may go."

The Kuro Oni is clearly not used to being dismissed like this. "That wasn't the plan—"

"It's one human girl. You've been paid. Leave us."

Akio gives me one last, somewhat sad glance, quietly muttering, "Such a waste," before spreading his wings and taking off into the night. After an exchange of looks, the guards turn and slink soundlessly into the darkness, leaving me alone now with the cyborg.

He moves forward with another determined *shunk-clank*, a broad metal foot eating a furrow into the ground with every step. "Enough talking," he grinds out. "Give me the seeds."

Gritting my teeth, I shove his blasters to the sky with a gust, applying as much mental force as I can to the top of his wings before turning to jump behind a rocky outcropping. A blaster shot demolishes the top of the rock an inch from my head, sending shrapnel searing into my already wounded forehead. I pull out my blaster, but before I can raise it, a loud *thunk* shakes the ground before me.

An icy metal hand wraps around my throat, lifting me off my feet, the bag and gun dropping from my slackening grip. The blaster lands on a rock, cracking into three pieces. "I said that's enough. This couldn't end any other way. Could you please stop making it so fucking difficult?"

The world darkens around the edges as my lungs burn, my hands clambering for purchase against the cold steel of his hand. I try to mentally shove his fingers open, and my nose gushes blood. His hand just tightens further.

Pushing through a growing pounding in my head, I slam a fist on his mech arm once, twice, with all my strength. I cry out in pain as the bones in my wrist snap. I stare into the cyborg's one human eye, and he watches back coldly and unmoved as he reaches into his pouch for something.

A blaster shot rings out, and dark orange-red blood spurts from the cyborg's right wing, covering my face and his. He drops me, doubling over in pain as half of the wing, the blaster included, lies useless and bloody on the grass at my feet.

I scramble away, letting out huge gasps of air, my head still pounding. The cyborg rounds behind him, turning toward the source of the shot.

"Well, well," Eiran says, stepping out of the gloom with a grin of gleaming, razor-sharp teeth. A black clawed hand grips the blaster, aimed at the cyborg's head. "Adrian Blackstone. Long time no see."

The cyborg, Blackstone, surveys Eiran, his human and electronic eyes both glinting in the low light. I scramble toward the elf, gravel and torn-up dirt eating into my palms as I struggle to my feet. The long grass scrapes my legs as I blunder forward. I need to put space between myself and the cyborg.

Air continues to come in burning gulps, my nose still dripping blood. "It's about time you showed up," I say in a poorly executed deadpan when I reach him, trying to think through the mental fog. Damn, my head hurts.

"Sorry I'm late. I was busy not having any clue where you went," Eiran mutters in reply. He eyes me up and down briefly, jade eyebrows tight as he surveys my injuries. "Oh, and being locked in a room that tried to dry-clean my lungs. Can't forget that."

"You?" Blackstone grinds out at Eiran, voice like a poorly maintained bicycle. Red leaks from the gash in his damaged wing, and he flutters it, annoyed, but with no further wince of pain.

"Hey Adrian." Eiran smiles that cool, detached grin of his and taps a couple of his black, pointed claws on the hilt of the blaster. "Have you gotten uglier? Because you sure as hell—"

"Enough of this," Blackstone spits.

Eiran dives into me as Blackstone fires with his one good wing, a crater forming where Eiran was just standing.

"You know him?!" I holler over a fury of blaster fire.

"You don't?" he asks searchingly. I shake my head, and he finally replies, "He works for Helix." Eiran and I scramble behind a tree as Blackstone lets out another flurry of shots. "Do you have a blaster?"

I motion to where it lay in pieces by Blackstone.

Eiran hesitates, and then hands me his. "Here. Take this and get out of here."

"But don't you—"

Eiran rounds out from the tree, fanged teeth bared in a vicious snarl. He holds his arms out wide, his claws splayed darkly. Roots begin to grow and stretch from the ground, roiling around him like giant snakes. He's an avenging god striding forward, his purple eyes blazing with fury. The roots follow, eating a rut into the earth and snapping at Blackstone. Creaking and dust fill the air; his outline is blurred in a cloud of debris. The cyborg fires, but the branches cross in front of Eiran, blocking the shot. The ends blast into splinters, but they quickly regrow.

I've never seen an elf wield magic like this. Didn't think it was even possible. The Valen need to touch a plant to make it grow. Everyone knows that. Eiran adjusts his direction, circling in front of the tree as if he's tethered.

"What are you doing here, Professor?" the cyborg asks. "Don't you have some books to read?"

"I could ask you the same question," Eiran growls. "What's Helix up to this time? Blowing up schools not doing it for you anymore?"

Blackstone sneers. "You'll never get it, will you? What we're trying to do. To build. The little fucking archeologist, ruining everything you don't understand. Well, not this time."

Before I can wrap my mind around the idea that Eiran was, at some point, an *archeologist*, the cyborg reaches between his wings. He grabs… holy fuck. It's the hilt of a wide, dark metal sword. A real, honest-to-gods sword. He shakes it, and a line of flickering blue plasma appears around the edge, giving him a sinister up-lit glow.

Yeah, I really should be going. I turn, but then see it. The duffel is lying a few feet from Blackstone.

"Why do you want the seeds?" Eiran asks, unfazed by the cyborg's theatrics.

"Yes," the cyborg grunts in what might pass for a disdainful laugh. "I'll tell you all my plans, shall I? Back off, professor."

As the two talk, I try to inch my way to the bag. It's heavy, but I try to summon it to myself, anyway. The bag doesn't even twitch. The pounding in my head gets stronger, and my bloody nose drips anew, globs turning the dirt a sickly black color. I'll get it by hand then.

As I slowly creep toward the bag, Eiran replies in an unconcerned tone, "Maybe it's not an explosion at all. Maybe this isn't even for Helix. Hoping for a power-up, perhaps? How much did it cost to have someone fillet a Zeridian and graft their exoskeleton to you?" He curls a lip in disgust.

"*You* made me this way." Blackstone steps forward, farther from the bag, and Eiran swipes at him with a root. Blackstone swings his fiery blade, sending the root flying. "You did this. Elves. Dwarves. Halflings. You're all the same. I know what danger you *freaks* pose. You alien scum and your fucking magic."

I can't let someone like Blackstone have the seeds. It was so incredibly stupid to take this job. I'm almost to the bag now, and I don't think Blackstone sees me yet. I reach out, wrapping my fingers around the strap.

Blackstone wheels around, swiping the sword at me. A searing pain burns across my arm and… oh gods. My… my hand, it's…

I can't process what I'm seeing. There's a blackened stump where my hand used to be. There's not even blood. Only charred flesh. And the pain? I can't think. Blackstone reaches down to the bag. With efficient ease, he removes the white hand still gripping the backpack. My hand. Blackstone drops it, and it lands with a sickening little bounce.

My body feels so distant. The world is so blurry. The blood loss. The magic. I feel…

"I really… gotta hand it to you…" I murmur.

Gods everything hurts.

Blackstone leans near me, his tone low. "Foolish girl." He's raising something toward me. Silver… an injector?

My head swims as blaster shots rain over my head. Blackstone pulls quickly away. There's a flurry of wings and a cry from someone yelling "No!" before I sink into blackness.

PART 2

THE TAYLOR GREY JOB

fuck the words you use to define me
the tiny lies that try to refine me.
chip off my soul in tiny piles
swept into corners of your confining
cage of lovely, soulless words
as you try to make me
the same

difference is my deliverance
yet you keep me detained
no, I'll remain the thing you fear
you carve out all that I hold dear
in the sacred name of Normal
well, fuck normal

—*The Journal of Taylor Grey*

9

RUDE AWAKENING

Did I fall asleep in my clothes again?

The thought's fuzzy, a vague ripple in the waves of sleep saying something's off. I push to the surface, fighting the currents pulling me under. The room slowly smooths into focus.

I'm lying on my back in a strange bed. I *am* still wearing my clothes, along with some sort of bracelets that—

I make to rub my eyes, but my hands won't move. That's when everything rushes back. The park. The cyborg. Eiran.

My hand!

I pry my eyes open and check. Okay, my hand's there. How is that possible? I saw it, saw what he did to it. Someone must have healed it, along with my broken wrist.

Sure enough, there's the tiniest trace of blackened skin peeking from the magnetic cuff. One covers each wrist, fixing them to the bedrails. What the hell? I pull, trying in vain to get my wrist to separate from the guardrail.

Surveying the room, I wrangle my brain back into my head, fighting the bright lights.

I'm lying on a hospital bed. There's a large window bringing in natural light and a succulent vine hanging in the corner. The natural touches feel foreign amidst the slow, harmonious beeping of the various readouts and monitors. Probably an elf's idea of therapeutic design.

"You're awake," a voice says from my left. Eiran, arms crossed, leans on the door frame with a frown on his face. His white button-down, free of the blood and tears from the lab, is a rumpled mess, the sleeves roughly rolled and the tail half untucked. The black hint of a tattoo peeks beneath the unbuttoned collar. He surveys me with either suspicion or concern. Maybe both.

"You okay?"

"I'll live."

Eiran closes his eyes for a moment, breathing. "What about your hand? Is it—" He steps forward, putting the tip of my finger in between his and wiggling it faintly. "Can you feel this?"

I nod, but he keeps checking each one.

His voice is sharp. Clipped. "I told you to stay out of this. I fucking *told* you. Then you locked me in that damn room and ran off—thanks for that, by the way. I barely evaded the guards. By the time I rushed over... if I'd been a few minutes later—"

"Where's Blackstone?" My tone's heavy, muscles shaking like I've run for hours.

Eiran drops my fingers and runs a hand through his emerald hair. It hangs in messy tatters, strands falling into his violet eyes like he's been doing that for a while now. "Gone," he sighs. "With the seeds. I tried to catch him, but he flew off too fast, and you were—" He motions helplessly.

"Sorry for the inconvenience," I mumble.

Eiran growls, baring those predator teeth. "If it had taken me any longer to get you here, you could've lost your hand entirely." He shakes his head like a grazehorn swatting away flies. He doesn't say more, and I don't respond to his baiting.

"What'd he want?" I ask, fighting my slow-moving thoughts. Eiran lets out a short, biting laugh. "I'm serious. I'd assumed the buyer wanted to steal the tech. You know, recreate seeds and sell them for cheaper? Kill the Valen monopoly? But a guy like that... well, he doesn't seem the corporate espionage type."

"So, that would have been okay, then?" Eiran asks in a low, tense tone. "Completely destroy the economy of your own country for a quick score?"

Gods, everything hurts so much. "You know, I'm too tired for this," I sigh. "So, you can take all your sanctimonious elvish self-righteousness and," I wave a hand flippantly, "stick it up your perfect olive-green ass or whatever."

Did I just say his ass was "perfect?" They must have me on some strong meds.

I don't even respond to the "your own country" bit. It's not like I'm a citizen. I'm basically a legal ghost. Besides, is he going to stand here and pretend I owe the Valen Republic anything? I try to roll over, but the cuffs hold me in place. "What the fuck is up with these, by the way?" I hold up my manacled wrists.

Eiran steps further into the room, closing the door behind him. "You're not going anywhere until I get answers."

I laugh without humor, staring up at a ceiling covered with hanging clover. "Answers? Really?" I raise an eyebrow at him. "Don't you think that's a little ironic coming from you?"

Eiran raises his own eyebrow back. "Who do you work for?" he asks calmly.

I sigh, wanting desperately to go back to sleep. "Am I under arrest? Is that what this is?"

Eiran shrugs, a smile playing at his maddeningly exquisite mouth. "You broke into a private facility and stole illegal technology with the intent to sell."

I laugh again. "Technically, *we* broke into a private facility. Unless you had a warrant."

At the mention of us working together, Eiran's eyes go as flinty as I've ever seen them. "How did you get connected with Helix?"

"Who?"

Eiran scowls. "Don't give me that shit. You're enhanced. You were meeting Adrian Blackstone. I'm not an idiot."

"You could've fooled me," I snap, voice rising. "Is this why you have me in fucking cuffs? That bastard—Blackstone, you said his name was—he wanted to kill me out there. Would have killed me if you hadn't shown up. And you think—"

"We don't know that he was trying to kill you."

I laugh at the ridiculousness of that statement. "We certainly weren't about to go for tea. That much was pretty damn clear. And you think I'm working with him?"

He crosses his arms, his face unreadable. Closer now, I can see that the black tattoo peeking out from his shirt appears to be leaves on a winding branch that continues up his arm. "Maybe you had a falling out. You've proven a pretty big pain in my ass so far."

"I'm sure having to put up with a 'geneblight' is a real hardship." The words feel like ripping my insides out, some vital chunk spat out between us.

Eiran stiffens at the slur. "I didn't—"

"Save it," I sigh, my voice raspy from lack of sleep. "Ever since you saw my ears at the party, you've been looking at me like some nasty insect you're worried will sting you. I'm used to prejudice. I've lived here my whole life. But yours seems… personal."

Eiran runs a shaky hand through his hair again. "No! That's not… I mean yes, it's that you're Enhanced. But not…" He trails off with a growl.

I deflate, nodding to the ceiling. Of course. Eiran took care of me. Again. He came and found me, brought me here, made sure I was okay… I guess I thought he was different. Clearly not.

"I told you. I'm used to it. I've lived on Vale my entire life. You're not the first racist prick I've met. You can save the rhetorical gymnastics."

Eiran growls, sounding tortured. "Aether save me, Grey. I don't give a shit about genetic manipulation. It's not… I thought…" He searches my face as if the answer is waiting to be discovered there. After a pause, he says, "What I mean is… I thought you were Helix. They work with a *lot* of Enhanced. And given the timing, showing up when you did… But you're right. Blackstone trying to kill you seems to imply otherwise… not that I'd put it beneath him to cut off an operative's hand to play some sort of 4D chess with me. But even so?" Eiran checks his watch. "If you were Helix, they'd have come for you by now, either to rescue you or to kill you to keep you quiet."

"Who's Helix?" I ask, too tired to be properly curious.

"A human terrorist organization based out of the Union of Independent Planets. They'd love to get their hands on some Valen tech. We've been trying to bring them down for years. Like I said, they use a lot of Enhanced. And I'm not just talking about improving your bone structure to make you more attractive or altering your musculature to make you faster than normal. I mean dangerous enhancements. Illegal enhancements."

"Like they did to Blackstone?" I ask.

Eiran nods. "And worse. Think of someone like Blackstone, but instead of mech… it's genetic engineering. Turning them into something inhuman. Dangerous. Something that shouldn't be."

"Like me."

"That's not what I meant." Eiran winces. "But you are Enhanced. Helix has done a lot of terrible things, most of them involving Enhanced operatives. Can you blame me for making assumptions?"

I'm not happy to admit it, but I really can't. Particularly when his hatred of this Helix organization seems so personal.

Eiran's mouth softens almost imperceptibly. "Who do you work for, if not Helix?"

With another futile tug at the mag cuffs, I groan. "No one. I'm a thief, okay? I'm fast, I'm smart, I'm enhanced, and I'm good at my job. I just made a big score when the Kuro Oni ambushed me and stole the artifact. Said to steal the seeds, and he'd give it back."

"That's it? You did this for some *artifact*? What sort of artifact?"

I scowl. "One worth enough to buy a new name and a life far from… well, you saw."

Eiran's eyebrows tighten. "The lab. Did they—"

"Yes." I turn away as best I can with the cuffs. "Anyway, I guess that was a lie. That's all I know. I don't know where the Kuro Oni is. I don't know where Blackstone is. I know nothing. I don't have the seeds, and I'm not getting paid. Now either arrest me or don't, but I'm going back to sleep."

"Ah, Miss Grey. You're awake. And just in time for your medicine."

I freeze as the pretty Valen nurse walks in, emerald hair in a tight bun, an injector gun in her hand. I couldn't process at the lab. Now, everything rushes back. The table. The needles. Blackstone's hand around my neck.

My severed hand lying useless on the ground.

Me useless on the ground.

Always useless.

A tear rolls down my cheek, and then another. A voice trickles back from the grave where I buried it: "*Okay, ready for the game, my starflower?*" My mom. She's here, an injector gun in her hand. A spike of pain sears in my head as I try—and fail—to pick up Dr. Puff. Over and over and over again. Until I pass out.

"Miss Grey—" Eiran says tentatively.

Blood trickles from my nose to my lip. I taste copper, and the familiarity breaks something in me. With a wrenching yank of mental and physical strength, I rip the arm rails from the bed. Eiran lunges forward. Too late. I swing, metal crunching against the side of his head. He crumples.

I leap up. A burst of air hurtles the nurse against the hallway wall. I vault over her and tear toward freedom, the taste of copper still sharp on my tongue.

10

BRINGING ME DOWN

I have to get out of here. Get as far as I can from this place and these questions and these memories. The words are a pounding beat in my head, timed to my footsteps ringing out in the hallway as I run. Go, go. Go, go.

"Miss Grey! Wait!" Eiran cries from somewhere behind me. It's all too much. Why can't he leave me alone? My heart burns in my chest, tracing fire up my throat. I can hear Eiran thundering down the hall after me. I push out with my mind, sending him sprawling. He hits the ground with a loud crash.

Good.

I near the end of the hallway, and the branch of a shrub brushes my cheek as I run past.

The scent of lorathar blossom hits my nose—except there is no lorathar in this hallway.

I'm in the garden, leaves grabbing for me as I weave in and out. The dappled light flickers gold and green across my arms as I run. Phina is behind me, chasing, laughing too harshly, her longer legs eating up the grass. My heart is pounding, not with fear but with something sharper. A need to outrun what's coming. I laugh too, because I can't cry in front of her.

"Taylor…"

The wind changes. Colder now. It smells of antiseptic.

Momma's calling to me, ready to play the game again. I don't want to play the game.

"Taylor!"

The laugh shatters like glass.

No. Wait. That's Eiran's voice. Right, I'm in the hospital.

Eiran grabs me by the neck, hauling me against his brick wall of a chest. "Wait. Please!"

Choking, I slam a foot down on his instep, and his grip loosens. Spinning, I throw him against a wall, shaking the space to the foundation.

Run. Run. Run.

Eiran glowers and wipes a streak of blood from his lip. Spitting, he reaches out his hands, and I feel the tree reach out for me.

Am I hallucinating again or… the branches bind around me, the rough bark grounding me in the now. They're not tight enough to hurt, but enough to keep my arms pinned, to stop me from running.

Bastard should have learned from his mistake.

With a tearing pain radiating from my wrist, I send shards of branches flying, embedding in the walls. With a scream, I round on him, throwing my fist flying at his chest with full strength. He jukes out of the way, my hand connecting with his arm.

"FUCK!" he cries as his arm gives with a crunch.

Pain sears up my arm from my wound, and I scream in tandem with him. "Didn't pull my punch this time, did I, asshole?"

Get out. Got to get out. Now.

I take a step, but quick as a flash, a branch reaches out. It wraps tightly around my arm, spinning me. I swing my free arm to break the branch, but another catches that wrist as well, stretching me out like a prisoner on a rack. I growl and spit as more branches bind my feet, legs, and torso.

Eiran holds out his hands placatingly, eyes wide. "It's alright, Miss Grey. You're—"

I reach out with my mind and slam him into the wall. Blood flows in a trickling stream from my nose as I lift him up, up, his feet dangling three feet from the ground. A burst of wind presses his arms and back against the wall.

"Leave. Me. Alone," I manage.

There's a millisecond of… surprise? Fear? But then it's gone. "I just—"

I growl at him, fighting the relentless branches. "Let me go."

"I will when you do," Eiran says calmly. His hands are open, outstretched, as if he can still touch me. "It's alright. You're okay. Put me down, and I'll let you go."

I hiss at him. I need to get out. Get safe. Back to my apartment. The park. Somewhere safe.

"Taylor. You're safe with me. I promise."

Something crumples inside me at the sound of my first name on his lips. My eyes sting. "I need to get out," I whimper.

I can't cry. Don't cry.

"Okay," he nods. "Okay, we'll leave. Let me down, and we'll get out of here. You're safe. I won't let anything happen to you." Slowly, I let him slide to the ground.

Eiran stalks forward, red blood stark against his temple, his arm dangling oddly. He winces as he stretches it out, the long, sinewy muscles of his shoulder writhing like disturbed snakes, something knitting back together beneath the skin—slowly, wrong. "Okay, I'm going to let you go, but don't run, okay? We'll leave together."

I nod faintly.

The branches loosen, and I drop. He reaches out quickly, his long, powerful arms wrapping around me, even the one I shattered.

"I've got you," he whispers into my ear.

"Your arm! You shouldn't—"

"It's fine."

"Eiran—"

"I said it's fine." There's a slight beep, and the weight on my hands lifts as the cuffs release, the metal bedrails clattering on the ground. "I'm gonna carry you, okay? Just for a minute. Then I'll put you down."

With no effort at all, I'm in his arms, and he's carrying me.

"I'm sorry," I mumble, the taste of salt in my mouth. "I'm sorry, I'm sorry, I'm sorry."

"Shhh," Eiran says quietly, and I lay my head on his chest.

We travel smoothly through the hospital, and I don't register the words surrounding me. Nurses say something. Eiran gives a low, commanding reply. None of it matters anyway.

There's fresh air, and I'm outside. Eiran's jogging now, his feet a quiet rumbling tempo. We reach a small hollow where a tree and a few flowers stand among the buildings. Eiran kneels, setting me down against the trunk. He grows the roots, forming a wall, blocking us from the world.

"Take a minute," he says, coming to sit next to me. "Breathe."

"I—"

"Breathe," he says again. "Breathe in the scent of the Luminar Essence. Exhale your contribution to the Aether. In through the nose. Out through the mouth." I give him a side-eye, the shock of it distracting me. He shrugs. "Aetheric Breathwork. It's just breathing, but it helps."

I smile slightly, an eyebrow still raised as I repeat, "Breathe in the scent of the… Luminar Essence?" He nods, and I take a breath through my nose.

"And exhale your contribution to the Aether."

I breathe in and out, pulse slowing.

"I'm sorry for crying," I manage, staring at the ground. I can't believe I did that in front of him, hurt him like that.

He cocks his head, frowning at me. "Why would you apologize for crying? You had a panic attack after an extremely traumatic day. I'd be worried if you *didn't* cry."

My mind replays all that happened today in fast forward. Oh gods. The lab. The park. My hand. The hospital…

"Breathe," Eiran reminds me again. When I resume the breathwork like he showed me, he smiles kindly. "I have some positions I can show you later. If you'd like."

Despite the fear of the moment, I can't help but say, "Oh really? What positions do you have to show me, Eiran?"

His mouth quirks, but I swear his eyes heat a bit, too. "I mean eldertree alignment, smartass. Center yourself. Align your body and mind to the Aetheric flow, yada yada. It helps."

For a bit, we sit in the cozy quiet. Nauktbirds coo a familiar, lilting melody, joyful in the cool evening air. I shiver, leaning into Eiran's warmth without thinking. He doesn't push me away.

Instead, he reaches out a hand in front of us, and a root from the tree slowly grows up from the ground, its movements precise and controlled. Eiran makes quiet movements in the air with his hands, and the root swirls in graceful arcs, bending in and out amongst the loops. I stare, fascinated, as the root dances in a stunning supernatural ballet, twining around itself.

Eiran stops, clearing his throat. "It's not my best work, but—"

"It's beautiful," I say, amazed by the Gruundlith sculpture.

Eiran flashes a brief smile. "The town I'm from is known for its artisans. Some of the best on Vale. I'd never be a great artist, but I couldn't help falling in love."

I'm amazed at how different our childhoods were, though I guess I shouldn't be. Without really meaning to, I say, "I grew up in that lab."

Eiran stills, his silence giving me space to think.

After a pause, I find the strength to continue. "I never got to see Vale. Not really. Not the way my mom did. But she always talked about it. Said there's something about this place. She called it… she called it 'the Vale effect,' like there was a magical pull that made it this paradise of mixing cultures. Like something about Vale draws people to it." I shake my head. "I've lived in the multicultural district for years. Never been off-world. I don't know that I ever understood what she saw in it."

"You always wanted to leave?" Eiran asks.

"Yeah. I mean, don't get me wrong. A lot in my life is good. A lot was good even before. Most of the time. The other kids were cruel. Some researchers too. Called me 'geneblight' and worse, but… but my mom loved me. And that made it okay. She was a scientist for the Initiative. She was so smart and super busy, but she always had time for me. But…"

"But what?" Eiran asks in a low tone.

"But she made me what I am." I stare at the ground, shame washing over me. I remind myself I'm not really feeling the prick of the needle in my vein. Not really feeling the press of a gun at my shoulder. It's just Eiran next to me. I'm safe. He said I'm safe.

"My mom made me a freak." I push the words out past this choking feeling in my throat. "She made me a freak, and not even a normal freak. Not just a geneblight doomed to live here in fucking judgment central, hated for being unnatural. No, she had to do more. To make me…" I can't finish.

"…the magic?" Eiran asks.

I flinch. "Yeah. She gave me all sorts of shots and injections. My entire childhood. Like… like a damn lab rat. If the Initiative found me…" Tears are running down my cheeks again. I let them roll unchecked. "And my mom did that. Put a target on my back that I can't escape. Not here anyway."

Eiran nods, like something's clicking into place. "The girl in the video. The thief from the jewelry store." His voice is quiet now. "The techs in my department swore it was a fake. But it wasn't, was it?"

A spike of adrenaline shoots through me at the mention of the video—but it fades quickly. Too quickly. (Not examining that right now, thanks.)

"My mom made me… whatever the hell I am. Why would she do that to me? If she loved me—she seemed to love me—then why? Why make me a freak, even among freaks?"

"You're not a freak," Eiran says, his eyes twinkling. "You're definitely a pain in my ass, but not a freak."

I laugh, something inside me cracking… or maybe mending. I bump his shoulder. "Takes a pain in the ass to know a pain in the ass."

Eiran grins that stupid, breathtaking, dimpled grin. "I can agree with that."

I laugh, and then sigh. "Why are you helping me? You're being… weirdly nice given I broke your arm a few minutes ago, especially given you accused me of working for terrorists. Not to mention you know I have magic, something that usually freaks people out." I hold my breath, oddly anxious for the answer.

"Well, first, we've established that you are not, in fact, a terrorist."

"Gee, thanks."

"And I'm not scared of you, either." I turn sharply to him. "I nearly lost it out there after what happened. You passed out by this point, but… the anger? The adrenaline? It can take over sometimes. We can go feral. It's called the Rökkurgrimm. The last time it happened… let's just say it's not pretty." He grimaces, but his face quickly smooths.

I pick up a stick, examining it as a memory tugs at me. "I saw a Valen boy attack another kid a couple of weeks ago in the same park where…" I take a deep breath, swallowing down the memories and the panic, fingers momentarily white around the stick before it snaps. I toss them aside. "Anyway. The Valen clawed the other kid's face."

Eiran nods. "Yeah, it happens a lot when we're little." His voice changes, cold and nearly silent. "And sometimes when we're older, too." Shaking himself, he says, "I pulled it back with Blackstone, but trust me: you may be capable and smart and have magic. And that makes you a badass." His eyes heat for a second, sending a strange thrill down to my core. The heat flares, then dies away. "But I know scary. You aren't scary."

Setting aside the terrifying thought of an adult elf going "feral," I do my best to laugh and say, "You're full of compliments today."

"As for why I'm helping you… it's my job. I help you, and then you help me."

I scoff. Predictable.

"Well, you're pretty good at talking me through my panic attack. So what? Do you also moonlight as a trauma counselor or something?"

Eiran laughs. "I've been trained on… well, this isn't my first time working with someone dealing with CPTSD. And I'm not an archeologist. That was my major in college, and that's how I started with the SRF originally. A consultant. Now that I'm a case agent, managing assets and CIs is part of the job description."

I pick up a loose stick and toss it. "A criminal informant? I already told you I don't know what's going on." Great. I'm not a suspect anymore. I'm a *snitch*.

"I know. But you have skills and connections I don't. I need your help."

"I'm not a spy, Eiran," I say, shaking my head.

"No, but you're a talented thief. One of the best, I'd bet, given you garnered the Karu Oni's attention. That's what I need. I may know the espionage circles. But for Vaeloria City's underworld, I'm going to need an expert. Blackstone's hurt, and he can't exactly go to a hospital. Ideas of where he'd go?"

Right. That's me. The expert asset. It's not his fault I'm so fucking damaged that I'm attracted to anyone who shows me kindness. I can keep it professional. In fact, that's immensely better than his being here talking me down because he is somehow actually *nice*. It's not like I want this Valen to be my friend, right?

So why did my stomach sink at the revelation?

"I might have some ideas."

Eiran nods and leans back against the tree. "Fair enough."

Quietly, I ask, "Eiran? About what I can do… it doesn't freak you out?"

He smiles a touch ruefully at that. "It's your turn to freak out right now. I'll freak out later." He lays back again, hands behind his head, his long arm a canopy above me as he stares out to the skyline glowing beyond his wall of roots.

I copy him, and we sit there for a moment longer. "So, you won't arrest me?" I ask.

Eiran contemplates that. "I'm thinking not. Not if you help me." He gives me a wild grin. "But if you're missing the cuffs, we can find other uses for them."

My cheeks go hot at that, although I'm at least mostly sure he's kidding.

I think.

I let out a laugh that's mostly a sigh. "So, what will *we* do then?"

"Talk to Kairo."

I turn to Eiran, horrified. "How do you… who?"

"You know, Kairo Ryūkishi? Your friend and associate? We know all about him, Taylor. We know Kairo is arguably the best fence on the continent, with connections to some very unsavory characters. We also know he's the only known Hitari on the planet—until his father showed up. And yes, we know that connection, too."

I groan. "If Kairo were here, he'd be offended that you didn't call him the best fence on the *planet*. And he's not in league with his father. Trust me."

Eiran's expression doesn't change. "I believe you. But he's still the son of the one Helix hired to set you up. And if he's 'the best fence on Vale,' he'll surely be of help. If he doesn't know something, someone he knows will. And you're going to get him to help me."

I'm sure that'll go well.

Eiran extends his hand, weakening the root of his sculpture. Eiran breaks it off, sending the root retreating into the ground. He tucks the thin loose end of the root behind one of the spiraling curls of his design and then hands it to me. "For you," he says. Then, without another word, he stands. With a wave of his arm, the wall of roots collapses, revealing the world beyond.

Eiran reaches into his pocket and pulls out a small, round wafer. "Here. Take this. It'll dissolve on your tongue."

"Kairo taught me not to take drugs from strange men in parks."

Eiran snorts. "It's a digestible tracker. Unless you want to sleep on my floor, it's the best way to make sure you don't run off. Don't worry. It wears off. Eventually."

"Not happening."

He shrugs. "Okay. Your choice. We can stop by your apartment and grab a pillow or something if you'd like. I don't have any bedding, so grab a blanket too."

"Fine. Let's go." I make to stand. It's not like I can't slip away once he's asleep.

Eiran grins, and I wonder if he suspects what I'm planning. "You don't mind putting the cuffs back on, do you? If you don't have the tacker, you'll need the cuffs."

Fuck.

How long will that tracker last? It's probably not worth asking him. He'd be stupid to tell me. I want to argue. But honestly, he'll track me either way. At least this way, he won't be physically breathing down my neck. I wouldn't want that. I don't think.

"You're a real prick, you know that?" I manage. With an eye roll, I open my mouth.

Eiran grins as he places the wafer on my tongue, and just to be an asshole, I run the top of my tongue over his finger as he pulls away. A fang catches on his bottom lip, and damn if that isn't the sexiest fucking thing. In seconds, the wafer dissolves, the salty taste of his skin somehow lingering long after the wafer itself. He motions, and I open, showing him it's actually gone.

"Excellent. You coming?"

"I'm going to sit here for a bit," I say.

Eiran nods. "Okay. I need this arm healed anyway. I'll meet you at your apartment in the morning. Don't even think of running, or I'll find you. Good night, Taylor." With one last backward glance, he disappears into the night.

11

TEAMBUILDING

What the hell was I thinking, letting Eiran meet me at my apartment?! Awakened thirty seconds ago by a buzz at the door, I rush around my tiny loft, throwing dirty clothes into a hamper, tossing takeout containers into a trashcan, and searching all over for my damn bra.

Warm pink light filters through the blinds, casting the room in a strange hue that's too cheery for this early in the morning. Piles of books, three different comm tablets, various plantlife, and a wide assortment of gifts and collectibles cover every surface, all lit in the odd light. That's always the first sign that the solar storms, which often plague Vale, are returning. The elvish mystics believe it's some sort of sign of impending doom, and given how this morning is going so far, I'm inclined to believe them.

"I know you're in there, Taylor. I have your tracker on my comm."

"Just a second!" A fern smacks me in the face (again) and I curse. Why the hell did I ever decide it was a good idea to embrace the elvish love of plants indoors? These things are a menace.

Eiran just chuckles. The bastard. "Do I need to come back later?"

"No! I'm just…" Ah, there's the bra, hiding behind an emberblossom plant.

Fuck. The emberblossom. Surely he won't get pissy about an herbal drug growing in my apartment, all things considered? It's barely illegal.

Throwing the plant underneath a table anyway, I slip the bra on, throw an old shirt over my head, and then say, "Okay, I'm opening the door, but if you say a word about my apartment or myself, I'm kicking you out."

"Okay, agreed." I frown as I open the door because Eiran sounds entirely too amused. He gives me a once-over, eyes making the down-and-up trek slower than absolutely necessary.

"Hi," I say self-consciously, running a hand absentmindedly through my mess of red curls. "You realize it's seven-thirty in the morning, right?"

"Yeah. Sorry I'm so late. Breakfast?" He holds up a bag of pastries and two coffees. I scowl at him, but take the coffee because I'm mad, not crazy. He chuckles again, closing the door behind himself. He inspects the small space with a slow, arcing gaze. That damn eyebrow raises at my tiny combination kitchen, dining room, and living room. "Your apartment is—"

"I warned you. I will kick you out."

"…nice."

"You weren't going to say 'nice.' Don't even lie."

Eiran inclines his head. "I was going to say 'quaint.' But it's nice. I like all the plants. Rare for a human apartment."

"You visit many human women's apartments?"

"Not really," he admits, amethyst eyes twinkling. "Why do you ask?"

"And… what about elves? Surely someone who looks like you…" I trail off. Where was I going with that sentence?

Eiran chuckles. "No one special. You?"

It's an innocent question. He means nothing by it. We're just making conversation… I think.

I swallow a boulder that's appeared in my throat. "No one. Not like that. With my past, I can't afford… friends." Coffee in hand, I head to the bedroom. I am definitely *not* fleeing. "Anyway, to answer your earlier question, I grew up on Vale. Feels weird without plants around." Stopping at the entrance to my bedroom, I turn and motion to the door, eyeing Eiran, who has moved to follow me. "Listen, I'm going to leave the bedroom door cracked so we can talk while I change. If I see you turning this direction, I *will* kick your hulking green ass."

"That's fair. Just hurry. We have a lot to do today." He shoos me off, and I head inside.

"Like what?" I call as I try to look a tad bit more presentable.

"I need to know everything you know. And I, uhh… may also need Kairo's help. Apparently, I caused a bit of havoc at work, and now

Thorne, my boss, is telling me not to use official channels until I have something solid. That I need to 'keep my head down', whatever that means."

I frown as I touch up the small amount of makeup I'm bothering to do today. "What happened?"

"Well, apparently my investigation into the Lorathar Initiative wasn't 'officially sanctioned'—though I know I told Thorne about it."

With an eye roll, I apply a touch of lipstick. Is this overkill for a casual day out? Why am I obsessing?

Realizing I should respond, I call, "Eiran, I'm sorry. That sucks."

"It gets worse. After you locked me in that damn lab, I called some friends in Environmental Protection, and they raided the compound."

I still, waiting for the shoe to drop. The Valen Environmental Protection Enforcement is notoriously ruthless, dealing out severe punishments for all violations, no matter if it's littering or dumping industrial waste. If they raided the compound… maybe my fear of the Initiative is gone! But then why the hesitation?

"They… the Initiative torched everything. All the seeds. All the research. Apparently, people are pissed about the lost research, even though it was illegal." I can hear the eye roll even through the nearly closed door. "So I shouldn't use official channels unless I want it to get squashed."

It's gone. The Lorathar Initiative, everything I feared for years… just gone. Without warning or ceremony, it's all gone. Except for my mom's journal. Could there be anything valuable there?

Do I really want to open up that can of worms?

Before I can decide if I dare mention it, Eiran says, "I brought you donuts, by the way. From that place you like. They're—"

My voice goes low as I walk out of the bedroom. "How do you know what pastry shop I visit?"

"I mean, I followed you, obviously. How do you think I located the… lab…" He trails off as I walk in the room. His eyes dip, roving over me before he gathers himself. I cross my arms, unsure if I'm more flustered at the idea he's been following me or the look on his face. He seems to notice he's staring, because he blinks rapidly. For whatever reason, his attention makes my heart rate spike, and I don't like it.

"Anyway," he says, voice normal again. "I can see why you visit there. The pastries are quite good."

Thankful for the change in topic, I laugh. "You eat pastries? I thought Valen were carnivores."

"Strictly speaking, Valen don't need pastries," he admits, voice dropping a notch. "The chlorophyll in our skin feeds us sugars just fine. Carbs are extra. Dangerous. They fade the color out of our skin, among other things As you can see…" He gestures at his lighter skin. "I've indulged more than I should. Can't make a habit of it, unless I want to bulk up in all the wrong places. But today? I figured we earned a little sin."

"Yes, extra weight is clearly a danger for you," I say dryly, surveying the fit of today's white button-down. It's annoyingly perfect, hugging his taut frame. I roll my eyes at the smug look that sweeps over his face.

Men. Honestly.

"But I agree on the point of deserving a treat. Plus, these are my *favorite*." I take a bite of a large fluffy donut and stifle a moan of pleasure.

Eiran grins. "I guess I chose well. Now hurry. We need to go meet Kairo and talk this out."

A frankly impressive thirty minutes later (given the state I was in when Eiran first showed up), the bell to Galactic Pages rings, announcing our entrance to the little shop. Kairo rushes from the back room. His eyes land on me and widen. "Taylor? What the hell? I thought you were going to message me after you went to the lab. How did it—" He lurches to a stop, seeing Eiran. "Who's this?"

"I texted you after," I say, holding out a hand, trying to calm him. "Your dad intercepted it."

Kairo stills at this. His wings materialize out of nowhere, billowing wide in anger. "He what?"

"The Kuro Oni is working with a cyborg named Adrian Blackstone," Eiran says, watching Kairo's response.

Kairo blinks in confusion. "A cyborg? And again, who the fuck are you?"

"Eiran works for the SRF," I explain. "He saved my life."

"You brought an agent from the fucking *SRF* to my—"

"Your father is working with a cyborg named Adrian Blackstone," Eiran cuts in, unbothered by Kairo's tone. "Genetically enhanced with stolen Hitari wings grafted onto his back. He's an operative for a human-first terrorist organization called Helix. Does any of that sound familiar?"

At the mention of the wings, Kairo's lip curls in disgust. "Are you telling me he's… no. Terrorists I believe. But someone like that—"

"They were there together last night," I say apologetically. I hesitate as Kairo shakes his head. "Kairo, Blackstone took the seeds and kept the lamp. He tried to kill me." Kairo goggles at me, rushing forward. "I'm alright," I say reassuringly. "Eiran saved the day. Got me to a hospital."

Kairo seems to mouth the word "hospital" but otherwise doesn't comment on the "saved the day" bit. Instead, he turns frostily to Eiran. "So, is that why you're here? This Blackstone guy?"

Eiran shakes his head. "You two stole one of the most dangerous weapons in the galaxy and put it in the hands of someone dangerously unstable working for interstellar terrorists. You're lucky I'm not throwing the both of you in a hole until you forget what sunlight looks like."

Kairo's wings flare again. "Why don't you try it then, Leaf Boy?"

Eiran's claws extend, that pointy grin returning. "I don't know. I might enjoy it."

"Okay, you boys can measure lengths later," I snap, exasperated.

Eiran chuckles. "No need to measure. I'm Valen. It's basic genetics."

Kairo lunges. "You son of a—"

I throw out a hand, stopping him just in time—though my brain is now flashing with warring mental images I absolutely did *not* consent to. "Kairo, he helped me. More than once. He hasn't turned us in. So maybe… I don't know. Maybe don't stab him just yet."

"Thank you for your restraint," Eiran mutters, leaning back against the table with those smug, infuriating dimples. I pointedly do not look at them. Or his slacks. Damn him.

"Eiran," I say, gritting my teeth, "you still haven't explained what's so dangerous about the seeds." "It's more than that," Eiran says, tone dropping. "The seeds are dangerous. Volatile. That's how we knew they existed. This group has been operating for thirty years right under our noses. We only found them because someone tested the seeds and… Did you hear about the stryder explosion a few weeks ago?"

"The Union-designed ones?" I ask. "Yeah, I heard. That was horrible."

The experimental vehicles imported from the Union had exploded in a building parking lot. Half of the building exploded. Fifteen people were killed, and many wounded. It was one of the driving forces behind the "Buy Local" movement—besides the VerdantBoost disaster.

"That's what I've been investigating. I don't think it was the vehicles' fault," Eiran says in that same quiet tone. "Somehow someone got a hand on one of these experimental seeds, and—"

"Holy shit," Kairo breathes.

"And that was just one powerseed. A small one at that," Eiran confirms. "Take a couple of full-sized ones and rig them properly? You could bring down a city. Easy."

I stare at him, horrified. "You're saying I put a potential city-leveling bomb in the hands of terrorists?!"

"It's not your fault," Kairo insists, but I shake my head.

"I stole the seeds for him. Plus, I forgot how confusing that place is. You couldn't have done it if you hadn't grown up there. Not without getting caught. How exactly is this not my fault?"

Eiran puts my hand in his, running a finger along the ragged black scar on my wrist that seems permanent. "What matters is that we recover them. And given Blackstone is working through Vale's underground rather than the spy network I'm used to, I'm going to need your help. *That*," he says to Kairo, "is why I'm here."

"Why should we help you?" Kairo asks in a dubious tone. "No offense, but you have your own people to do this shit, and my father is dangerous as hell. If this Blackstone is worse—"

"The mission is off the books. I'm getting no backup from central. As for why you're helping, is staying out of prison not enough motivation?"

Kairo rolls his eyes. "When the alternative is death, no."

"I'll get Taylor the documents she needs to get off-planet," Eiran says quietly.

I gape at him. "How did you—"

He shrugs. "You wanted off-planet. Interplanetary is expensive, but not prohibitively so. If you're still here, it's because you can't leave. You're a ghost. I know that much from my failed attempts at researching you. Setting up a false ID and back-history believable enough to get you safe passage into the Union or beyond? Now *that's* expensive. Unless you know someone in the SRF."

My brain is reeling. He's once again nailed me in one.

"You... you can do that?"

He nods.

I turn to Kairo. "Look, you make your own choice, but I'm helping."

"Fine," Kairo grumbles, but then he shrugs. "Spy shit. Awesome." He grins, though the shine doesn't quite meet his eyes. A wooden shelf creaks slightly as he leans against it. "So, what can we help you with, Leaf Boy?"

Eiran's eyes narrow. "That nickname will *not* become a thing."

"I was thinking 'beanstalk', because you're tall and green, but in the end, I figured Leaf Boy would piss you off more," Kairo says cheerfully. "Looks like it worked."

I grin. "Leaf Boy needs me to finger some underground doctors that might help fix up Blackstone. Not sure what he's wanting you for, though. I like the name, by the way."

Kairo laughs. "Knew it."

"What I need," Eiran says in a long-suffering tone, "is intel on your father. Why Blackstone would work with him."

"If you figure out my father, let me know," Kairo says with a growl. "We haven't spoken in about a decade, and I promise you if I had it my way, it would've been longer." Then, he sighs, wings curling a bit. "But his working with this Blackstone guy is surprising. At least it should be."

"Because of the wing thing?" Eiran asks.

Kairo exhales through his nose, a sound somewhere between a laugh and a snarl. "Yes, if by 'wing thing' you mean cutting off a Hitari's wings and stitching them onto some cybernetic butcher-monster. It's beyond sacrilege. It's desecration. Like setting fire to Hikario and dancing around the flames."

He flicks his wings in annoyance, light rippling strangely across the surface.

"Hikario is the god of light and knowledge," I explain to Eiran. "Chief god of the Hitari religion."

"You don't strike me as the religious type," Eiran says with a raised eyebrow.

"I'm not," Kairo replies in a flat tone. "But my father *is*, believe it or not. At least—" he clenches his jaw before taking a breath and continuing in a calmer tone. "My point is, cutting off someone's wings violates everything the Hitari stand for. Even at a cultural level, it's just… wrong. And yet, you say my father is working with this Blackstone.

Someone cut the wings off a Hitari, grafted it onto this bastard, and now my father is *working with him?* Fuck, I should be surprised, but honestly I'm not. Compromising everything he's supposed to believe in for a long-term gain is pretty standard for how Akio operates. Tell me more about this Blackstone guy. Maybe that'll help me understand what his play might be."

"You two have a history, right?" I say to Eiran.

He seems distant now, staring at one of Kairo's elvish sculptures like it holds the answer to all the universe's truth. He eventually turns back around to us, face grim. "Alright look. I'm not super proud of what happened, but—"

Kairo's mouth grows into that lopsided smile of his, the bookshelf groaning again as he steps away, moving closer to us. "What'd you do, Leaf Boy?"

Eiran sighs, leaning an arm on the register counter. "Okay, eight years ago, I'd finished school with an archeology degree and was doing some consulting work for the SRF. Cases where historical artifacts came into play, that sort of thing. Anyway, I was advising on this case, Operation Chimera. Big joint operation with the Union. No artifacts involved. But by this time, I had other, um, *talents* they'd identified."

"The using magic without touching plants thing?" I guess, and Kairo's eyes widen.

Eiran inclines his head and continues, "There was a scientist, Dr. Alexander Kane, who was huge within the cybernetics community. Super influential. A genius, really, if a twisted and evil one. Anyway, Kane had been working on some off-the-books research."

"That doesn't sound good," I say wearily.

"No, it really wasn't," Eiran agrees. "Kane was working with a Valen. They were looking for a way to meld biotech seeds with human anatomy. To use seeds as a sort of 'power-up' for human cyborgs."

"Oh, gods," Kairo groans.

"Exactly," Eiran confirms. "I can't even imagine the potential impact of putting that power within a single person. And biotech is, by definition, biological. The cyborgs would become living rechargeable batteries. With blaster rifles."

Kairo's look goes keen. "So, what happened?"

Eiran grimaces. "You need to understand. The Valen that Kane was working with? It was Seranthil Vaelorian."

My eyes widen. "Vaelorian? As in the Vaelorian family, founders of Vaeloria City? Those Vaelorians?" The Vaelorian family was a rich and influential family, with several family members in influential positions in government and business circles.

"They're the ones," Eiran confirms. "Seranthil was one of the youngest in this big influential family, and he was often overlooked. So, he joined in with Kane, buying into his lies. He was enamored with the prospect of making a name for himself, of pushing the boundaries of technology and magic."

"Got to make Daddy proud somehow," Kairo mutters, and I wonder if he's thinking of Akio.

"At some point, Seranthil realized Kane's intentions. Understood the potential consequences of merging cybernetics and powerseeds. He tried to back out, but… it didn't go well. Everyone blamed the task force for Seranthil's death, and there was this push for a quick resolution."

Eiran pauses, eyes distant. "So, I went and found their facility where Kane was working. I infiltrated the mainframe, and when I reached the core of the experiment, I disabled the security protocols and made the seeds self-destruct. But—"

"They were working on someone," I guessed.

"Blackstone?" Kairo asks.

"Yeah," Eiran confirms. "He was a soldier originally. Was severely injured on his first mission. It was the skirmish on Caldrakus. Maybe you're too young to remember. It was a big deal some twenty years ago. Anyway, he was severely burned. Kane offered him hope. And twisted his anger for his own ends."

My insides go cold. I've been there. Know what pain and bitterness can do.

"So, he became a cyborg. And then when you set the seeds to self-destruct—"

"Yeah," Eiran confirms. "It was a controlled implosion, but still. Adrian lost an arm and a good part of his cybernetics, and Kane somehow died in the chaos that ensued afterwards. Blackstone disappeared for a couple of months, and then popped up again, working for this dangerous terrorist organization out of the Union."

I nod. "Helix."

Eiran shrugs. "It's not surprising, really. He hates the Valen. Blames us for what happened to him, to Kane. So, of course, he's going to align with an organization wanting to end the superiority of magic users. An organization you can be sure has terrible plans for those seeds."

Kairo groans. "And whatever that plan is? That's dear old dad's play here. He likes the long game. Opportunities. It's never one job."

"I don't understand why someone like Adrian Blackstone would do that to himself," I say. "I get why he was drawn to Kane originally. If I went through what he did… but why turn himself into *that?*"

"Well," Eiran says after a pause. "I think what the Caldrakes did to him made him feel weak. Helpless. Humans are the only major race with no magic. We Valen have our nature abilities. Hitari have light magic. Zeridians have geomancy, the Quiblins have their psychic powers—"

"Did someone mention Quiblins?" a squeaky voice says from behind me.

12

SYLARA THE HUNTRESS

Two short, gray-skinned aliens in matching aprons shuffle in from the back room, the faint scent of ozone and warm metal clinging to them. Their large bat-like ears twitch as they peer over a cluttered display table, whispered clicks and static noises coming from the strange goggles perched on Frank's oversized eyes. Standing at barely three feet tall, Quiblins are among the smallest of the intelligent races, but what they lack in height they make up for in intelligence and magical ability.

Eiran stiffens. "Who's this?"

"Greetings!" the Quiblin grins. "I'm Frank. This is my twin sister, Emma. Pleased to meet you!" Frank stands as tall as he can, holding a long-fingered, gray hand out expectantly.

"They work for me," Kairo explains as I give Emma a brief hug (which she kindly endures).

Eiran raises an eyebrow and shakes Frank's hand. "Well, it's nice to meet you then, Frank. Pleased to meet you, Emma." Eiran turns, holding out a hand to the diminutive gray-skinned female. After hesitating, she shakes it briefly, looking away, most of her face hidden behind a large fur-lined hood.

"Emma is not fond of talking, sir," Frank explains. "She prefers to speak mind-to-mind. Go on, Emma. Say hi."

Frank gives Emma a shocked look, and I know she must have said something rude to him over their telepathic connection. But then she makes eye contact with Eiran.

He startles, but says, "Uh... hi."

Her eyes turn to me, and her soft mental voice brushes mine. *"Hello Miss. Are you okay?"*

I think back, *"Oh! Hey Emma. I wouldn't exactly say okay, but I'm getting there."*

Emma's enormous eyes seem to widen slightly beneath the hood. I've only attempted psychic communication with her a few times. I hadn't even realized I could do it until recently. Another mysterious gift from Mom, another secret to hide. Frank chimes in, "So, now that the introductions are made, how can we help?"

"Oh, no, Frank," Kairo says quickly. "Sorry, we were talking and mentioned your people in passing. We weren't asking to—"

"But we would like to help," Frank insists, dark eyebrows forming a V against his silvery skin. "Let us help with this Blackstone person. And this Kuro Oni."

Eiran's eyes flash at Kairo, who frowns at Frank. "Have you been eavesdropping, Frank?"

Frank's massive eyes go, if possible, even larger, the edges disappearing behind the goggles. "Oh no, Mr. Ryūkishi, sir. We have not been eavesdropping, sir. But we were listening, I must admit." He grins sheepishly. "With our ears, it's hard not to sometimes, sir." He wiggles his long gray ears in explanation.

Eiran has a small smile forming at the corner of his lips now. "That's alright, Frank. How do you think you could help with Blackstone?"

Frank seems to crumple in relief. "Oh, well, we could help you find him, sir. If you would like. Find his ship."

"I doubt he's still here," Eiran says. "The Eclipse Consortium never sticks around after a job, and Blackstone's probably already in Union space by now, too."

"No, they're not," Kairo replies. "Haven't you seen the news? The solar storms are dreadful, and getting worse. All interstellar travel is closed for at least a month. Maybe two."

Vale's star is notoriously temperamental, and storms are not uncommon. While there's tech to manage effects on Vale itself, interstellar travel gets shut down completely when it acts up. It's never this bad, though. Two months of travel stopdown is huge.

But speaking as someone who's been trapped on this planet their entire life, I can't say I'm too sympathetic.

Eiran's eyebrows rise in surprise at the news. "How would you find

Blackstone's ship?" he asks Frank.

"There will be a trail in the system," Frank says confidently, his little chest sticking out a bit in pride. "Even arriving under a false name, there is still a record if we look properly. Finding things is Emma's expertise. Isn't that right, Emma?" Emma bobs her head once in confirmation.

"I'm sure Eiran has his own people that can track such things," Kairo says, glancing between Eiran and me.

"I don't, actually," Eiran admits, frowning slightly at him. "Off-the-books op, remember?"

"No," Kairo says, shaking his head. "Not happening."

"I want to help," Frank repeats, tiny gray hands on his hips now.

"Just let him help," I coax, baffled why Kairo's opposing this.

"No," he repeats, voice tight and urgent, his fingers twitching against the worn fabric of his sleeve. "I'm not getting someone else roped into this shit. I already let you get involved, and you nearly…" His shoulders hunch, wings folding protectively around him like a shield, the faint scrape of leathery hide against fabric filling the silence.

My heart aches at Kairo's words. "That wasn't your fault." I pass his wing and put a hand on his shoulder. "You didn't *let* me do anything. I'm a big girl. I can make my own decisions."

"Bad decisions."

I laugh. "I can make those on my own, too."

"Why are you so eager to help?" Eiran asks Frank. "This is a dangerous situation. Kairo's right. This isn't the sort of thing I want you involved in. I shouldn't have agreed so quickly."

Frank looks over at his sister before saying, "It is hard for Quiblins to find jobs outside of factories or ships after what the Zeridians have done to us. We have no home. Nowhere to go." The twins stare at the ground. Frank reaches a hand to his sister, and my heart breaks yet again.

Decades ago, the Kingdom of Zeridia claimed Hyouko, the icy Quiblin homeworld, in a hostile takeover. The opportunistic Zeridians justified it as "necessary for the survival of the Zeridian people."

Fucking dwarves. They always say that.

Quiblins like Frank and Emma became refugees with nowhere to go unless they made themselves "useful" somewhere. With their near-instant telepathic communication and strong aptitude with electronics, they typically ended up in engineering roles. Businesses have hired them by the hundreds, paying them next to nothing.

"We want to stay here," Frank insists, eyes pleading with Kairo now. "I will not let my sister spend her life toiling away in a factory or traveling on a starship. This is a good job. You are a good boss, Mr. Ryūkishi, sir. If you and your friends are in danger, I want to help. I want to keep this job."

Kairo deflates at the statement. Running a hand through his constantly messy black hair, he groans, "Okay, fine. You can help. But stay hidden," he adds to Emma. "Don't leave any digital trace of who you are. We can't let on that someone's looking for Blackstone."

Emma stares at Kairo for an unwavering beat before heading to the back. Frank gives another sheepish smile. "I apologize for Emma. She does not have the extraordinary gift of speech that I have, Sirs, Miss. She prefers to focus on her work, which she is very good at, I assure you. If there is any sign of Mr. Ryūkishi's father or this Blackstone person, Emma will find it. I will leave you now and go assist her in this."

With a low bow, Frank heads into the back room with his sister.

"His name is… Frank?" Eiran asks Kairo softly once the door shuts.

Kairo's mouth quirks. "Quiblins don't have their own language. They 'think' their ideas and feelings telepathically with each other. They didn't even know 'language' existed, in our concept of the term, until the Hitari came and discovered their planet about five hundred years ago. They need vocal cord surgery if they want to speak at all. So, they borrow names from other species. Not always effectively."

"I hate the idea of involving them in something this dangerous," I say as Kairo leads us toward the door.

"I'll keep an eye on them. You two watch out for each other. I'll see you at lunch." With a nod at Eiran and a wink at me, he disappears inside, a tinkling bell his final farewell.

"He really cares about you."

"Yeah, he worries too much." I smile despite myself as we walk past a row of shops. "After my mom died, I… well, long story, but Kairo took me in. Taught me everything I know."

Eiran laughs as I round the corner of the next block. "Some role model."

"To be fair," I say a bit defensively, turning around to glare at him,

"I was so freaked that I tried to run off twice. He caught me hacking credits from the register for the third time before he gave up. Said if I was determined to be a thief, I should at least be a good one."

Eiran clearly disagrees with that philosophy, but he doesn't argue. "Where to now? Want to go check out those doctors you were talking about before we meet Kairo for lunch?"

"Sure, but if you're dragging me all over Vaeloria City, I'm going to go take a shower, since someone woke me up at the ass crack of dawn."

Eiran chuckles. "Fair enough. Clean up. I'll pick you up in an hour." With a last glance, he walks off, disappearing among the trees of the greenway.

I turn another corner, heading for my apartment when, without warning, there's a sharp prick at my throat—thin and surgical. My thoughts begin to splinter, but a cold, coppery-red hand latches onto my arm and a familiar oily, sweet musk hits me.

Then, a whole new sort of dread sucks me in.

The Zeridian pulls me to her broad chest, the tip of her stinger never leaving my neck. "Too bad Kairo never actually taught you to be a *good* thief, Taylor," a clicking voice says into my ear. "If you were, then I wouldn't be here to catch you. Now, would I?"

"S-Sylara?" I manage past the spike at my throat. "How… how are you doing? Uh, long time, no chat." If Sylara the Huntress is here, then things got a lot worse. I glance around the mostly abandoned side street nestled between shops. No one can see us. She picked her ambush point well.

As always.

"Don't even think of trying anything," the renowned thief, bounty hunter, and problem solver says in her slithering tone. She steps behind a large boulder, drawing us further out of sight. "You really stepped in it this time, Taylor. Sloppy. It's not like you."

"You know me," I say with a shaky laugh. I can feel the hard press of her exoskeleton on my back as she pulls me against her, the grooved texture of her engravings digging into me. "I never have my shit together like you. Come on. Cut me a break, Sylara… you… you owe me for the Harmonix Crystal job. I helped you out on that."

Sylara lets out a mirthless laugh. "We worked together on that job. It wasn't a favor. Besides, you cheated me out of the take."

"Because you left! And got a friend killed if you recall," I spit back.

"In fact, I think I told you I'd kill you the next time I saw you. So why don't you let me go, and we'll call it square?"

"I tell you what," Sylara says, not commenting on the accusation. "Since we have history, I'll make you a deal. You see, Ryland Corvane is very upset with you. Very upset indeed. With these solar storms, he's stuck here for several more weeks. And he really wants his artifact back."

"I don't know what you're talking about," I say reflexively. "He must have me confused with someone else."

"Oh, I don't think so," Sylara says, her thickly armored forearm like a steel bar across my chest. She's not gripping to hurt, just to keep me immobilized, but unfortunately, she's doing a damn fine job of it. "He saw your face, remember?"

"But how…" I disabled all the cameras. Even seeing my face, there's no way he'd be able to identify me. No one knows who I am.

"Quiblin mind scan," Sylara explains.

"Oh, dammit," I groan. The invasive process involves Quiblin magic and some rare tech, and it's painful as hell. But it can perfectly render an image from even an imperfect memory. "And you so kindly ID'd me."

Sylara raises a thick, chitin-covered shoulder in an unrepentant shrug. "That's right. But, like I said, I'll make you a deal. Corvane is stuck here for at least the next few weeks. So am I. You return the item you stole before he leaves, and we'll call it even. I'll tell him I roughed you up a bit. That'll be enough for him." I relax a fraction. So she won't kill me yet. Then she cocks her head in suspicion. "You do have it… right?"

I tense again, and I am sure Sylara can feel it. Still, I say, "Of course."

Sylara curses, sensing the lie. "Well, you'd better get it back. If not? There's nowhere in the galaxy I won't find you. And when I do… I *will* kill you." She pushes me into a nearby tree, barely giving me time to regain my balance before she crawls menacingly into my space. "It's nothing personal, Taylor. It's just business. But you know I mean it." I nod because I know for certain that she does. Without another word, she leaps straight up, landing on the roof of the three-story building above me. Giving me one last warning glare, she disappears onto the roof.

13

LUNCH DATE

"Ugh, how can you drink that?"

Eiran eyes me from over his glass, leaning on the rickety table. "It's lunchtime. Perfectly respectable to have a drink. I mean, you're drinking." He motions to my glass of ice wine.

To be fair, it's probably a strange order in a bar like this. The leafy touches and magically grown wood bar may mark it as Valen, but the bevy of scratches and smell of old drinks and stale nuts speak of a mostly human clientele. It wasn't my first choice of lunch spots, but Eiran insists that the Union-style burgers here are excellent.

"This wine is barely alcoholic," I say, rolling my eyes. I won't mention it's my second glass. "Besides, that wasn't my point. I couldn't care less if you drink. After the past forty-eight hours—hell, after the morning we had—you've earned it." We went to three different underground doctors that handle patch jobs at the severity Blackstone would need, but all we'd gotten for our trouble was blasters in our faces as soon as they figured out Eiran was a fed.

"I mean… how can you drink *that*?" I motion to the glass of bubbly, faintly pink liquid.

"You don't like anthalas?" he asks, surprised, motioning to the popular elvish beverage.

I wrinkle my nose. "Not at all. If I'm going to have a beer, I'll have a beer."

"Don't call anthalas beer," Eiran says, sounding pained. "I don't see how anyone drinks that Union beer. It tastes like you're drinking bread."

"It's an acquired taste," I reply primly. Truth be told, I'm not too fond of beer either, but given the choice, I'd take the beer over the anthalas. The drink may be strong, but much too floral. I mean, it makes sense, as it's literally made from lorathar blossom, but still. Weird.

Plus, you know, lorathar.

I sigh, trying not to dwell on Sylara. As one of the best hunters in the galaxy, I'm not surprised Corvane hired her to get the artifact back. Meaning I need a way to buy her off. There's no way in hell I'm giving the artifact to her—even if I had it.

I'll think of something.

"Where'd you go?" Eiran asks.

"Sorry," I grimace. I can't let Eiran find out about Corvane. If he knew what I stole, what Akio had in his possession…

With a burst of blaster fire, the front door to the bar explodes. Glass and wood go everywhere, tiny shards like acid rain on my skin. Eiran leaps on top of me, knocking me off the stool and onto the hard stone floor. We slide with the momentum, and my head slams into the bar's edge. My ears ring. I blink, trying to bring the room into focus. Through the dust and my blurry eyes, I see the edge of wings come into focus, one lopsided and strangely shaped.

It's Blackstone.

He stomps forward, grabbing Eiran and throwing him through the gaping front of the shop before hauling me to my feet by the arm. "Hey! What the… let me go, you metal-brained barbarian!" I yell. The elves in the store all goggle at us, several pulling out comms devices to film the strange altercation.

"Eiran!" I scream. Branches from the walls of the bar grow, wrapping around Blackstone, pulling him, but the cyborg refuses to let go. He moves, purposeful but unhurried, grabbing a small tool that looks like a gun. After a moment, I recognize it. No! No! No!

A tendril of wood wraps around Blackstone's arm, but a blast from his wing sends splinters flying. I thrash uselessly as Adrian Blackstone puts the medical gun to my neck. He leans in close, and I feel his rancid breath on my cheek as he says in a tone I can barely hear, "You made this so difficult, and to what end? This is all I wanted. Your blood. But since you made it so difficult, I'll take it all." He pulls the trigger and leaves it there.

I scream, the terror wrenching from me, until there's a blinding light, and I slam my eyes shut. Hollering in pain and annoyance, Blackstone lets go of my arm and stumbles back. There's a tinkling, thumping crash as he apparently upturns a table, sending drink glasses shattering against a wall. The floor shudders as he slams into the hard ground, the wooden branches cracking free. I open my eyes to see Kairo standing in the doorway, his large black wings filling the frame. "Hey, you ugly son of a bitch. Stay away from her."

Blackstone squints at Kairo with his one human eye for a moment, and then without warning fires off shots at him and Eiran, sending them scrambling for cover. Blackstone starts toward me again, but Kairo and Eiran both pop back up, trying to get around the fallen tables to intercept him. I scramble along the stone floor against the bar, trying to hide, my back digging into the metal footrest as I try to put distance between us. The males are twin storms barreling toward the cyborg. Blackstone grins in anticipation.

With a loud crunch, the floor begins to split and splinter, a ridge of stone appearing between the cyborg and me. I turn, astonished, toward the doorway. Sylara is there, a blaster in one hand trained on Blackstone. The other lifts from the slate floor. "The girl is mine," Sylara spits. "I don't care what you do with her after. She has business with me first."

"I don't give a fuck what business she has with you, you scorp bitch," Blackstone says, his one remaining blaster pointing toward her.

I clamber to my feet as Eiran pulls his own blaster on him. Searching for a weapon, I notice the glistening glass shards on the floor.

Now, that could work.

I touch as many of the pieces as I can with my magic, raising them to form a floating glass spear aimed at Blackstone's head.

Blackstone grins, a terrible, inhuman thing. "That's fine. I got what I wanted." Suddenly, his remaining wing blaster shifts and sends an arc of shots to the ceiling above us. As we all dive out of the way of the raining shards, he slams straight through the wall and onto the street beyond. I send my shards of glass flying, but his injured wings widen and he flies off jerkily into the distance.

Kairo steps toward the hole, his own wings unfurling.

Eiran grabs his arm, pulling him back. "Too risky. He'll blow you out of the air."

With a parting glare at Eiran, I turn my ire to Sylara. "Why?"

"Get the item," Sylara says to me, her blaster swinging back and forth between the three of us. Her mottled red exoskeleton is brilliant in the bright sunlight. "My fee's higher if I retrieve it. But if you're dead, I still get paid, so I won't save you next time." The crunch of glass mingles with the sound of our exhaled breath as she leaves as well.

***

I slurp my beer as obnoxiously as I can and glare at the two overprotective assholes escorting me. While I finally relented to Kairo's insistence that I "get off the street immediately" after Sylara showed up, I still can't believe his "safe house" is his storage warehouse.

I exhale loudly, hoping it's suitably annoying. Kairo rolls his eyes as I stomp along the concrete and steel hallway. At least irritation has burned away the terror of what just happened.

The gun on my neck. Just like... no. Focus on being mad. Mad is good. Mad is alive.

"It's for your own good," Eiran says yet again. The warehouse, drab in any context, is particularly stark amidst all the elvish architecture in Vaeloria City. It fits my current mood.

"We'll talk when we get inside," Kairo says flatly, stomping forward past an endless row of roll-up doors.

I can't contain my groan this time. "This is stupid."

"I told you to shut up." Kairo pulls out his comm device and unlocks the electronic padlock to his storage unit. With a clatter, Kairo lifts the rolling door about halfway, beckoning me to go inside. Ducking under the door, I enter the surprisingly well-lit space, Eiran crouching to follow behind me. Once Kairo is inside (somehow making the process elegant despite the wings), he closes the door and reengages the lock.

"Seriously, this is so unness—" Kairo holds up a hand, cutting me off.

"Frank," Kairo says.

I'm surprised to find Frank and Emma both here, toiling away at a row of Union-style computers, the screens balanced precariously on a stack of crates. Frank waves a hand, not turning away from the monitor he's looking at. "Sound dampening is in place."

"Frank's skills go beyond tech," Kairo says fondly, walking over to sit down on a box labeled "Histories 1 of 4," the wood cracking ominously under his weight. "He's found a way to use his magic to block sound."

Frank frowns slightly. "Actually, Mr. Ryūkishi, sir, that's not quite correct. As you know, our magic is not one of the mind, per se. It is one of wind…" (a light wind ruffles our hair at his words) "…and of electricity." Frank raises a hand, and faint blue sparks roil across his fingers. "We've always been a peaceful race. We focused our talents and studies on understanding the workings of the mind and of moving objects around us. Not of combat, espionage, and so forth. But we now have innovations like the voice implant. If we ever hope to get our homeworld back, we need to evolve. It is not a popular opinion among my kind."

I smile at the subtle bravery of the halfling. He could get kicked out of Quiblin society for saying stuff like that. Even as refugees, their culture is one of isolation and neutrality.

"The point is," Kairo says, clearly trying to get back to our reason for coming, "with Frank's help, we can speak freely here without worrying about being overheard." Frank nods, beaming widely. "Now… what the hell is Sylara doing on Vale?"

"Sounds like… our mark contracted her to get back the artifact we stole," I sigh, finding a seat on an empty container of romance novels, the illustrated abs from over a dozen species peeking out from within. This must be where Kairo keeps his extensive selection of smutty fiction.

"The artifact that *you* stole," Kairo counters.

Eiran's eyes narrow.

"And now he wants it back before the solar storms are over, or she'll kill us," I say, impervious to his griping. "Can we pay Sylara off? She's not exactly… loyal." What happened with the Harmonix Crystal proved that much.

"Maybe," Kairo says dubiously. "Depends on how much we offer. I'll see how much I can pull together."

"What did you steal, and from whom?" Eiran asks in a dangerous tone. "Who is Sylara working for?"

"You don't need to know," I say firmly. "It's unrelated to this case."

"Not if your life is threatened or we can't move freely. If you're not helpful, I can simply arrest both of you."

"And make Taylor a sitting duck?" Kairo huffs.

Eiran stares at me, his eyes firm but vaguely pleading. "Tell me. Maybe I can help."

Kairo says quietly, "Maybe he could arrest him. Give him something else to worry about."

"Arrest who?" Eiran asks, eyes ablaze.

Sighing, I turn to meet his gaze. "Ryland Corvane."

"Fuck," Eiran mutters. "You really are insane, aren't you? What'd you steal?"

"Ask me no questions and I'll tell you no lies." I cross my arms, glaring at him.

Eiran crosses his right back. "Okay, then. Who was your intended buyer?"

"A Night Realm chick," Kairo supplies. "Done business with her a few times."

"Not human? No one enhanced?"

"No, Eiran. I told you. Now, can you help with Corvane or not?"

Eiran scratches his neck. "I have an idea. Nothing's ever stuck, but—"

"Yes?" I ask, rolling my eyes.

"It's classified…" Eiran begins, but a glare from Kairo and me has him adding, "…Corvane's started smuggling Union weapons to the Zeridian separatists."

"Shit," Kairo breathes. As ruthless as the dwarven royals are, the rebels are worse. At least, that's what it says in the news. The last thing they need is powerful Union-built weapons. No one knows how to destroy shit quite like a human.

"The team in charge put off the arrest because they're trying to nail his supplier. If we bring down Corvane, someone else will start doing the transactions. We need the source. If you had some time, you'd be okay. A couple of months from now, the SRF will be deeply engrossed in his business, and you'll be the least of his worries."

"Wonderful," I grouse. "We'd be dead by then."

Eiran leans against a concrete pillar. "If you told me what you stole," Eiran says, "maybe I could help. Something of equivalent value, tied to someone the SRF already wants to take down."

"Tempting," I say, turning to Kairo. "But I'll pass. Right now, I'm more concerned about Blackstone."

"As you should be," Eiran replies ominously. "It takes special skills to deal with a human cyborg, and that would be hard to find on Vale. If you're sure we checked the most likely underground docs in the area, then he must have someone else on his payroll on-planet. And if he isn't alone, then we should—"

Eiran's comm rings. He pulls it out and mouths, *"My boss,"* before placing a finger to the biotech interface. "Yes, sir." Eiran listens as his boss speaks, a crease deepening between his dark green eyebrows. "I don't understand. You mean someone from the SRF was—"

Eiran gestures for silence, and then a male's boisterous baritone voice comes loudly through the comm's speaker. *"...was as surprised as you were. Believe me, I couldn't fathom anyone in our ranks thinking it was a good idea to partner with the Lorathar fanatics. But now? Everyone's scrambling for cover. Which explains why the flak for bringing them down. The place is crawling with shadows. You can't trust anyone right now—not even people you've worked beside for years."*

"This is bullshit, sir."

"No argument here, but that's the situation. Keep this case off the books. Quiet. Clean. The SRF agents involved probably thought it was a smart way to fast-track biotech R&D, but cloaked under Initiative funding. It blew up, and now they're hoping it doesn't trace back to them."

Eiran hesitates. "I was bringing in an asset—"

"Don't. I know who you mean. If you bring her in, she's a loose thread. You don't want her tangled in this mess. Keep handling her on the outside. No records. No names. Don't trust anyone, Eiran."

"Fine," he mutters.

"And Eiran?" A pause. *"Watch your back. You're loyal. That makes you dangerous."*

Without responding, Eiran ends the call.

"Is that... normal for where you work?" Kairo asks hesitantly.

"Unfortunately. Welp, I guess an SRF safe house is out. But we still need to send you into hiding."

"What?" I cry.

Wait, did Kairo nod in agreement with him?!

Eiran pinches the bridge of his nose. "I know, I know. You deal with dangerous people all the time. But Blackstone is different. We were lucky all he got was a sample of your blood. If Sylara hadn't come when she did... You can't make yourself an easy target."

"I'm not hiding," I say, shaking my head. "Not a chance."

"No, he has a point," Kairo says. "It's too dangerous for you on the streets. I'll deal with Corvane. Eiran can work on the seeds. You lie low. Now where can we stash her?" he asks Eiran.

"Well," he replies, considering. "I was thinking that—"

"I'm *not* hiding!" Both males fall silent. Even Frank and Emma look questioningly at my outburst. "I'm sick and tired of you two talking like you can run my life. Particularly you, Eiran. I've known you for what, a few weeks? I appreciate your talking me down the other night. But that doesn't mean you can tell me how I live my life. And Kairo," I add, rounding on him, "same goes for you. I'm a fucking adult, and I don't need you two making decisions for me."

"I'm your friend," Kairo replies in a low, firm tone. "I care about you."

"And I love that, Kai," I say, my tone softening slightly. "But if you're my friend, then you need to back my play. And I'm not running away. I've spent the last eleven years in hiding. I'm finally free from those bastards, and I'm not running *again*, particularly not from some metal-brained asshole. Besides, you heard him. He got my blood. And that's scary as fuck, but it's done."

"Okay, you're right," Eiran says, raising a hand placatingly. "Hiding isn't the right term—"

"If you don't stop it with that crisis intervention shit—" I growl, remembering how he had that same damn hand out last time, as if I was a wounded animal he was trying to keep from biting him.

Eiran lowers the hand. "I meant we need to lie low and regroup. We aren't stopping, and we aren't hiding."

Frustrated, I stand and begin pacing. "Okay, that's a total line, but it's a good line, so I'll allow it."

"We need a little breathing room," Eiran says, eyes creasing. "We need to put Corvane off until the SRF makes its move."

"What if…" I say, a plan forming. "What if we stole something to buy us time?"

Eiran shakes his head. "Even if I ignore that it's, well, illegal, anything valuable enough to steal would be too heavily guarded. And would take too long to plan. *And* be too dangerous in Corvane's hands."

My grin widens. "Not if it's not actually worth anything. Not if Frank can help us dress it up."

"Oh no," Kairo says to Eiran. "I know that look. She's thinking of doing something stupid."

I shake my head. "No… It's not stupid. It's fucking brilliant."

14

BAD IDEA, RIGHT?

This is a terrible idea.

My pencil taps out a steady rhythm against my journal cover. The words I meant to write abandoned me minutes ago, thoughts slogging through my brain like mud through pipes.

Eiran comes over and stands next to me, leaning against the vine-covered alley wall. "Nervous?" he whispers, eyeing me while Kairo preps for the infiltration.

"Me? Never." Why does this man insist on making me lie to him?

He runs a hand down my arm, my heart stilling and racing in equal measure. "I always get nervous before an op. Every time."

I turn to him, surprised. "You never seem fazed by anything."

"I get in my head," he admits, hair mingling with the leaves. "Think about what could go wrong." His eyes look haunted, and I wonder if he's thinking of Blackstone.

"Me too." My voice is so quiet I can barely hear it myself. "Normally, writing helps." I motion with my closed journal before sliding it into my backpack. "But I'm too jittery today. I can't get the words to stick."

Eiran smiles and raises an eyebrow at the disappearing book, but otherwise doesn't comment on it. Instead, he says, "When bad things happen, I overcompensate by trying to make sure everything always goes right. Prepping for every eventuality. Sound familiar?" I nod, and he raises a hand, running a finger along my cheek.

I turn away, watching as Kairo's tank top and jeans melt into a full Vaeloria City Police Department uniform. The illusion even has a department-issued blaster and the stupid hat. The weirdest part is the elvish green skin and pointed ears. Kairo's still under there… and yet not. It's disturbing.

"Kai, maybe this was a bad idea after all," I try.

He shakes his head in exasperation. "It was your suggestion!" An echo of his words to me before the Corvane job that got us in this mess.

"I know, but—"

"Listen, it'll work. I've got this. It'll put off Corvane, and it may tempt Blackstone out of hiding too."

"Is it a stupid idea?" I ask Eiran.

"I've done stupider. Kairo's right. It'll work. Assuming you can escape the holding cell."

I scoff. "That doesn't even deserve a response."

Eiran grins. "Then you'll kill it. You're a badass." The words are like straight adrenaline. The lift they give me should worry me, but they do the trick. I'm ready.

Fifteen minutes later, Kairo and I storm through the large glass doors of the central station of the VCPD with my wrists cuffed and his hand tight around my forearm. "Get your filthy green hands ov'me, you p-pointy-eared azzole," I yell, pushing and pulling against Kairo's firm grip. I slide a bit on the slick tile floor of the space, my voice echoing off the expansive foyer that is fairly sparse by Valen standards, save for the giant eldertree growing right through the center of the space.

"Hey, you two, come help me with this one!" Kairo calls to the two Valen officers sitting behind the reception desk.

An older officer (who is slightly pudgy for an elf) stands, frowning, and says, "What's this about?"

A second, younger cop jumps off his seat and comes running to help. "Looks like someone partied a bit too hard."

"No such thing, sexy," I slur to the younger cop. "Why don't you and I go party right now, huh?" His cheeks brown slightly in embarrassment, but he keeps glaring at me.

Kairo yanks on my arm (a little too hard, if you ask me) and says, "Come on, princess. Let's get you into a cell."

"A cell!" I shriek. "Do you know who my daddy is? He is going to fillet you alive!"

"No, we don't know who your daddy is, and we don't care," Kairo says, pulling me forward and "accidentally" tossing me onto the older of the two cops, sending the two of us tumbling to the ground.

The younger cop moves to help, and Kairo sticks out a foot, sending him toppling. We're a confused pile, and neither officer is aware enough to notice the tall janitor walking down the hallway without showing ID.

"Now," the young cop spits when we finally untangle ourselves. "Are you going to behave?" The older cop grabs my upper arm, glaring at me while he uses his other hand to make sure I didn't take anything.

I bite my lip to stop the grin.

As I am about to respond to the younger cop, I see Eiran, in his janitor outfit, still at least ten feet from the end of the hall. Tracking the older cop's eyes, I see that he's about to notice Eiran.

Instinctively, I kick him hard in the shin and make a break for it, running for the entry doors. I am, of course, caught by Kairo a few seconds later. It's all the time Eiran needs.

"Hey!" the younger cop shouts, slapping me hard across the face. "That's enough of that."

"Watch yourself, Alaric," the older cop says, limping over to push him away from me. I spit in Alaric's face, and the older cop has to pull him off me. "I'll take her down to holding," the older cop says to Alaric, taking me from Kairo. "You get her checked in. Unless you want the collar, Officer…"

"Tielyr. Fourth precinct," Kairo says. "And no, I don't care. I just want this bitch off me."

"Fair enough," the older officer says. Turning to me, he asks, "What's your name? And no jokes. Tell me straight."

I grunt in annoyance, and then say grudgingly, "Sarah Ableton."

Alaric nods, glaring at me in a way that makes it clear what he'd love to do to me if he could get me alone. Thankfully, we soon leave him to Kairo (who, I hope, has some plan for exfiltrating himself from Alaric) and wind our way through a short maze of vine-roofed corridors to a row of clear-door holding cells.

When we get near the row of cells, I slip, slurring, "Whoops!" and letting out a little giggle to hide the faint clatter.

The older cop rights me without comment, leading me to the doors. With a simple warning to "behave," he closes the thick bioplastic door, the metal frame clanging shut in my face. I wait, shoulders clenched, until he rounds the corner.

Once he's clear, I lurch forward, reaching out with my mind to find Alaric's keycard where I threw it. Finding it half-slid under a chair leg, I coax it toward me on the faintest thread of air, careful not to let it scrape or catch.

I've used my abilities more openly in recent days, but I still don't want to go broadcasting that a sort-of human has magic. Not here. Not in a Valen precinct with a shit-ton of cameras and half a dozen surveillance spells. As the card nears my cell, I notice the vynthra vines that coat the ceiling coil like snakes. I glance over to see a janitor mopping an adjacent hallway.

No longer worried about the cameras now blocked by vines, I raise the ID card with magic and press it to the lock. The door opens with a beep, and I run out. I know Eiran can't keep the vines in front of the camera forever (otherwise it'll be way too suspicious), so I take two broad strides and then leap, grabbing the edge of an air vent hidden among the roiling vynthra leaves. In moments, I'm inside.

Struggling to reach into a pocket, I pull out a small comm device and stick it in my ear. "I'm in."

"All clear at the moment," Eiran's voice says, and I tell myself to ignore the goosebumps trickling up my spine as I make my way along the tight metal space.

There are two electronic beeps, meaning all is clear. I guess Kairo hasn't ended his conversation with the young cop. For a few minutes, I crawl in silence.

The thing I love and hate most about this job is the long stretches of silent crawling or climbing. It's peaceful to be alone with your thoughts… but then sometimes that means, you know, being alone with your thoughts.

The vent dead-ends, and I stare at the air grate, preparing myself with a deep breath. "Breathe in the scent of the Luminar Essence," I mumble. "Exhale your contribution to the Aether." Eiran's low chuckle sends another warm shiver trickling down my bones.

"The fuck?" Kairo whispers, amused, apparently clear of the officer now.

I open the grate and lean through, placing my hand splayed onto the ceiling. With a firm mental grasp, I use a small current of wind to press my arm against the rows of vines, holding myself there. I feel several of the vines thicken, and I know that if I were stupid enough to look down at the floor that is almost twenty feet below me, I'd see Eiran's form somewhere close.

Relying on Eiran's magic as much as my own, I slowly make my way across the large, dusty room. A Valen officer sits behind a half-height door, not seeing or hearing me. There's a faint shimmer, and I can tell that Kairo has made his way to me now, and he's using his ability to hide me from view. I crawl quickly and silently, sliding past the fifteen-foot-high cage wall separating the evidence locker from the rest of the precinct.

Out of sight of the officer, I drop, making my way to the fourth row of evidence boxes. It doesn't take long to find the charred remains of a small powerseed, the very powerseed that blew up and destroyed part of a building.

Will it work? No. Will it help me with Corvane? Absolutely.

Before I leave, I look straight into the camera that I know hides in the top corner of the space, feigning shock and fear. I make sure it gets a good shot of me.

Boxes of evidence are strewn open on the floor in a perfectly crafted tableau as I move back across the vines. I'm clambering into the grate when my foot makes a loud, all-too-intentional "thunk" against the side. I imagine how the evidence worker's head must have snapped to the sound.

Not bothering to be quiet, I scurry back along the vent. Following my mental map, I crawl past several grates, ending in a narrow offshoot. I open the grate and drop, landing next to the tall form of a Valen officer. "Got it?" Kairo asks.

"Yep," I say, showing him.

"Alright. Let's go." I feel the ghostly touch of his wing coil around me, and I know his glamour is now hiding me again.

"I'm clear," Eiran's voice says in our comms.

"On our way," Kairo says, and we move in unison toward the exit.

"Hey, Officer Tielyr," Alaric's voice calls from the reception desk. "You want to grab some anthalas? I'm off in ten."

Kairo puts on his trademark grin and says, "I'd love to, but I'm working a double. Maybe next time."

Wordlessly, we slip through the doors and out of the building, the key to stalling Corvane tucked under my arm. Just as we vanish from sight, the alarms erupt behind us.

15

IT'S ALL IN
YOUR HEAD

"Okay, so…" I begin.

"Please wait," Frank says distractedly as Eiran, Kairo, and I stand helplessly around the storage container, watching him work.

"How is it going?" Eiran asks.

"Please wait," Frank says again, not turning from the small worktable where he's toiling away.

Kairo's quirked mouth broadens slightly. "So, are you done yet?" Frank flicks a hand, and a book goes flying off a nearby stack, aiming for Kairo's head. He ducks, but it glances off his wing. Kairo lets out a loud curse. Emma and I exchange a look, hiding our grins.

"*You seem better today,*" Emma says in my mind.

"*I am,*" I think back. Emma frowns at me. "*What?*"

"*Your mental voice sounds strange. Like you're shouting. Perhaps you need more practice. I can show you if you like. We will practice soon. If you don't mind my asking, how did you get the gift?*"

I take a deep breath, and then say, "*My mom was a doctor. She… injected me with… something.*" The old ache in my chest that I keep buried is raw and fresh. The powerseed Frank is working on, the damage it caused? My mom was part of that. Helped these people. Despite everything she did to me, I've clung to the belief that, on some level, my mom loved me. I remember how she helped me when Phina was being horrible, would wipe my tears when I fell, and generally did 'mom things' that she didn't have to do if she was some psychotic evil scientist.

How could she help them do this?

Thoughts of my mother remind me of my mom's journal. I still haven't told Eiran about it. It feels too much, too personal, to have in Eiran's hands. While he's proven trustworthy thus far, handing him the truth of my past and how I came to be? That seems insane.

Not that I'm sure there's actually anything on it. The file's encrypted, and I've had no luck cracking it. Maybe I should ask Emma.

Before I decide if I can bring myself to even do that, Frank cries, "Finished!"

Eiran moves forward, taking the partially repaired seed. A fresh batch of glowing yellow liquid sloshes in an unbroken vial, pulled from a different small seed now lying in pieces on the table next to the biotech key I stole. Frank mixed the small amount of enhanced liquid in the key with the normal liquid in the cannibalized vial, creating a passable fake.

Eiran tilts the fake seed, moving it this way and that, scrutinizing it. "Excellent work, Frank," Eiran says, and the Quiblin beams. "No way Corvane knows this was altered. At least at first glance."

"Yes," Frank confirms. "With the traces from the key added in, even initial testing will show it differs from a standard seed."

"I still say this plan is insane," Kairo says, laughing. "Brilliant, but insane. We're going to give Corvane a *fake* enhanced powerseed, tell him it's the real seed, and then hope he doesn't figure it out before the SRF comes calling for him. Like, it could work, but also… man, it's risky."

I shrug. "What's the worst case if it doesn't work? Someone wants to kill me? What else is new?"

"Speaking of that," Eiran says, raising a green eyebrow at me. "It's a good idea to lie low now, particularly because you weren't exactly quiet in the PD last night."

"I had to make it obvious! We need the word out that it was stolen. How else will Corvane believe we have it?"

"I get it," Eiran says, conceding the point. "But Blackstone's in the wind, Corvane wants to kill you, and there's still the possibility that the Initiative isn't as dead as we hope."

I gape at him. "What?"

"I mean, we *think* we've got everyone, but it's been operating for three decades. There could be more cells, though that's a what-if. Blackstone remains the biggest threat, and we can't find him."

"We found Blackstone's way onto the planet," Frank offers. Eiran turns, excited, but Frank holds up a hand. "It was on the Eclipse Consortium ship. But they left before the attack at the diner."

Eiran deflates. "Another dead end."

Kairo shakes his head. "Maybe not. He'll need another way home. We could track is ways off-planet. Not that he can leave for a few more weeks."

My comm blares suddenly, causing the Quiblins to jump. I shake my head at Kairo, letting him know it's an unknown messenger. Eiran motions for me to answer it.

"Hello?" I say, answering on speaker.

"Well, well, well," Sylara's silky voice says through the comm. "Someone's been busy."

"I don't know what you mean," I say, glancing meaningfully at Eiran. That was fast.

Sylara is unfazed by my denial. "I heard about those powerseeds. I'm surprised there was anything left to steal."

I walk around the concrete room, welling up the right level of nonchalance. If I'm nervous, Sylara will know something's up. "I guess your sources aren't as good as mine. Not surprising."

Sylara lets out a chuckle that sends chills up my spine. Apparently Zeridians do laugh, and it's as horrible as I imagined. "Is that so? Well, given the timing, I'm assuming the item you stole from Corvane was sold?" I don't respond. Better to let her think it's sold than stolen by someone else. "Thought as much. Well, I've been instructed to give you a counteroffer. Turn over the powerseed, and we'll call it even. But if you ever go near Corvane's operation again—"

"I understand," I manage. Eiran makes a stretching motion with his hands. "I'll get you the seeds. I need a few days to let the heat die down. I can't very well give them to you if I get arrested as soon as I set foot on the street."

"You have forty-eight hours," Sylara says flatly. "I'll send you the drop-off location. If I don't get it by then... well, I know where you live. And that Hitari friend of yours." Kairo grimaces as if he's suppressing a growl.

"Fine," I reply, hanging up. "Well, that's settled."

"You still have a lot of heat on you," Kairo says. "I'll get the seed to Sylara. Just let me know the drop-off."

"So, what? I'm supposed to hide out and do nothing? We need to find Blackstone."

Eiran shakes his head. "He can't go anywhere right now. We'll lie low and work in the shadows a bit. We need to figure out why he wants this powerseed so badly. I have some SRF files we can try. Maybe there's a pattern. I prefer working in secret, honestly. I know subtlety isn't your style."

"Asshole."

He grins, and again my nerves do that little spine-prickle thing. The shiver goes lower and sinks to places that have no business tingling.

"So, where would you hide her?" Kairo asks, thankfully shattering the moment. "Your boss said you can't trust putting her into a safe house."

"I have an idea," Eiran says, but doesn't expand further. He stares at me, clearly considering something. "For my plan to work, you'll need an implant."

"What?!" I say, horrified. I can't explain my fear of getting an implant. Part of it is the idea of needles, the invasiveness of another procedure. But part of it? The idea of having something Valen inside of me has always seemed so abhorrent. Of course, then I glance at Eiran. Perhaps there are *some* Valen things I'd be okay with having inside me.

Where the hell did that come from?! Nope. Don't think about that. Not at all helpful. And definitely not happening.

"You don't have to do anything you don't want to do," Kairo says quickly, glaring reprovingly at Eiran. "We'll find another way."

"I want to take you outside the district," Eiran says, ignoring Kairo. "For an extended period."

"You have to be Valen," I say, confused at this suggestion. "I could get a short-term pass to go explore the forest. Going much farther would be impossible. Maybe if you had access to the SRF's resources, but—"

Eiran shakes his head. "Taylor… I was able to get your ID sorted."

"But… we haven't found Blackstone yet."

He shrugs. "I'm hoping you'll help anyway. Do you really want that bastard to have the powerseeds? Or your blood?"

I cock my head at the question. I've never exactly been altruistic, but it would probably suck if the entire galaxy was thrown into war. And that might happen if Helix gets its way.

"No."

Eiran smiles, something warming within him. "I thought not. Now, one thing about your official identity. I… okay, look. I know this is complicated, but you're Valen, legally speaking. You were born here, so by Valen law, that makes you Valen anyway. Not elvish. Just Valen."

"Valen?" The idea crashes through me in waves. I'm Valen. I'm *Valen*?! It's just "legally speaking," but still. "After what the Valen did to my mom…" I can't finish, can't put it into words.

Eiran steps forward, placing a hand to my face, his thumb tracing along my cheekbone. "What the Initiative did to your mom," he reminds me. "I know your feelings about your mom are also… complicated, but you clearly loved her. And no matter what she did, what happened to her was horrible. I get your reluctance. But there's no reason to trap yourself in the multicultural district."

In a too-quiet voice, I ask, "What do I have to do?"

"You just need to register. Now, implants are mandatory for non-elves, but—"

My hands tremble at the words. An implant? Implants mean needles. Fuck no.

Eiran keeps his voice even. "Valen systems are all biotech-based. The interface links you to identification, travel permissions… everything. It's fast. Safe. I brought a sterile injector from my loft in case you said yes. I'm trained. Five minutes, tops. But it's your choice."

"Today?!" This is all moving too fast. "I don't—"

"I hate to rush this, but I'm worried about operating in the open, particularly in Vaeloria City," Eiran admits. "We don't have to do this. You could hide in this storage shed until Blackstone is caught. But if you want the interface, I can do it right now. It wouldn't be my first time. I'm trained, and it takes five minutes. The choice is yours, though. What do you want to do?"

With a groan, I nod. Slowly, he reaches toward his bag and pulls out a small metal injector gun. My eyes widen at Eiran, but he steps slowly, showing me the tool and making no sudden movements. He reaches out to grasp my hand reassuringly, taking my frightened grip in stride. A cool prick touches my neck, and I jump. My breaths come in rapid gasps.

"It's alright," Eiran says soothingly. "It's just an implant. You're here. You're safe. I've got you."

I nod, staring into his mauve-colored eyes, and say, "Breathe in the scent of the Luminar Essence. Exhale your contribution to the Aether. Breathe in…" I keep chanting, staring into those eyes and ignoring the spike of pain in my neck.

"Done," Eiran says, pulling away.

I reach up, feeling the strange disc shape on the side of my neck. Kairo hands me a mirror, and I hold it up, staring at the slightly pale circle below my ear, only half visible among my red curling hair. I pull the strands back, getting a better look at my new addition.

A sharp pain lances across my neck at the spot. I stare in horror as strands of dark green branch out from the spot, curling up behind my ear and down my neck to my chest. A huge spiking pain stabs through my head, and I hear myself scream. The last I recognize is Eiran yelling my name in panic before everything goes black.

PART 3

THE LOST
LIBRARY JOB

the truth is a thing with claws
with teeth that rend in tiny bits
that dribble drip from crimson lips
I lay in shreds as Verity grins
she is myself
I see—I am
the monster

—The Journal of Taylor Grey

16

YOU CAN NEVER GO HOME

Eiran

There's nothing but the quiet hum of the stryder skimming over the land to intrude on my thoughts as fields of grassland slide past the window in a verdant blur. I glance over at the human girl sleeping in the seat beside me, marveling that we're here together. Marveling at how beautiful she looks, her hair glowing in the sunlight.

I can't believe I'm doing this. Going back. Taking her to *them*. Facing them after what happened. They'll probably think I—

Sleeping, I remind myself. It's not a coma. The doctor was sure.

I shouldn't care so much. I know that she's just an asset. Keeping assets in line and on board is part of the job. And sure, sometimes they get attached. Sometimes *you* get attached. But you're not supposed to. I'm supposed to keep it professional.

But I can't. And is that stupid? Absolutely. With my luck, she's probably a fucking double agent, some mole specifically crafted to bait me. None of that seems to matter. I can't stop worrying about her. I keep glancing at the monitor on her wrist, checking her vitals every couple of minutes. Keep glancing over like she might disappear.

This incredible, smart, annoying, funny, dangerous, sexy woman who loves nothing more than pushing my buttons. When she one-ups me, does something completely outrageous and infuriating... damn it if I don't get so turned on that I could practically burst into flames where I stand.

Aether save me. She has to be okay. She has to be.

A pain racks my chest, a panic so intense it's like a cyborg is gripping my heart. What the hell did I do wrong? Why do I fuck up anyone who gets too close? Isn't what happened when I left home evidence of that?

I knew better. I should've let her go, but no. My dumb ass had to find an excuse to keep her on the case, keep talking to her. And now she's going to—

No, Eiran, you idiot. Stop that. Lirion will know what to do. He'll help her.

I won't give him a choice.

Eventually, trees intersperse the grassland. Familiar broad-leaved quithra trees mark the edge of the Siberwald, the large forest that stretches across the southwest corner of the continent. Soon, taller quithra will come into view, thick trunks covered with vynthra vines. Their silhouettes looming in the distance signal my return to the town I haven't seen in seven years.

It's another half hour before the actual town of Silberwald comes into view. The squat, overgrown houses and bushy, rough-hewn shops are a sharp contrast to the sleek, cultivated green space of Vaeloria City.

I drive past the familiar stores and restaurants, and it's like rewatching an old vid you only half-remember. Occasionally I pass faces I can't place but surely knew for years. I wonder if any of them recognize me in my expensive Nuvaleheim-built stryder that is so different from the flatbed utility stryders that are so common here.

A tall building with a smoking chimney comes into view, the large sign out front declaring it to be "Valtir Metalworks." Dark wood twines around the swirling metal in an intricate pattern to form the familiar words, and I repress an old ache, remembering who made that sign.

I breathe in a huge, shaking breath as I exit the stryder, rounding the side to head to the forge. Thank the Aether, the Valen tourists haven't shown up to work on whatever knives or tools they selected to make. This encounter, at least, should be okay. I can handle my uncle. Aunt Maelara is another question, but she should be—

"Eiran Valtir, as I live and breathe!"

A tall and stately Valen woman comes sweeping out the open door to the popular tourist stop like she owns the place. Which I guess she does. My aunt is as striking as ever, her wavy green hair thrown up into a messy bun, loose strands falling to intermingle with the intricate pattern on her traditional-style tunic. I haven't seen her in years. Barely spoken on the phone even. The sight grabs me by the chest and wrenches me into the past.

Locking the old memories back into the box where I keep them, I plaster on a smile and say, "Aunt Maelara! You haven't aged a day since the last time I saw you."

"Oh, you charmer," she grins. "It feels that way because you've spent so much time among those fast-aging humans. But I'm glad you finally came home. A vid call every few months hardly counts."

I keep my smile at the jabs, and definitely don't point out that comm calls go two ways. Or that it's possible to travel to Vaeloria City too—something Elowynn figured out years ago. Though Maelara never understood why I left. None of them did.

"You're looking pale, dear. Are you getting enough sun?"

"Just a fondness for sweets, Maelara," I say, and before she can comment further on my lack of a suitably Vale-green skin tone, I add, "Where's Lirion? I need to see him."

"So that's why you're here?" my aunt asks with a raised eyebrow. "I should have known it wasn't to come see your—"

"Lirion is at his office," says a sharp tenor voice. I turn to see my uncle, Roderic, walking toward me, burly arms straining against the sleeves of his blue tunic, bald dark green head glistening with sweat. Roderic surveys me, his overgrown goatee hiding what I know is a frown, amethyst eyes keen, missing nothing. They're my father's eyes. My eyes. "I've already called him to let him know you're here. He's on the way. What's up?"

I turn and open the passenger door to my black stryder, swinging it wide to reveal Taylor, passed out on the seat, a portable health monitor beeping away on her wrist. Taylor's head lolls over to the side, pale human skin a strange greenish white. Her curls have fallen behind her in a heap, revealing fading green tendrils along the long sweep of her neck and, more importantly, her pointed Enhanced ears.

My aunt and uncle stare in shocked silence for a long moment. Then Roderic says, "I'll go check on Lirion," and turns to head back inside the open forge. I know without him saying more that he's going to tell him to hurry, and also warn him of the strange human girl I've brought into their midst.

"What—" Maelara begins.

"She's in trouble," I say, cutting her off. "She needs a quiet place to heal and rest."

My aunt surveys me for a moment, her eyes always seeing too much. She says nothing about the trouble I've brought to their door. She doesn't ask questions, doesn't even mention the years filled with nothing but a few awkward comm calls. Instead, she smiles sadly and says, "Poor thing. Lirion will know what to do."

"Don't I always?" a booming voice says behind me. I turn to see a long-haired Valen male, the broad curves of his shoulders and arms straining his long-sleeved tunic top. Several long, thin chains hang beneath a brown leather vest, and above the low V of his neckline, I can make out the edges of what I know to be a large tree tattoo. The same tattoo I have myself.

"Hey," he says flatly, seeing me finally.

"Hey."

My best friend throughout childhood and university stares as if he doesn't know me. "You're back."

"I'm not back. I'm just back for the moment."

"Good." Lirion cocks his head, and then slams a fist into my jaw, knocking me to the ground.

"Shit, Lirion." I spit a red glob onto the gravel.

"That's for leaving."

Massaging my jaw, I stand uneasily to my feet. "Are you done?"

Lirion surveys me for a second, his anger warring with something I hope is at least modestly friendly.

Eventually he shrugs. "Nope." He slams a fist into my temple, and I push him back.

"Boys!" Maelara gasps. "Stop—"

"Okay, asshole." I wipe the blood leaking into my eye. "You get two. That's enough."

"I think I get to say when it's enough," Lirion growls. He lunges at me, but I block this time, landing two quick punches to his midsection. He grunts and then headbutts me.

"Fuck, you idiot. Damn it." I massage my head before running and tackling him, bringing him to the dirt. With a rearing cross, I smack him across the temple as he brings two fists down on my back.

"I told you I'd kick your ass if you ever came back here," Lirion growls, flipping us.

I allow the move because we don't have time for this. And well, I deserve it.

"Damn it. Will you fucking calm down? I need your help."

Lirion pauses, raising a disbelieving eyebrow, a familiar scar cutting across it. I know where that scar came from. I can guess what he's thinking. After what happened, why should he help me now?

He might have a point.

After a moment of hesitation, he moves, letting me up. Spitting more blood, I rise to my feet and motion to the open door, where Taylor moans slightly.

Lirion frowns as he steps forward. "What happened?"

This, I remind myself, is why I came. Because I knew, some part of me knew, that despite everything, they'd help. However pissed Lirion may be at me for everything—for leaving, for the scar, for abandoning him and our life here to go "play spy" as he'd called it—I knew that if I asked, he'd help.

Because unlike me, Lirion's a good man.

I glance at Taylor, and the panic takes over again. I breathe it down.

"She was getting a biometric implant—"

"As an adult?" Lirion says, surprised. "How old is she?"

"Twenty-two," I reply, meeting his keen brown eyes. He tosses his long umber braids off his shoulders and strokes his braided goatee as I explain. "One minute she was fine. The next… these streaks started forming on her neck, and…" I trail off, remembering the way she screamed. It was… horrible. "I did the injection." I refuse to look away from Lirion's gaze.

With a raised eyebrow, Lirion turns back to Taylor and inspects her neck with a frown. He traces a finger along the now fading lines, poking at them lightly. "No bulge. That's not just an adverse reaction. It's like it… dissolved. Like a carbon tablet in water. I've never heard of this happening. Ever."

"Yeah, well. She's…" She's what? Special? Unique? Infuriating? "… different."

"Different how? More than just Enhanced, you mean?" Lirion asks, raising that scarred eyebrow again.

I hesitate. Taylor's secretive about this, and I don't want to freak everyone out. Eventually, I say, "She has magic." My aunt and uncle exchange startled looks, while Lirion's eyes narrow.

"What in the Aether's breath did you bring down on us?" he asks. "And don't give me any of this 'classified' bullshit. You came to me for help. You tell me everything. Or fuck off."

I know what "classified" means to Lirion. What damage that word has done to him. Not seeing a way around it, I give the very, *very* abbreviated version of Taylor's history, telling only the parts that apply to her current condition. I'm not thrilled about Maelara and Roderic hearing this, but I know there's no way they'd leave either. My aunt would make me tell them, anyway.

When I'm done, my former friend says, "So, she's on the run from this psycho—"

"Lirion," Roderic warns quietly.

"Two psychos," I clarify, doing my best not to rise to Lirion's tone.

He laughs without humor. "Right. Forgot about the smuggler, who *also* wants to kill her. And you try to give this petri dish of a human an implant, and then—surprise, surprise—everything goes sideways. And now she's passed out, near comatose, and you need me to tell you how badly you fucked up. That about right?"

"That about covers it," I grind out. Okay, so maybe "not rising to Lirion's taunting" isn't going great.

Lirion scoffs, rubbing his temple. "You always did have a hard head." Groaning, he walks past me to examine Taylor. "Well, I'll need to get her back to my office to do a full workup. I have no clue why getting an implant would make her faint, but at first glance, she might be anemic. She looks a bit green. As for the other symptoms? I don't know yet."

"Thank you, Lirion," I say in a low tone.

"Oh, don't thank me," he says with a shake of his head. "And don't let my sister know you're in town. Not if you don't want your head ripped off your shoulders and shoved up your ass. And that's exactly, word for word, what she said she'd do if she saw you again. Fair warning."

"Noted," I growl, annoyed. I knew it was stupid coming back to this damned town. I'll need somewhere else to stash Taylor after Lirion checks her out.

"That'll be tough to do," Maelara says, interrupting my thoughts, "since they'll be hiding out at our place for a spell."

"Is that right?" Lirion asks, eyeing me. "You're planning on hiding the girl… here? Not some fancy SRF safe house?"

I notice the look on my aunt's face. There's no use in trying to change plans now. Dammit. "Yeah. Just for a few days."

Lirion laughs again. "Alright. On your head be it then."

17

OUT ABOUT TOWN

Taylor

"Not that I give a shit, but she is right, you know."

"Shut up."

My whole body feels impossibly heavy. My legs. My hands. My eyelids. I lay in the soft bed, listening to the strange voices around me, struggling to care enough about what they're saying to wake up.

"Either you're spending too much time inside some fancy SRF office or you're eating too much human food. You're not nearly dark enough to be—"

"I thought you didn't give a shit." Eiran. That's Eiran's voice. My brain's so fuzzy. Where am I?

"I don't." A different male voice. Definitely Valen, the lilt thick and unmistakable. "I'm just saying. Looks like city life is bad for your health. As I said."

"Well, you're not wrong."

"You should have come back home. At least come to visit."

"After what happened? I knew what my reception would be. At least you did me the service of actually giving me the greeting I deserved."

"You always were a dumbass, Eiran."

I finally get my eyes open, taking several rough blinks to get the gunk out. My vision clears, and I see that I'm lying on a large magic-hewn bed, thick quithra branches winding in a beautiful display. The soft cotton sheets and thick quilt wrap me in so much coziness that it's a bit of a struggle to pull myself back awake.

"Hey," I say, and my voice is faint enough I'm surprised anyone hears me.

Eiran turns, though, his bright violet eyes roving over me. One is blackened and slightly swollen. Did he get into a fight? And more importantly, is Eiran wearing a T-shirt?! Yes. Yes, he is. It's a black Union-style V-neck, and the fit over his tight chest, the swooping curve of his neck? Once again, it's entirely too distracting.

Behind him stands another male, this one with long brown hair that hangs in wavy braids that mirror the twining branches of some elf-magicked tree. The matching brown stubble along his strong jaw gives the refined features of his race a rangy, slightly wild appearance. His arms and shoulders are broad and intensely muscled, with a dark green skin the color of forest leaves. He also has a split lip. Ah. The other party in the fight, I guess.

After surveying me a moment, the other Valen says, "I'm Dr. Lirion Beutwinn. How are you feeling?" His intense brown eyes continue to skewer me to the bed, piercing, but not unkind. As he waits for my response, he traces a finger along the scar that splits his left eyebrow, adding to his ruggedly handsome look.

"Okay," I say, voice still hoarse. "My neck is sore, and my head hurts a bit. What happened? Where am I?"

"Silberwald," Eiran says. "My hometown. My aunt and uncle have agreed to let us stay here for a bit." The two males exchange a look I can't read. "As for what happened… you passed out. Something went wrong with the implant and… Taylor, I'm sorry. I—"

I wave him off. "It's fine. Not surprising that it wouldn't work after all my mom did." I don't miss the fact that Dr. Beutwinn doesn't seem nearly as confused as he should be about this. "I guess that means he told you?"

"He did," Beutwinn confirms. "But we don't know if that's what caused your reaction. I've never heard of someone reacting like that, even Enhanced. We'll need to keep a close eye on you."

"What about Kairo?" I ask Eiran.

"He made the drop-off of the fake powerseed. Now, he and the twins are working on tracking down Blackstone." Before I can ask, he adds, "He was freaked out, obviously, but with you like you were… bringing you here was the best idea either of us could think of."

"You can worry about all of that later," Dr. Beutwinn says. "For now, let me examine you closer, and then we'll get you something to eat. Eiran, do you mind tracking down some food for Taylor? Human diet, of course. You should be good at that."

Eiran scowls, and I wonder if the doctor meant it as a dig. Eiran certainly seems to have taken it that way, stomping off while Dr. Beutwinn—or Lirion, as he insists I call him—takes me through the usual checks—temperature, blood pressure, reflexes, and other vitals.

"Despite what's happening on your neck, you seem fine, clinically speaking," Lirion says, sounding somewhat baffled when he finishes. "You do look a little jaundiced… or maybe…"

"Maybe what?" I ask, scalp prickling at his hesitation.

Lirion shakes his head. "I don't know. Your coloring is a little weird. Probably need some food and a bit of sun. I'll keep running more tests on the blood sample I took while you're out, but I also need a sample from the wound itself—" He reaches into a bag and pulls out a large syringe, angling for my neck.

I'm standing in the large sterile room.

The heavy scent of lorathar.

My mother's hand on my shoulder, comforting me…

Holding me in place…

"Be brave, my starflower…"

I throw a hand out, sending the syringe flying as I knock Lirion over a chair with a mental shove. "Get your fucking hands off me!" I shout. When did I stand up? And why is the chair upended?

Eiran is instantly at the door. "Hey. What happened?"

"My fault," Lirion says, holding a hand to a slightly bleeding forehead. "I need a sample of the wound and… well, I surprised her."

"Yeah, it is your fucking fault," Eiran says, his normally bright eyes the shade of dark wine, his glare hinting at violence. "A syringe to the neck? Really?"

Oh, gods, I attacked him. He was trying to help, and I attacked him. Cheeks flaming in shame, I say, "Eiran, it's fine. Lirion, I'm so, so sorry. Are you okay?"

"No problem at all, Taylor," Lirion says kindly, holding a hand to the faint cut, and it disappears. His tone sharpens slightly as he adds,

"It's not the worst cut my face has seen." He glances—so briefly I almost miss it—at Eiran as he says it.

Eiran clearly didn't, because his smile sharpens. "It helps when you get it healed right away so it doesn't scar."

Lirion's face darkens, putting the long mark across his eyebrow in sharp relief. "Yeah, as long as you're not busy picking up the pieces when someone—"

"I'll get the sample," he snaps. "Maelara is asking for you, anyway. She is preparing a big batch of food, but of course isn't listening to me when I tell her that vynthra salad isn't enough carbs for a human. She wants *your* opinion."

Lirion laughs faintly. "Alright. Extract some of that green stuff from her neck if you can." Before leaving, he walks over and puts a hand on my arm. "Take it easy, okay? Let me know if you feel *any* symptoms, however small. It sounds… it sounds like Eiran is keeping a good eye on you."

I glance over to consider Eiran. Lirion's right. I wonder why that is. I suppose he needs to protect his assets, but am I worth all of this effort?

Eiran walks forward, his nearness overriding my senses. He reaches out a hand, gingerly tilting my neck to examine the wound. "Lirion seems nice." Eiran grunts. "Is he married?"

Eiran's hands still for a moment. "Why?"

Both confused and slightly amused at his tone, I say in a too airy voice, "Just wondering. He's very attractive."

Eiran makes an annoyed laugh and says, "Well, I don't think he's married, but then, as you probably gathered, we aren't in touch, so I wouldn't know. But if you're so interested, I'm sure my aunt could set you up."

The cold, sad tone in Eiran's voice has the humor dripping away like melting ice. "What happened between the two of you?" I ask. When he doesn't respond, I say, "You're about to jam a needle into my neck. I need you to distract me."

Eiran runs a finger along my wound, the touch sending shivers down my neck to twist in my gut. My breath catches, and thankfully, he finally speaks. "We were friends growing up. My parents died when we were young, and my sister and I moved in with my aunt and uncle. We were close to the Beutwinns. Even went to university together. But then… well, I left. Lirion stayed."

"And he's mad at you for that?" I ask, confused. Without warning, there is a huge stabbing in my neck, and memories again threaten to overwhelm.

Before I can lose myself in them, Eiran replies, "Yeah, sort of." There's the briefest of pauses before he says, "I left him. Left everyone to join the SRF. Lirion got pissed. We got into a fight. I lost control a bit and…" He trails off, shrugging.

"He was that mad about you joining the SRF?"

"People here feel a duty to this place." Avoiding my eyes, he pulls the syringe out, and then puts a hand on my neck. I don't push him for answers. He's revealed so much of himself already. His eyes stay fixed on my wound as he heals the small puncture with his magic.

"So…" I say as he steps away, wanting to preserve his boundaries but unable to bear the silence any longer. "You really have a sister?"

Eiran laughs, and I'm heartened to see him pull out of the dark place that my questions drew him. "That's your takeaway from that story?"

"The rest of it I guessed. You're not as hot and mysterious as you think you are."

Eiran's cocky grin is back in full force, and the impact of it leaves me breathless again. "Oh, trust me. I am." I roll my eyes, scoffing to exhale the nerves tendriling along my spine. "And to answer your question, yes. I do in fact have a sister."

"You mean you have the best, most *amazing* sister in the world." Eiran and I turn to see a Valen girl with long dark green hair and amethyst eyes like her brother's, a broad grin on her pretty face. She looks around my age in years, putting her at the equivalent of around eighteen or nineteen in human development.

"Elowynn!" Eiran says with the first proper smile I've seen since waking up here. He opens his arms to her, and she runs over to hug him. "This is my sister Elowynn," Eiran explains unnecessarily.

Elowynn eyes me shrewdly, a mischievous glint crinkling the corners. "Eiran, you brought a girl home! You didn't mention a girlfriend on your last vid call."

Eiran growls. "She's not… nevermind."

My cheeks burn, and from the satisfied gleam in Elowynn's eye, our reaction seemed to confirm some sort of suspicion for her. I didn't want any suspicion about that topic to be "confirmed." Fuck. "We're working together," I explain. "Nothing else."

"Mhmm," Elowynn says, unconvinced.

"No, really! I've known him for only a few days. And besides…" I trail off, glancing at Eiran.

He raises his eyebrows, crossing his long, thick arms. "Besides what?" He sounds annoyed, but there's a tugging at the corner of his mouth that looks suspiciously like a suppressed smirk.

I open my mouth to say that he's not my type, that I don't even like elves, much less date them, and even if I did, I wouldn't date someone like *him*. So tall and cocky and annoyingly handsome. But before I can say anything, a voice calls from the kitchen. "Eiran, dear. Lunch is ready. Why don't you and your friend come and eat?"

At the sound, Elowynn bounds into the kitchen. Before I can follow, he says into my ear, "I'm very sorry for subjecting you to my family."

Whatever that's supposed to mean.

I follow Eiran and Elowynn into an eat-in kitchen, where an ornate table dominates one corner. It's beautiful if imposing, made of thick woven branches somehow magicked into a flat surface. Standing near a small island counter is a short-but-imposing woman who is undoubtedly Eiran's aunt.

Something about her broad, knowing smile and sharp, all-seeing eyes get my hackles up. I've had a few wannabe mother figures cross my tracks in recent years, and it always ends with someone with the best of intentions trying to tell me how to live my life.

"Hi," she says, smiling kindly. "I'm Maelara. I'm glad to see you up and around. How are you feeling, dear?"

"Better." I remember the ruckus I made in the bedroom, and internally wince. But if Maelara heard, she says nothing about it.

"That's good, dear. I've made you a sandwich because Lirion says you need carbs. We rarely keep carbs in the house—don't need them, you know— but luckily, we had some bread in the stasis hold. It's from a party a couple of years ago, but should be fine."

Maelara continues rambling fussily, taking the sandwich and arranging and rearranging it on the table for me. I sit, trying to eat to appease her. "Now you need to eat it all, including the bread. Lirion's orders. Then y'all go walk around town. He said that even if you aren't

Valen, you still need the sunshine. Smart man." Eiran frowns slightly at the fond way his aunt refers to Lirion, although I think I'm the only one who sees it.

"We could go shopping!" Elowynn appears in the doorway, grinning excitedly at the prospect.

"No," Eiran says in a growl. "She's supposed to be hiding out."

"Oh, come on," Elowynn pleads. "Aunt Maelara only likes *practical* clothing, and Gaelarya's never around. I need someone to go with me. Plus, we could get you some new clothes if you like."

I'm tempted to ask who Gaelarya is (there are so many unfamiliar names to learn!). Instead, I smile and reply, "I'll be fine. Eiran. No one knows I'm here, right? And I can wear my glamour bracelet. I need some vitamin D. Besides, I don't even know if I have anything else to wear."

"I packed you a bag," Eiran says, sounding slightly offended.

I stare at him in horror. "You went through my things? And packed me a bag? Of clothes?" He shrugs, unconcerned with my tone. Oh gods. What did he pack? Did he pack my *underwear?* And… oh no. What *else* did he find rummaging through my drawers?

"Oh, hell no," Elowynn says, snorting incredulously. "We need to take you shopping."

"The idea of the poor girl being stuck with only whatever you packed her sounds a bit dreadful, dear," Maelara concedes. "You three go walk the square and stop in some shops. But get as much sunshine as possible."

"So we're taking Eiran with us on this outing?" I say dubiously.

"Or you don't go at all," Eiran grumbles.

Elowynn beams. "We need someone to torture and tease on the trip, anyway. It would be dreadfully boring without him." Eiran scoffs again, although the corner of his mouth twitches. But when he looks away, the light in his eyes dims.

Concern blossoms in my chest. I wish I could talk to him. He checks on me. If only I could—

An idea strikes, and I reach out with my mind, trying to replicate the feeling from when I was talking to Emma. *"Are you okay?"* I think to him. Eiran startles, glancing at me. *"Coming back must be hard."* He looks surprised at the question, but then shrugs. I give him a small smile. *"Thanks for taking care of me. You sure go all out for your assets."*

Eiran frowns slightly, and I wonder if he's hearing me at all. I've never tried with anyone but Emma before. "Let's go."

Without further encouragement, Elowynn bounds out of the room, dragging me along with her.

***

I have to admit, it's hard to be upset around Elowynn. She's like a flaming ball of joy, warming everyone around her. She flits and bounces down the sidewalk, explaining about everything and everyone, leaving me warm and buzzing beside her. The spring day is gorgeous; the sky, a vibrant greenish-blue from the solar storms, shimmers in swirling waves above us. The warmer southern weather heats my skin pleasantly, and I can't help but smile as Elowynn prattles on.

"…and that's the vynthra wrap place, Thaliron's. We've *got* to go there. So good. The selection is kind of crap, but everything there is amazing. The seasoning is… ung. I'm hungry now."

Eiran laughs. "You just ate."

"So?" Elowynn says, turning and putting her hands on her hips before snarking, "Besides. You haven't been home in seven years. Don't come and judge my eating now." She smiles tauntingly at him and turns, flicking her long hair in his direction.

She seems happy he's here, and likely didn't mean it as harsh as it came out, but the jab landed. Eiran's amused, dimpled grin slides from his face like oil. "Yeah, well. We need to stop by the metalworks, anyway."

He nods to an old building standing slightly apart from the rest, a wide-open space rather like a garage on the left side, smoke billowing from smokestacks above. Heat blooms from the forge in waves, making me feel faintly feverish. The sign above the shop declares it to be "Valtir Metalworks," and the beauty of the sign and general ethos of the place makes me both excited and nervous.

I remember Eiran's woodworking from the other night, and say, perhaps stupidly, "The sign is beautiful. Did you…"

Elowynn freezes at the question, glancing nervously at her brother. His lip twitches like he's trying to smile, but can't manage it. "Nah. My dad made that. Well, him and my uncle. He was… incredibly talented."

"That he was," a male voice with a thick Valen accent says. I turn and see a broad-shouldered elvish male. He's unmistakably Eiran's uncle, with the same piercing eyes and tall, almost lanky frame. But unlike Eiran, his uncle's arms are thick and dark as summer leaves, with hands that speak of many years swinging a hammer.

"Pleased to meet you, Taylor. I'm Roderic. I'd say welcome back, but since you were asleep last time you stopped by my shop, you probably don't remember it."

I laugh. "No, sorry. It's amazing though."

"I'll have to let you make a knife," Roderic says as he wipes his hands with a cloth that only seems to make his dark green skin even dirtier. "The tourists love it. You can't come to Silberwald without the full experience."

"She'll have to do that another day, Uncle," Elowynn says quickly. "We're going shopping today." In a false whisper, she adds, "Eiran packed all her clothes."

"Oh!" Roderic says, laughing in surprise. "Then yes. You'd better go and rescue the poor girl."

"I'm completely capable of picking out a few nice outfits," Eiran says, annoyed.

"Don't go telling people that, son," Roderic says dryly.

"I won't even touch on how many ways that's offensive," Eiran says in a tone quiet enough that Roderic could pretend not to hear it. Still, the air goes taut as a bowstring.

"Why don't we go shopping before Elowynn bursts into flames?" I say, laughing to make it a joke.

"Yes, let's!"

Elowynn's eyes widen as she spies something behind me. "Oh, hey! Do you want—"

I turn as a beautiful Valen woman with long wavy brown hair slaps the ever-living shit out of Eiran. "You son of a bitch. I spent a year and a half negotiating that sale, and you screw me over! I'm going to kill you." Elowynn looks in utter shock, while Eiran stands utterly stiff, more like a tree than a person. The woman's fiery gaze finally lands on me. "Who the hell are you?"

Elowynn says, "Gael, this is Taylor, a… coworker of Eiran's who is staying with us for a bit. Taylor, this is Gael… er… Dr. Gaelarya Beutwinn. Lirion's sister."

I expect Eiran to say something. To yell, or at least stick up for himself. Instead, he stands there, holding his cheek. Frozen. Not cowed or embarrassed. Just… waiting it out. Waiting her out. Like he's learned when speaking only makes things worse.

Something about the sight annoys me

Deciding Eiran won't stand up for himself, I say, "You're the little sister of Eiran's best friend? And so that somehow means you get to slap him like that?"

I'm shaking, not from fear, but fury. Fuck her. Who does she think she is? Who slaps someone like that? What is this, some stupid romcom vid?

Mentally reciting Eiran's stupid Aetheric breathing mantra, I say, "Look. I don't know what happened, but I've had a long fucking day. Week, really. Month. And so whatever ancient shit you have, can you stow it, please? We have bigger problems right now than small-town bullshit and petty grudges. I've kind of had my fill, honestly."

Gaelarya seethes for a moment, her claws extending in anger as she tries to figure out which bit of that she wants to respond to.

"Gael…" Eiran says, but she holds up a clawed hand in his face.

"You know nothing, whoever you are, so I'd keep your little human mouth shut."

Then, stepping closer so she can tower over me and use her Valen height to full advantage, she adds, "And to be clear, my brother was never his best friend. Those two always competed like idiots. Lirion was always Kaelen's friend. Eiran's best friend? The one that listened to him when he was a kid, who tutored him through college? The one always on his side? Who had his back every day until he fucking *left*? Me. I was the best friend. And then he ditched us to go chasing after his stupid older brother and the false dreams of glory that Kaelen spun for him."

I stand horrified and frozen, unable to move, unable to fight back against this woman. I turn again to Eiran, but he's hanging his head in shame.

Finally, I find my voice. "Friend?"

Eiran shakes his head at Gael. "Don't."

"Girlfriend, right?" The nervous tick in her shoulder and sparkling at the corners of her eyes gave it away.

Gaelarya shrugs. "Once upon a time." Then, with a bitter little laugh, she adds, "But he was too scared to set a date."

My eyes go wide. Engaged? Holy shit.

Eiran growls. "Dammit Gael. We never—"

"That was a long time ago," Gaelarya says over him, strength returning to her tone. "That was before Eiran ran off to play spy. When Lirion told him to stay, that he was being an impulsive idiot, as usual, he nearly killed him."

Eiran's body goes rigid. In words so soft I doubt Gael hears him, he says, "That's not what happened. I didn't—"

Gael tosses her brown locks in a frustrated flick. "Anyway, I'm a different person now, so you can wipe that stupid pleading look off your face, Eiran. I'm not interested."

His eyes become an inferno, roving from her to me. "That's not why I'm here."

Gaelarya gives Eiran a look that should kill him on the spot. "That's not why I'm here, either. I need to talk to you. Alone. Now."

Eiran's gaze slides to me again for some reason. "I don't think that's—"

"This isn't about us," she spits, sounding disgusted. "It's important." Baring her teeth when he still hesitates, she adds, "*Now*, Eiran."

18

CLAWS OUT

Eiran

I can tell Gaelarya's blow landed exactly as she wanted. Taylor looks hurt, confused, and all because of… well, perhaps "lie" isn't the right word. But how far do you get to stretch the truth before it becomes false? Gael and I were basically broken up long before Kaelen asked for a consultation. We were never mates. I never claimed her.

I didn't want that life. I told her, but she wouldn't accept it. The fight got so bad that I doubt Lirion will ever forgive me fully. And now Taylor thinks…

Get your damn head on straight, Eiran! Why do I even care what she thinks? I don't love Gael. But Taylor… Taylor would be a mistake, too. She's reckless, wild, beautiful… and entirely wrong for me. Besides, she's my asset. No fraternization allowed.

Even if fraternization with Taylor sounds really, really nice.

Fuck. I can't let her walk off thinking that I'm still pining for Gael.

And no, we won't investigate why that's so important.

"Fine, let's talk, Gael," I say with cold steel. "But I need a minute."

"No, Eiran. We need to—"

"I said I need a minute." Gael takes a step back, but I don't care how wide-eyed she is at my tone. The guy she bossed around as a kid is long gone.

I turn to Wynn, who still looks almost comically shocked. "Call Lirion and ask him to come walk you both home and then wait for him. Got it?"

She nods, looking from Gael to me.

Exchanging glares with Gael, I grab Taylor by the arm and pull her over to the side. "Look, I'm sorry about this. I hate to drag you into my family's mess, but I didn't know what to do. Lirion was the only one I could think of that…" I run a hand through my hair, growling.

Taylor grabs my hand and pulls it away from my head. "It's fine, Eiran. I'm the last one to say anything about weird family shit. You know that."

"It's not the same," I grumble, too weak to pull away from her. She's my asset, damn it. I can't do this.

But then why does her touch do… whatever the hell it's doing to me?

"She was never… Gael and I weren't together. Not like that. I mean, we dated, but we weren't engaged. We weren't mates. We just…" Taylor's eyebrows raise at the word "mates," but I move on, not feeling like explaining that particular ancient tradition at the moment. "I'll tell you more later. I promise. Anything you want to know. But for now—"

"It doesn't matter, Eiran," she says, looking uncomfortable. "It's none of my business. I'm not your girlfriend, no matter what wrong ideas Wynn gets into her head. You don't owe me anything."

Aether save me, why does that feel like a gut punch? That should *not* bother me. She's right. My personal life isn't her business, any more than her personal life is mine.

Still, I stand, unwilling for this moment to end.

"You'd better go before Gaelarya breaks something," Taylor prompts, stepping away.

Nodding, I motion for her to follow Wynn. "If you see anything suspicious—anything at all—then call me immediately. And stay with Wynn and Lirion. Don't wander off on your own."

Once she's out of sight, I stomp back past Gael to a nearby grove. She follows with stomping feet and a stiff jaw.

"What?" I ask, crossing my arms. I've been nothing but ragged about leaving since I got here, and I'm getting pretty sick of it at this point.

"You screwed me over," she spits again, repeating what she said earlier before she slapped me (impressively hard, I must admit). "I spent a year and a half tracking down lost Valen artifacts, trying to make connections, and then we finally find it. Sale nearly finalized. Just needed to verify the artifact's authenticity. But no. It all goes to hell, thanks to the damn SRF."

Of all the things I imagined Gaelarya saying, this definitely wasn't one of them. "W-what?" I splutter oh-so-eloquently. Way to play it cool, Mr. Superspy.

"You heard me," Gaelarya breathes in a furiously quivering tone. "The EPE arrested my contact, and now I can't find out what happened to the artifact."

"Wait. What?" I say, regaining my voice. "Arrested by Environmental Protection Enforcement?" She has to mean someone from the Lorathar Initiative.

"That's what they're saying, but I have a contact in Environmental Protection. She told me this whole thing is super-secret and has SRF written all over it. I've been searching for this artifact for years, Eiran. Finally found someone who knew its location. He and I were negotiating with Ryland Corvane—trying to repatriate it for the university."

My eyes widen. "You were working with *Corvane*?!"

Gael scowls, as if I were being willfully ignorant. "I was trying to recover stolen artifacts, not throw in with him. After years of chasing rumors, I met someone. Dr. Eilrach Feylon. He brokered the deal. But before it closed, your people arrested him. So now the deal's dead, and the relic's vanished." Gaelarya glares at me, stepping into my space. "So where is it, Eiran?"

Alarms start ringing faintly in the back of my head. Something's off in her voice. Paranoia, maybe. She sounds like…

Trying to remain calm, I ask, "Where's what, Gael? I have no clue what you're talking about."

She growls like an animal, her feral nature just below the surface now. "Don't play dumb with me. Where did the SRF hide the Eldralume?"

The question lands like a punch. "The… Eldralume?"

She's looking to recover one of the most valuable religious artifacts in all of Valen mysticism. From a fucking mobster. Of course she is.

Damn it. I knew Gael had stayed in archeology when I'd left the program to join SRF full time, had gone on to get her doctorate. But never suspected she was risking her life tracking down stolen artifacts.

Treasure hunting was always *my* dream. It was the reason we broke up, in fact. She was the quiet academic, while I craved adventure she never wanted. But that was before. Before a breakup and a death changed everything. Now here she is, risking her life, but without Taylor's skill or her cunning. Taylor may be in this job for the money, but at least she's calculated in her insanity. It's one of the things I find so sexy about her. But Gael… well, if I know anything about Gael, it's that she's a true believer. A zealot.

Of course, given how she grew up, it's no surprise.

"You've been looking through your mother's journal again."

Gael flinches momentarily but then brushes this off. Advancing again, she says, "So what? The university may not have listened to her. The Council. My father. But she was fucking right about this. I've been searching for relics related to Thalindor for years, and I'll take insights where I can get them. Now shut up and answer the question. I know you have the Eldralume."

"You're saying that Corvane… Corvane had the Eldralume Relic?" Cold fury drips down my spine. My brain buzzes in numb horror as truths from the past few weeks connect in my head. The Lorathar Initiative. Eilrach Feylon. A beautiful girl in a silver dress. A hand in a jacket pocket…

Gaelarya gapes at me like I'm an idiot. "Yes, among other things. I found a lead in Mom's journal about who might have stolen it two centuries ago. After years of hunting, I was about to buy it off Corvane and bring it back into safe hands. But now it's *gone*. Where is it?" I try to push past her, but she grabs me by the arm. "You're not going anywhere until you tell me where the relic is."

"I have no clue." Which isn't entirely a lie. I don't have the answer *yet*. Not for sure.

Gael refuses to let go. "Stop acting like you know nothing about this. Feylon arrested. Relic gone. I can add, Eiran. I know the kind of shit that you do. The work Kaelen did. Don't pretend you weren't involved."

I turn to Gaelarya, my shock feeding my anger. "So, is this what you're doing with that archeology degree? You rail on me for leaving, broke up with me for wanting to explore the world, and now here you are. You're—"

"—gonna end up like my mother?" Gael's voice drops to a

dangerous timbre. "You really think so little of me?"

Despite all that's happened between us, the implication stings. "Like I give a damn about the opinions of some stuck-up academic assholes. Chase whatever theories you want. But making deals with scum like Corvane? Do you have any clue how dangerous he is? He's one of the biggest criminal kingpins in the sector!"

Gaelarya pushes me into a nearby tree, and I let her get her anger out. Her claws extend, and she bares her teeth. Growling, she stalks toward me. "Yes, I am risking my life for my passion. Just like you. But at least I come back. I always come back." There's a pause, a breath of exhausted pain, like the festering of an old wound. "You… were supposed to come back."

I let out a sigh. I never wanted to come back. To where he lived. To where we were all happy. To the world of "before."

I'm only here for Taylor. And she has no idea.

"Gael, I'm sorry that—"

She lunges, pinning me against the tree with the tips of her claws. "No. You don't get to pity me. At least my work matters."

My former compassion leaks out of me, and I laugh at this, actually laugh right in her face, unable to help myself. "So national security doesn't matter, then?"

This entire conversation is ridiculous.

I need to talk to Taylor.

Gaelarya looks like she's ready to slap me again. "Don't you dare look down your nose at me, Eiran Valtir. And don't give me that national security nonsense. I've read books. I know the—"

"You know nothing." I bare my teeth at her, growling.

She flinches, stepping back in fear. "What are you gonna do, Eiran? Attack me like you did Lirion?"

I don't mention that Gael looks pretty close to attacking *me*. That her brother picked a fight with me just hours ago. I let the verbal blow land, the old guilt, like I did Lirion's punch. Because I deserve it. For leaving everyone. For not visiting my family. My friends.

It was all too hard.

I shake my head in disgust. "You're messing with shit more dangerous than you can imagine. You're going to get yourself killed."

She presses her claws into my shoulder, nearly breaking the skin. "Does the SRF have the Eldralume?"

I see the briefest flash of red in the bushes.

"No," I reply, my eyes lingering on the spot for half a second before returning to Gael.

My brain is buzzing with revelations. I need this conversation over. "No, we don't have it. I swear. And that you think I'd let something so important be hidden away is really fucking insulting, Gael."

And I mean it. It's going into a museum as soon as I get it back.

Something in my words or conviction breaks through her haze of anger. She retracts her claws and steps away in a daze, looking lost. "Then it's gone again… probably forever. The most important spiritual relic in Valen history… and it'll never be seen again." She shakes her head and turns to walk off. After a step, she pauses, not turning around. "I was so close."

Gaelarya slinks off, and I wait for her to disappear around the corner before calling, "Miss Grey. Come out, please."

"We're back to Miss Grey, I see." Unrepentant, she rises from behind the bush where I so briefly spied her. Grass and twigs cling to her clothes and hair, and I push down my instinctive reaction to her effortless cuteness. "What gave me away? I'm downwind. You couldn't scent me."

"A lock of your hair must have blown in the wind. I saw it for like half a second. Just long enough to notice."

"Damn this hair," she grumbles, her normal playful tone sounding forced. "The only thing I got directly from my mother—and it's a total pain in my ass. I normally wear a cap."

I don't let myself grin. This is what she does.

"You heard what we said?"

"The tail end of it," she shrugs. "I had to lose Elowynn. Sounds like Gaelarya is *really* mad at you."

My lip curls at her cavalier confirmation. Keeping my tone as even as I can manage, I ask, "The thing you stole from Corvane. What was it?"

"Eiran, I told you—"

"Yeah, how about I tell you, and you can let me know if I got it right, okay?" Taylor cocks her head, looking confused, her short red hair bobbing. I don't buy the act. "The item was Elvish. Over a thousand years old. Wooden branches woven together with Gruundlith, with a core of Zeridian crystal."

"I… I…"

I throw out a hand, and a nearby tree cracks. A huge branch goes flying, landing with a crunching thud some twenty feet away. "The fucking Eldralume Relic?"

Bring it down, Eiran. You can't lose control. Not here. Not with her. I flex my fingers, retracting the claws that have slipped out at some point.

Taylor doesn't even flinch at the crashing sound. "I don't know what you're talking about."

Anger rises at the words, but it's more than that. The realization of what Taylor has done… hurts. And that's a very stupid thing to feel. Trying to keep my voice level, I growl, "I'd say I can't believe it, but the truth is? I can. I can believe it. You stole the fucking Eldralume. You're a good liar, Taylor, but I can read you now. I can see it on your fucking face."

She shrugs, unfazed. "You're wrong. I have no clue what it is you think I stole, but you're wrong."

The line's smooth. Almost enough for me to believe it. But I'm not buying what she's selling. Not this time. "Do you have any idea what recovering that artifact would mean to the elves?"

Finally, her mask cracks. Taylor's eyes narrow, and she steps recklessly closer. "Honestly, Eiran? I don't give a shit. I can't."

I laugh, the sound half-crazed, because this is anything but funny. Aether save me, Gael was right! I should have trusted my gut rather than my dick. She played me. But then, she's a thief. What did I expect?

"That's exactly your problem, isn't it?" I manage. "You don't give a shit about anyone or anything. You stole the most revered artifact in all of Valen mysticism, lost for centuries. Taken from our most sacred temples. But so what, right? Who cares if the elder mystics say it served as a key to unlocking 'the profound secrets of the Aether' or that it 'ensures harmony with the Luminar Essence?' What does it matter if a priceless object of invaluable cultural relevance stays lost in the hands of whatever scum you would have sold it to, as long as you make a quick buck? Why should any of that concern you?"

"Exactly." Taylor's voice is so low I almost don't hear. "You think I give a flying fuck about the elves after the hell they put me through? After the way they treat me? At least with what my mom—" Her voice breaks, and she clears her throat. "At least I got something out of it. All

I've ever gotten from you elves is pain. And you're telling me I should care about how important some damn *lamp* is to them?"

"It's not a lamp—"

Taylor barrels on. "You don't know what I went through. I'll do anything—and I mean anything—to get away from arrogant, simple-minded elvish assholes like—"

"—like me?" I snap. With deadly calm, I say, "That's what you mean. Because you don't care about me either. There are moments when I wonder if this was a game from the start."

Taylor stares in stunned silence before managing a barely audible, "What?"

"Maybe you're a double agent sent by the Kuro Oni. Some attempt to distract me, to keep me off the trail."

I know the words are crazy. They're crazy. I think. But the fact that I still have doubts, still wish my words weren't true, compels me to continue.

"It would explain everything. Remember, I've seen your work firsthand. Maybe Helix sent in the pretty face with the sob story to play off what happened to Kaelen. Is that it? Did you fucking *play me*?"

Finally, something snaps in Taylor. Growling, she steps forward to slap me across the face. Searing pain as her nails—no, her claws—tear into me. I collapse onto the grass, head swimming. Blood drips onto my shirt, red smearing my vision.

Taylor's grimace turns to dread as she stares at her hand, my blood dripping from her black claws.

"Eiran?" she whispers, pleading like a child.

I stare into her helpless eyes.

At her claws.

My blood.

Then...

Nothing.

19

FUCK NORMAL

Taylor

Oh gods. Oh gods. What have I done? What's happening to me? I stare at my hands, the crimson blood stark against the black gleam of the very elvish claws. All anger has flooded out of me, replaced by repulsion.

Eiran is lying amidst grass and fallen leaves, cursing quietly as he tries and fails to "man" his way through having his face torn open.

I did that. My claws did that to him.

I need to call someone. I need to… need to…

Elowynn bursts into the clearing. "Taylor, there you are. I got us two teas with milk and extra sugar for you. Carbs, remember? Are you ready to… Eiran! Taylor, what happened?"

I look at the girl pleadingly. "Elowynn. I…" I hold my hands up, fingers… no, claws… still dripping crimson.

That's… that's Eiran's blood.

"Eiran!" I yell, stepping over to him. But his mangled face, the ruins of what I did to him, wrenches like a blaster shot to the gut.

I'm going to be sick.

I lean over and hurl up the remains of Maelara's stale sandwich while Elowynn pulls out her comm. Her face lights up in relief as someone picks up. "Gael? I need your help!"

Oh shit. Not her. But then, what else did I expect?

"We're still in the clearing. I know you're pissed, but something happened and… Please come?" Satisfied, she hangs up, calling someone else.

A wave of exhaustion hits, and I can't bring myself to care who she's calling now. Everything's fucked. My cover, my life in Vaeloria City? Fucked. Friendships? Fucked. Any chance of getting off Vale? Fucked.

Everything I touch? Fucked.

I mean, look at me. I have claws. Claws! What's happening to me? And Eiran! Eiran is…

Fuck, what if I killed him?! The wound is so deep.

"Eiran!" I call again. He doesn't respond. Just moans softly.

That's it. I've killed him.

I really am a monster.

"Lirion!" Elowynn says into the comm, her voice desperate now. "You need to come downtown! We're in a little clearing by the shops. Eiran's hurt and Taylor's… just come! Please come!"

Elowynn and I collapse in front of Eiran. Elowynn's hands rove over her brother's face, checking the wound, but I can't seem to move. I'm staring at the rise and fall of his chest. It's moving, so he's alive. That's all I can process.

I should do something. Help. Eiran's in pain. Eiran's hurt!

My breath comes in tiny, broken gasps as past and present blur.

Geneblight.

Freak.

Monster.

Elowynn puts a hand to her brother's face, trying to seal the wound with magic, but he waves her off. "I can do it, Eiran," she says, teary and annoyed. "Lirion showed me how."

"I don't want… to scar," Eiran says, and the sound releases another floodgate of relief and exhaustion. His voice is frighteningly slurred, even as he tries to chuckle. "Look like Lirion. The ugly ass."

"You're bleeding too much," Elowynn says, nearly sobbing now. "We've got to—" Eiran shakes his head stubbornly. He's not thinking straight. He's lost too much blood. In too much pain.

Mustering up some strength to be in the moment, I mutter, "Oh, for gods' sake, let her help. It's not like you wouldn't be annoyingly hot, even if you had scars. It'd probably make you even hotter, given how unfair the universe is."

Eiran stares at me, his gaze somewhat glassy, and I return an equally glassy stare, shrugging. I can't seem to care that I called Eiran hot. Again.

"What the hell?" I don't turn to see who it is. It doesn't matter. Somewhere in the back of my mind, an instinctive warning tells me it's an elfin voice, but for some reason I'm not afraid.

Eiran's words from earlier come floating back to me. "You were born here, so by Valen law, that makes you Valen anyway. Not elvish. Just Valen." I laugh, though I'm not sure what's funny. I guess I really am a full-fledged, claw-carrying elf myself now.

Shock. I'm in shock.

"Is he…" the elf behind me asks. Whoever she is.

"He's fine," Elowynn replies. "I've got him stable. Lirion's on the way. I don't know about Taylor, though."

He's fine. Stable. But still hurt.

"Alright, you watch him. I'll take her," the stern elf says. An arm reaches firmly under my shoulder and lifts me up. Still hazy, I see Gaelarya standing there, a tight crease on her face.

"I can't…" I try to say, searching for Eiran. I need to see that he's okay. That I haven't…

"I have him," Elowynn says with a watery smile. "I promise."

Gaelarya lets out a tiny, disgusted sort of sigh. "Come on. Let's get you cleaned up and checked out." Insistent without being rough, she pulls me toward a nearby shop.

The other shoppers stare at me, horrified and gawking. Poor, weird, crazy, messed up me, dripping blood across the carpet of some fancy local boutique. I look away.

Gaelarya leads me wordlessly across the shop and into the small bathroom at the corner of the store. When we get inside, she turns the water on hot enough to steam, and puts my clawed hands underneath the near-scalding spray. I barely feel it.

I've tuned out the whirring thoughts, and a hushed silence falls over the world like a heavy blanket. Her mouth a thin, hard line, Gaelarya meticulously washes each finger, cleaning the blood off the black claw before putting the slightest bit of pressure on the tip, causing it to *snick* back inside.

Satisfied with the hands, she turns me toward her, wetting a towel and cleaning my face. "So, you're Enhanced, huh?" Gaelarya's tone is dispassionate. I nod anyway. "You know Eiran hates Enhanced humans, right? After Kaelen? Is that why you attacked him? Was he being… Eiran?"

I shrug, too exhausted to get into it now. Part of me wants to ask what she means, but I'm too tired to even attempt comprehending any answer she might try to give me. So, we stand here in silence, Gaelarya (for reasons incomprehensible to me) cleaning me up in mute efficiency.

And minute by minute, the crimson stains of blood slowly wash away, taking the looming haze and numbness with them.

"Thanks," I say when she's done.

Gaelarya laughs bitterly. "I'm doing this for Wynn."

We leave the room, and a willowy old Valen woman watches us with a furrowed brow. "Is she alright, Gael?"

"She's fine, Greta," Gaelarya says, giving the lady a brief, apologetic smile. "Sorry about the carpet."

"Don't worry about it," the shop owner, Greta, says, tone still anxious. "You two… um… be safe."

As we exit the store, it's hard to miss the small mass of people huddled on the street corner. Elowynn, Maelara, and Roderic stare in tense silence, watching Lirion, who has two fingers on Eiran's temple.

Relief floods me at the sight of him. He's shaky, but whole.

Of course, with the shock worn off, I wonder why I was so terrified. I mean, he's my… handler or whatever the term is. We're working together. And sure, he's a good guy, if a pain in my ass. It's not like I want him dead, particularly at my hands.

That must be why my heart feels like it's being stitched together with a knitting needle.

Lirion's magic knits the last of Eiran's gashes together like new. "There," the doctor says when he finishes. "Had to get it back perfect so I could break your face next time. It's not fair if you're already messed up."

Eiran smiles slightly at the attempted humor and then eyes me warily. I brace for the disgust, for the cries of "monster" or "geneblight freak." But he just says tentatively, "Are you alright?"

"I'm fine, Eiran," I say, shaking my head. "I'm the one who… gods, I'm so sorry."

I want to run to him. To touch his face and make sure he's really alright. To feel the steady breathing in his chest.

But as I told him minutes ago… I'm not his girlfriend. And I won't confuse that in front of all these people.

I look down, eyes focused on the grassy greenway, avoiding any potential judging stares.

His closeness takes up my universe as he stands in front of me. The others blur into the periphery, and it's just him. Just me. He places a finger under my chin, pulling my eyes to him. Fire races along that contact, calming and igniting me in equal measure.

"I'm okay," Eiran says in a tone low enough only we can hear. I know they're all watching us, but he slides his hand to my cheek, forcing me to look at him. I stare into those amethyst eyes, stable and kind. Always centering, like a touchstone. An anchor in a storm. "It's really fine. I'm okay. It was an accident, and now Lirion has me right as rain."

"I hurt you," I whisper, my voice a breath.

"Well, I hurt you first," he replies in a broken tone. His eyes are tortured, not from pain, I realize. But from guilt. Of course, he would make this his fault. "I'm so sorry. I shouldn't have said… listen, I get what you're saying. About why you did what you did."

"You can have it back," I blurt, not planning the words until I say them. But after everything… can I go on pretending that I don't care? "What I said… I didn't mean that either. I wouldn't—couldn't—let myself think about it. But I can see why it—"

"We'll talk about the relic later," Eiran says, glancing around.

Oh, right. We have an audience.

"Right now, we need to figure out what's happening to you. I need you on this case."

"What case?" Lirion asks.

Gaelarya's eyes go sharp as razors. "You stole the—"

"What's happening to her?" Elowynn asks Lirion.

"She looks nauseous," Maelara notes, stepping forward to grasp my hand.

Gaelarya rolls her eyes but then focuses on me. She frowns, her eyebrows in a tight V. "She looks green."

"That's the same thing," I say, but everyone's scrutinizing me, more heads tilting in confusion.

"Umm…" Lirion begins. After a pause, he continues, "You know how I said your coloring looked off? Well… you look more…"

"Elvish," Eiran says, frowning at me. "You look elvish, Taylor."

My jaw must be on the floor. This *can't* be happening. First claws, and now…

Nope. No way.

"Well, more like half-elf," Roderic disagrees.

Half-elf? Am I… was my dad…

"Have you ever actually met a half-human?" Gaelarya asks with a shake of her head. "I taught a half-human, half-Valen a couple of years ago, and they're a lot taller, no offense."

Oh, offense one hundred percent taken.

"Their ears are also a lot more pronounced," Gaelarya continues, either unaware or unconcerned with my building frustration. "They're almost as long as a full-blooded elf. Not those short, tapered things the Enhanced humans have."

Finally, I find my voice.

"I'm an *elf*?!" My hands fly to my face. My ears. No way. There's no way. Valen are… I couldn't be a…

"You're still human," Eiran says, putting a hand on my shoulder. "That's what we're saying."

"Your basic physiology is still that of a genetically enhanced human," Lirion explains. "Muscles? Height? Bone structure? All human. But some changes are… unexpected."

"I think the word you're looking for is 'freak,' Lirion." I smile like I mean it as a joke.

"You're not a freak," Eiran says firmly, a subtle anger at my words held on a tight leash. In an admission that pains him, he adds, "You may not be completely *normal*, but—"

"—but 'fuck normal,' right? It's a favorite phrase of mine. But then, it's easy to say when you've never *been* normal."

"What do you mean, you've never been normal?" Gaelarya probes, eyes shrewd.

"This isn't the place for this conversation," Eiran replies, glancing around.

"So, let's go somewhere where we can have it," Lirion says, eyes equally flinty. "Sounds like there's quite a bit we need to catch up on."

"No," Eiran says emphatically.

"Here it comes," Gaelarya spits. "National security. Just like

Kaelen."

Eiran looks tortured. "I'm trying to keep you all safe. Safe from this. From me."

Lirion crosses his arms and shakes his head. "It's too late, Eiran. You brought us into this."

I say quietly, "They're a part of it now. And who else can we trust now? The solar storm won't last forever, and then we'll lose Blackstone."

Eiran groans. "Fine. Lirion and Gael only. Aunt Maelara, can you take Wynn home? Uncle Roderic, I love you, but I need you out of this. I need someone on the outside to protect Maelara and Elowynn." He nods, but Elowynn scowls.

"You're not leaving me again, Eiran."

"I never…"

"You *left*. And you never came back. You can leave still… be here."

Eiran glances at Lirion for the briefest of moments before returning to his sister. "I'm here now."

Her tears sparkle, and she swipes at them angrily. "Are you? You call, and we talk about school and boys and trivial shit. You never let me in." For the first time, I can see that hurt lurks beneath the bubbly surface. "I'm not letting you shut me out again. I'm staying."

"I'm just trying—"

"I'm old enough to choose the risk. I'm not a child."

"Elowynn, dear," Maelara starts, reaching for her shoulder.

Elowynn shakes her off. "I'm staying, damn it."

The stare-down between Elowynn and Eiran is brief but fierce, and I'm not surprised that Eiran breaks first. "Whatever," he sighs.

"If she goes, I go," Maelara says, but Roderic shakes his head this time, and I can see it in the exchange of looks he and Eiran have. They don't want her to worry.

"No, Eiran's right. Let the kids handle this. They're adults, even Wynn." She gives a half-hearted nod, clearly not thrilled.

"Alright," Eiran says, and then, to my surprise, turns to Gaelarya. "Let's take this to the clubhouse."

"The clubhouse!" Elowynn says excitedly. "You'd never let me come growing up."

"You were too little," Eiran says.

"It's nothing special," Lirion laughs. "Don't get your hopes up."

20

THE CLUBHOUSE

Taylor

"The clubhouse" turns out to be a secret childhood play spot in the middle of freaking nowhere. It takes walking through the edges of Silberwald Forest for half an hour before we find it. Unlike the Aelfswelth forest, with the massive but sparse silvery trunks of towering eldertrees littering the landscape in irregular patterns, the Silberwald is a tightly packed warren of quithra trees. Broad leaves spread across the forest like a blanket, obscuring the path. Eiran motions over a ridge, and he laughs as Elowynn scampers forward.

As Gaelarya follows, Lirion puts a hand on my arm, holding me back. "Before we go in there… you shouldn't beat yourself up about what happened."

I shake my head. "You weren't there. I attacked him. What I said… what I did…"

"Eiran provokes many things. Most of them are deserved. Trust me." He grins at me kindly. "But I want you to know. Sure, he can be a dick. Hell, I decked him the minute I saw him."

"I kind of guessed."

"But he knew what he was facing. He knew the reception he'd get, knew I'd want to hit him and Gael would want to kill him. That Maelara would guilt-trip him into the next century. But he came. For you. He plays the hero, sure, but he's never brought anyone here. Ever. But I got twin medical degrees in elvish and human anatomy so I could be the lead doctor in a tourist town like Silberwald. Eiran knew that. He came here, faced everything, so that he could get my help. With you. And I punched him in the face as soon as I saw him. He deserved it, but still. I just thought you should know."

Before I can even begin to process that, he walks off without another word. "There it is," Gaelarya calls from somewhere in front of us. There's an odd tone in her voice, somewhere between wary and wistful. She motions to a pair of quithra trees where the branches and roots have been magically woven to create a wooden cave barely large enough for all of us to stand.

Elowynn's mouth turns down at the small, common-looking space. With a shrug, she leads us in. The tiny room's little more than a dirt-floored hollow with a low ceiling and flat, curving benches roughly magicked from the trees. Somewhat awkwardly, we sit.

Lirion clears his throat and leans his large frame forward. "Now, I want to know everything. Everything. You swear it?"

Eiran gives a sad grin. "I'll tell you everything I can." Lirion glares at him, but he holds up his hands in apology. "It's the best I can promise."

"Fine," he grumbles.

"But first?" Eiran retorts with a raised finger. "Taylor."

Gael scoffs. "Of course."

"Yeah. I've been thinking about that on our walk over. The implant," Lirion says, cocking his head at me as if he hasn't heard Eiran. "It had to have done this… somehow." Wordlessly, he pulls out a medical comm. Placing one hand on the med comm's biotech pad and the other to my brow, he reads my vitals.

"Doesn't the implant use Valen DNA to work?" Elowynn asks.

Lirion glances at her, surprised. "Yeah. Spliced sequences—engineered to interface with Valen biotech."

"So if Taylor's body reacted to it, maybe it's rejecting the foreign DNA?"

Lirion frowns. "No, rejection is a rare but normal reaction. We know what that looks like. This isn't rejection. There's no redness. No swelling. None of the normal markers. Even the green veining is going away. The implant's still there, but there's no bump or white patch of skin. It's like the body… absorbed it. Here, look at this." He shows his medical comm to Eiran. "See? It's more like… adaptation. Her cells should fight the DNA, but instead? They're breaking it down and using it."

"Using it how?" Eiran asks, tone sharp.

"That's the problem," Lirion says. "I don't know. But if her system is integrating Valen markers, that could explain the changes. Facial structure, ear shape, even minor neurological shifts."

"That shouldn't be possible," Gaelarya mutters.

"It shouldn't," Lirion agrees.

"Well…" Eiran says with a small grin, his twinkling eyes turning to me. "It sounds like Taylor can do many impossible things."

Gaelarya's eyes widen, looking me over in confusion. "What does *that* mean?"

I motion for Eiran to go ahead, and he recaps everyone on what's happened.

***

"So… let me make sure I understand this," Lirion says, frowning at Gaelarya when Eiran finishes. "You found the Eldralume Relic, and you didn't tell me you were going to buy it from a dangerous smuggler and gunrunner?"

She gapes, clearly not expecting to be the first to face the firing squad. "I… I…"

Before she can say more than that, he turns to me and continues, "But before she can buy it, *you* steal it?"

I nod, feeling no shame at this.

Lirion raises a scarred eyebrow. "And then the head of a dangerous criminal organization—who also happens to be the father of your best friend slash older brother figure… father figure… whatever. He takes the relic and says you'll only get it back if you steal super-powerful powerseeds that could blow up a city."

I shrug.

Shaking his head, Lirion continues, "Enter Eiran, who is also investigating these seeds. You get the best of Eiran—"

"That's my favorite part," Elowynn chimes in. She seems much less disturbed that I stole a valuable Elvish religious icon than Eiran or Gaelarya.

"She didn't 'get the best of me.' She cheated," Eiran grumbles.

Elowynn laughs.

"Anyway," Lirion continues doggedly. "You meet up with said dangerous criminal head, only to get your asses handed to you by a freaky cyborg. A dwarven bounty hunter comes into play somehow. There's that bit about stealing—excuse me, *pretending* to steal another super-powerful seed. Now you're on the run, hiding here in this small town, hoping the cyborg doesn't find you and the bounty hunter doesn't realize you lied to her. Does that about cover it?"

"Except I'm not on the run," I say.

Eiran groans. "Taylor—"

"The Initiative is *dead*," I insist. "You heard Blackstone. He got what he wanted. Who'd come for me now?"

Eiran's smile is as brittle as twigs. "Blackstone got what he wanted *for now*. And we don't know the Initiative is actually dead. We destroyed the lab and got the workers we know about, but they've been operating in secret for over a decade before even the SRF found out about them. Who knows how big they really are?"

Lirion lets out something between a laugh and a groan. "Let's agree to 'may or may not be on the run from one or more forces', shall we? Anything *else* I missed?"

"You forgot the bit about the Zeridian woman blowing up the coffee shop," Elowynn says helpfully. "I liked that part."

"Yes," Lirion says dryly. "We can't forget that part. Not to mention, your mom's experiments during your childhood have given you psychic magic akin to a Quiblin, along with claws and green coloring like a Valen."

"That covers everything we know," Eiran says before focusing on me. "Now let's talk about what we suspect."

"Eiran thinks I'm working for the Eclipse Consortium," I say, raising a defiant eyebrow at him.

"Not the Eclipse Consortium." Eiran crosses his arms, surveying me. "Helix. It's the kind of shit they'd get up to."

The words are a slap in the face. "After what Blackstone did, you thought—"

"No," Eiran says quickly. He runs a hand through his hair in frustration. "Sorry, I was being paranoid. After all that's happened, it's hard not to be. But I shouldn't have accused you."

"Wait, Helix? The human terrorists that you said are trying to turn people into dangerous Enhanced?" Elowynn asks, sounding horrified.

"Are they the ones that—" Lirion begins, but a glare from Eiran cuts him off.

The fuck was that about?

Elowynn wrinkles her nose and asks, "Is it because Taylor's Enhanced? Because… that's kind of racist."

"You're right, Wynn," Eiran says, his eyes on mine. "I'm sorry, Taylor. I just… it's hard to trust people in my line of work. So many people have betrayed me. And honestly—"

"You don't have to explain." Something inside twists at his pleading, beseeching me to listen to him. To understand. I don't have the strength to fight the urge. "I haven't given you ample reason to trust me. I get it. I'm definitely not the trusting type either. And I'm not Helix, for the record. I've never worked for Helix or the Lorathar Initiative."

"I believe you," Eiran says. "And good thing. I need your help to figure out what Blackstone wants with the enhanced powerseeds. Whatever it is, it can't be good, particularly if he hired a firm as ruthless as the Eclipse Consortium to retrieve it. Is he trying to power himself up again? Making a bomb for Helix? And what does it have to do with your blood? We need to know more. I want to look through some of Helix's known associates. Maybe there's a link we aren't aware of."

"What if… what if Blackstone finds me before we find him?" I ask quietly. Shit. That sounded way too weak. "Not that I'm convinced anyone's actually after me at this point."

Eiran scoffs. "Taylor—"

My hands are shaking now, a familiar trembling creeping up my neck. I take a deep breath, shoving it down. "Then fuck 'em. I'll be ready."

Lirion cocks his head. "We could… practice your magic, if you're up for it. Because… I wonder if you have Gruundlith now."

"Gruundlith?" I say, leaning back into the wood root wall as if I could run from this conversation. "You mean elvish magic?"

"Sure. Why not?" Lirion shrugs. "I mean, you can already use Quiblin magic to manipulate air and electromagnetic fields. They tap into the Aether to alter electrical signals in the brain, manipulate the air to lift things. And you can do that. Our magic works the same way. Our affinity is just focused on manipulating the chemical processes in living things like plants and animals."

"You should try!" Elowynn says, bouncing in her tree-branch seat. "Go ahead!"

"I don't…" I begin.

Lirion laughs. "Yeah, maybe best to try outside. Let's get out of this cramped space before we attempt anything. It's much smaller than I remember."

"You're larger than you were when we were last here, big brother," Gaelarya says, patting him on the shoulder as they move to the exit.

I stay rooted, as if I'm now part of these trees myself.

Eiran turns, and whatever look of fear he sees stops him. "I want to work with Taylor a bit. Why don't you all go on? Lirion can get back to work. And Gael? Would you mind helping Elowynn pick out a few things for Taylor? Since apparently everyone has doubts about my packing skills."

Gaelarya doesn't reply, but after a long moment, gives a curt nod and takes Elowynn gently by the arm, leading her back along the trail toward the town.

21

AGAIN

Taylor

"I can't do this."

Eiran smiles. "If so, that's fine. There's not a test or anything. I'm just saying we should try."

"Try," I echo, wincing at the weakness in my voice. I take a breath and try again, putting steel into my tone. "My mom called it the game." I've never told anyone this. Not even Kairo. Never spoke of it. "She'd take me into that lab, the one we saw. She'd lock the door. 'Our secret,' she'd always say. And then... she'd make me 'try.' For hours and hours."

"I'm so sorry, Taylor," Eiran says. "What she did was horrible. I know she did nice things, too. I'm not saying she was a horrible person, but... what she did? That *was* horrible. Doing that to a child. But this isn't that. You can say no. It's your choice."

"I just wanted to make her proud." My fucking voice quavers traitorously. I take a big sniffing breath, sucking it down. I'm not crying today. "But you're right. If I do this, I'm doing it for myself. Let's try."

"Okay," Eiran says. No questions, no offer to wait. I could tell him I was done. We could go home now, and he'd be fine. But now that I've decided to try? He'll let me. He'll support that choice.

"I... don't know what to do," I admit.

Eiran grins that dimpled grin that does weird things to my stomach.

He reaches out, gently grasping my hand, sending electric shocks down my arm as he leads me over to the trunk of a short tree. He has me reach out so I'm touching one of the winding vynthra vines and says, "I'm no expert, and I'm no believer in the old mysticism either, but I'll tell you what I was taught. Maybe it'll help."

"Okay," I sigh, a little unevenly.

He reaches out to the tree, running his hand along the bark. The tendrils of thin green vines that cover the tree reach out and play with his fingers. "The mystics always taught us the Aether connects everything. It's like… the bond that ties all things together. And different things have different bonds. They sing at different timbres. And different races, we resonate at those different timbres."

He turns to look at me. My confusion clear, he explains, "The Zeridians resonate with the stone and earth and the metals. Quiblins resonate with the air and the psychic forces. The Hitari resonate with light, and the Valen? We resonate with the living forces." He plays with the vines again, coaxing them into twirling shapes before letting them drop. "Now how you change your resonance? How you connect with living forces rather than psychic ones? I don't know." He groans. "This would be easier in Aelfswelth forest."

I frown. "Why?"

"The luminar essence, the living manifestation of the Aether, is strong in Aelfswelth. It's what causes so much to glow there. That's what the mystics say, anyway. But we're in the Silberwald. So, we'll try a vynthra vine. They're thin, grow quickly, and rarely fight against the push of the Gruundlith."

I stare at the tree, the sight of them playing with Eiran's fingers still gripping me. "Gruundlith. Elvish magic."

"Your magic," Eiran says, stepping forward.

"You don't know that."

His solemn purple eyes survey me for a moment. "Perhaps… but I have faith."

"Misplaced faith, but I appreciate it," I say with a quiet chuckle.

Eiran shakes his head. "Reach out like before. But this time, rather than moving the object… make the object move itself."

I close my eyes, reaching out with my mind as usual. The vine lurches beneath my fingers. I get excited for a moment, until Eiran chuckles and says, "Don't move it. Make it move."

"Right." Grimacing, I admit to myself that maybe I'm thinking of this the wrong way. I'm doing elvish magic now, not halfling. I need to (gods, I can't believe I'm saying this) think like a Valen. And Valen (well, everyone but Eiran) have to touch a living creature to enchant it.

Rather than reaching out across the air from my mind, I picture magic emanating from my hand. I feel the pulsing of the vine, the slow processes within the plant flowing under my fingertips. The touch opens up the plant's entire world to me. I try to make a small bud grow into a new leaf. A tiny shoot of green appears, and I hit a wall. The vine itself is fighting against me.

I feel a slight twinge under my eyelid as I mentally push against that invisible wall of opposition in the vine. It's like trying to lift a boulder. My ears start to ring, a telltale sign that I'm nearing my limit. Finally, hesitantly, the bud awkwardly grows before bending in on itself, misshapen and ingrown. I release the Gruundlith, nearly collapsing from the effort.

"That was too much!" Eiran snaps, eyes wide and nostrils flared. "You're going to hurt yourself if you try to go that fast so soon."

"I can… do it…" I heave. Surreptitiously, I swipe away the tiny trickle of blood from my nose.

"You can try again tomorrow," he says, scowling. "That's enough for today."

"Again," I say. Eiran starts to argue, but I just repeat, "Again."

This time, the bud grows into a tiny leaf before browning at the edges. There's a pounding behind my right eye, and Eiran steps forward again. "Okay, Taylor. We proved the point. We don't have to—"

I glare at him, not bothering to wipe the trickle of blood this time as the faint copper taste tinges my lip. "Again."

And so we try again. My headache gets worse.

And again. Exhaustion threatens.

And again. Flowers—and my confidence—grow.

An hour later, I don't protest when Eiran's patience gives in and he makes me stop. "Keep practicing. But *slower*," Eiran says with a smirk. "Perfect it, and I'll take you to the pottery class."

I stare at him, mouth agape. "Pottery class?"

"There's a Gruundlith pottery class at the college every Friday. You grow wooden bowls and vases from the trees. Elvish tourists from Nuvalenheim and the rest of the Republic love it. Keep working on your skills—without killing yourself—and I'll take you."

"Uh… okay," I say, oddly pleased at the prospect of doing something as normal as taking a pottery class—if a Valen pottery class counts as "normal."

"It's a date then," Eiran says, his ears browning slightly at his choice of words.

Wiping away a tendril of blood still dripping from my nose, I say, "Well, at least you don't have to buy me flowers for the date." I collapse amidst the small patch of lorathar and emberblossoms I've magically grown. My head spins slightly. Eiran lies down beside me, and we stare up at the waning sun shimmering slantways amongst the trees. The green swirling is darker today, an effect of the intensifying storms.

I move to grasp his hand, but his arms are too long for it. At his height, his hand is somewhere around my calf. The moment broken, I laugh, and he turns his head, puzzled but amused. I grasp his muscular forearm instead, and he smiles in understanding. He reaches over with his other arm and grasps my hand, and we lie there as the evening cools.

"Thank you," I say eventually.

He turns to frown at me. "For what?"

I chuckle again. "For saving my life. More than once. For following me to that park. For bringing me here. For telling me the truth, for letting me in. I…" I have to pause. There's something in my throat. "I only ever had Kairo. Nobody else watched out for me like that."

"And you two never—"

"Did you and Gaelarya ever?" I retort.

"Well…" his cheeks brown. "I mean, we dated for most of high school, and you're evading the question."

"I'm just teasing," I say, smiling.

"We were never engaged, to be clear."

I turn, and his eyes are on me, searching.

"But it was… umm… pretty hot when you went to defend my honor."

"She slapped you!" The memory pisses me off all over again. "And you just stood there and took it like… like you deserved it."

He turns back to the sky, his emerald hair blending with the grass. "I did deserve it. And worse. Not because of her specifically, but… what I did to my family. My friends. Lirion… I'm dangerous."

"Eiran!"

"I am, Taylor." His face hardens, eyes tightening. Glistening. "Gael and I dated in high school, but it wasn't long into college before it was clear she was more interested in research and staying close to home. One day I finally told her I didn't love her, said horrible things to push her away. Push Lirion and Wynn and everyone away. It was… a tough time, and I wasn't handling things well."

My heart tightens at his tone. "Tough how?"

"My brother'd just passed, and I needed a change. To get out. I was all messed up, and Gael… it's not her fault. But I was upset and hurting, and I said terrible things. Lirion showed up. Got in the middle of it and—"

"What happened?" I prod.

Eiran sighs. "Remember when I told you about the Rökkurgrimm?"

I blanch. "You went feral?"

"Just for a second. Lost control and swiped at Lirion. Gave him that damn scar. Gael screamed, and that sort of pulled me back to myself. I tried to help, but Lirion told me to 'get out and stay out. Never come back.' And so I did."

"He didn't mean it," I say. "He still cares about you. They all do."

Eiran shrugs. "Maybe. But that doesn't mean he wasn't right. I'm dangerous. I get people hurt. Look at what happened to you."

"Eiran, that wasn't your fault!" I say, taking his cheek in my hand. "You're not dangerous. You're safe. I've always felt safe with you."

He winces, like the words are whips, and then turns away. "To be fair, it's not like I tried really hard to come back. Gael blames the SRF, but the truth? I always dreamed of exploring. Figured I'd grow up to be a treasure hunter, finding lost relics like someone from a book."

"And Gael didn't want that," I guess. Stupid, stupid heart. Don't get so damn hopeful.

"No. That wasn't who she was. At that time, anyway. She wanted to stay home, stay close to her brother and her parents, and I wanted… a challenge. Something… someone who would challenge me. It took me a while to realize it, but I figured out that wasn't Gael. When I told her, we had a huge fight about it. I guess she assumed I'd come back one day. Return to this idealized small-town life that she imagined. One I'd never said I even wanted. But I still feel bad. I may have moved on, but I still want her to be happy. Find someone. I'd rather her not hate me. She was my friend long before we got together. And she's Lirion's sister and close to Wynn and—"

"I get it. And to answer your earlier question, no. Kairo and I's relationship isn't like that. He's been watching over me since…"

I trail off, eyes on the purpling sky. If Eiran can share his history with Gaelarya, I can discuss this. "Growing up with my mom was… well, you know. But at night, she was mine. She was kind, and… just a mom. Until one night, she got a call. She was arguing with someone. Dr. Lirael, maybe? But she said, 'I can't do this anymore.' I remember it so clearly now. She was so angry. She said she wouldn't do it. Wouldn't work for them anymore. She didn't want to keep doing what she did to me."

"Taylor—" Eiran says, as if trying to warn me off a dangerous train of thought.

"It's just… that night? That night, she snuck me out. Drove into Vaeloria City and dropped me off at the Hitari embassy. She gave me this enormous hug. She was crying, and I… I never saw her again."

"The Hitari have a neutrality law," Eiran says, understanding. "They don't get involved in conflicts. If you took asylum there—"

"I lived in the embassy lobby for a month before Kairo found me," I reply with a teary laugh. "I was a complete nuisance. There wasn't a ship scheduled for Kagēkami, and I didn't want to go to the Hitari homeworld anyway. But they'd granted me asylum, and my mom made me promise I wouldn't leave the embassy. So I stayed until Kairo came in one day. I terrorized him like everyone else. He took a liking to me. Said he could keep me hidden. I could tell somehow that I was safe with him. So, he snuck me out, and I've been with him ever since."

"And what happened to your mom?" Eiran asks, although he likely already knows, squeezing my hand reassuringly.

A tear rolls down my cheek. I don't stop it. "The Valen police found her in an alley a week after she dropped me off. I didn't even know before they shipped her body back to the Union." I sigh. "You're probably wondering why I'm telling you all of this."

"No, I—"

"I just don't have many people I trust. And so, I'm glad I have you."

I sit up in a snap, regret instantly drenching me. Walk it back. Walk it the fuck back. Taylor, I swear. You and your damn mouth. You'll freak him out.

I scoot away from him. "I mean, I'm glad I can rely on you… for the job. The mission or whatever. I've worked on crews before, but I've never trusted them. It's why I work alone."

Eiran sits up as well, giving a too-understanding gaze. "Well, you're not alone now." He extends a hand to me, and his words somehow feel like a promise. Like a vow.

I take his hand and squeeze. He pulls me closer to him, protecting me from the chill of the evening. I watch the twilight shimmer through the branches like frozen raindrops suspended in time. "So, do you do this with all your assets?"

"What? Lie in the grass and watch the sunset?" Eiran grins, flashing those predatory teeth in a way that sends my heart racing. "Only the pretty ones."

My face tingles with heat, and my smile is probably full-on goofy. But frankly? I don't give a shit.

Eiran reaches out, running a hand through my curls. I breathe in the scent of mint and elderwood, the scent of him. Slowly, he leans over and brings his mouth close to mine. His lips hover there, his hand shaking hesitantly. Slowly, ever-so-slowly, he pulls away. He gazes at me, his eyes reflecting the magic of the Silberwald at dusk.

I begin to reach out, to pull him back to me, but he shakes his head. "Sorry."

Something inside me shatters. "For what?"

With an apologetic smile, he stands, reaching down to help me up. "You're an asset. I shouldn't... there are rules."

I scoff as I stand, though the glow of the moment is quickly fading. "Fuck the rules."

He laughs ruefully. "I'm not surprised you'd say that."

"And I'm not surprised you'd risk your own happiness for the sake of someone else's rules." I cross my arms, challenging.

He steps away. "Touché. Now, we'd better get back. Aunt Maelara will have a fit if we miss supper."

Letting the conversation drop for the moment, I admit, "I will too, honestly. I'm starving."

Eiran laughs. "In that case, let's go."

I take his arm, and he leads us back through the forest toward civilization.

BEDROOM CONFESSIONAL

Taylor

The next two weeks pass in a blur. The last vestiges of spring fade to summer as the days get longer and muggier, buzzing insects a constant menace. Still, Silberwald delivers on the subtle majesty and quiet charm that is quickly beginning to feel more comfortable than anywhere I've lived before.

Eiran hasn't tried to kiss me again, but we spend our days talking, laughing, and cursing our inability to find a lead in Eiran's extensive files on Helix. Maelara gives me space (something that seems a Herculean task for her), while Wynn gushes like I'm her new best friend and Gaelarya avoids me like the plague.

It's all become entirely too normal. And that is fucking dangerous.

This morning, I sit with a cup of coffee and a tiny potted tree, trying to magic it into a corkscrew shape. It's basic for a Gruundlith sculpture, but it's giving me trouble.

"Still working at that?"

I jump, and the growing trunk lurches off, ruining the spiral.

"Dammit, Eiran! You scared the shit out of me."

"Come on," he laughs, dimple making a brief appearance. "I ran a search and pulled some files for us to look at."

I groan. "More Helix files? I thought we'd seen all the SRF's reports by now."

That damn dimple deepens. "Not this time."

Curious, I follow him through a small door I've yet to open.

Crossing the threshold, it's immediately clear whose room this is. The walls are covered with sculptures, trinkets, and books. Children's books about great adventurers and magical treks line dust-free shelves, and beautiful sketches and paintings are haphazardly pinned at odd angles.

"This was your room," I say in awe.

"For twelve years." Eiran picks up a small pot. I realize the head-shaped sculpture is actually a tiny flowering tree with bright yellow flowers for eyes.

"Trying to show off?" I ask, thinking of my pitiful ruined tree.

"Maybe a little." His smile falters, turning sad. "Looks like Maelara is keeping up the enchantments."

"How'd you end up living here?" I ask before I can help myself.

Eiran runs a finger along a golden petal. "I made this a week after my parents died. They went on an anniversary trip to Hyoukō. They never came back."

I gape at him. "They went for a vacation to the Quiblin homeworld? But the Zeridians occupy it now. I didn't think they allowed visitors, particularly elves."

Eiran laughs distantly. "They don't. But my dad was ex-military. Never let something as trivial as permission get in his way. He'd mostly retired from his wandering ways after getting out of the army. Became an artisan at the college. But he wanted one more adventure, I guess, so he and Mom scheduled a hiking trip. There was a cave-in and… well, I guess it didn't work out like they planned."

I reach a hand to his shoulder. His shirt is smooth and cold under my fingertips as he stills for a breath. "I'm so sorry, Eiran. Where was Kaelen during all this?"

"Vaeloria University." After a moment, Eiran sets the pot down, staring at a charcoal sketch of a silberwolf like it's some portal to the past. "Kaelen escaped. Escaped this town, its hold. Maybe I should be mad at him for that, but the truth is… I envied him."

"If you're looking for someone to make you feel bad for wanting to get away from the place you grew up, you're talking to the wrong person," I laugh, sitting down on the old bed. Looking to change the subject, I say, "So, this is your old bed, huh?" I pat the quilted sheet. "The stories this thing could tell."

Eiran grins begrudgingly. "Do you really want to know?"

I picture him and Gaelarya in this bed, and my stomach drops. "Not really."

He snorts. "Anyway, I've been thinking. Perhaps we should rethink our approach. We really need to figure out why Blackstone wanted your blood. We need…" He trails off, looking awkward.

"…need to figure out what my mom did to me?" I finish with a nod. Something twinges inside at the idea, but I've been thinking the same thing.

Eiran nods gratefully. "Exactly. Maybe the answer isn't with Helix, but with the Initiative. So, I got some files to look through. If you're up for it."

I take a breath, then nod. "Let me go grab my glove and goggles."

"Actually, I was wondering if you wanted to try your implant."

I suppress a shudder. We hadn't attempted using it to access the biotech files after the reaction I had, instead using my biotech glove. "You think that's a good idea?"

Eiran reaches out and tucks a stray strand of hair behind my ear, his thumb tracing a line along my cheek. My heart stutters at the contact.

"Lirion thinks it's time. After all of your magic-wielding practice? You'll be fine. You can do this." He holds out a small metal slate about the size of my hand. In the center is a familiar mossy green pad. After a second, he prods, "Just reach out with your mind. You'll feel it."

Placing a finger on the pad, I feel a faint twinge in my neck. It extends up, growing like a mild headache. Suddenly, an iridescent tree floats into view in front of me, the illusion translucent and vaguely shimmering. Eiran places his hand over mine to access the pad as well, and my skin burns everywhere we touch. I don't think it's the biotech. Heart racing, I glance at him, those purple eyes blazing momentarily before he turns to the floating interface.

With practiced movements, he swipes throughout the tree, branches expanding, shrinking, and lurching out of the way. He plucks one of the ephemeral teal leaves, flicking it larger as the rest of the tree vanishes into sparks. Words shimmer into view. A list of names. "It's a list of some of the staff from the Lorathar Initiative. I thought we could dive into their backgrounds, see if it gives us some idea of what they were working on beyond the seeds. We could look at their expertise, backgrounds, and that sort of thing." He pinches off a section of names and throws it to me.

Tapping the first name on my hovering list, I dive into a bottomless tunnel of research. The most boring part of the job, but the most vital.

A while later, Eiran stills, eyes fixed on the scrolling photos of Initiative freelancers.

"Taylor?" he asks, his voice strange.

"Yeah?" My heart is in my throat. What now?

"You know how you said you weren't working for Helix or the Initiative?" Eiran smiles somewhat sadly. "I suspect you'll find that neither half of that statement is true."

My eyes widen. "What?"

Eiran holds up a hand and pulls out his comm. After a few moments, Kairo's voice comes through. *"Hey, Leaf Boy. Find something?"*

"Maybe." Eiran clears his throat, and then says, "I need you to tell me about this buyer from the Night Realm. What race?"

"Louponisian," Kairo says.

"Werewolf?" I ask, intrigued. "I've never met one."

"Wolf shifter, if you want to use such terms," Kairo says. *"Do not call her a werewolf to her face. Of course, she's probably already off-world, so there's not much chance of that. Why are you asking? Is Sylara still hassling you? I thought we took care of that."*

Now, Eiran has gone very, very still. "No. It's something else," he says. "I don't want to talk about it over comms. We can talk when you're in for the bonfire on Friday. But I need any details about the buyer you can get me."

He reaches up and taps one of the floating pictures. It expands to reveal a larger picture and two details:

NAME: Isra Darrow
RACE: Louponisian

I examine the photo of the attractive woman as Kairo admits, *"I know little about her. I've facilitated a few acquisitions for her in the past, but she's pretty cagey."*

"You mean you've helped arrange some thefts," Eiran says, ever the agent.

"I've facilitated acquisitions. I've met her once or twice."

"Ever seen her in her wolf form?"

"Thankfully no. I've heard rumors of how bad it can be, but she never directed her ire at me. I think she has a soft spot for attractive males." I can hear the lopsided smile even over the comm.

"Then why would she be interested in you?" I quip, and Eiran laughs.

"What's she look like? Her non-wolf form."

There's a pause. *"Long dark hair. The usual yellow eyes. Really hot—"*

Matches the photo so far.

"Any distinguishing marks?" Eiran says quickly with an exasperated sigh. "Anything near her ears or cheek?"

I notice it just as Kairo speaks again.

"Yeah, now that you mention it. She has a small tattoo of a fang beneath her right ear. It's such a stereotypical wolf shifter thing to do that I'd forgotten about it."

Holy shit.

"And... her name?" Eiran asks, sounding hesitant.

"Isra," Kairo says. *"Isra Farthing."*

Eiran looks at me meaningfully. "And she came looking for the relic?"

"Yeah. She knew Corvane had it but didn't have a contact with a thief skilled enough to pull it off."

Eiran bites his lower lip, fang tracing over it in a way so distracting that it becomes impossible to forget I'm sitting on a bed with him. "And... when was this? When did she reach out to you?"

"It was..." Kairo trails off, getting Eiran's point. *"It was about a week after Taylor's video went viral."*

"Okay, thanks, Kairo. I'm going to send you a few more details about Darrow. Have your Quiblins see if they can find her. She may have left the system already, but if we're lucky, that storm kept her in orbit. We need to locate her."

Disconnecting, Eiran glances at me and says, "Isra Darrow, alias Isra Farthing, alias Isra Fanghurst, alias Elara Fanghurst, alias Elara Darrow... and a bunch of others. I'll pull up her file. Give me a second."

He makes a few swipes and shows me the file. I realize what he's saying, and the rock it sends into my gut is heavy and cold. I was about to sell to the *Initiative*?! But that would mean...

I cock my head. "So, the Initiative wanted the Eldralume?"

Eiran looks away, then back to meet my eyes. "Not necessarily the Initiative. Darrow is also a little-known operative for Helix. Does odd jobs that they want to keep quiet. So we don't know who wanted the relic."

My heart is racing now. Solve the problem. Focus on that. "Okay, but again. Why?"

"I'll have to get Gael to do some research," Eiran says. "Its value is as a historical and religious relic. It was used in ceremonies by elvish mystics, but there's no evidence of any true power beyond symbolic value."

I nod, then tilt my head. "I don't know why the Lorathar Initiative would want it, much less Helix."

"This whole situation still doesn't quite add up for me," Eiran says. "Despite the illegal element, most of the Initiative's staff were geneticists, aetherologists, biologists... all about what you'd expect. In fact, it's your mom that's the outlier."

I eye him suspiciously, and he clarifies, "I don't mean because she's human. Because she's a genetic engineer. I feel like there's an element I don't understand. And... maybe that element is you."

Sighing, I flop down next to him, crawling up the small mountain of pillows (what guy has this many pillows?). Eiran reaches out and runs a hand along my arm, goosebumps prickling in his fingers' wake. He gives a soft, warm smile that melts my insides, but I roll to my back, surveying the small bedroom. "Eiran, I... I need to tell you something."

He stiffens, jaw working. "Okay."

"Well..." I smile sheepishly. "When we were at the lab... I stole my mom's diary. Maybe it could shed some light on things."

Eiran's eyes widen in annoyance. "What? When? Why didn't you say anything?"

"I honestly forgot at first," I admit. "I mean, it was like the fifth most world-shattering thing that happened that day."

Eiran gives a rueful chuckle. "I suppose getting your hand chopped off by a crazed cyborg is a little distracting."

Relief floods. I can't handle a barrage of questions and accusations right now. I laugh softly, and man, does it feel good. "The issue with the diary is that it's encrypted. I tried breaking it but didn't have any luck."

Eiran glares for another minute, then sighs. "Do you think Emma could hack it?"

"Sure, she can help. But we'll need to prioritize between finding Blackstone and this. You're sure the SRF can't do it?"

Eiran shakes his head. "Thorne, my boss, said not to trust anyone at the SRF right now. But if we have to pick… I don't know. What do you think?"

"The diary," I say. Eiran surveys me, but he doesn't disagree. "She won't get much farther on Blackstone without a lead. Let's get her working on the diary, and in the meantime, we'll try to come up with something."

Eiran grins. "You're the boss."

I chuckle softly. "Somehow, I doubt that. You seem the type who likes to be in control."

Shit. I did *not* mean for that to slip out.

Eiran's eyes heat at the comment. "I do enjoy it. But I can also let someone else take charge. Someone… I trust." He leans forward ever so slightly. Whether it's an invitation or self-restraint, I can't tell.

"Same," I reply softly. Without thinking about it, I lean forward, and he moves to meet me.

Our lips touch, light as a feather. His hand trembles where his fingers graze my arm, his quiet strength somehow vulnerable. I inhale the mint and rosemary taste of him, of his shaky breath, before pulling back. "I'm an asset, remember?"

Eiran leans forward, planting a soft kiss on my temple before putting his forehead to mine. "Fuck," he mutters. With a shaky breath, he leans back. "Alright. Back to work."

23

FENKLAU BOIL

Taylor

"It's hideous."

"It's not hideous. It's… cute."

"No, it's horrifying," I say as I grab more stray branches and hand them to Eiran. "Even after three weeks of practicing Gruundlith, my first genuine attempt ended up a complete disaster. Your aunt put it in a closet. She didn't even pretend to set it out in some pity gesture. The worst flowerpot ever in the history of flowerpots."

"It was fine," he says, picking up several thick fallen logs. "Besides, you can't be good at everything."

"You can. Your pot got the flowers."

"I'm the nephew. And my dad was an artist. It's not the same thing."

I halt then, frowning at him. "What are we doing, Eiran? You said we weren't hiding, but this feels a whole lot like hiding." I motion to the purple-pink sky. "We have two or three more weeks of solar storms before we lose Blackstone!"

"We're not hiding. We found that lead on Darrow. Kairo and the twins are searching for her and Blackstone, and Gael is tracking leads on the Eldralume Relic. We'll figure something out. But in the meantime? Kairo is on the way here. It's fenklau season. Don't worry so much."

I pick up a quithra cone and throw it at him. "Stop that. Stop pretending that everything is okay. I'm not some fragile piece of glass that is going to break. I've spent my whole fucking life on the run, Eiran. I'm not weak, and I won't spend my days hiding and refusing to live."

"No one is saying you're weak," Eiran says, picking more sticks and logs for the bonfire we're apparently doing tonight. "But we're up against some dangerous forces, and no matter what Adrian says, I don't think he's done with you. Being safe doesn't make you weak or breakable."

"You won't even allow me out of your sight," I say, motioning to the forest clearing where we're gathering wood—fallen branches only, of course. A very elvish bonfire. "The other women are all prepping things for the fenklau boil tonight—whatever that is—and I'm gathering firewood."

Eiran pauses, hiding a wince.

"What?" I ask, crossing my arms.

He hesitates. "Well, I mean… I saw your pantry."

My eyes widen. "You don't think I can help with the cooking!"

"If we were ordering a delivery of vynthra wraps, I'm sure you would be super helpful."

"Asshole!" I cry, picking up more cones to chuck at him.

Eiran cries in defiance, dropping his load of wood to gather his own arsenal of cones to lob back at me. I dodge, and he runs forward, leaning over to tackle me, pinning me against a tree.

"Truce," he says into my ear. His body is pressed against mine, and I can feel him everywhere. He leans forward, one hand on the tree above my head, the other on my waist. His lips are so close to mine. Eiran raises a hand to my neck and runs a single claw down it. I shiver, though from terror, or something else, I can't tell.

I grab a fistful of his hair and pull him down to me.

His mouth crushes eagerly against mine, tongue and hand roving in equal measure. The taste of him, the scent. It's not enough.

Finally, he pulls away, and I can't seem to catch my breath.

"I thought… you couldn't… with an asset."

"Shouldn't…" he gasps into my ear. "Not couldn't."

"Are you done with that wood?" Lirion's voice calls from beyond the clearing.

Eiran jumps back as Lirion enters into view, but from the way his eyes flick between us, it's clear Lirion can see what he interrupted.

"I don't know," Eiran says, his mouth quirking as that mask of his slides back into place. "Taylor, are you done with the wood?"

Lirion snorts, and I give Eiran a glare. "We'll be there in a second."

"Don't," Eiran says to Lirion, cutting off whatever smartass retort he was about to make about "wood" and "a second."

He laughs. "Alright. But you two hurry up. Supper's almost ready."

A few minutes later, we drop our load off by Roderic, who is busy building a fire in the clearing behind his house. Maelara, carrying out a large bowl of some sort of hearty grains, gives me a relieved grin. "Oh, Taylor dear. Perfect timing. Can you help Gael and me bring out the rest of this from the kitchen?"

Apparently, I'm not capable of cooking the food, but I can help bring it out.

"Sure," I say, and I hurry to follow her. We enter the warm kitchen, where Gaelarya is busy meticulously assembling a board of meats, cheeses, and fruit.

"Grab the blue bowl, and put these tubers in it, please." Maelara motions to a metal platter full of some bulbous purple veggies, and I notice a faint crescent mark on her wrist. It's a bite mark.

"Maelara, what the hell—"

She laughs. "It's a mate-mark. Have you never seen one? Well, I guess it's not done much in the city these days. Everyone prefers rings like the humans—no offense. Anyway, everyone has their strange traditions, I suppose. Hurry and get those in the bowl, dear. Everyone is waiting for us." As I begin scooping, she says, "So, Eiran tells me you're a thief."

I still at the sudden change in topic, and Gaelarya's hands falter.

"Oh… um… I mean, yeah." Is she worried that I'll steal something? "But not that kind of thief. I wouldn't ever take anything from—" Gaelarya rolls her eyes.

"Oh, I know, dear." She motions to another pot. "Let's put these peppers in that red dish there. No, I wondered… why steal things? You seem a very smart and capable girl. And Eiran says that this Kairo owns a bookstore in the city. Surely you don't need to steal to survive."

"Well, no," I admit. "I mean, it's something I'm good at. But also, the jobs I do… they get me a lot of money quickly."

Maelara waves a spoon at me. "The beans go in that bowl there.

Then I think we're ready to carry this all outside, if Gael is planning to be done with that board sometime this century. Now, let me tell you something I've learned over the eighty-five years I've been around, girl." Valen aging still amazes me, even though it shouldn't. Maelara doesn't seem much beyond middle age, though I suppose eighty-five years *is* about middle age for an elf, given their lifespan. "Money isn't everything. It won't buy you happiness."

"It'll buy a life off Vale, though."

I snap my head toward her, instant dread and regret blooming. I didn't mean to admit that. Maelara's calming, disarming presence is like a superpower. There's a loud *shunk* as Gael's knife stutters mid-cut, a piece of sausage flying to the floor.

Maelara cocks her head at me. "Why would you want to leave Vale? Seeking adventure?"

I turn my eyes down to the platter of beans. "No. I... my mom died when I was eleven. Kairo took me in, taught me how to be what I am. And I'm grateful for that, but... it's past time I left."

"You were eleven, and this Kairo turned you into a thief?" Gaelarya asks. "This is the guy who's coming here later?"

"He's my mentor. My family."

Gael scoffs, almost too quietly to hear. "Some family."

I don't reply. Don't bother explaining how much I begged Kairo, how he decided he could show me the ropes or let me get arrested. I just stare at the beans as if they can resolve my lifetime of drama. Like they might hold the answer to the ultimate question:

Can I really leave Kairo?

Hell, could I leave Eiran after all that's happened?

Yes. I have to. Even if no one was after me. I need distance from what happened here.

"Taylor." Maelara x-rays me, her chocolate-brown eyes seeing too much. It must be where Eiran gets it. "I'm sure you experienced more than I could imagine, but take it from an old woman. You can't escape bad memories, not even in a starship. You just replace them with good memories and good people."

The fuck am I supposed to do with that?

"Roderic is about done with the fenklau, Aunt Maelara!" Elowynn says, waltzing in (almost literally).

Oh, thank the gods.

I rush to grab a platter. And no, I'm not running away. I'm being proactively helpful.

Not looking at Maelara, I go with Gaelarya and Elowynn to bring out the food and paper goods. As we carry various dishes out, Elowynn prattles on about what everything is, her purple eyes shining in the falling light.

In her usual excited tone, she says, "Of course, the real meal is the fenklau."

"I gathered that much from the term 'fenklau boil,' Elowynn."

"Oh, Wynn. Please," she says with a wave of her hand. "Have you tried fenklau before?"

"I can't say that I have." I do my best to cover my trepidation. I'm not the world's most adventurous eater.

"Oh, they're so good," Wynn assures me. "They're seafood… but not fish. They're… here. Let me show you." She leads me over to where Lirion is tending a large steel pot over an open flame near where Roderic is building the fire. "Show her a fenklau, Lirion."

"Sure thing." He removes the lid of the pot and pulls out a large, ugly bug thing with a fat finned tail and bulky claws. The foot-long creature's thick exoskeleton is mottled dark green and brown, and I have no clue why anyone first tried eating it.

"The season is only for a couple of months, so it's lucky you're here right now," Lirion says, dropping the bug back into the pot so it can finish cooking and then, somehow, I'm supposed to eat it. "They live in the Glythman Fen, the wetlands that border the Silberwald. They catch them in the shallow waters and mud, but only in the late spring and early summer."

"And then… you cook them," I say, unable to hide my dubious tone.

"They're fantastic, I promise," Wynn says again. "They boil them with all of these spices and stuff along with peppers and tubers and… I hope you don't mind spicy food. You're not a wimp, are you, Taylor?"

"Of course not!" I say, although I am definitely a bit of a wimp with spice. "But… you'll need to show me how to eat it."

"Oh, you'll pick it up. I'll show you."

And true to her word, eating the fenklau wasn't as complicated as I expected. She showed me how to pull the tail off the bug and get the succulent meat inside. The claws also contain meat, but Eiran took pity on me and helped me with them, letting me do the tails. That is, until I got bored with that, too. I probably lost some country girl points in the eyes of Eiran's family, but honestly, I didn't care. Because they didn't care.

We eat together, beginning to work our way through the seemingly insurmountable pile of hardshell seafood. Then I halt as it hits me. This is what family is like. And for some reason… I feel like I'm part of it. Even if it's just for a little while.

***

The evening went amicably like that, everyone laughing and talking as they finished up the fenklau and drank copious amounts of anthalas. Even I drank some of the elves' floral-tasting alternative to beer, leaving me buzzing nicely. It was almost possible to forget all that's been happening. Except everyone has a blaster within reach.

Apparently, the country has more than its share of guns.

I ended up sitting next to Gaelarya, and the two of us sat without saying much before I tired of it. Slowing on the fenklau before the others, she'd brought out her comm and started reading a book.

Glancing over at her, I raise an eyebrow. "What are you reading?" That's a harmless conversation starter, right?

"Just a book," she says, turning the screen away. She sounds annoyed, or… embarrassed?

"Girl porn," Lirion mutters, and Gaelarya glares at him.

"First, just because it's a *romance* doesn't mean it's—"

"Romance is not girl porn," I say to Lirion. "Don't be such a guy." He shakes his head, and Gaelarya looks at me appraisingly.

"And my book isn't *just* a romance. It's an adventure story. There's this princess who's secretly a treasure hunter. And she meets this band of circus performers who—"

I gasp. "*The Clown Prince*? I've read that one. It's great. Yeah, Lirion. That's not even really a romance. I mean, there's romance *in it*, but—"

"—but yeah, it's not the main plot," Eiran finishes. Gaelarya and I gape at him, and he shrugs. "I've read it. It's good. It's a treasure-hunting book." He nods at Lirion. "You need to expand your horizons, man. Like Taylor said. Don't be such a *guy*."

Gaelarya and I chuckle, and Lirion raises his hands in defeat. "I have been thoroughly chastised and have learned my error. I'll have to check it out, I guess." He glances at Eiran. "Are there… scenes?"

"Oh, yeah." He glances at me, and I bite my lip, my cheeks going a bit warm.

I turn away, desperate for a change in focus. "So Gaelarya. Where are you in the book?"

She sighs slightly, sounding resigned to something. "It's Gael." Maybe it's the anthalas, but after that, things seem to thaw between us.

24

THE *CHRONOLIS*

Taylor

"Don't let Eiran tease you about shelling the fenklau. He was terrified of them as a kid."

"I was eight!" Eiran protests, and Wynn and Lirion burst out laughing.

Gael gives a satisfied chuff, and says, "When they were little, Kaelen would chase Eiran around the yard with the fenklau."

"Mom would get so mad," Eiran says, smiling a little sadly at the memory.

"Kaelen?" I ask. "That's your brother?"

"So, Gael, have you found out anything about the Eldralume Relic?" Eiran says.

"Awkward," Lirion mutters before his sister elbows him in the ribs.

"No, actually," Gael says, hesitant now. "I wanted to discuss that with you."

"Oh, here we go," Lirion says. "I wondered when she'd bring this up."

"Shut up, Lirion," Gael says with enough bite that he holds up his hands in surrender.

"What's this about?" Eiran asks.

"I can't find anything in any records about what the Eldralume actually is," Gael says, like her research failing her is somehow a personal affront. "So, I think… I think the answer must be in the lost library."

"I'm going to go get the fire started," Lirion growls, tossing a half-eaten fenklau onto the grass.

"I'll go help you," Roderic replies, and the two of them quickly disappear from the table, but not before Lirion gives Eiran a meaningful look.

"Elowynn, can you help me bring some of these plates inside, please?" Maelara says, looking pointedly at her niece. She nods, and the two flee quickly from the table.

"The lost library?" I ask, confused.

"It's a myth," Eiran says, glaring as if he could somehow stare some sense into Gaelarya.

"It's not," Gael retorts just as firmly.

Eiran takes a deep breath and reaches for her before thinking better of it. "Do you really want to go down this road?"

"I'm already down it."

I can barely catch Gael's words, but can't miss the watery, fiery gaze.

Eiran sighs, trying to rein in his frustration. "You know what happened. She was sick. You can't trust—"

"You don't get to say that to me. You don't—" She cuts herself off and takes a breath. In a contained, diplomatic tone, she continues, "I know my mother was sick. I know I can't trust everything in her journals or all of her theories. But some of it was right. The library exists. And I've found it."

"Umm…" I manage, loathed to interrupt, particularly since Gael is being nice to me. "I'm sorry. What's the lost library?"

"The supposed lost library of Thalindor," Eiran replies, his eyes still on Gael. "It was supposedly a grand castle located deep within the Silberwald, built from living stone if you believe the legends, along the Himmelstor River."

I glance between the two elves, sure there's more to this argument. Hoping she won't suddenly make me call her Gaelarya again, I say in a tactful tone, "Okay, let's set aside the whole 'living stone' bit. I'm not great at geography, I'll admit. But the Himmelstor River doesn't go through the forest. The mouth is miles north of here… at Himmelstor. It's sort of where the city gets its name? Right?"

"There was a quake! My mom found a map—nearly three millennia old—showing a different path for the Himmelstor River!"

Eiran takes another breath, as if fighting not to roll his eyes.

She shakes her head. "Okay, I know what you're thinking, but it's not just from my mom's journal. There's proof now. Around 1,500 years ago, a quake happened. I had geologists confirm it. There was a huge landslide and ground cracks. It redirected the path of the river. I have a satellite map, and I think I know where Thalindor Castle is."

Eiran rubs his temple. "Vale is the most studied planet in the entire republic. They've searched for Thalindor Castle for centuries. But you somehow know exactly where it is?"

"Yes, actually. You can see it on the satellite map. It's hard to recognize unless you're really looking for it, but it's there."

Eiran frowns. "And no one's stumbled onto it before?"

"It's *enchanted*," Gael says. "Add in how dense the Silberwald is, and you'd probably have to walk headfirst into it before you realized it was there. And it *is* there. I just need to go prove it."

My head already hurting, I say, "I'm sorry, but you two still aren't explaining. What's Thalindor Castle? What's this lost library? And what's the tie to the Eldralume Relic?"

Gael surveys me, making me squirm. Wynn said Gaelarya was a professor at the local Silberwald College, but she didn't look the part until now. "Thalindor Myrthar was not just a castle. It was also a monastery, home to revered mystics who delved into the fundamental nature of magic. These ancient scholars sought to understand elvish magic. More than that, they studied the luminar essence, the nature of magic itself, working with magical scholars from all over the galaxy. They created an object said to bring 'balance to the Aetheric flow across the universe.' A magical object so sacred it combined the work of dwarven and elvish mystics and artisans in a way never seen before or since."

I blink, the pieces falling into place. "They built the Eldralume."

"Yes," she says, nodding. "But the same quake that redirected the river also destroyed much of the castle. The library *should* still exist within the ruins. Everything's just overgrown, lost to history until recently. Until my mom found it."

"Your mom?" I prompt, curious but not wanting to pry.

Gael smiles sadly. "She was a historian. One of the most renowned in the entire Valen Republic. She spent her early career in top academic circles, the foremost expert on North Valen history. But then she started attempting to prove something no one wanted to believe: that Thalindor Castle really existed. Her theories got… eccentric. Her popularity faded. And then… she got sick. Something in her head… her theories got wilder. She lost her job at the university, her friends, her husband…"

I glance at Eiran, who shakes his head, telling me not to pry into that.

"She was welcomed here at Silberwald. Taught some at the college. Then, died in obscurity."

"I'm so sorry," I say, and she shrugs.

"It's fine. I found her notes. I'll prove her right. Thalindor is real. The library is real."

"If this place exists… it might tell us why the Lorathar Initiative wanted the Eldralume."

Gael nods, and then, a moment later, so does Eiran.

I shrug. "So, let's go. Let's find it."

Gael smiles sheepishly. "One slight problem with that."

"Here it comes," Eiran says.

"It's… well, it's illegal to get anywhere near it."

"It's not just illegal," Lirion says, returning to the table. He hands Eiran and me fresh bottles of anthalas, avoiding Gael's gaze. If he's upset that she's pursuing the theory that broke up their family, he clearly isn't interested in talking about it. "It's death, or worse, for anyone who goes within a mile of that place. Bonfire's ready, by the way."

Eiran's eyes go stony as we walk as one to the large fire. "You're talking about the *Chronolis*."

Oh shit. The *Chronolis* incident was some seventy-five years ago, but it's still a topic of political and social debate. A band of pirates crashed in the middle of the forest, creating widespread damage to the local ecosystem.

"It's not radioactive anymore," Gaelarya says quickly, sitting down on one of the mishmash of portable chairs around the large fire.

Eiran grabs my hand and pulls me down onto a small bench barely wide enough for the two of us. He puts a hand over my shoulder, and surprised as I may be, I lean eagerly into his warmth.

Maelara glances at us momentarily, the corners of her mouth twitching in a pleased way before she looks back to the two Beutwinn doctors arguing.

"That's not the point, Gael," Lirion says, sitting down next to her. His tone makes it clear this isn't the first time they've had this argument. "The *Chronolis* was running a modified quantum propulsion engine."

"Because they were on the run from the Zeridians," Gaelarya snaps back, her eyes glowing fiercely in the firelight.

"It doesn't matter," Lirion says, throwing a small stick into the already glowing blaze. "The mods were illegal and dangerous. When the ship crashed, it contaminated the area. It'll take 20,000 years to clear that out. But also—"

"Scientists say the radiation is safe for quick visits if you don't go near the crash site."

"…but *also* the temporal disruption is permanent. There are temporal anomalies all over that area, Gael. Stuff unlike anything we've ever seen before. What if a time loop sticks you reliving the same three seconds for the rest of eternity?"

Roderic tips his anthalas bottle in agreement. "Boy has a point."

Gaelarya throws up her hands in exasperation. "So, we deal with it. There's tech out there to deal with temporal distortion that we can modify. I've done the research, and I have an idea that should keep us safe. I just need someone to make it work."

"Frank could do it," I admit. "Halfling inventor who works for Kairo. If anyone could do it, he could."

Lirion groans. Wynn's eyes flick from Gael to Lirion to Eiran, but she wisely stays out of it.

"That's not all, is it?" Eiran says quietly. Lirion motions to Eiran in a "thank you" sort of gesture, clearly grateful someone else in the conversation is talking sense.

There's a pause as Gael stares into the flickering flames, her own bottle of anthalas sitting undrunk in her hands. "I can't get it approved," she admits. "The Environmental Protection Enforcement's Safety Council denied my request to try."

"Of course he did," Lirion mutters. I don't miss his use of the word "he" rather than "they," but no one else addresses it.

"How many times did he reject it?" Eiran asks shrewdly.

Gaelarya fiddles with her bottle nervously. "…six." Eiran rolls his eyes, and I deflate. Gael adds quickly, "But I thought you could flash your badge around, make some calls…"

Gael looks at Eiran pleadingly, and he finally says, "Dammit. Fine. But you're not going alone."

Lirion groans, and Maelara glances nervously at her nephew.

"Yeah," I say, and I can tell from the tightened arm around my shoulder that Eiran was hoping I wouldn't chime in. "We're going with you."

Gael actually smiles at me, giving me the tiniest of cheers before downing a chug of anthalas.

Eiran's firm voice in my ear makes me jump, the tingling vibrations sending shivers down my spine. The anthalas speeds up its travel to areas I don't need tingling right now. "Taylor, can I talk to you alone for a minute?"

"Uh… sure?" We stand together, and Wynn gives me a baffled look—which I return. Together, we walk into the nearby trees. The sounds of the forest quickly drown out the easy chatter of the group as we dive deeper into the dense darkness of the foliage.

What's this about? Is he mad at me or something? Going to give me the overprotective speech about how I can't help? How it's too dangerous?

Or is this something else? Is he going to finish what we started before Lirion interrupted? Or will my "asset" status keep blocking us?

Okay, I'm too tipsy to unravel this right now.

When we reach a distant clearing, Eiran turns and groans, "I'm not sure about letting everyone get involved in this."

I guess it's not to finish anything. Maybe it was my brain having issues with us being so close together. Apparently, he's too busy worrying about *Gael*. Something dark and oily slithers into my mind, and I don't like it.

But I can't shake it.

"Okay, fine," I sigh.

"What's that tone mean?"

"Nothing," I say, shaking my head.

"Taylor, for someone who's such a skilled thief, you're terrible at lying about stuff like this. Out with it."

"You're protecting Gaelarya."

It sounds stupid. Petty. But I mean, would he really choose me when he could choose someone like Gael?

Eiran gives me an odd look. "Yeah, because she's hurting. And she has no clue what the fuck she's doing. Her mom… it got bad by the end. So I worry she's making decisions she doesn't know how to deal with. She's not like you."

"She's what? The damsel, whereas I'm just the asset?"

"Fuck, that's not what I… Look, I mean it scares the hell out of me when you go off and do stupid shit, but I also know you can handle it. I've seen you in action, and you're damn impressive. More than impressive. Gael's smart, but she's not you. You're—"

"What? I'm what, Eiran?"

He watches me for a long moment before glancing away. Eyes still on the stars, he says, "Taylor, just because I don't want her to get herself killed doesn't mean I don't care about what happens to you. You know that, right?"

He cares about me. That should be enough. It should be. But it's not.

Eyes on the rough ground, I repeat, "You care what happens to me."

Eiran steps closer. "Of course."

He's so near, but I can't look at him. His shoes are too fascinating. Union-style athletic shoes. What size are they? They're massive. "Because… because I'm an asset."

I'm being petulant, but I can't let the thought go.

He puts a finger under my chin and raises my eyes to meet his. "Not just because you're an asset."

I feel like screaming at the half-spoken words. "What then, Eiran? I don't understand what you're saying."

I want to shake him, but also I don't want to *force* him to open up. But just say it for Hikario's sake!

Eiran clears his throat, but keeps those gorgeous amethyst eyes on me. The corners of his mouth go rigid, as if preparing himself for a battle. "What am I saying? I'm saying that they're not as awesome as you. None of them. How could they be? Your strength? Your capability? Your brilliant, hilarious mind? It's… well, it's really fucking hot. You take my breath away. I've met no one like you. I couldn't even if I searched the entire galaxy. And that's terrifying, and yet…"

I can't look away, frozen by the conviction of his words. "…and yet what?"

"And yet… for the first time in my life, I trust someone implicitly to have my back. And that's the scariest thing of all."

Eiran reaches forward, holding my head in his hands. For a long moment, he stares, his eyes blazing. Then he drops them, just for a second, to my lips, his hand bracing firmer on my hip. His claw traces along my chin, under my ear, and into my hair. Pulling me to him, he leans down, and suddenly his mouth is on mine.

It's slow at first, his lips soft and inviting. His thumb traces along my cheek as his fingers entwine with my curls. I open my mouth to him, and his tongue plunges in, impaling me. He places a hand low on my back, drawing me into him.

Unsatisfied, he dips his hand lower, lifting me up and slamming me against a tree. I wrap my legs around his waist and draw my hands up into his hair as he drops kisses down along my jaw to my neck. Slowly, he pulls away, his breath mingling with mine. I stare at him in surprise, in amazement. I move forward to renew the kiss, but he pulls away, lowering me to the ground.

"You're not just an asset… but you *are* an asset." He steps away, but I grab him, spinning him and pinning him against the tree this time. He leans forward, but his mouth is inches from mine. Like he's holding himself back. I close the distance, tasting his jaw before flicking my tongue against his earlobe. He gives a shaky little chuckle at the reminder of our tussle in my mom's lab.

"Fuck the rules," I whisper into his neck, as I run a hand down his side. He shivers at the light touch. Tracing along the firm lines of him, I reach down and grasp him through his slacks. Gods. "Basic genetics" indeed. Eiran groans as I run my hand up and down his considerable length. "This guy seems to agree with me."

Quick as a flash, he grabs my wrist, turning me so I slam against his wall of a chest, his hardness pressing against my back. I reach again with my other hand, but he seizes it too. He pulls them together above my head, one massive hand binding them.

We stand there for a second as my breathing slows. I wait for the panic, but the racing of my heart isn't a stampede. It's racing forward. Toward him.

I lean back into him, pressing to feel his smooth, hard lines. Our bodies have a silent conversation. His arms entrap me like vines, head leaning forward as if drawn there. His lips trace lines along my neck. Fire sears in their wake.

His hand glides down my stomach as his mouth plunders the hollow of my neck. I tilt my hips, begging for him to continue his trek. Slowly, his hand disappears beneath my waistband.

"Fuck," he hisses as his hand finds my core, tracing slow circles through my heat.

I whimper, "Eiran…" My voice is little more than a moan.

Those magnificent fingers freeze as I wait in aching anticipation. "I'm sorry," he sighs, pushing me gingerly away from him. "We've been drinking. We shouldn't—"

My eyes widening, I round on him. "I don't care!" I try to push forward again, but he holds me off.

He closes his eyes for a long moment, like he's steeling himself. "Not… not while you've been drinking. You have enough reasons to hate me. You have my back. I have yours—even from yourself."

Something crumples in me slightly, stupidly, at that. Why does he have to be so fucking noble? Irrational or not, noble or not, it still feels like rejection. "Fine."

"Taylor."

"We've got to get back. I'll keep Gael and the others out of the line of fire."

"Taylor, I—" But I don't look at him. I just turn and leave.

25

PARTY CRASHING

Taylor

"Okay, so your dad was the wood artist and Roderic was the metal artist?" I say some time later, glancing between Erian and his uncle for confirmation. Eiran hesitates, then nods. We're still sitting next to each other. I wish he'd sat somewhere else, but then that would make it impossible to act like what happened in the forest earlier never happened—which we apparently have silently agreed to do. So now I'm stuck here, the contact more scorching than the fire.

Maybe this anthalas *is* getting to my head after all.

That's fine. This is better. I'll sit here, his warm, powerful body pressed next to me. I'll just pretend I don't know the feel of his mouth on my neck, his hardness against me, and his fingers…

No. Stop it, Taylor.

"Gruundlith artist," Roderic corrects mildly. "And my brother was one of the best in the area."

"And that's saying a lot," adds Maelara. "Silberwald College has one of the top Gruundlith art programs on Vale. Eiran might have been better than his father if he'd kept at it."

Eiran purses his lips at this statement and says, "My aunt exaggerates. And I still make art. We have trees in the city, too."

"Yeah," I chime in, deciding to save him from this conversation, even if I am still slightly annoyed at him. "He made something for me recently. It was incredible."

"Really?" Maelara says, her eyebrows raised in surprise.

"It was just a quick sketch," Eiran says, scratching his neck.

"You'll have to show me your real work sometime, then. After all of this." There. I threw it out there. The possibility of an after. Even after leaving me like… that.

Eiran's eyes widen. "I'd love that."

There's a snap somewhere in the woods. Lirion and Eiran grab their blaster pistols, and Roderic picks up a rifle, handing the second one to his wife. "It's just a… sage hare or something?" Wynn tries.

Lirion shakes his head. "Too big."

She gives an unconvincingly hopeful grin. "Silberwolf?"

Eiran stands, stepping cautiously toward the sound. I pull out my own blaster (well, one that Lirion lent me), and follow him.

A blaster shot fires. Searing pain burns across my shoulder. Damn, that hurt.

"Taylor!" Eiran yells, shoving me behind him.

Out of nowhere, Sylara drops into the middle of us, a blaster in each hand, her mottled copper and burgundy coloring barely visible in the gloom. "I missed on purpose," she says before anyone can fire. "That was a warning."

"Warning my ass," Eiran says, his eyes blazing. Branches begin to grow, and the ground beneath us shakes in response. This could get ugly really quickly.

I place a wall of wind in front of Eiran, halting him as I step around. He's probably staring daggers at me, but before he can ask me what the hell I'm thinking, I ask, "What are you doing here, Sylara?" I take another step forward, and I wonder if Eiran will pull me back. Instead, he steps to my shoulder.

The Zeridian's antennae twitch as her head swivels, waiting for someone to make a wrong move. "Did you think no one would notice?" Her voice is like snakes over rocks. "Did you think you could slap together a fake powerseed and no one would figure it out?"

I grip the blaster tighter. "I kind of hoped."

Sylara grunts in annoyance. "You made me look like an idiot. I do not appreciate that, Taylor."

"Well, I don't appreciate your fucking *shooting me*, but yet here we are. Hurts like a bitch, by the way."

"You know, we just ate a bunch of things that look an awful lot like you," Lirion says, motioning to the pile of shelled fenklau. "Friends of yours?"

"Lirion," Gael admonishes, grabbing her brother by the arm. "Don't be an ass."

Lirion laughs incredulously. "She shoots Taylor, and I'm the one being an ass?"

Sylara stills more than I've ever seen her go, and I can tell Lirion's jab found a home. I know little about Sylara outside work, but she's never responded well to taunts about her race. And there's a lot of them. "The shot was a warning. Find the item, Taylor. Don't make me regret it further." Sylara spits, her abdomen buzzing in anger now.

"Do you know what it is?" Gael says.

"She doesn't care," I say. "In fact, I bet my stealing it doubled the value."

"Tripled," Sylara clicks. "So, you need to either get the item, or get me something worth the *current* value, or I won't have a choice, Taylor. Because you know what else is worth triple the original value? Your head. And not just from Corvane."

There's a bounty on my head. Blackstone.

Wonderful.

"How did you find us?" Eiran says, mouth a thin line. Sylara grins. She's the Huntress. She can find anyone.

"Well hell. I didn't know it was a reunion." With a burst of unnatural light, Kairo emerges from the forest, sending the Zeridian's form into sharp relief. "Better get out of here, Sylara. You know what happens to a bug under a magnifying glass?" He focuses his light down into a tight beam that sizzles slightly, leaving a black mark on her rust-colored exoskeleton.

"Don't tell Corvane anything," I cut in. I hold up a calming hand to Eiran before he makes this worse. "Sylara, I don't know you well, but… when we worked together on the Harmonix Crystal thing—" Sylara hisses, and I hurry to say, "Look, that ended badly. What you did… hell, what I did… I'm not trying to rehash it here. I'm just saying that when we were on that Zeridian warship, you could have killed those guards."

"They were skilled warriors."

"You're better. You could have killed them. It would have been easier, and with your, umm, history… I wouldn't blame you if you'd killed all of them."

"I don't kill unless there is a reason," Sylara says, her large black eyes glinting.

"And there is reason to kill Taylor?" Kairo asks, disgusted.

"Money's reason enough," she says, but her usual flat tone quavers. "Someone will do it. Better me than some of the sadists out there."

I look at Eiran. She left me on the Harmonix Crystal job, and it had some dire consequences. But if we can hold Corvane off until the SRF begins their takedown… Eiran finally says, "We're working to get it back. We just need a couple more weeks." Hopefully, by then, Corvane won't be a problem.

Sylara stands preternaturally still, the way only her kind can do. "I'll run interference for you with Corvane," she replies eventually. "The solar storm is *still* going on, so I can buy you until it ends. No more."

"What if we can't find it by then?" Kairo asks.

"Then I'll be back," Sylara says coolly.

"Trust me. You don't want to try it," Eiran snarls.

"You really want to die so needlessly?" Sylara lets out a bone-chilling little chuckle.

There's a quiet creaking as everyone's hands tighten on their blasters, this powder keg seconds from exploding.

Sylara's scaly mouth kicks up at one corner. "Do you know why my people expelled me from Zeridia, boy?"

My eyes widen slightly at the question. I know only bits and pieces, mostly through rumor. None of us replies.

"My caste was bred to be hunters. I was doing it centuries before you were a thought. And I was good at my job. The best. That's why I was chosen to recover a valuable artifact. The Rythmus Shard."

Kairo's eyes widen at the name.

Sylara scoffs at him. "You've heard of it? Well, it's more powerful than you can imagine, and I was so close to recovering it. But there was an attack and Ankáriel…" She trails off, staring at the dark trees before continuing. "My mate was in trouble. I tried… I tried so hard, but… I couldn't save him. I went to recover the artifact… but it was gone. It hasn't been seen since."

The huntress falls silent, scowling. After a few moments of heavy breathing, she continues, "I failed. I made the one mistake we were taught since we hatched never to do: I let personal feelings cloud the mission. It cost me everything."

The sound of the wind shaking the leaves is the only backdrop.

A small, reluctant part of me understands Sylara a little better… though I'll never truly forgive her. Not after what happened with Marcus.

He was kind. Funny. The first person to really see me. The Harmonix Crystal was the big-ticket item I'd been after back then—another job, another score. But somehow, Sylara and I ended up working together, along with a human named Marcus. He wasn't like the others. He never flinched when I used magic, never looked at me like a threat or a stray.

He was the first one besides Kairo who told me I had potential. That I mattered.

And I believed him.

But Sylara double-crossed us. She and I made it out. Marcus didn't.

Sylara looks from Eiran to me as she reaches down to pick up her blaster and holster it. "Don't make the mistake I did." She stares straight at me. "Sometimes people die. Even the people you're close to."

Horror and anger and old lingering hurt rush over me, blotting out the sympathy. Sometimes people die?! Did she seriously say that to me?

I gawk at Sylara in confused anger, unsure if that was a warning, an explanation, or an apology. Wordlessly, she leaps thirty feet into a nearby tree. "You'd better pay me," the Zeridian calls. "Storms won't last much longer. Get me something, or I'll be back. Your life, and my reputation, are on the line." With another gigantic leap, she's gone.

I stare at the treetops for a long time after. I should be more scared that there's a bounty on my head, but somehow Sylara's revelation about her past held more impact.

Maybe I've been in hiding too long.

"Well, that was dramatic," Kairo says, unfurling his wings as his light dims. "Hey everyone! Sorry I'm late."

"Kai!" I run to hug him before a spike of pain lurches in my shoulder.

Kairo wraps me in his massive arms, his wings folding around me a moment before releasing me. "Are you okay, kid?"

"I'm fine," I say, stepping back with a wince. "Other than Sylara finding us, we're all okay."

"Speak for yourself," Gael mutters shakily.

"She shot you," Kairo agrees.

I shake my head. "She wasn't really trying to hurt me."

"Didn't look like that to me," Eiran says, rushing forward, eyes tense.

Before Lirion can reach me, Eiran has a hand on my face, and the wound in my shoulder knits together. Finally, the pain and tension leave me, and he relaxes.

"You'll be sore for a few days," Lirion adds from behind me.

I wave that off. "Gives us time to track things down."

"We have a lead," Eiran explains to Kairo. He quickly fills him in on Gael's thoughts about the Eldralume and the lost library of Thalindor.

Kairo looks Gael over appreciatively. "Nice. So, you're a treasure hunter?"

"Archeologist," she corrects self-consciously before crossing her arms and glaring at him. "And you're the fence."

"Kairo Ryūkishi," he says with a flourishing bow, his grin devilish. "It's a pleasure to meet you. And your name?" Gael crosses her arms, unimpressed.

"This is Gael," I offer. "And this is—"

"It's Gaelarya," she says icily. "Dr. Gaelarya Beutwinn. My friends call me Gael. You can call me Dr. Beutwinn."

Kairo's eyes narrow, that grin sharpening dangerously. "Do you have a problem with me, Doc? With my job?"

Gael's eyes are red and twitchy, still shaken from the encounter with Sylara. But she doesn't back down from the challenge. "I don't care what you do. But after what happened, I do care who you buy from." Her eyes dart—ever so briefly—to me.

Kai takes a prowling step forward, a silberwolf tracking prey. "You gonna judge me, doc? You don't even know me."

"I know enough."

"Kairo is the one that got me off the streets," I say to Gael, slightly baffled. I know Sylara showing up rattled her, but still. "He's the one—"

"—that took an impressionable young girl and turned her into a thief. I got it." She curls her lip and turns her back on him.

Kairo shrugs, holding out his hands to concede the point. "Taught her everything I know. It's why she's the best."

My heart warms a bit at Kairo's praise, but why is Gael taking such offense on my behalf? Eiran watches her, strangely wary.

Waving her anthalas bottle like a weapon, she spins and scoffs, "And such an outstanding role model you ended up being. So kind of you to use her like a tool. You'll forgive me if I don't have a lot of patience for men who lead innocent young people away with visions of grandeur, ignoring the risks."

"I did the best I could!" Kairo says hotly, wings rustling in fury. "She was lost and abandoned. Such a traumatized little thing. Just waiting for someone like my father to come and snatch her up."

His eyes burn at the memories, and the anger and pain break something in me.

Kairo glares at Gael. "You know she didn't talk the first month? And then just short phrases here and there. A tiny 'no, sir' or a terrified 'thank you.' The most tragically polite kid you ever met. The proudest day of my fucking life was when she first flipped me off. Stood up for herself. And I'm not apologizing for that."

I let out something that's either a laugh or a sob. I can't tell. Maybe both. This is why I love the big idiot. I give him a watery look, and he gives one back, the closest to tears I've ever seen.

Gael is unmoved. "This is what you're proud of? Having her end up on the run from… how did Eiran put it? One of the biggest criminal kingpins in the sector?"

"I didn't—"

"You're how old? Sixty?"

Kairo blinks, scowl deepening. "Fifty-seven."

Gael laughs incredulously. "Wow. And Hitari reach adulthood at what? Forty-five, right? So you were barely an adult yourself when you got it into your dumb head that you could raise a child *by yourself*."

I open my mouth to cut in, to defend Kairo, but nothing comes out. Yes, he was young. Too young. But at least he cared. I didn't have anyone else. I should say something, but… I can't. Partly because I don't understand why Gael is acting like this. Somehow, I feel like this isn't about me.

Kairo gapes at Gael. "You don't think I regret it? You don't think I wish I'd done something different? I wanted to keep her away from people like my father. And where did she end up? Going right back to that place. She ran right into my father's arms and… I let her."

Oh gods.

Kairo flings his arms in helplessness. I flinch, and he winces, realizing too late what he'd said.

I'm not mad at him, though. He's right. I'd been so, so stupid to agree to the Kuro Oni's offer. What the hell was I thinking?

The question eats at my gut like a tapeworm.

Gael scowls at Kairo, arms crossed tight. A shield. "Boo. Fucking. Hoo. Save your regrets for someone else. They're too little, and too late. And you know what? Don't try that *charm* on me, either."

The accuracy of the statement, given Gael just met Kairo, skewers him. And she knows it. "Oh, I know guys like you. You mean well, but you just lead people astray. I had your number as soon as Taylor told me about you. You're just like Kaelen."

"Gael!" Wynn gasps.

Kaelen? What the hell?

"It wasn't like that," Eiran says quietly, eyes on the fire. "Kaelen never—"

Gael rounds on him, tears in her eyes. "Wasn't it? We had a plan—"

"*You* had a plan—"

"We had a plan! Had a life. Then here comes your brother, the big bad SRF agent. Just wants a consultation on a job, needs the help of an archeology expert. He paints this picture of excitement and mystery and the big city. 'It's just one job,' you'd said. But then there was another job. Then another. And then…"

Gael's voice breaks, and she takes a deep breath. "And then Kaelen dies. Those bastards killed him and… I lost you forever. We all lost you. Really, we lost you the day Kaelen came calling about that first consult."

Eiran's breaths come in ragged gasps as he glares at the ground, trying to regain composure. Without looking up, he says in a tone so low I can barely hear, "You have no clue what you're talking about. When I heard Blackstone was alive, heard the shit he did for Helix? I *begged* Kaelen to keep letting me help. To dig deeper. Because Adrian was right. I made him. I pushed him into Helix's arms. Pushed him to become that… thing."

My ears ring, and Maelara gives a tiny gasp. "Eiran—"

But he continues as if he didn't hear. "You know what it got me? Blackstone didn't just kill Kaelen. He eviscerated him. Helix ripped him apart, dissecting him like a lab experiment. I made him into that monster. The thing that killed Kaelen. And now it's my responsibility to bring him down."

Oh gods. Blackstone… Helix had done that. Helix, haven for Enhanced, butchered his brother, his hero, from the sounds of it. No wonder he hates Enhanced. Given what the Lorathar Initiative did to my mom… I can relate.

I squeeze Eiran's shoulder in solidarity, and he leans into me for the briefest of moments before straightening again to look up at Gael. His face is murderous… desperate… pleading. Maybe all three.

"So, I ask you, Gael. Was I supposed to let it go? Should I have just gone home and acted like nothing happened and spent my time studying old books and making art projects? I never wanted that, even before. Told you time and again. You couldn't let go. Wanted me to stay home and be okay and act like they hadn't fucking *killed* Kaelen. Like I hadn't… I asked you to come with me to the city. You said no, so I moved on."

Gael's face is an anguished mix of fury and defiance. "You weren't thinking straight! Your life was here. My life was here."

Eiran wields his own bottle now, pointing at her from across the fire. The orange flames reflect strangely on his olive skin, putting his anguish in a weird relief.

"See? That's the point. I'm sorry about what happened. I lost control, and Lirion…" He turns to his friend, whose eyes are watering too. "I'm so sorry you got hurt. You could have…" He takes a deep breath, his eyes shimmering but gaze steely. "There's no excuse for how I responded, but I don't regret my decision. And I think that upsets you most, Gael. You talk about my choices, but you made one too. And honestly? I'm fucking sick of apologizing for mine."

"Same here," Kairo says, crossing his arms, his jaw set in a hard line.

A single tear rolls down Gael's forest-green cheek, but she ignores it. The forest is still, full of the sound of rustling leaves and Gael's heavy breaths.

"I'm sorry about Kaelen, Eiran. He was my friend. Like a brother. But that? That's easy to say when you're not the one living with the consequences of those choices." She takes a shaky breath. Putting on a brave, watery smile, she says, "Thanks, Roderic, Maelara, for having me." She clears her throat. "I had a great time… until the end."

Eyes above Eiran's head, she adds, "If I find out more about the library, I'll let you know."

With more grace than I could probably muster in her place, she walks off into the darkness, leaving Eiran and Kairo both glowering after her. I watch her disappear into the dense foliage, another victim of caring too much.

***

It's quiet at the fire after that. No one really feels like talking. Eiran and Kairo confirm details they both already know about the case, as one by one, the rest of the family slips away. Even Kairo slips off to his designated space on the couch, leaving Eiran and me by the fire.

I stare into the dancing depths as the warmth slowly dies, sipping anthalas as the chill of the late-night breeze eats into me. Eiran never forces me to speak, just sits there next to me, lending me his body heat in a shield even the night can't overcome.

At some point, Eiran begins reciting one of his mother's stories, a tale of a space pirate, a hidden chest of jewels, and the high-born lady he seduces away for an adventure amidst the stars. I listen absentmindedly to the winding narrative, letting the worries slip away until the world slows and the edges darken.

Eventually, I feel him pick me up, the chronicle still flowing softly from him as he carries me inside. The warmth of my bed envelops me. Softly, tenderly, he pushes a strand of hair away from my forehead, planting a soft kiss there before whispering, "Goodnight."

Some small part of me awakening amidst the haze of alcohol, I grab his arm and mutter, "Eiran?"

He stills, his mouth quirking in that way it does when he thinks I'm cute. "Yeah?"

"Thank you. For everything."

The quirk expands into a smile, both dimples making an appearance. "Anytime."

And with a wink, he steps away. I watch contentedly as the door closes before slipping off into a heavy sleep.

26

BRACELETS & BEDSHEETS

Taylor

The scent of old oil and the clattering noise of vintage electronics compete in the tiny workshop. Whirring, buzzing, ticking, and beeping crash from every direction, the not-so-subtle chorus of the various refurbished gadgets and gizmos that make up the "tech emporium" part of Galactic Pages, Rare Finds, and Tech Emporium. Rising above it all, though, is Frank's insatiable chatter.

"The parts for the device itself were fairly easy to come by. A few of them were… well, I am surprised Dr. Beautwinn would suggest violating Valen legal—"

"Frank—" Eiran smirks, laughing as Frank's long, gray ears wobble in excitement.

"—guidelines, but of course Mr. Ryūkishi has many such connections. I could not manipulate the enchantments on the components myself, but thankfully—"

I laugh, exasperated, at the halfling, whose squeaky voice continues unperturbed. "Frank!"

"—that was not required here. Only adaptation of the spells. No, the true difficulty was obtaining a time-pocket generator to test that it works. Only the Kanlóng can create the enchantments for such devices, and they've been hunted to near extinction by the Zeridians.

The dwarves refuse to even admit that the 'space eels,' as they call them, are even a thinking species. But they are aware, Miss. I have not had the privilege of speaking to them myself, but I've heard tales—"

"*Frank!*"

Emma's telepathic voice booms in our heads, making Eiran and me wince in pain. Frank stares agape at his sister, his already overlarge eyes even wider in his magnifying goggles. With a rustle of fabric, the Quiblin female lowers her bulky hood to give her brother a stern look. *"That's not what they meant by asking how the devices work."*

Frank grins sheepishly. "Apologies, Miss Grey. Agent Valtir. You simply tighten the bracelet around your wrist by pulling this strap—"

"The time-pocket compensator, Frank," Eiran says, his impatience almost burning through his amusement.

Frank jumps at the admonishment, though Eiran barely raised his voice. "Yes, sir. Quite right, sir. This knob here is for temporal adjustment. The farther to the left, the more positive temporal compensation the device emits to the wearer. The farther to the right, the more negative compensation. So, if the time in the pocket passes slowly, you turn it to the left, and if it passes faster than normal, you turn to the right. Here, I will show you."

The Quiblin adjusts a humming device that looks like a giant egg. "This is the time-pocket generator. I was able to borrow this from…" He glances at his sister, and then trails off. "Anyway, there's a small pocket of frozen time here. You just can't see it. That's why you have this."

Frank adjusts a toggle on the bracelet, and a tiny quavering holographic sphere appears in the space above the egg. With a glance at us, he places his small hand into the sphere and then yanks it hard. It doesn't budge. "Time is frozen here. But if I adjust the compensator knob to the left—" With his free hand, he tweaks the knob on the device on his wrist. Moments later, he's able to wiggle his fingers and then easily remove his hand. "—it compensates for the rift. If the rift is faster than standard time, you adjust the knob the other way. Simple."

"Brilliant, Frank," Eiran says, and the halfling beams. "Simply brilliant. We'd never make it without these."

"Just be careful with them," the tiny Quiblin warns, shaking a long finger at Eiran. "This is experimental technology. Don't go banging it around."

"We won't," Eiran says, though he gives me a side-eye. Where we're going, we can't promise that.

"*Good luck, Miss Grey,*" Emma says to me, placing a hand briefly on my arm.

I give her a small smile. She's never been one for physical affection, so her initiating contact like that is a big gesture. Hugging Frank and promising to give our hellos to Kairo (who has been off "researching" something or other ever since the bonfire), I lead a gadget-laden Eiran out of the bookshop and into the warm afternoon air of Vaeloria City.

"So, back to Silberwald?" I ask, holding the door of the stryder open for Eiran. "I know you don't like me out in the open."

"I don't," Eiran agrees, placing the box onto the backseat.

It took a lot of convincing—and a fair bit of shouting—before Eiran let me go with him to the city. I was so tired of being cooped up, and as I reminded him, I've been hiding from people half my life. I can fly under the radar. Finally, my observation that I'd be safer with him in the city than alone in the country won him over.

Closing the stryder door, Eiran looks up at the shop and frowns. "So, explain again what 'research' Kairo had that meant he couldn't make this trip for us."

"I'm not really sure," I admit. "But if I know Kairo, it's probably about money."

Eiran raises an eyebrow. "Money?"

"Yeah," I shrug. "He mumbled something about the shard, and before I knew it, he slipped off for research. That was three days ago."

"Shard? Like the Rythmus Shard that Sylara mentioned?" Eiran asks, sounding annoyed. "So your life is threatened, the galaxy is in danger, and he's planning another heist?!"

"Yeah, if he has a lead on it. It'd be the perfect way to pay off Corvane. I may not know what Kairo's up to, but I trust him."

Eiran looks like he'd like to reply to that, but says, "To answer your question, we're not heading back yet. First, I need to stop by my flat and pick up some clothes. We haven't all shopped at every boutique in Silberwald to pad our wardrobes."

I give him a little shove before digging my hands into his white button-down. "Pointy-eared asshole."

Gods, the scent of him.

Eiran gives me a playful shove in return, pressing my back against the smooth frame of the stryder and sending my heart into my throat. He leans into my space, leg sliding between my thighs, which open willingly for him. "Peach-skinned pain in my ass," he growls into my ear. My hands move from holding his shirt to tracing the powerful curves of his chest beneath it. His hands grip my waist, long fingers biting wonderfully into the soft skin.

Fighting down a moan, I force myself to smirk up at his beautiful face, that cocky dimple in full force. "So, we go back to your apartment?"

"Yes."

"Want me to come in with you? Or will you run in?" It's an offer. A question of a sort. The closest I can bring myself to ask.

The curve of those luscious lips becomes absolutely sinful. "I'd love to show it to you. If that's alright."

I stare into the eyes that hold such tenderness, such understanding. Survey the man who knows all of me and still wants me. Even parts that are broken, ugly, and… well, unlovable. Or so I thought.

I know what he's saying. What he's offering in return. And what it means. We haven't discussed the night of the bonfire. Not his proclamation four days ago that I'm "more than just an asset," nor what almost happened after. But this? This is his way of saying he meant it. All of it. And still does.

I let my own smirk widen a tad, even as my voice shakes from suppressed nerves. "I'd love to see… anything you have to show me."

***

At first, I was confused by Eiran's choice of apartment. A top floor at the edge of town, it's a pricey space in a decidedly unglamorous neighborhood. But before I can question him about spending so much to live at the city's fringe, he opens the door to his open-concept flat, and I see the view from the large floor-to-ceiling windows.

And then I understand.

There's no vista of the city. No imposing vine-covered buildings or windy, yellow-lit greenways. Instead, his windows frame Aelfswelth Forest. Beyond the trickling string of run-down buildings at the edge of town, the expansive canopy billows in a roiling, endless green sea.

It's like I'm back in the Silberwald.

Because, despite what his family thinks, despite what he even tells himself… he still misses home.

"It's beautiful," I gasp, admiring not just the view, but the eclectic-yet-tasteful selection of artwork in his apartment—tiny details that stitch touches from a dozen cultures.

"Yes, you are," he replies.

I can't help but laugh at the corniness of that, leaning against an intricate stone-and-wood dresser, surveying him in all his smirking glory. "Oh, my gods. Is that really your closing line?"

He strolls toward me, taking all the time in the world. Reaching out, he grabs a belt loop and ever-so-slowly draws me to him, amethyst eyes never leaving mine. I press myself against him. The firmness digs into me as I look up at him, lost in his depths. "Well," he says, with the slightest hitch in his voice. "Is it really a line if it's true?"

With a caressing drag of his fingers, he cups my cheek. "You are so beautiful, Taylor. I've been mesmerized, enchanted by you from the moment I saw you in that garden. The way the sparkling lights flickered in your hair? The way you looked in that dress? Aether save me, I almost forgot the entire mission then and there. All I wanted was to take you in my arms and taste you."

"Eiran—" My voice is a rasp. A plead. I can't take this. My heart can't take this. The overwhelming feeling in my chest. The sweet pain of it. I'm going to shatter.

"Then I saw you take that key. Saw what you were." Eiran scoffs at himself, shaking his head. "I knew I shouldn't, couldn't trust you. But you know what? Even then, I didn't care. I almost gave in anyway. Because if you were going to destroy me… what a wonderful way to go."

I'm crying now, tears running down my face. "I thought I was just an asset."

"Fuck, Taylor. You were never just an asset. I wish you were. It would be easier. Safer. I'm dangerous, Taylor. I get people hurt. I promised I'd keep you safe. But I'm done trying to keep away from you, even if you'd probably be safer far from me. I'm done trying to be a good person. Maybe I'll try embracing what it means to be bad. If you're willing to try with me. To be with me."

Gathering myself, I plant my cocky grin back in place, because if I don't, I'll be a weepy mess. Reaching up, I tangle my fingers in his emerald locks. "I love the speech, Eiran. Really, I do. But respectfully?

Shut the hell up and kiss me."

Eiran growls at that, and with one swift movement, I'm in his arms. Wrapping my legs around his frame like the trunk of an eldertree, I climb up to reach his mouth. He crashes his lips against mine, tongue sweeping in to claim me. His taste is like nothing I've experienced—warm, sweet, and spicy all at once. Supporting my weight with one arm, he tangles his fingers in my curls, the world slipping away.

At some far-off level, I can tell he's carrying me across the room, but I'm so lost in him I barely notice. Eventually, he breaks the kiss, and I realize we're at the foot of his giant branch-poster bed, green vynthra vines winding up and around to create a verdant canopy. His eyes wide with awe, he lays me gently on the mattress.

In silken movements, Eiran crawls up the bed to meet me, his weight pressing me into the soft sheets. I can feel his length on my thigh, my sundress riding up. He seems to sense my thoughts, and his eyes darken with heat as he sees the expanse of skin.

Eiran kisses me deeply a moment before tracing a line of kisses along my neck. My breath trembles in tiny gasps as he moves the kisses along the curve of my breast, brushing against the cloth-covered peaks as he continues his descent. His fingers slide under my skirt, my calves aflame in their wake. With reverent slowness, his fingers slide under the hem of my panties.

He pauses and looks up at me, eyes wide with a question. I nod, and he slides them down, revealing me to him. "Beautiful," he mutters, his roving glances branding my skin. He reaches up, running a single finger along my center. "Ready for me, I see." In a steady, agonizing rhythm, he slides that finger up and down my core for a moment, making my back arch as he circles where I need him.

Tension builds, and then suddenly he's gone. I grumble, and he chuckles darkly. "So impatient."

My breath catching, I watch in decadent fascination as he brings that finger to his tongue, his eyes on mine as he tastes me. "Mmm. I need more."

I sit up, raising my arms above my head as he lifts my dress off me, and then lays me back on the pillow.

For a moment, he gazes at me again, taking me in and making me feel I could actually somehow be beautiful. I'm aching for him to move, to touch me again, but he stays there for one more second, lingering.

With a chuckle, he leans forward, trailing kisses along my thighs that make me whimper. Then finally, fucking *finally*, he traces that gorgeous tongue across me.

"Fuck," I gasp, arching off the mattress. That earns me another laugh as he lazily drapes my legs across his shoulders. His claws give the tiniest pinch, not quite breaking the skin, as he grips my hips. His tongue circles and sweeps in agonizing arcs, and I rise again. "Shit, Eiran. I can't take—"

With a lazy wave of his hand, vines reach from the headboard, holding my wrists to the bed. He pauses, raising an eyebrow. The breath of his chuckle warms my skin as he says, "Are you going to be still like a good girl so I can finish this? I told you. I've been waiting months to taste you. I'd like to take my time. Well?"

Heat gushes to my core, and I give a jerky nod.

"I need the words, Taylor."

"Just fucking do it, Eiran," I hiss.

He laughs again. "Such a brat." But without another word, he continues his ministrations.

As he laps languidly, he slides two fingers in, curling them as if beckoning the rising tension out of me.

"Oh, gods," I moan, and then my words devolve into senseless muttering, my sounds only emboldening Eiran further.

The corded vines around my wrists fall away, a leaf trailing like a feather across my skin. I'm aflame at the touch, my brain unable to compute the heady mix of sensations as the vines encircle my breasts. The edges of the leaves caress my nipples, my insides tightening.

With a cry, I break apart, my body racking with wave after wave of pleasure. Eiran slows, but doesn't stop, riding it out with me before I finally settle.

As the waves recede, a wrenching ache is left in their wake. Eiran crawls up next to me, pulling me over so my head rests on his shoulder, my arm around his waist. I slide my hand between the seam of his shirt, feeling the smoothness of his chest.

Suddenly, inexplicably, I remember lying with Marcus in another moment like this one. Where everything felt perfect. And the juxtaposition is too much.

"Eiran..." My voice breaks, and I don't understand it, can't explain the tears that begin to prickle and well. "That... was so beautiful. So amazing. You're amazing. I…" I wipe my eyes, pulling myself up. "Sorry. I'm being a girl. Emotional and everything. Just give me a second and I can—"

"Taylor." Eiran wraps a hand around my forearm, halting me. "It's fine."

"It's not fine," I complain, motioning around to the perfect room. The perfect evening. The perfect man. And the stupid girl who's *crying during sex*. "We're here. We have a plan. We have time alone for once. I'm fine. I'll be fine. I know you want—"

"All I want is you," he says, his voice heavy with sincerity. "Whenever you'll have me. However you'll have me. I got to taste you. I'll keep that memory forever, Taylor. The rest can wait."

Something about that loosens something in me. I don't deserve this man. His care. With a shaky hand, I reach down to his waist, determined to ignore his words, even as the tears continue to roll.

He places a gentle hand on my wrist. "My only expectation was spending time with you. I got that."

The consideration of that breaks me. The way it makes me feel so selflessly taken care of? It's something Marcus would have done. The first man to make me believe in a future. The thought is bittersweet, yet somehow comforting.

"But what about…" I glance at what still presses against my thigh.

Eiran gives a faint grin. "I promise I'll be fine. We'll take it slow. We have time."

I smile, drawing him down to lie beside me, his head on my bare chest. But as his weight drapes across me, my thoughts slip back to Corvane and Blackstone.

Because I'm not sure time is on our side.

27

THE STRANGE PASSAGE OF TIME

Eiran

"Ugh! Should've brought more bug repellent," Kairo complains for the fifth time.

"It's a swamp," Taylor laughs from the front of the group, turning to eye her friend as she wades through thick ferns. "What did you expect?"

"Not a swamp. I thought the castle was in a forest."

"It's both," Gael scoffs, thick boots squelching in the mud next to me. "The *Chronolis* crashed sort of on the border, where the Silberwald transitions to Glythmar Fen. The fen is the easiest route. Unless you want to hike through silberwolf territory. Which you are most welcome to do."

It's been over a week since the bonfire, and Gael's attitude has barely thawed toward Kairo, despite her apologies when she sobered up. She forgave me fast enough (the argument was tame for us, in the grand scheme of things), but Kairo was still pissed at Gael. And of course, that pissed her off.

It's also been three days since Taylor and I… shit, I can't think of that right now. A hard-on is the last thing I need.

Kairo mutters an indistinct curse from the rear as he swats another bug. "Are we there yet?"

"We should be," Gael says, checking the holographic three-dimensional map her comm is projecting. Yellow lines overlay the entire space, a glowing trail leading off past a bend in the path.

"Well, it's about time. I'm getting pretty—" The leather and metal contraption on Taylor's wrist beeps loudly, and we all halt, staring warily at the spot in front of her.

She reaches down to grab an acorn and tosses it. About two feet in front of her, the little brown seed passes through an invisible barrier, and the unseen temporal anomaly throws it forward at top speed. The acorn slices right through a nearby tree, sending splinters flying as it carves a large hole in the middle of the trunk.

"Fucking hell, Taylor," Gael complains, wiping a small streak of blood from her cheek where a shard grazed her.

"I guess… time speeds up in that anomaly…" she replies haltingly.

Kairo throws up his arms in exasperation. "Ya think? What if time reversed? It could've come flying at your head."

I walk up to her, nervously adjusting Frank's temporal compensator. "Well, time to give these a try." I try to put strength and cocky positivity into the grin I give Taylor, but honestly? These things seem held together with twine and tree sap. "Wish me luck."

If this works, I should pass through the anomaly in near-normal time. The less the rift affects me, the quicker the battery runs down, so I need to be conservative with how much I use it. Eyeing the splinters of wood left in the acorn's wake, I step forward.

I hear Taylor's cry of "wait" as I cross the barrier into the anomaly.

The outside world glistens and ripples beyond the barrier to the elevator-sized rift, like I'm trapped in a tiny water bubble. Taylor's mouth is moving in ridiculous slow motion as she continues, her voice sounding a long "yoooooooo…" into the otherwise silent void of the rift. Her arm slowly moves, as if she's going to reach forward to grab me. I watch her for one second, amazed at the way her red hair glistens golden in the morning light, before crossing to the other side of the barrier.

"…ou don't have to… oh." Taylor stares in shock as I stumble out of the anomaly, the force of my momentum almost knocking me to the ground. Frank's wristband could prevent the worst of the effects of the anomaly, but clearly, it wasn't a perfect process.

"I'm fine," I say, raising my arms to demonstrate. "Come on. Let's keep moving."

"That was needlessly reckless," Taylor says.

I laugh. "You're one to talk about being needlessly reckless. Anyway, we had to test it out somehow. At least we know."

"Well, better you than me, Leaf Boy," Kairo says, trudging forward. "Now let's get moving. I'm getting eaten alive out here."

Taylor hesitates for the briefest moment, and I raise an eyebrow. Fear fading at the challenge (as I knew it would), she steps forward after me. One second, she's six feet away, and the next she's being shoved forward, falling into my arms.

"I got you," I say, her hands gripping my biceps as I hold her upright, my skin somehow aflame at her cool touch. She looks up at me, her eyes wide and shining. Her taste lingers heavy on my tongue, the memory flooding the here and now.

And I let her see it. See how much I still want her, despite what she shared. It only makes her braver and more beautiful in my eyes.

"Alright," Gael sighs, drawing us back to the moment. We turn to her, and the two of us catch her in unison as she steps through the rift. Kairo just takes off, flying over the rift to land behind us. He winks mockingly at Gael, who turns wordlessly and continues hiking in the general direction of the crash site.

We continue like that for a while, avoiding anomalies where we can. The ones we can't either send us lurching forward or slow us down unbearably. Thankfully, Frank's gadgets work, and we can enter and exit the anomalies without issue.

The forest opens onto a clearing near a large hill. There, half-buried at the base of the hill, is the *Chronolis*, its large boosters dark halos amidst the shade of the nearby trees. Moss and vines have overtaken it, and the semicircular shape of the craft's rear section is barely discernible amongst the foliage. The large rut the ship dug when landing is overgrown now. There's a small creek trickling down through a large rift. The floating leaves and branches loop over and over again, never reaching the bottom.

Gael attaches a cable between her comm and Frank's wristband invention, and the area lights up with holographic shapes of varying sizes.

Rifts.

Even with Frank's gadgets, the way through will suck. And with more rifts littering overhead, flying's out too.

"Stay close," Gael says, and we all nod, moving forward as a single tight mass, leaning this way and that to avoid the maze of anomalies.

"So, where's this castle?" Kairo grumbles. His wing's stuck on an anomaly for the third time in five minutes. The slower passage of time forces his wing to slide through like quithra sap, despite his tugging.

Gael adjusts the readout on her comm. "It should be… here?" The display adds a holographic pin amidst the trees and ferns. It looks the same as everything else. Aether save me. This was a waste of fucking time.

Before I can say something suitably derisive, Gael holds up a hand, typing on her comm. "Hold on. Hold on." Suddenly, the display overlays the lines of a ruined castle onto the chaotic undergrowth.

I'd never have seen it without the hologram. Bits that I took to be branches, rocks, leaves… they all rise in the line of a wall. It goes beyond the Lorathar Initiative's clever camouflage. The walls seem to be alive. I watch in awe as a small creature jumps from branch to branch of a tree I realize isn't even there. The creature isn't even there.

"The living stone," Gael says in awe, stepping forward toward the wall. "It's real." Reaching the surface of the ruins, she puts a hand to it. "It's… it's like bark. A tree magically altered beyond any I've ever seen. The enchantments still linger even millennia after their casting. As do the walls themselves. Despite the passing of time, despite the damage and decay. It lingers." She turns to me, her eyes shining in a way I haven't seen since we were kids. "We're here! We've found Thalindor Castle."

I incline my head, and I can't withhold a returning grin. "It seems I owe you an apology." Her eyes are bright, blazing at me for one more second before she turns in amazement to the castle ruins, walking forward with Kairo to look for a way inside.

Taylor smiles slightly, watching her dart off. "Gael seems excited."

"We've been talking about Thalindor Castle since we were little," I explain as we walk toward the ruins, still avoiding the rifts that continue to complicate our path. "Between her mom's work and my mom's love for adventure novels, how could we not? Before she got sick, Laida would tell us stories about the legendary Thalindor Castle and other myths like that… I guess not entirely myths."

I hold out a hand, unable to run a finger along the woodstone wall.

"And then we'd go to my house and my mom would load us down with books full of treasure hunters and swashbuckling space pirates… between that and my dad's love for ancient architecture—his day job was as an environmental engineer—how could we not grow up to love archeology?"

Taylor smiles, the grin as fragile as fall leaves. I wonder what she thinks of my happy childhood, given the hell she grew up in. "So… what pulled you away from it?"

She seems hesitant to ask, and I'm not sure if I should be madder at Gael or myself for making her feel she can't ask these questions.

"Kaelen worked at the SRF before me. After I graduated, he had me consult on some projects. Needed the help of 'a big bad archeology expert,' he said. After that job, there was more… and I found I liked it. But the thing is, the hunt's my favorite part. I love tracking things down, finding what was lost."

The tiniest ghost of a smile coasts across my face, like the haunting of times past. I lower my voice so Gael can't hear. "Gael was the academic, if you can believe it. My work for the SRF… it delivered on the promise that dream always held. Plus, a better paycheck than a college professor. Then after Kaelen died… I signed up full time. I had to track down the bastards responsible. To bring down anyone doing that to people."

I glance at Taylor, wondering if the blazing anger I usually hide scared her.

Apparently not. Somehow, her empathetic expression remains. Feeling completely seen and accepted? It undoes me.

"Uh… Taylor?" Kairo's tone makes both of our heads snap in his direction. "You… may want to come see this."

"What is it?" Taylor asks warily.

"You two just… come look," Gael replies. Her bright brown eyes warn I won't like this.

We follow Kairo and Gael to a break in the wall, the jagged edge of the massive enchanted tree grown over with dark brown bark. We duck through, where the space opens into a giant open foyer.

Kairo creates a small ball of light to hover in front of us, illuminating a long set of stone stairs overgrown with moss and lichen. In an endless loop, the stairs crack, crumble, and fall. They then fly back, crumbling once more. A portion of the wall seems frozen mid-collapse, an entire section leaning at an impossible angle. Bits of rock float midair.

The entire castle is riddled with time rifts.

Taylor sighs, glancing at me. "Well… this just got more complicated."

28

WHEN LIFE CLOSES A DOOR

Taylor

"Fascinating," Gael says, scraping away debris and moss to better examine a carving. "We're the first ones to walk these halls in three thousand years." Her breaths kick up dust motes that hang in the air like tiny ghosts, the remnants of the ones that came before.

She wanders down, examining the carvings. Kairo grabs her by the shoulder, pulling her out of the way before she can walk straight into a rift. "Watch where you're going, or you'll be walking these halls for the next three thousand years." He shakes his head angrily and then sends his floating ball of light farther down the dim passage. It casts twisting shadows like black serpents slithering and twining along the engraved walls. "How do we find the library?"

"That's what I'm trying to see," Gael replies, raising a fierce eyebrow at him. "The legends say the library—"

"…lies at the heart of the castle, its knowledge the cornerstone of the realm and the foundation of where the lord sleeps," Eiran finishes, and I know he's remembering the stories his mother told him as a kid.

A mother who read legends at bedtime and a father who taught him to love art—both things I never had. My heart aches for Eiran. And myself.

I think of his tiny room in his aunt and uncle's house. Of the living sculptures with enchantments she diligently maintained for years. They did their best to make Eiran and Wynn feel loved. But it's not the same. I know from experience.

Do I miss Mom? Not really. Not anymore. As much as I insist she loved me… the difference is striking.

Refocusing on the task at hand, I say, "So… the library is below?" My voice comes out a little too bright for the damp stone around us. Eiran and Gael both look at me. "The cornerstone… that's the bottom corner of a building, right? And the foundation… sounds like it's under the lord's quarters, maybe near one corner of the structure?"

Eiran shrugs. "Worth a try."

It takes an hour of searching for a way down before Kairo calls, "Found it!" Pulling apart an overgrown tangle of thick, woody vines, he floats the orb into the hole and reveals a winding set of crumbly stairs that look dangerous at best to walk on. The air grows cooler as we peer into the hole, the taste of old stone on the air.

Kairo starts to hack at the vines with a plasma blade before Eiran says, "Hold on." With a raised hand, he concentrates on the knotted mess. The vines loosen like ropes being released, and after a moment, they slowly unwind, framing the opening.

"Show off," Kairo snarks in a quiet tone, the corner of his mouth tugging.

Looking down into the stairwell, he says, "Damn Valen. I can barely fit."

He pulls his wings in tightly, but before he can go through, I call, "Wait! Let me go first. Check it. If it's blocked, you'll never turn around down there."

"Taylor," Eiran says in warning, but I roll my eyes. "I'm good. I got this." He grits his teeth, but nods.

Carefully, I wind my way down the steps, Kairo's orb floating with me like a friend. The tunnel is long, with large wooden slabs lining the path, covered in paintings illustrating what appears to be all of Valen history. They're in amazing condition, given the state of the rest of the castle. Even the stairway itself is barely functional, and I spend most of my time avoiding gaps where stones have fallen onto the steps below— just to climb those rocks when I get to them further down.

About halfway down the long spiral tunnel, there's a massive section where the stairs are missing altogether. I stare at the gap. It's short enough to jump, if it weren't for the large temporal pocket blocking half the stairwell. I could make it past. Gael maybe, but Eiran and Kairo definitely couldn't. And if you tried jumping through that pocket… even with Frank's gadget, you'd risk losing your momentum and falling. Plus, there's some debris from the stairs above, so finding a safe landing spot would be tricky in the best of conditions.

I eye the rubble lining the hole's far edge. If I could move it… yeah. That'd work. And the path's clear after this.

"You guys go ahead and come down!"

Hearing the stomping of feet above, I brace myself and then leap across. Keeping an eye on the glowing projected edge of the rift, I twist in the air, avoiding it to land on the other side. Rocks slide under me, and I roll forward, head banging on the stairs as the stones tumble down to the floor below. Standing with a wince, I begin moving the rest of the rubble away, clearing a path.

The crunching of feet gets closer, and I loop off to see Kairo staring wide-eyed at the gap, his wings pulled in as tight as they can get in the cramped space. "Taylor, what the hell? How are we—"

"Just hold on," I cut in, waving a placating hand. "I need your help."

More grinding steps announce Gael and Eiran's arrival as I turn and run farther down the stairs to the next painting in the series. My enhanced muscles still straining with the effort, I remove the giant wooden panel from the wall. The wood is curved to match the angle of the wall, making it awkward, bulky, and heavy as hell. But it'll do.

"Taylor, what are you… you are not doing what I think you're doing." Gael stares at me, appalled, as I bring the priceless piece of Valen art over to the gap in the stairwell. "We are not going to *walk* on that. Do you know—"

"Grab this and lay it as flat as you can," I say to Kairo.

"Taylor, you can't!" Gael insists. Kairo and Eiran help guide as I weave it through the gap, avoiding the rift as much as possible. "Eiran?"

She looks to him hopefully, but he shrugs, yanking the painting through the edge of the rift and laying it down. Shaking her head, she turns to Kairo. "It's invaluable. We can't—"

"National security, Doc." He smiles sadly at her, and then heads across the artwork, paint chipping away under his feet. Eiran follows, and then finally, closing her eyes once and taking a deep breath, Gael crosses as well.

Soon, we are at the bottom of the stairs, which open onto a winding set of corridors and open spaces whose purpose is difficult to decipher. After another two hours of wandering, Gael gently scrapes at another engraving. This one appears to be some sort of marker for the stone doorway she's found. She motions with her hand, and Kairo brings his orb closer to light up the ancient door sign.

"It says… entrance beware, or…" She frowns, trying to make it out.

"…or you will die a horrible death, essentially," Kairo says, reading over her shoulder. "Cursed by the Aether to… well, it's bad." Gael gawks at Kairo, but he ignores her. "Only the revered fathers are allowed entrance, if they can… prove their worth. Sounds like traps. Because of course there are."

"Yeah, it does… how the hell do you know ancient Valen?" Gael is still staring at Kairo like he has three heads, and at least one of them tried to bite her ear off. "What else haven't you told us, Bat Boy?"

"I own a vintage bookstore," he says, as if that explains it. When she keeps glaring at him, he adds, "Some are… umm… really vintage. Now, should we go and see what fresh horrors this library has in store for us?"

I laugh. "Yes, let's."

We open the door, filing into a small antechamber about six feet square. As soon as we enter the space, the stone door slams behind us—a sound like a giant mouth closing over something alive. Our heads snap toward it, but there's the loud scraping of stone, and we turn back to see one wall slide up, revealing a small hallway.

"Should we go?" Kairo asks.

Before anyone can respond, the wall slams back down, shaking the space and sending dust floating. A moment later, the right-hand wall slides up, revealing a different hallway.

"It's a maze," I breathe, stunned.

"So which way?" Eiran asks. "The monks knew it by heart. How do we—"

"They'll have had some way for acolytes to learn the path," Kairo says, watching as the right wall closes and the wall in front slides up to reveal a third corridor. "That's how these people work. Got to indoctrinate the next generation somehow."

Gael's eyebrows knit, but Kairo ignores her.

"There are engravings!" Eiran says, pointing to a small marker on the door. He moves closer to read it, but before he can, the wall slams back into place. "There are phrases…" he says, turning. "They must mean something."

Gael, Kairo, and Eiran go to check out the carvings, waiting as each is briefly exposed, trying to puzzle out what they might mean. I just stare at the center door.

"Why don't we try one, and if it's the wrong one, we'll go back and try again?"

"And risk getting lost?" Eiran looks from the wall to frown at me. "Besides, there could be traps punishing the wrong answer."

"We don't have time for this," I say, shaking my head. Take a step forward, thinking of trying one, before reconsidering. Picking up a large stone that's fallen from the ceiling, I toss it through the center door. When the stone crosses the threshold, massive roots burst from the wall, pulverizing it. The smell of earth and a choking cloud of dust linger the air.

"Okay… so it's not that one," Kairo observes.

Gael scowls at him. "Let's figure out the trick to this room before we try that again."

"Why would the room try to kill us, though?" I ask, glad I decided to throw a rock instead of jump through myself.

"This place has been untouched for centuries," Eiran says, and from the burn in his eyes, I can tell he noticed my step toward the door. "The enchantments have gone wild."

I imagine a student's legs wrapped in roots, waiting until someone comes along and rescues them. Brutal. Then, I picture myself pulverized in a cloud of red…

"Okay, so… let's look for clues," I suggest, and Gael rolls her eyes, returning to her investigation of the doors.

I start studying the spiraling patterns on the floor when… there! Beneath the creeping undergrowth, words curl in the same undulating script.

"Guys," I say haltingly.

Gael and Kairo's eyes widen when I point to the floor. They move quickly to read.

Walking in a circle along the spiraling floorwork, Kairo reads, "Who is Thalindor, the silent witness that observes the cosmic ballet?"

He looks at Gael, raising an eyebrow. "The fuck?"

"It's elvish mysticism. Let's see. The door in front says, 'The Earthshaper.' We know that's not it." She gives me a pointed look before continuing. "Now, let's see if I can remember. It's been a bit since I reviewed Mom's notes on this stuff. Is it 'the whispering wind'…" She points to the path on the left. "…or the watchful guardian?"

"That one," I say, pointing to the left, repressing the heat on my cheeks. I should've waited, but having the patience—and trust—for them to figure this out is hard. Security infiltration I can do. Deciphering ancient traps? Not really my thing.

Except this one I know.

Gael raises an eyebrow at me. "Now, Kairo knowing ancient Valen is strange enough. If you say you're a mysticism expert—"

"Lorathar is the watchful guardian, so it's not that." I glance at Eiran. "When you grow up around elvish fanatics, you learn a thing or two. Rituals. Symbols. How to pass unexpected tests that are likely to kill you."

"She's right," Gael says to Eiran with the faintest hint of surprised approval. "On the symbology at least."

"Alright," Eiran replies with a nod. "When that door opens, *I'll* go through first and make sure it's clear."

We watch, waiting for the "whispering wind" door to swing open again. When it does, he walks through, and I brace for something to happen. When he seems okay, he nods to us, and we hurry in behind him.

We head along another dark stone passage, Kairo's glowing orb sending eerie blue shadows across the cobbled walls. Spiderwebs litter the corners of the cramped space, and I'm relieved when we empty into a second room.

This time, the walls slide up and down faster, the thundering slams shaking my bones in time with my racing heart. Eiran and Kairo stare at the doors like stalking predators, shoulders hunched in concentration as they try to register the shape of the engravings before they disappear again into the ceiling.

"Within the roots of eldertrees, what echoes the heartbeat of the Aether?" Gael reads from the engraving on the floor as Kairo reads the writing on each wall.

"The Lethara Harmony, the Verdant Resonance, or the Luminar

Essence?" Kairo asks me.

"Luminar Essence," Gael replies before I can.

Kairo nods, waiting for the door straight ahead to open, and then jumps through. He turns back to us, and the wall slams closed before Eiran can follow. Ready now, we go through the small divide one at a time.

"That wasn't too bad," Kairo grins.

Gael smacks him on top of the head. "Ugh, don't say that! You'll jinx us!"

"Too late," Eiran says, coming to a halt at the third set of doorways.

This time, the doors are sticking and jerking, slamming down at weird intervals. Gael makes a couple of adjustments to her comms, and then three different rifts display in shimmering yellow light, each blocking part of at least one doorway.

"They've converged," Gael says.

"It's messing up the timing of the doorways," Eiran says, surveying them with blank intensity.

"When shadows embrace the glowfruit's radiance, what path leads to the realm of dreams?" Kairo reads.

"Ziralian reflection," Gael says absently. "That one." He points to the right.

"Of course it is," I mutter. The third door is the most erratic. Two different anomalies overlap, screwing with the mechanism. It slams down once, then moves halfway before rising, and then slams down three times in quick succession.

"But how—" Gael says.

Before she can finish, Eiran runs and leaps, sliding under a closing door, the wall slamming down inches beyond his head. "Idiot!" Gael yells. Eying the door like it's an angry toddler, she jumps forward, praying audibly as the door slams behind her.

"This trap is not wing-friendly," Kairo complains. "I'm going to need to talk to the disability accommodations department." Sighing ruefully, he leaps.

The closing wall clips the bottom edge of his wing, and he curses loudly.

"Kai!" I holler, horrified. I've never heard him scream like that.

"I've got it sealed," Eiran says from the next room. "He'll be alright, but we should hurry. We need to get him to Lirion."

"Coming!" I say, and I leap through. The rising door abruptly stops and begins closing once more. I reach out desperately, and two powerful hands grip my forearms. Eiran yanks me through, and I can feel the wall scrape the sole of my boot as it closes.

I exhale, looking up blearily at Eiran, breath coming in shaky gasps. "Well, that was fun."

29
THE LOST LIBRARY OF THALINDOR

Eiran

Kairo's wing is an absolute mess. My magic is keeping the blood loss and the worst of the pain at bay, but it still must be killing him, the mangled tip sticking out at an unnatural angle like the crumpled corner of a dropped book. As we head down the rubble-strewn hallway, he keeps reaching back to hold the edge of his wing, as if he can somehow straighten it out.

"Maybe you should—" I breathe, but he shakes his head.

"My wings have endured worse. Besides, I'm not going back." He glances briefly at Gael, then Taylor, as they enter a large open cavern.

"They won't think less of you," I reply in as low a tone as I can manage, pausing before we follow.

Kairo gives me a look, then whispers, "I don't give a shit if they think less of me or not. I'm not leaving them here."

"But I'm out of luck?"

Kairo shrugs. "From what I've seen, you can take care of yourself." Without another word, he walks forward into the large space, joining Taylor and Gael as they approach an opening half-blocked with rubble, the ceiling hanging at a strange angle.

I stare at Kairo for a moment. That's the closest thing to a compliment he's given me.

"Be careful going through here," Gael tells us as I join the group. "Don't touch any of the walls. It won't take much to bring this down on us. Kairo—" She surveys his large wings.

"I'll go last," he says stubbornly.

"That's not—" Gael begins, but he cuts her off.

"Don't worry about me, Doc. I can crawl if I need to. You make some progress, and then I'll follow." It's a stupid plan, but from the set of his jaw, it's clear to everyone that he's not changing his mind.

Gael rolls her eyes in disgust. Taylor turns to me, shrugging silently. I wink back, and her cheeks flush a bit.

How is it that even in a collapsed ruin, she looks beautiful?

Gael cautiously looks at the angled ceiling, then crouches her six-foot-four frame to enter the narrow passage. Taylor follows with no need to bend, and she turns in the half-light, giving me a cocky little grin. I can practically hear her saying, "*See, being short can be a good thing sometimes!*"

I grin back, her playful glance sending a fist around my stomach. Sighing in mock defeat, I bend, following her inside.

We are a few feet inside the passage before Gael screams. Panic grips me at the too-familiar sound, a steely coldness stiffening down my spine.

"What's wrong?" Taylor hollers, running forward. Then she screams as well.

I chase after them through the low tunnel, but I quickly see what the situation is. Gael and Taylor are both shuddering and slapping at themselves, trying to pull off large black insects with long spindly legs and large pincers, tiny luminescent white spots lighting them both up like an eerie disease.

I lurch toward Taylor and Gael, grabbing at the bugs when something lands on my back, legs skittering up my spine. Panic flares as I claw at my neck, desperate to tear it off before it bites.

With a smack, Taylor kills it, leaving a smear of wet, sticky gore across my shirt. Needing no further prompting, we flail and slap at each other in a frenzy. Huge, skittering spiders pour from cracks, shadows—everywhere and nowhere at once. Sickening crunches fill the world.

Then Gael hollers in pain.

Taylor stills, and suddenly the bugs erupt outward in a black cloud of splattered insect parts. Gael winces, all of us dripping in bug guts.

"Yuck," she says, eyeing Taylor.

"You alright?" I ask, and she shrugs, limping slightly.

A large red welt is growing on her calf. "They're not very poisonous, but it hurts like hell."

We walk forward to where the tunnel ceiling is still in place, and Gael and I stand with a sigh. Taylor looks at me apologetically, and I reach up to pull part of a leg out of her hair, laughing in a low tone. She grins in a slightly humiliated way, and I try not to laugh at how disheveled she looks.

"Uh… guys?" Gael's odd tone makes us turn. The hallway slowly lights up in a wave of tiny dots of light. Tiny chittering, like fingernails, rises in a wave, tickling my spine.

I glance at the two of them, and then holler back, "Hey Kairo? How's it going?"

A grunt echoes from up the passage. "Fine. Almost there."

"You might want to hurry," Gael says.

"What about the walls?" he asks. "I thought we didn't want—"

"Hurry!" Taylor calls.

"Run," I agree.

We sprint down the passage as the insects drop in a wave. Kairo hollers, and I know he's reached the bugs. The place shudders as someone—probably Kairo—hits a wall. Bits of debris fall along with the insects, and now it's an all-out dash for the dark opening. Chunks of the walls and ceiling rain down in earnest, and the three of us are vomited out onto another open area in a heap.

We turn as one to see Kairo clambering after us on all fours. The passage collapses behind him, blocking the way we came.

"Okay," he gasps, pulling bugs off him. "Maybe… this… was a… bad… idea."

"There it is," Gael breathes, drawing all our eyes across toward rows and rows of shelves, leather tomes barely visible.

"But… how are we getting there?" Taylor asks.

We don't need Frank's holographic display to tell us there's a rift. The bridge that led over the large canyon ahead of us was caught in mid-collapse. Huge chunks of the bridge float, suspended in time—or at least moving at an immeasurably slow pace. Gael adjusts her comm anyway, and the largest rift we've encountered yet lights up the entire path ahead.

Taylor glances up, then looks at Kairo. "I guess you can't—"

"Not with this thing," he says, wincing as he tries to adjust his damaged wing. "Sorry."

"Don't be sorry," Taylor says, shaking her head and putting a hand on her friend's shoulder. She then pulls it away quickly. "*Ugh!*" She reaches up and grabs a lingering bug from his back, tossing it on the ground and stomping on it.

Kairo's eyes widen, and I laugh. He turns and surveys the bridge, concern furrowing his brow. "So, what do we do?"

"We'll have to leap across," I say, looking to Taylor. "But we don't want to get the timing wrong, or everything will fall. We'll need to tune Frank's temporal compensators to the precise fluctuation of the rift itself, so that we can move in real time rather than get stuck."

Gael gives me a surprised look. "And you can… do that?"

I reply defensively, "I paid attention in physics class. I also *read the message* Frank sent further explaining how they work." I glance down at the strange gadget on my wrist and adjust the various knobs and dials. "Okay, according to the scanner, this should be the correct setting. If I'm doing this right, the temporal anomaly shouldn't affect me. There are no rifts within the library itself. So, if we get through this—"

"What if you're wrong?" Taylor says, her eyes knitting in concern. "And don't give me that damn grin and try to tell me it'll be fine."

I step forward and reach out to cup her cheek, lost in those beautiful azure eyes. "I'll be careful. We've got to finish what we started the other night." Her cheeks flush pink as her eyes flit to my mouth.

I wink and then turn and leap into the rift.

There's the briefest of moments where I'm sure it won't work, that I'm going to be stuck in eternal freefall. There's a tiny tug, and the gadget pulls me into the timeline. I land on a large, slightly slanted chunk of bridge. I turn to the group and motion for Taylor to follow. She braces herself, and then leaps, her enhanced strength allowing her to land smoothly beside me.

Gael follows shortly after, slipping with her bad leg. Then, with a small flutter, Kairo lands, his wing slamming against her leg.

She howls in pain and slips right off the rock. She screeches in terror, but with a flurry of flapping, Kairo is suddenly there, arm outstretched to grab her. He grunts with pain as he pulls her up with his injured wing.

"Oh Aether, please protect us!" Gael mutters in a crazed tone. With a flop, Kairo drops her on the rock, landing behind us.

There's no reprieve before suddenly the rock tips. Taylor and I react the quickest, landing on the next rock and sending it slightly spinning. Our hands instinctively find each other, and we take a leap together, with the thud of Kairo and Gael landing close behind us, Kairo gripping Gael. Swiftly, we land on the next rock, reset our stance, and prepare for another jump. We move like that, leaping from rock to rock to rock before landing on the solid ground of the lost library of Thalindor.

After a moment to catch our breath, I follow Gael's numb plod into the library, staring at the books in awe. Kairo raises the orb of light, illuminating rows and rows of magically preserved wooden shelves and hundreds of forgotten tomes. The scent of dust and old paper fills the air along with the faint hum of some powerful enchantment. Something preserving the books, even after all these centuries.

"I never thought…" I say, walking forward to read the names on the multicolored spines.

"…me either," Gael replies as she strolls from shelf to shelf, running a finger along the leather bindings.

"I can't believe it!" Kairo says, thrilled despite his pain. "So many were thought lost. The value of these books… the knowledge… it's priceless."

Gael stares at him with an odd look on her face.

"Again," he says, faintly exasperated. "I own a vintage bookstore."

"It's amazing," Taylor agrees, reading a few of the titles. Several of these books would sell for a big profit on the black market. Enough that Taylor could travel anywhere. And yet, the way she's looking at these books isn't predatory. It's reverent.

Maybe I'm a fool. Maybe my gut is shot. But when she turns and smiles brilliantly at me? All I sense is wonder.

I turn to Gael. "I'd love to spend hours looking through all of this, but…"

She shakes herself slightly. "You're right. Let's find something on the Eldralume Relic."

Half an hour later, Gael cries out, "I found something!" She comes running over, stumbling on the injured leg, to show me a book with an illustration of a very familiar item.

"That's it," Kairo says, leaning over my shoulder.

"What's it say?" Taylor asks.

Gael shrugs, looking baffled. "It's… code? Or a dialect I can't discern. Figuring it out will take time."

"Well, we'll need to sort it out fast. We need to figure out what the Lorathar Initiative wanted with it. I can't shake the feeling that there's some clue we're missing." Glancing around the massive library, I add, "But first, we need out."

"I've got a way," Gael calls from somewhere farther in the library. "But you won't like it."

PART 4

THE DARROW JOB

i made a home in the roots of trees
enveloped by a nest of shadows
drawing from the earth, the source
and hiding
past and future, loss and power
all that makes me
me

—The Journal of Taylor Grey

30

GETTING OUT OF THE GUTTER

Taylor

"I need about ten showers after that," I say, shuddering as we crawl our way to sunlight.

"The sewer lines are thousands of years old," Gael replies, rolling her eyes. "Anything left broke down ages ago."

"Yeah, into dirt," Kairo chimes in with a grunt. We're all caked in mud and grime, but Kairo got the worst of it with his wings.

"At least we're out," Eiran says, turning toward the trees to check that we're clear. He grabs his tattered and mud-drenched shirt from the back of the neck, pulling it over his head. His shoulders tighten in a near-obscene display, the black branches of a vast tattoo rippling with the movement as though waving in the breeze. They stretch over his right shoulder, disappearing onto his chest.

He turns to put the shirt into his pack, and in the golden evening light, I'm breathless, in awe of him. The branch stretches over his powerful shoulder to join the trunk of a massive quithra tree. I can't help but follow the tree's journey past a row of impressive abs to where the roots disappear into...

"You're drooling," Kairo whispers.

"Shut up," I murmur back.

"Can't blame you, honestly," Kairo grins, then grimaces as I elbow him, forgetting for a moment about his wing.

"Oh, I'm sorry!" I say quickly, but he raises a hand, forestalling my apologies.

"Come here," Gael sighs, motioning for Kairo.

"I'm fine," he grouses.

"Come over here, you big baby. I don't want to hear you whining the rest of the way back." Muttering something unflattering under his breath, he stomps over to Gael, letting her examine his damaged wing.

I don't notice his silent approach until I feel the heat of him close to me. I turn to see Eiran just feet from me. My eyes follow along the gorgeous lines of his chest to his face. His mouth turns down in a concerned frown. "You okay?"

"Yeah," I shrug. "I like your tattoo." Unable to help myself, I reach out, tracing a branch along his shoulder and down toward his ribs. I allow it to glide farther down than I should, close to the waist of his pants. His eyes fall to mine, a beat too long. I let my hand fall before making a bigger fool of myself. "Always wanted a tattoo."

Eiran's mouth quirks. "What would you get?"

I shrug noncommittally. "I always wanted a flower. I know. Cliché, right? Not that it matters. Needles, you know?"

"I don't think it's cliché at all. You know, you should get a lorathar blossom." I let out a faint laugh. "No, really. Reclaim it. It would be a nice 'fuck you' to the Initiative."

Oh my gods, he's serious. Oddly, I kind of like the idea. Except…

"If you want to go, I'll take you. Keep you distracted from the needle. If you want."

Leave it to Eiran to read my mind. Something swells in me, giving me enough bravery to ask, "Where should I get it?"

His eyes burn dangerously, a predatory grin sending heat to my core. "Well, you could do the shoulder…" He traces a single claw slowly along my shoulder. I resist a shudder as my breath catches. "…or you could do your back…" He runs his hand along my spine, and this time I do shudder, my eyes slipping closed. "…or, my favorite. The hip." He lightly grips my hip, the tips of his claws just pinching. I let out the tiniest of gasps and lean into him…

Kairo's comm blares, breaking the relative quiet. Eiran and I jump apart as Kairo checks it, his face brightening. Clicking it to speaker, he answers, "Hey Frank!"

Frank's squeaky voice comes through the comm, and his excitement is, as always, infectious. *"Hello Mr. Ryūkishi, sir!"*

"Kairo," he corrects with a sighing laugh.

"Yes, apologies, Mr. Kairo, sir. I have excellent news!"

Kairo's eyes widen in surprise. "Did you find Blackstone?"

"Unfortunately, no, sir," Frank says, sadness creeping into his voice. *"Still no sign of Adrian Blackstone, sir. But we will find the fiend. I promise you that, sir."* The excitement snaps back into Frank's voice so quickly it gives me whiplash as he says, *"But I found Ms. Darrow, sir!"*

Eiran and I hurry forward. "Excellent work, Frank," Eiran says into the comm. "Where is she?"

"Thank you, Mr. Valtir, sir. The wolf shifter is staying at the Eldrahaust Inn. That's what I have at the moment. I'm searching for more as we speak."

Kairo exchanges a look with Eiran. "Thanks Frank. Excellent work."

"We need to get there now," Eiran says after Kairo hangs up, his voice sharp, in planner mode.

"We need to be smart," I reply, hastening back to our stryder. "Don't go in half-cocked. Let's put together a plan. Attacking her without understanding her intentions, without knowing what's going on, would be a disaster. Does this mean Helix is the one who wanted the Eldralume Relic? We should recon first."

"We need to get over there before she slips away again," Eiran disagrees, his long legs easily keeping pace with me.

I steal a glance at him, trying my best to ignore his almost nakedness so close to me. But I can't deny the truth. He is absolutely gorgeous. Even if he is a stubborn ass sometimes.

I reach out a hand, pausing him with a touch to his thick, powerful arm. He turns, his violet eyes aflame as my hand warms against his sage skin. "We need to track her, but we can't engage. Not until we know more."

His eyes search mine for one more moment before he nods, stepping away. "You're right."

"I'll do it," Kairo says, but then he stumbles on a branch, and his face collapses in a flash of pain.

"Heal first," I say sternly. Before he can protest, "I know what you're going to say. I'm sure your illusory magic makes you ideal for tracking, but we need to get you healed up if you're going to be any use to us."

"I'll watch first," Eiran says as we make it to his sleek black stryder. He puts a hand on Kairo's shoulder and adds, "Once Lirion sets you straight, you can come take over. Alright?"

Kairo nods, relenting and looking a little relieved. I suppress a smile, oddly thrilled that Eiran and Kairo are getting along. We clamber into the stryder, Kairo taking the front seat and struggling to situate his injured wing, and then we all make the trek back to town.

***

A few hours later, Lirion has Kairo comfortable, but insists he needs to rest at least for the night. After more complaining than necessary, Kairo takes a draft that knocks him out.

In the meantime, Eiran leaves for Vaeloria City, trying to locate Darrow. From his texts in the hours since, it sounds like all he's found is her empty room. There's a strange emptiness here without him, but there was a gift on my bed that helps: a small bouquet of the flowers we practiced growing on my first day of learning Gruundlith. Plus a card that reads simply, "Be sure to miss me. -E". And smartass or not, I do miss him already.

Boy, am I in trouble.

After Lirion treated her spider bite, Gael disappeared to decipher the book, leaving me to fill Wynn in on all that happened. Thankfully, she convinced her aunt and uncle to go searching for pasta to make for supper (a "Union-friendly dish," as she put it). So, we kept from traumatizing them too much with the details of what happened.

That said, even Wynn seems nearly shocked into silence when I finish my story. "You could have been killed about ten times over," she breathes, eyes wide.

"That's lower than average, to be honest," I shrug.

Wynn goggles in amazement, but then says, "Still… I want to go next time."

"Wynn—" I reply, but she cuts me off.

"I'll stay away from anything serious and do exactly what you say. I can be on comms or whatever. Honestly, I'm not looking for danger. But staying home?" Her lavender eyes, so much like her brother's if a bit lighter, begin to water slightly. "Not knowing what's happening to you all? I don't think I could handle that."

"I don't think you can go on the job itself," I say, and she deflates a bit. "But you could help set things up, and we'll check in before and after."

Wynn embraces me like I've promised the moon, and then straightens, taking a deep breath. "Okay, so now the real question. What's going on between you and my brother?"

My brain spins with the whiplash of the question. "I… I don't… what?"

"Oh, don't play dumb," Wynn says with an exasperated sigh—the master of the sneak attack, just like her aunt. "*Something* is going on. The tension is palpable. But I want to know the details."

"Wynn, no offense, but it's not—"

"Not any of my business?" she asks, raising an eyebrow. "He's my brother. What if I don't approve?"

"There's nothing to approve of," I groan. "This is really—"

"Okay, so you're not together," she says, thinking to herself before her eyes sharpen on me. "Then what's going on? Unrequited love? Did you reject him? Why do you hate my brother?"

"I… I don't hate him," I say quickly, laughing yet taken aback. "He's very… hot… I mean… nice. Kind. Whatever."

Elowynn grins like a fiend. "So, you *do* like him, then."

"I'm going to kill you," I grouse, but her energy is infectious. I've never had a close female friend to talk about men with. Kairo, a barely reformed man-whore attracted to anyone and everyone, might comment on how hot a guy is, but he's never keen to gossip about someone I'm looking to date. Says the very idea is gross.

"But you win. Yes, I like him."

"Have you kissed?" she asks keenly. "Had sex?"

I laugh, incredulous. "Getting right to the heart of things, huh?"

She shrugs. "I want him happy. So?"

"Yes, we kissed. As for the other—" I trail off, thinking of our one night together.

There hasn't been time to do anything more.

She smirks. "I'm taking that as a 'sort of', then."

I shake my head. Clearly, while Kairo may have hang-ups about his "surrogate little sister" and sex, Wynn has no such issue. Sighing, I admit, "I've only known him for a couple of months, but… he's unlike anyone I've ever met. That doesn't mean I know what this is."

Wynn gives me a look. "Please. Have you seen the way he watches over you? It's like you're gravity."

It's a marvelous—yet frightening—suggestion.

Wynn smiles at my expression, but it fades quickly, replaced by something heavy and serious. "Just… don't hurt him, okay?"

Her eyes lock on mine, and her voice softens. "He's been through a lot. We all have, but Eiran… he took on everything when Kaelen died. Even leaving was his way of stepping up, of filling the hole Kaelen left at the SRF. And Gaelarya not going with him? He can't do that again."

The words settle like a boulder on my chest. "What are you saying?"

The walls close in on me. What about my dream to leave Vale—and the years of questionable actions to make it real? Would I sacrifice that? For him?

And Eiran? His life, his family are here. Would he give that up? Could I ask him to?

If there's no future, should I risk a relationship?

Since when did I care about good ideas?

"I'm just saying…" Wynn says a bit sadly, "that if you aren't all in… don't do it. You're so smart and funny and… I can tell it would be easy for Eiran to fall for you. If he hasn't already. If you won't be there to catch him, that's okay. But if you're not in, you've got to walk away. He can't handle another heartbreak."

Maelara and Roderic burst in, pasta in hand, bright smiles breaking the tension. "Who's hungry?" Maelara beams. I jump up to help them bring in the food, trying to ignore Wynn and her comments. Still, I know her eyes are on me, her words sinking down into my gut.

The pasta—and the weight of the day—sits heavy in my stomach. Sleep won't come. The unspoken questions press down, harassing me late into the night until I finally collapse from sheer exhaustion.

31

THE VALE EFFECT

Taylor

The shrill silence within the stryder is palpable as we glide along toward Vaeloria City. I take a quiet bite of the cookie, half-fearing my munching is too loud, half-hoping it's annoying as hell. Indistinct forms of buildings loom faintly in the distance as we pass the city of Himmelstor, and I absently study their blurry shapes, searching for details as if answers to this gulf between us might lie there.

Eiran's back is stiff, his hand gripping the nav stick between us like a throat he wishes he could choke. I wish Gael and Lirion rode with us, but Gael had to stop by the university first, so they said they'd meet us there. Now it's just Eiran and me. Together. Alone in the stryder.

So, I keep munching on the cookies Eiran's aunt baked for me, trying not to feel like complete shit after she thanked me for bringing Eiran back home "despite the circumstances."

With a soft sigh, I throw the half-eaten cookie back into the decorative tin. Guilt gnaws at my gut. With the way I've been acting the past couple of days, Eiran must be hurt and confused, even if he hides it. He has no clue why I've barely spoken to him. He came back home after Kairo relieved his Isra-watching duties, and I just… avoided him. He even tried to kiss me. He pulled my hair away from my face, smiling that fucking dimple. My heart slammed painfully in my chest, but I forced myself to pull away.

I took a cold shower and went to bed. Hardest thing I've ever done.

But I made myself do it, because Wynn's words keep echoing around in my head. Getting off Vale, away from narrow-minded elves and torture-tinted memories and… everything? It's all I've wanted since I was eleven. The look in Kairo's eyes before he told me my mother was dead? I knew then I had to leave.

I've been dreaming of it ever since. Of moving to the Union of Independent Planets, where I could live among humans. I even picked the place. The planet Dallas is supposed to be one giant city—a crowded haven of sports, gambling, and shows. Millions of tourists. Enough marks to keep my bank account full for life. I have a plan.

And Eiran? He doesn't fit into that plan. He couldn't survive on a planet like Dallas. Hell, he'd never leave Vale. He left his family to move to the city, but off-world? I can't imagine him doing that. And even if he would… I'd never ask him.

No, Wynn's right. I need to finish this job and walk away. Until then, we keep it professional. No reason to make it any messier than it already is.

And, gods, is it messy. I can't think about that night. About the feel of his hands on my skin. Of his tongue in my center. A wave of warmth threatens to pull me under, to shatter my resolve, but I clamp my jaw, close my eyes, and force the memory into that locked box deep inside.

Breathe in the scent of the Luminar Essence. Exhale your contribution to the Aether.

Desperate to break the silence, I ask, "What news do you think Kairo has? What can't he say over comms? Is it related to whatever the hell he was researching about the shard? Or something else?"

Eiran sighs softly, breathing in and out in a calming rhythm. A flicker of pain hits his eyes before getting lost in that green sea of forced calm. "I don't know," he says, his tone the consummate spy. "It's either great news or terrible news."

A small laugh escapes my lips. "Given our luck, terrible."

Eiran glances over at me, something tugging at his delicious mouth. Gods, don't think of that.

"I don't know. It hasn't all been bad luck."

I try to bury it, to deny the power those words hold over me, to ignore how that smile makes my insides tingle. It's like fighting the ocean. No matter how much I push back against the waves, the force bowls me over, lapping around the edges and seeping into me anyway.

He seems to sense something in my expression, because that smile falters for a second.

"Eiran," I murmur, looking away from him. "There's too much at stake. We need to stay focused."

"I *am* focused," Eiran says, and I know if I turn and look at him, I'll break. I'll see that intense, burning gaze I know he's fixing on me now, and I'll break. I'll give in… and then I'll break him. I can't do that.

"We need to focus… on the mission. We can't afford to get distracted."

"And what is that supposed to mean?" he asks roughly.

"It means…" My traitorous voice breaks, and I pause for a second to catch it. To gather my strength and rebuild those walls. Slip back into the mask of Taylor the thief.

"It means that I'm leaving, Eiran. When this is done. I'm going to the Union. And you're staying here. Nothing will change that."

Don't look at him, Taylor. Don't look at him. I stare at the blur of green beyond the window.

"You said we'd try," Eiran growls, the hardness flickering like a flame in the wind. Like the briefest gust will extinguish it, leaving only devastation in its wake.

"I did," I say, watching the trees as they pass, swallowing down the shaking. Finding my cool. "But that was wrong. I'm sorry."

"You want this too," Eiran insists. I can feel the pleading beneath the anger, the words reaching out like fingers. Desperate for me to look at him. To come back to him. "I can tell you do."

I have to lie to him again. That's what I do, right? I fucking lie.

"I don't want that. I'm attracted to you but… we shouldn't waste time on things…" I swallow my pounding heart. Swallow the dangerous truth trying to claw its way out. All of it.

Just fucking say it, Taylor. Woman up and do the right thing.

"We shouldn't waste time on things that don't matter."

Eiran lets out a strangled little cough. The words ring in the car between us. *Things that don't matter.*

"Okay," he says in the quietest sort of gasp. "Okay. Fine. But I still think you're full of shit."

"Think what you want," I whisper. "Just… respect my wishes, please."

Eiran nods, and we travel the rest of the way in silence.

***

It's late when we arrive at the bookstore, but apparently that's by design. I ask about Darrow after giving Kairo a hug. "No sign of dear old dad. He must have slipped off. But Darrow's fine. Every day, it's the same thing. She gets up from the hotel. Works out. Goes and changes, and then leaves with this case—"

"A case?" I ask sharply.

"Yep," Kairo confirms. "Doesn't go anywhere without it. Takes it to the tea shop. Then goes to the *prison* where she's been working. Then she leaves with the case, eats somewhere, and heads back to the hotel. Does it every day. Frank's watching her now."

I raise an eyebrow. "So, this case. Think the relic's in there?"

Kairo shrugs. "Could be. It's definitely something she doesn't let out of her sight."

"Wait, go back. She works at a what?!" Eiran asks, startled. "There's no prison in Vaeloria City… unless you mean Horizon Correctional? I didn't think it was open yet."

"That's the one," Kairo says. Horizon Correctional is a new, privately owned facility that popped up a few months ago. The details on it are sketchy at best. "Emma did a quick search. It's owned by NovaGuard Solutions."

He frowns. "The SRF did a whole deep dive on this. They're some Union conglomerate working with the military. It seems legit, from what I can tell. They house mostly political prisoners, though there's supposed to be some sort of mental facility there as well. There aren't many details, though, because, well, military."

"Well, the operation may be legit, but—" Kairo trails off as the door jingles. Gael and Lirion walk into the shop, Gael's mouth gaping like a fish.

"This place is… wow."

"Glad you like it, Doc," Kairo smirks.

She quickly snaps her scowl back in place for him. "How many of these were stolen?"

He smiles that dangerous smile of his. "Wouldn't you like to know?"

"What about the prison, Kairo?" Eiran prompts.

"Right," he replies, refocusing. "Anyway, the prison itself might be legit, but there's definitely something going on there, and I'm actually surprised the SRF didn't find it."

Eiran's mouth is a sharp line. "Find what?"

Kairo ruffles his wings at the tone. "It's no surprise Darrow has been going to the prison. It took some digging, but Frank and Emma found a trail linking NovaGuard with—"

"Don't tell me," Eiran mutters. "Helix."

"Exactly."

Shit.

I look at Eiran. "We need someone on the inside."

Kairo shrugs. "There are back channels I can pull if you can put together a decent fake backstory, Leaf Boy."

Eiran frowns. "As what?"

"It looks like they are trying to recruit a couple more guards."

"Okay," I say, my gut clenching tighter with each passing second. "We can talk about Darrow and the prison later. That's not why you called us all here. What's this about?"

Kairo takes a deep breath and then lands his intense stare on me. "We…" he looks away, clearing his throat. "Emma found something. In your mom's journal. She cracked it."

It's like there's a ringing in my head. Warning bells.

"You… you might want to sit." He motions to the reading nook, the one I normally love to collapse into, but I need to stand. To keep moving.

Sensing this, Kairo continues. "Your mom…" he glances at Eiran, and the wariness in that gaze sends my fear skyrocketing further. "… your mom worked for Helix."

Eiran's face turns to stone, but I barely notice. There's no sound. No emotion. No… nothing. As if unable to help himself, he moves closer to me, a granite wall of fury.

"What?" is all I can say.

"She… she worked for Helix," Kairo continues. "And you…"

My gaze snaps to him. Please stop talking. Don't say whatever's about to come next.

"Taylor? Taylor, I'm…" He clears his throat, eyes watering at the edges. "There's no easy way to say this. You were an experiment, kid."

I let out a gasping laugh, although there's nothing remotely funny about this. "Well, we sort of already knew that. Right?" Still, the words, put so bluntly, hurt more than I would have expected. "I mean, my mom was experimenting on me most of my life, and—"

"No, Taylor." Kairo shakes his head. The sadness in that simple gesture, the faint fear in his eyes, like I'm a sage hare ready to bolt… my hands start to tremor.

"Kai…" I breathe. "What—"

"You're a clone. Your mo… Dr. Grey cloned herself. Altered her DNA. You were a… project. For Helix."

Out of the corner of my eye, I see Eiran go still, shoulders locked, the muscle in his jaw flickering.

"Fucking hell," Lirion mutters.

The sound in the room is muffled, like I'm underwater. Drowning. Must be why it's so hard to breathe. The edges of my vision blur, as if the air itself has thickened. Pressing against my skin.

I'm a clone? Not even my own person, just a copy of someone else. A twisted, corrupted copy.

Eiran's jaw works. His eyes flick toward an ornate bit of elvish sculpture on a shelf, as if he needs somewhere to put the rage, but his shoulders stay angled toward me. One hand braces on the edge of the table, close enough that his knuckles brush mine—barely there, but enough to anchor me for a heartbeat. "It doesn't matter," he mutters.

I pull my hand away. "The hell it doesn't," I say just as softly.

Eiran takes a step away then, giving us distance. "What was the goal?" His voice is as cold as I've ever heard it, brittle like thawing ice. The words drop like stones, his fury at Helix a physical blow.

Kairo winces. He turns to me and says hesitantly, "They want… magic."

I nod. It all makes sense. It's the one thing the humans never had. The one thing no amount of tech or genetic modification could overcome. This magic I have? It's what I was *made* for.

No long-lost father to track down. The passing traveler my mom would tell me stories about as a kid? Just one more lie to hide the truth. That I'm an experiment. A test and nothing more.

"How?" Eiran says in the same clipped tone.

"Well, at first Grey tried to isolate whatever genetics were behind magic," Kairo says. "But that didn't work."

"People have tried for centuries," Lirion nods.

"Right," says Kairo. "Magic is metaphysical. You can't simply isolate a few genes and replicate them like that. But Grey made you... I don't know. Receptive?"

"I... don't know what that means," I admit. None of this makes sense. Or maybe I'm not able to process.

Kairo shrugs, as if he can't really put it into words either. "She made you able to absorb abilities from foreign DNA without knowing the genetic origin. To absorb the best qualities of another race. Of another species. The Aether affects every race differently. We don't know why, but... somehow you can absorb every species' magic if you come into sufficient contact with it."

"Like... like a Quiblin's wind magic?" Gael asks.

Eiran nods, his hand tracing for a moment over my finger before pulling away. My hand trembles at the loss of contact. "Or an elf's Gruundlith abilities."

"Exactly," Kairo sighs. "Grey, she... she found a way to trigger the ability to resonate with multiple species' magical traits without losing stability."

"Because messing with the foundations of magic has terrible side effects," Gael adds in a quiet tone. "If you believe the lore, anyway."

Kairo keeps giving me that sad, apologetic look that's so unlike him. It's weirding me out more than this entire conversation. "Grey told Helix it could be the key to adapting magical abilities across species. She called it 'The Vale Effect'."

"The ability to draw the best of all worlds to yourself," I say faintly. "My mom... Dr. Grey talked about it all the time. I thought she meant the charm of the planet. I never..."

I look to Eiran, tears in my eyes, desperate for him to understand. "I hated it. Hated this place. Because she loved it. The place where everyone hated me! So, I wanted to leave. And now? You're saying it didn't even mean anything. Just mom... just Grey's way of telling me what I was... what she made me. A geneblight. A freak."

"Taylor," Kairo says, but I cut him off.

"No, I am. It's like I'm some leech of magic, stealing from those around me." I stare at them, expecting someone to step away, to be fearful that I'm drawing from them somehow.

"I don't think that's how it works," Lirion says kindly.

"Do we really have any idea how any of this works, Lirion?" Gael asks. "You haven't read the same lore I have. You're thinking like a doctor, but this is my world we're talking about here. And the ancient mystics say that bad things happen when you fuck with magic."

At a loss, I look to Eiran, hoping he'll say something.

Please tell me I'm not a freak. Say the right thing, like you always do. Make me feel better.

But he keeps that damn mask of calm in place. It doesn't fool me. I see the roiling emotions in his eyes, but he's not touching me anymore. I know it's because he's giving me the space I asked for, but I can't stop the nagging voice telling me it's because he's revolted by me.

If he's not, he should be.

Before I can find anything halfway intelligent to say, Kairo adds, "There's more."

Because of course there fucking is.

I turn slowly back to Kairo, not sure I can take "more." But it's not me he's looking at now. "Eiran," he says. "There are references to Blackstone in this. He was Grey's contact at Helix."

Eiran goes lethally still. In a deadly tone, he says, "What?"

Everyone looks to the ground, avoiding this moment. They all know what this means. In some weird, fucked-up way—Eiran was right all along.

Willingly or not, intentionally or not, I've been working for Helix my whole life. A product of two Helix operatives, one of whom killed his brother.

Ears ringing strangely, I manage, "But if Blackstone knew my mom, if my mom was working with Helix… why would they need me now? Why would they need my blood?" I ask, confusion breaking through my trance. "Shouldn't they know everything already?"

"That's a good question," agrees Gael.

"You know what's a better one?" Eiran says, his tone a mix of surprise, rage, and dawning horror. "Is The Vale Effect connected to why Helix wants the enhanced seeds? And does it tie to the Eldralume theft?"

I stare down at my claws, extending them with a flick. Was Eiran right again?

Could this all tie back to me?

"Actually," Gael says hesitantly. "I have something that may help shed some light on this."

32

THE LUMINAR ESSENCE

Eiran

"You're going to wear a hole in the floor," Lirion says to his sister. Gael paces across the room, her mumbling blending with the odd rumbling of the various gadgets. Her footsteps squeak on the old wooden planks, a soft, abrasive rhythm that's like a thorn in my brain.

Yet there's something strangely familiar in the scene. I glance at my onetime best friend, and Lirion gives me a quick grin. It's the closest to a friendly glance from him in years.

"Yeah, Gael," I say, slipping into the old conversation pattern. "You've walked a mile and not gotten anywhere. Maybe less pacing and more talking."

"She'd have to open her mouth to do that," Lirion replies, looking up from the weird shelf of electronic knickknacks. "And she looks like she might throw up. You know how she gets stage fright."

"That happened *once*," Gael says hotly, and Lirion laughs.

The exchange is like an apparition from a past life, an echo of a different man with a different center of gravity.

I can't help but look at Taylor, still a magnet I can't escape. She leans against an ancient, human-made music player and raises an eyebrow, confused.

I raise the corner of my mouth in an apologetic smile. "We were all in this drama class during our freshman year of college. No clue what insanity led us to take a drama class, but—"

Lirion laughs again, and Gael grimaces. "Do we have to tell this story?"

"Anyway," I say, ignoring her, wanting to share this part of me with Taylor. To bring a touch of light after so much heaviness. "Gael got stage fright something *terrible*. Threw up backstage. Got it all over her costume—and the stage manager. Gods, it stank."

I just said, "Gods." I guess even Taylor's expletives have slipped into my vocabulary now.

Taylor smiles at the story, trying to laugh along, but her gaze keeps slipping to the pitted wooden floor, her shoulders hunching from the weight of it all. It makes me want to close the space between us, to shoulder some of it for her.

My frown returning, I give Gael a small glare. "Okay, seriously. What did you find?"

"Right," she says, looking a little sheepish. "Sorry. With what you've told me about Taylor's mother—"

"Dr. Grey," Taylor says flatly. "She wasn't my mom."

The words are so soft, so straight, yet edged sharp enough to draw blood. I wince at the impact. I think of my mother. She wasn't perfect, but at least I had someone. Had my parents and Wynn and Roderic and Maelara. She just had her mom… and now even that wasn't real.

I want to go to her. To hold her. But I doubt she'd let me. Not when she's too busy trying to convince herself that all the time we spent together doesn't matter. So, I look away. Look back at Gael, hoping somewhere in that big brain lies an answer. A way to put this shit behind us.

There's a long pause after Taylor's words. Finally, Gael says, "Right. Sorry. I'm trying to organize my thoughts here. It was confusing even before this news about Dr. Grey and Helix—" She trails off into silence.

My eyes return to Taylor then. Drawn to her yet again. The smooth mask is back, but she can't hide the pain behind that detached smirk and "give no shits" posture. Not with me. Not anymore.

"Why don't you tell us, and then we can *help* figure out what it means?" Kairo suggests, sounding exasperated.

"Right. Right." Gael nods to herself, and then says, "Okay. Sorry, this is a lot." She finally stops pacing and turns. "Why are outsiders not allowed in Aelfswelth Forest?"

We blink at her. What sort of question is that?

"Because it's sacred?" Lirion replies, clearly confused.

"Yes, but why?" Gael prompts.

Kairo ruffles his wings, clearly not enjoying being treated like one of Gael's university students. "The eldertrees."

Gael points at him excitedly, seeming surprised. "Exactly. What's so special about the eldertrees? Why are they sacred?"

"The luminar essence, right?" I raise an eyebrow at Gael. Turning to Taylor, I explain, "The luminar essence makes the forest glow. The bioluminescence is believed to have many mystical properties. But what's the connection to the Eldralume Relic?"

"I'm getting there. I'm getting there," Gael says. She continues pacing around the back room of the bookstore, wheels turning in her head as the smell of oil and rusty metal hangs heavy in the space. "Okay, so the Aether is the magical connection between all things, right? Mystics say the luminar essence is the 'physical manifestation of the Aether.' But what does that mean? What does the luminar essence actually do?"

"It glows," Lirion shrugs.

Gael gives her brother a baleful glare. "Other than that."

"Didn't you say it makes it easier to use magic?" Taylor asks me, my neck sweating at a single glance. With all the news hitting her today, maybe she's forgotten to push me away.

The words from the stryder earlier still echo in my head. *Things that don't matter.*

Fuck that. They matter, damn it. And I'll make her remember. We'll sort the rest out.

"Yeah," I reply past the lump in my throat. "That's what the mystics say, and it seems to be true. You probably noticed it when we were at…" I trail off, realizing it's not a good idea to mention the Lorathar lab.

Sure enough, the brief light in Taylor's eyes shudders, and she says faintly, "Yes. I did."

My fingers twitch, desperate to reach for her, to smooth that hurt look away.

"Right," Gael says, redirecting the conversation back to the topic at hand. "The luminar essence enhances magical ability."

"You're talking about it like it's a real thing," Lirion says, looking incredulously at Gael. "It's just mysticism."

"It's real, Lirion," Gael breathes. She turns to me and says, "What was the Eldralume for?"

"It unlocks the secrets of the Aether," I say, nodding.

"Yes," she says. "And it's because it *contains* luminar essence."

Kairo scoffs at the suggestion. "But how could it—"

Gael overrides him. "I've been reading, and what I've discovered is... the luminar essence is... they're microbes. *Magical* microbes. Powerfully magical. They live in the roots of the eldertrees, and they enhance the magical environment around them. At some point in antiquity, the mystics figured out how to harness the essence. Capture it. They housed some in the Eldralume Relic, left untouched and preserved. The rest... the rest have been cultured. Made more... *powerful*."

"Are you trying to tell me..." I ask, horror dawning, "...that they've taken the luminar essence... and turned it into powerseeds?"

"I'm afraid so," Gael says. "When the microbes die, they release a burst of magical energy. And it powers everything. The essence that's in commercially available powerseeds has been crafted over centuries through careful hybridization. No genetic engineering, of course. Just good old-fashioned breeding. But there are limits to that."

"Enter our friends at The Lorathar Initiative," Lirion mutters, and Taylor shudders. I give her my best comforting smile, but I'm not sure it's making it through the fog.

"So, the enhanced seeds. That's why The Initiative wanted Grey?" Kairo asks. "She helped them make the essence even more magically powerful? Bigger boom when the microbes die?"

"Which again," Gael reminds, "is extremely dangerous if you believe the lore."

Taylor frowns, cocking her head at Gael. "Okay, I'm confused. Even setting aside the class on elvish mysticism I've just been forced to take, I don't understand. Why would Helix want the Eldralume Relic? Eiran, are you sure this is about a bomb?"

The question is like drowning in ice. Could I have been wrong?

"What else would it be?" I ask, my voice barely audible even to myself. If I'm wrong about this... we have no clue what they're doing. How are we supposed to stop them before—

"Maybe Helix needed a control," Lirion says just softly.

The question snaps me out of the mounting gloom. "What?"

"A control," he repeats, and I'm reminded that my childhood friend is not just a local doctor. At his heart, Lirion is a scientist. "If they had the seeds and a control, a sample of untreated luminar essence… they'd be able to reverse engineer centuries of genetic development."

"Genetic development," Gael adds, "that made living creatures unimaginably magically powerful."

Lirion nods. "And if they had that… and they had you…" he says to Taylor. Fuck. I glare at Lirion, willing him to shut up.

"The leap from microbes to people wouldn't be hard," Gael adds, her mind lost in the puzzle of it all. "The Eldralume Relic and modified seeds explain how to make someone more magically powerful. The Vale Effect tells them how to use the magic of another species. Of all of them. Put those together…"

"And humans become the most magically powerful species in the galaxy," Taylor finishes, her eyes wide with devastation. "That's what they want. They want the Vale Effect. But better. Or worse, depending on how you look at it. They want their experiment back."

Gael and Lirion seem to realize the effect their words are having on Taylor, but it's too late. Taylor's vacant, desperate eyes ruin me. Something inside me shatters and crudely reforms, the pieces coming back together in ragged lines. I'm all sharp edges.

"So… what now?" Gael asks.

In a voice I don't recognize, I say, "Now, Taylor hides."

A pause stretches thin, a beat too long before Taylor's devastation hardens into fury. "No way in hell."

Glad some fire is back but hating how her mouth is freezing in that stubborn curl it gets. "Taylor…" I try.

"No, Eiran."

I stare at her, pleading but hopeless. "Taylor, if they get your blood—"

"They already have it," Kairo points out.

I turn to Taylor, trying one last time, my heart racing as the fear threatens to break its leash. "I know that. But what if they need more? What if—"

"I said no," she replies flatly. "Unless you want to tie me down— and we both know I'll just break out—then you'll need to work with me."

A memory of a penthouse bed and vines around wrists comes to mind, and my blood heats.

Her breath catches for a second at my look, but she quickly recovers, that thief mask back in place. "I bet Isra has the relic. I bet there's some sort of lab inside that prison, and she's in there doing some sort of experiments on it. I need your help to stop her. We need to bring Helix down. For what they did to Kaelen. For what they did to me. Hell, for what they did to fucking *Blackstone*. He may be a monster, but they're the ones who made him. I know a little something about that."

"You're not a monster, Taylor," I reply, permitting no disagreement in my tone. Doesn't she realize how incredible she is? How brave and kind?

Her tightened lips say she doesn't, but thankfully she doesn't argue either. I have the time to convince her. Make her understand her worth. What she means to me.

Shrugging, she says, "Well, either way, Helix has a lot to answer for. And I kind of *like* the galaxy, so I guess I'd rather not see it get destroyed in some interstellar war."

The humor in her tone, however half-hearted, sends a flood of relief. "So that's still the plan, then?" I ask, crossing my arms and smirking back at her. "Get the relic back from Isra and see if she leads us to Blackstone?"

Taylor nods once.

"Any ideas on how to do that?" I raise an eyebrow at her, already knowing the answer.

For the first time in days, a true grin spreads wide across Taylor's face. One I return. "Oh yes. I have a few."

33

DINNER AND A SHOW OF FORCE

Taylor

It took longer than it should have, given Kairo's claim that Darrow has a "soft spot for attractive males," but he finally secured a date with the infamous wolf shifter. This might be our one chance to separate her from that case she takes everywhere, so I'm glad we got it worked out, though it had more to do with a clever glamour, an staged meet-cute at the tea shop, and a dash of Frank's psychic help than any innate charm of Kai's.

After a day of doing… whatever she does at the prison, Isra heads back to the hotel to change. An hour later, she emerges, finally separated from that damn case, on her way to dinner with a disguised Kairo.

It'll probably be half an hour at least before she realizes he's not coming.

"Okay, she's heading to the restaurant," Kairo says over the in-ear comms. "I'll keep tailing her. You three, make this quick."

"Got it," I say, glancing at Eiran and Frank. The little Quiblin nods once, uncharacteristically serious.

Silent as death, we hurry to Isra's room. Frank puts a long, knobby-fingered hand on the door, closing his eyes. A small burst of electricity sparks from his fingers into the crack in the door, and moments later, there's a click as it swings open. "I've been practicing!" Frank beams with a tiny hiss, and I wink at him.

Eiran leads us inside. Frank's fingers fly over the keys, and a moment later, he nods. I'm not sure if that means there aren't cameras or that he's disabled whatever ones are here. Either way, I take it to mean we're good to continue.

We spread out to explore. Little adorns the space beyond the usual bed, nightstand, and holo display. Fanning tendrils from a large plant creep from the ceiling in the corner of the otherwise sterile room.

Despite being here for weeks, she's still living out of her suitcase. Eiran checks it anyway, rummaging through Isra's undergarments with an ease that makes me, frankly, a tad uncomfortable.

In the middle of the room, dropped off somewhat haphazardly, is the rolling case. I nod for Frank to go check it out. The Quiblin closely eyes the box, which is nearly as large as he is. There's a large screen on the side, normally dark, that is glowing an ominous red.

Frank leans close to read the display and then sighs. "This is not good."

Eiran and I exchange a look. "What's not good, Frank?" Eiran asks.

"Biometrics. Genetic," Frank says, and Eiran curses.

I run for the bathroom as Eiran says over the comms, "Kairo, we might need a bio sample."

"Hold on!" I call. "I'm checking toiletries here first."

To my surprise—though perhaps it shouldn't be much of one—Isra's toothbrush and hairbrush are clinically clean. A UV cleaner, illegal in the Valen Republic, sits on the counter. No DNA to be had here.

"Ugh," I groan. "No dice."

"Then Kairo," Eiran says, "you'll need to figure out a way to—"

"It wouldn't matter," Frank says, eyes still on the box. "It also has a geolocation lock."

I sigh. "So it will only open at a preset location. Likely some safe space."

"The prison," Eiran says.

"Can you bypass it?" I ask Frank.

He shakes his head. "It requires a passcode, and I doubt Ms.

Darrow will give it to you, ma'am."

I groan. "And the anti-intrusion enchantments would destroy whatever's inside if we try to brute force it. Plus, likely kill us in the process. Wonderful." I knew it couldn't be this easy. "Do you think the relic is inside the case?" I ask Eiran.

"Maybe. Regardless, we need to get inside that prison."

"The problem is, we don't know where she goes. You tracked her to those secure doors, but once she goes past them, we don't know what sort of security we'll face. And since you can't get us into the secure area with your guard access—"

"The box could tell us," Frank chimes in. "It goes through security every day."

Eiran sighs. "Frank, how is a box going to—"

"We add a bug," I say, getting Frank's point. "Something to record its movements, detect tech around it as it goes through checkpoints. Do you have something like that, Frank?"

"No," Frank says with a shake of his ears. "But I can make one quickly." He glances at the holo-display. "Is there one of those in Mr. Ryūkishi's room?"

"There is," I grin, knowing Kairo will be pissed once he finds out Frank has cannibalized his holo display for one of his gadgets.

"Give me fifteen minutes," Frank says. With that, he disappears through the door.

"She's leaving the restaurant," Kairo says urgently over the comms.

"Shit," I groan. "Kai, you need to intercept her. Tell her you're so sorry. You got busy at work. You know the drill."

"Like she'll go for that," Kairo growls.

"We need a couple of minutes," I insist. "Make her slap you if that's what it takes. Be a pushy asshole. You're good at that. Just buy us time. As much as you can."

Despite the urgency of the situation, Eiran laughs. "I think you enjoy torturing him."

"It's how I show my love," I say.

"Well, you must *really* love me, then," Eiran snarks—then sputters. "I mean—"

My cheeks burn at the slip, but I rush to the door, watching for Frank. Too many minutes later, the tiny gray male comes bouncing down the hall toward me, a misshapen disc in his hand.

"This should do it," Frank says. Pulling out a tool, he quickly removes the cover from one of the boxes protruding from the side of the case, revealing a mess of wires and control boards. Frank slips the disk in amidst the control boards and then closes the case back. He flashes a Union-style thumbs up.

We rush down the hall toward Kairo's room. Just as we reach the door, the elevator chimes. There's no time. We're all exposed.

Without warning, Eiran grabs me. He shoves Frank against the door, hiding him from view. Wordlessly, he grips my neck and draws my face to his.

Eiran's mouth crushes against mine as the elevator doors open, and he turns our heads so our faces are out of sight. His lips are soft and inviting; the feel of him is strong against me. His hands hold my face, and he cups my cheeks like I'm the most precious prize he's ever held. I run a tongue against his lips, loving the taste of him and wanting more, wanting him deeper.

But he pulls away. "I think she's gone," he mutters, sounding out of breath.

I remember Frank as he clears his throat. "Yes. She's in the room now. Getting a strong signal." Eiran motions toward the door, and we walk through it, my thoughts spiraling.

Shit, shit, shit. I'm supposed to be staying away from him! Wynn said I need to stay away from him. But that kiss… it was so…

No, I can't think about that. I just need to forget the most amazing kiss of my life.

"Sorry," Eiran spits out, his back as straight as a board. He certainly doesn't look like his world's just been rocked by a planet-shattering kiss. He looks… uncomfortable. "I didn't mean to do that without warning. It was the only cover I could work on short notice."

Right. It was a cover. Just a cover. I've kissed people as part of a job before. I'm a professional. I can do this. Pull yourself together, Taylor!

"No problem." I give my best attempt at a reassuring smile. "That was quick thinking."

"I mean… I know you said to focus on the mission. It's just that when I'm around you… it's hard."

I let my eyes drop, and in a quiet tone say, "I noticed." His eyes widen in a mix of shock and desire.

"Did you get anything?" Kairo walks in, harried and rubbing his cheek.

Eiran pulls away in a breath, leaving a cold emptiness in his wake.

"We planted a tracer," I say, recovering quickly. "We'll need to be inside the prison to open it. Frank put together a brilliant little tracer that will record the security checkpoints and let us know what we're up against."

Kairo looks at Frank, appearing impressed. "Great. So, Plan B is a go, then?"

"Yep," I say. "You ready?"

Kairo groans. "I'm more of a 'work from the shadows' kind of person. I don't enjoy being the center of attention."

Eiran chuckles. "Somehow, that doesn't fit my understanding of you at all."

Kairo shakes his head but doesn't disagree. Then, he glances around the room. "Where's my holo-display?"

34

CAUGHT IN THE ACT

Taylor

"B Team, come in! Do you read me, B Team? Kai?" All I hear is static. I look pleadingly at Frank, who frowns, typing away at his screen.

It took a few days to set things up—particularly Eiran. Still, the initial infiltration went off well. Kairo pulled off a huge illusion in the prison parking lot: a traveling circus with performers behind a velvet rope. The guards went over to investigate and tell Kairo to leave, and the rest of us slipped silently past using Eiran's access card. Once inside, though, the comms went down, leaving us unable to reach Kairo for our exit or Eiran for the next phase.

"I do not know, Miss," Frank says as he types away at his comm. "I can't get a signal through, which makes no sense. We—"

I cut him off. "Perhaps it's interference from the prison comm systems." I glance from Frank to Gael, hoping he understands my point. Eiran tested that several times, but Gael doesn't need more to freak about.

"How are we supposed to coordinate our extraction strategy without comms?" she asks in a rush as her eyes dart around the corridor.

We huddle in a tiny corner of the prison section under renovation, trying to determine what to do. I need to calm her quickly. "We have a plan," I try to inject calm into my voice, although I'm unnerved by the sudden interruption in our comms too. "Clock started when we lost comms. We have two… well, one hour, fifty-eight minutes, and thirteen seconds until he will be set up and waiting to help in our escape."

"Okay," Gael says, voice shaking a bit. "But how do we contact Eiran?"

"Hey! Who goes there?" We all jump as a tall Valen guard looms through a nearby door and enters the dark hallway, silhouetted by the lights of the prison block beyond. I prepare to attack when the figure comes more into view, wearing a trim uniform and an ear-mounted mic.

I sigh. It's Eiran.

"Convicts aren't allowed in this area." He nods to a nearby duffel, and we scramble to don the bright yellow jumpsuits. While Eiran's earlier recon confirmed there are no cameras in the wing while under renovation, his ear-mount comm is still always on and monitored.

When I finish getting dressed, I walk up to him, and he grasps my hand and mouths, "You good?" I nod and wink, and to my surprise, his dimply grin deepens briefly before his all-business mask returns. "Come on, you three. Get your asses in here now."

"Yes, sir," we all say in unison. Just as we practiced.

Eiran grabs Gael and me, Frank leading the way. "I'm afraid it's solitary for you three, sneaking off like that. Two days in the hole. Each. That'll teach you to run off to areas you don't belong."

We walk through the doors and into the prison at large. It looks nothing like the prisons I've seen on holovids, and yet… it's undeniably a prison. We walk along a raised awning, the clear doors of the cells we pass left half-open. High above us, way out of reach of the prisoners, vines and ferns hang from planters, giving life to the otherwise impersonal space.

The prisoners in the low-security wing walk around unescorted, some sitting in their cells listening to music or watching holovids, while others eat, work out, or read in the open commons area below us. Only the burly, well-armed guards make it clear that these are prisoners.

When we reach the end of the corridor, Eiran takes us down a flight of steps and into the mass of "less dangerous" criminals. I'm trying not to panic, not to dwell on where we are. But the silence is killing me.

This is too real. In a way, I've been in cages my whole life. Whether it was the lab or the multicultural district of Vaeloria City… I've always felt trapped. And now we're in a literal prison, the worst version of my nightmares. My palms itch with the impulse to bolt.

As we walk past inmates sitting to eat, Eiran gives me a little shake and says to another guard, "I caught these three in the remodel area."

"Is that right, convict?" the other guard says to me, his tall, broad frame looming even over Eiran. "You need to be… punished for that."

Eiran stiffens for one second at the insinuation, an echo of my own horror, but he says, "I'm taking them to the hole. You can find them later if you want." The guard grins, and I'd really like to punch his teeth in.

Eiran's own grin sharpens almost imperceptibly. "But really, you should thank your buddy, Anton. He's the one who gave me the tip." He nods to a tall, thickly muscular human sitting at a nearby table. The prisoner and his three human tablemates wrench their heads around. Eiran motions to the table with his head, not turning to look at them. "You were right," he says to the guard. "He's been a significant source of info. And cheap too."

"I didn't say nothing to no one," the prisoner says, kicking his chair back as he stands.

A nearby table of large Valen inmates stands as well, the biggest and ugliest of the bunch, saying, "You're the one that turned me in? I'm going to kick your ass."

"No!" the human insists, turning purple. "Did you tell him I was a snitch?!" he yells at the guard. "You tell him. You tell him I didn't say anything."

"You're mine, pinky," the Valen prisoner says, launching himself at the human as he launches at the guard. The large Valen misses him completely, and there's a tangled mess of green-skinned bodies as he collides with another table. Several people are throwing punches now, and alarms blare from somewhere. Eiran grips my arm firmly and leads the four of us toward a far set of doors.

As we make it through, we come across the black, nondescript entrance to the prison's mental ward, two guards standing out front.

"Riot!" Eiran calls as he passes them, making to head farther down the hallway. "You'd better get out there! I'll stick these three in solitary and then meet you." The guards glance at each other, and then run toward the screams.

Eiran pulls us farther along the hallway until the guards are out of sight. When the coast is clear, we rush back to the abandoned door. Frank rushes forward, his spindly fingers flying across the keypad by the door. There's a loud beep, and the large sliding door opens with a too-fast swoosh. Gael steps through, then Frank. I go next, and then Eiran moves to follow us.

Without warning, the door slams shut right in his stunned face, blocking him from view.

"Get it open!" I yell at Frank.

Eiran pounds on the thick door. I can barely hear him shouting. "Taylor!"

"Hold on, Eiran! Come on, Frank," I plead.

The Quiblin's fingers fly over the keypad on his screen, a frown deepening. "I… I can't. I'm sorry. The door is locked out. It's a one-way passage. Must be a security protocol. You exit on the other side, or—"

"Guys," Gael says in a strange tone, her finger on a biotech interface on the wall. "I can't see the grid."

I round on her. "What?" Fear, like cold water, trickles down my spine. "Eiran checked that."

"Mr. Valtir has guard-level access," Frank says in a soft tone. "Dr. Beutwinn does not."

"Well, give it to her," I say, my voice severe from tension.

Frank shakes his head. "I do not have time to hack the security level permissions. It's why Mr. Valtir infiltrated this place to begin with. If I had a week…"

"Then get the door open." I turn away from him before Frank can respond. I know he's doing all he can. But the last time things fell apart like this? It was the Harmonix Crystal job.

"Taylor!" Eiran cries, banging on the door.

Stop it. Focus on the issue at hand. "Go find Kairo!" I call through the door. "Meet us at the exit. We've got this." There are three more violent pounds on the steel door, and then silence.

"Hopefully he listens," Gael mutters.

"Alright." I turn back to the room and start talking it out, though the heat from the intense skin-searing beams is making me sweat, muddling my thinking. "There's a button to disable the lasers. But you need to hold it the whole time. And it's biotech, so we can't magick it from here. We'll need to traverse the grid somehow."

I reach into my bag and pull out a small tin of hand chalk. I blow on the tin, and the stream of lasers momentarily comes into view before the cloud of dust dissipates. I glance at Frank, and he nods, understanding. After a breath, I toss the chalk into the air, and Frank catches the cloud with magic. Slowly, he spreads it into a fine haze that fills the space, revealing a tight web of laser beams.

"Okay," Gael says hesitantly. "That helps, but the floor has pressure sensors. It's not like you could climb your way through. Could you fly through?"

I try not to grumble at the negativity. "We can figure this out. To answer your question, no. They're too close together. But there must be another way."

"Right," Gael says, pacing as well, breaking the problem down. Gone is the scared young woman from earlier. Now she's in her element. Solving puzzles. Besides her historical knowledge, it's her best asset. She finally stops and turns to one of the hanging plants by the door, frowning. Although you couldn't have any plant life in the actual laser grid, leave it to elves to stick them at each end. "If I had Eiran's ability, I could use one of the plants over there."

"You could do that with a biosensor?" I ask, surprised.

"Sure," she shrugs. "You can send your mental signal down the plant to the sensor. If it's alive and touching the sensor, it'll work. But it doesn't help us. I can't do what he can."

"How *does* he control plants without touching them?" I ask, although I know it's not the right time.

She shrugs. "No clue, honestly. I have some theories, but they're conjecture at this point. I'm still doing research. But at any rate, I can't do it. I am still stuck with touching the plants."

I nod to the plants near us. "Use them."

Gael laughs. "And navigate that without hitting a beam? Not likely."

"I'll help," I say. "You grow them, make them as rigid as you can, and I'll guide you and support it with magic. Frank, are you good holding the cloud of dust a while longer?"

Frank gives an affirmative shake of his ears.

Gael grins at us. "You know? This might work."

"Don't get ahead of yourself," I say. "Game faces, everyone." They both nod, and Gael moves over to a shrub of a plant with spindly branches and small, silvery leaves.

"Alright," Gael says. "Let's do this." She touches a branch, and a tendril snakes out from the bush, flitting through the beams. It goes slowly at first, but soon we get into our rhythm, the branch dancing between the beams in graceful arcs.

When we reach the other side of the room, Gael moves the branch at a determined pace, encouraging it to grow smoothly, straight to the biotech interface. One leaf grazes the surface of the metal disc, and then a few moments later, the beams turn off.

"Well done, Gael!" I cheer in a loud whisper. "That was amazing."

"I guess we work well together," she shrugs. "Who knew?"

Once we cross, we break the branch down, and then pull off our prisoner garb, stashing it as best we can. Straightening the white nurse uniforms we had underneath the prisoner wear, we head into the psych ward.

***

It's the most un-elvish space I've seen on Vale. No plants. No wood surfaces. No life. Just cold metal walls, a warm brown glow barely lighting the space. I wonder if the lack of stone or organic material is by design. The last thing you'd want is someone using magic here.

The air is thick, stale, and tastes faintly of antiseptic and rust. An eerie silence hangs heavy, broken only by the faint, mechanical hum of unseen systems. It's as if the very walls are watching — cold, unfeeling, and utterly devoid of mercy.

We pass through the first metal door, marked with a long series of nondescript Valen numbers. I step closer, and beyond, there's a soft scraping noise, like branches against a windowpane. I step away, glancing nervously at Gael and Frank.

We continue our progress too slowly, and I can't help but wonder why there isn't enough light in here. The shadows twitch and stretch, swallowing the edges of the hallway like hungry mouths.

Or maybe that's my imagination.

Bang! Something heavy launches itself against a nearby door, and we jump.

Maniacal chuckling emanates from the next door down. *"Hehe. Hehehehehe!* They are coming. *Hehehehe.* The whispers… *Hehehehe…"*

I wrench my eyes from the door and jump. A dark silhouette fills the end of the hallway, looming. Gliding forward.

A nurse.

Frank twitches a finger, and they walk on, barely noticing us.

How do we find Darrow in this maze? We explore blindly, turning this way and that until the corridor dumps out into a large space so horribly familiar that Gael and Frank both grab me before I can collapse or bolt.

It's a lab, with that sickening sterile scent that brings up flashes of things I wish I could keep forgetting. Animals sit in metal cages, and something short and snakelike is floating in a large cylindrical tank. Gael squeezes my hand. "You okay?"

I nod, pushing past my fear.

Isra is here, her back to us. The attractive wolf shifter is hunched over a microscope, a tall Valen standing next to her explaining something in low tones. And there, in the middle of the floor, is the rolling case, the lid open to reveal a large, strange wooden box.

Eying Isra and the box. Gael creeps over to the nearby set of cages. I reach out to grab her, but she darts away. In one cage, there's a sage hare, its long, pale green ears barely discernible. It's curled into a ball, apparently asleep. Gael places a finger against the animal's side, closing her eyes in concentration. After several moments, she steps away, frowning. She motions for us to move out of sight.

"Okay," she breathes into my ear. "I don't know what they've done to that hare, but it didn't feel normal. But it should still work. Open the door to that cage." I nod, unsure of what she's planning. Mentally, I search across the space, trying to concentrate only on detecting the feel of the lock, suppressing a shudder as mental fingers trace over the shape of an injector gun. With a gasp of relief, I find the lock and slide it open.

A second later, there's a flurry of motion and sound as the animal awakes, jumps out of the cage and starts leaping around the room, knocking over papers and metal vials. Darrow and the Valen doctor shout in surprise. With a scrabbling of claws against metal, the sage hare rushes through the right-side door. Darrow and the doctor are quick on its heels.

In a rush, we run over to the case. Even together, we barely lift the heavy wooden box out of it.

Setting it on a nearby table, Gael lets out a groan. "Well… this complicates things."

"What is it?" I ask, stepping closer to the ornately engraved case.

"It's a Gruundlith puzzle box," she says, frowning. "It's original, not a remake. The box itself is an important artifact. And inside—"

"Hold on," I say. "I couldn't sense anything through the case, since it's built with modern tech and enchantments, but this…" I reach out with my magic, letting it trace between the cracks in the box. After a second, I can feel it. Familiar curving wood, and beyond that, a heart of strong crystal. I glance at Frank, who's also checking the contents of the box. He nods. "It's in there," I agree, and the idea that the relic is so close sends my nerves tingling. "We need to get inside. Can you crack it?" I ask as the sound of footsteps comes from the nearby hallway.

"With these enchantments…" There's a slight pause, and then she concludes firmly, "Yes. But this will take some time."

A moan trails in from the right-side hallway, sending the hairs rising on my neck. Frank and I turn, trying to block the much-taller Gael as through the door walk Darrow and the scientist.

THE SCANNER

Taylor

The pair don't see us at first, their focus trained on a bleeding wound on the doctor's leg. "Why did you have to kill it?" Darrow says in a sharp, dangerous tone.

"The bloody thing bit me!" the scientist says in an odd accent that marks him as being from the southern continent. "What did you expect me to—"

"That's why we have the VerdantBoost, you—"

I send Darrow flying into the far wall. The doctor yells, turning to run. Frank stretches out his spindly gray fingers, and the doctor freezes mid-step. Frank drops his chin, his face going as chilly and determined as I've ever seen as he holds the doctor there.

Darrow's jaws lengthen, hair growing up her neck and onto her face as she starts to shift. With a huge magical shove, I pin her against the back wall.

I growl to Gael through gritted teeth. "Get that lock open!"

"I'm on it," she snaps back, sounding distracted and annoyed.

I take a slow, steadying breath, forcing my panic down under the roaring surface of my emotions. I have to trust Gael has it handled.

Darrow's lip curls in a sneer, revealing long, glistening canines. "Grey," she says, her voice barely recognizable beneath the snarling overtones. "Took you long enough."

My gut twists at the words, but I press her farther into the row of cabinets, a huff of pain cracking her demeanor.

"The fuck does that mean?"

I don't care about the answer. Anything she says can't be good and will probably be a lie, anyway. But we need to stall them to give Gael time. We may have them pinned down for now, but it won't last.

"Did you think I didn't notice Kairo?" she sneers, her clawed paws reaching and scraping against invisible bonds. "I'm a shifter. I'm good at detecting who lies beneath… physical changes."

"So, all of this…" I say, horrified.

"A trap?" she shrugs. "Pretty much."

"*Don't believe her, Miss,*" Franks says in my head. "*The artifact is in the box. You said so yourself. And this trap doesn't appear to be going well.*"

Guy's got a point. What's the goal of this exactly? I take a step closer, trying to ignore the prick of pain in the back of my head as I continue to press her against the wall, fighting against her increasingly violent attempts to break my hold.

"How's it coming, Gael?"

I glance briefly to find both her hands on the box. Pieces of it spiral off and then back on as she fits them back together in different ways using magic.

"Almost… got it…"

Darrow takes advantage of my momentary distraction, breaking free to lurch forward, claws and teeth flashing. I struggle to regain control of my magic, but before I can, Darrow flies back again, her wolfen arms and legs now pinned as well. Her furry head slams at an odd angle, and she blinks in surprise. Apparently, that's all she can do. "I do not think so, Miss Darrow," Frank says.

The doctor, now free, starts to run—or rather limp—down the hallway, but with his bite, he's not able to go very fast. With a swipe of magic, I knock his good foot out from under him, sending him toppling. He groans and stays down.

I turn to the wolf shifter, who is growling now, looking nothing like the prim human she pretends to be. Drool drips from her fangs, yellow eyes glistening.

"Talk, Darrow. Why are you here? Why did you try to lure us?"

"Allow me to answer that," says a low voice like chains on sand.

A red laser sight traces along my chest, and I jump, but too late. A blaster shot to the shoulder sends me toppling, my side banging fiercely against a counter. I whimper, limping away from the cyborg trouncing in from the right-side passage. More blaster shots send bits of floor and Isra's case flying in all directions. Blackstone's red glowing eye stays trained on me, even as his other glances over to Gael.

This will not happen again.

"Taylor!" Frank says, and the use of my first name draws my focus. "Take Darrow." Before I can even comprehend what he's saying, the shifter drops and Blackstone is shoved back several feet, his heavy metal feet scraping long ruts into the ground.

"Frank! No!" I holler.

"Stop Darrow," he grunts, straining against Blackstone. "Help Gael."

There's no time to argue with the tiny Quiblin. Darrow leaps for him, but I jump in front. Grabbing her, I use my physical and magical strength to push her back. Long claws rake against my back, scraping along the fresh blaster wound on my shoulder.

Darrow leaps forward at me again, and I meet her claw for claw. All I can manage is a quick glance at Blackstone, who is rooted to the ground, body straining and head shaking as he fights off Frank's wind and psychic magic at once.

The image gives me an idea.

My claws dig into her arms until they run hot with blood. She howls with pain, and while she's distracted, I push out with my Gruundlith magic. Grappling with Darrow as a living being, I use my elven magic to send the command to sleep. To stop.

At the same time, I reach with magic. After a second, I can sense a roiling ball of words and images I'm not able to penetrate. I push against that ball with halfling magic, again pressing the idea that she is tired. That she needs to sleep. That she should stop.

Suddenly, there's a give in her defenses, like a buckling wall. Darrow slows for a moment, eyes fluttering. I press further, sending a spike of magic at her. Darrow shakes violently, and then collapses, eyes rolling into the back of her head. She continues to seize, head lolling and form returning to the humanoid female she was before.

Did… did I kill her? I push away the thought. With a heave that seems to take all of his considerable might, Blackstone takes a jolting step toward Frank. I raise a hand to help, but then Gael screams.

Shit! The box has grasped both her arms in long wooden tendrils carved to look like snakes. They begin to tighten, turning her normally green arms a dangerous shade of rusty brown. A third tendril has wrapped itself around her neck, and I see it beginning to squeeze as well.

"Trap," she gasps, and the vine condenses. "Torture… box…"

"Oh gods. Hold on!" I slam my hand against the wooden serpents, but to no avail. They're too thick. Frank yells in frustration, pushing back Blackstone. A trail of black blood trickles down the halfling's tiny nose.

I send a single shove on Blackstone's side, catching him unbalanced, and forcing him to lose a step. Frank takes the chance to press forward. I glance around the room, unsure what to do for Gael. I need an axe or something. Something to break these vines—

That's when I see it—a large container of VerdantBoost. From what Darrow said, they must be attempting to use it as a counteragent to whatever dark magic they're testing here. I grab the canister and run over to the sink.

Filling the half-full can of fertilizer with water, I close the lid and shake the mixture up. I run back to Gael. Her arms are almost black now, her face going a strange, pale shade. Without another word, I pour the entire canister over the puzzle box.

Nothing's happening! What am I… wait.

The tendrils loosen, flopping with a *thunk* onto the floor. There's a loud creak, and the puzzle box opens wide, revealing the Eldralume Relic.

Gael collapses, taking huge gasps as she points tremulously at Frank. I round on him, and see that Blackstone has the Quiblin by the neck. Strange, orangey blood is trickling out of Blackstone's nose and ears, his entire body shaking as he fights against Frank.

"Halfling… trash…" Blackstone manages through clenched teeth.

I turn to Gael, who is trying to stand, but I hear a sickening crunch. I snap my head back, expecting the worst, but Frank is still moving, still fighting. Black blood gushes from his large ears, but he's grimacing in determination.

The crunch came from Blackstone. He lets out an anguished scream as more orange blood pours from where, a moment ago, his one remaining human eye had been.

"Go! I'll buy you time," I yell to Gael, taking two shaky strides toward Blackstone. Ignoring me, she runs toward Frank, but there's nothing she can do. I grab her shirt, stopping her advance and pulling her to me. "GO!" I scream.

"I…" She hesitates. This is taking too long. "Come with—"

"Go," I plead. "Take the relic." At least she can get out.

Her flopping footsteps recede behind me, running for the recycling pickup that's our extraction point. I try to send a blast of magic at Blackstone, but I'm too weak. I've used too much.

Blood is rushing freely from my nose now, mingling with the red covering my shoulder and chest. Blackstone shakes slightly at the magical barrage, but never breaks his silent war with Frank.

I try to run forward to stop him, but I can't. My knees… my legs… I collapse on the ground.

"No…" I say, begging the gods, the Aether. I drag myself forward over debris, bits of glass and large chunks from the demolished case scraping my already wounded hands and stomach. My ears are ringing, my brain in a fog. Too far. I've pushed myself too far.

This can't be happening again.

I can't lose another one.

There's a crack. It's a quiet sound, barely audible over my own sobs. With an unceremonious thud of flesh, Blackstone tosses Frank's body aside.

"Now," he says, turning to me. "Let's get this done."

The scraps of glass crunch under Blackstone's steel heel as he plows inexorably forward, a looming inevitability. I scramble backward, hands trailing blood as shards bite into my skin.

Frank stares back at me, judging, his huge glassy eyes unseeing. My heart disintegrates, my insides rending themselves to pieces as thoroughly as this glass is rending my flesh. It's just like the Harmonix Crystal job. My insides go cold.

I always blamed Sylara for that, blamed her for what happened to Marcus.

The three of us went to steal a Quiblin artifact. Sylara split to create a distraction, but never returned.

She had an objective of her own.

I blamed her for that. For not being there when we got in a jam.

But maybe what happened to Marcus wasn't her fault. Maybe I'm the reason everyone around me gets hurt.

At least Gael made it out.

I'm sorry, Frank.

Steeling myself, I force myself to turn away from him, looking up to the cyborg who seems in no hurry. When he reaches down to grab me, my hands wrap around a stray bit of the demolished case. I grip it and swing the jagged edge wildly. There's a loud crack that reminds me sickeningly of opening a fenklau as Blackstone's stolen exoskeleton fractures.

The end of my makeshift weapon flies off, and I have a second to recognize what portion of the box I'm holding. I curl in on myself, going small. Fetal.

Hiding my hands.

Blackstone reaches out with his metal arm this time, and a steel finger digs into my shoulder, hauling me up, my legs dangling. I swing wildly with both arms, tearing at him as if I could somehow make him release me. Bits of the metal tear away, and black oil begins to trickle from somewhere.

I have no longer than a breath, a flicker of distraction, to slip the tiny board among the other loose bits of electronics in his arm. The next second, he's grabbing my shoulders with both hands, squeezing so hard I can feel my bones grinding against each other. I scream as he carries me over to slam me onto a long metal table, holding me with one hand as he straps me down.

This is too much. Too much. Past and present swim together in waves.

"Okay. Are we ready for the game, then?"

No. Not that. Stay in the now. The danger is now. Fall apart later.

Bound to the table, I can do nothing but holler. Blackstone hesitates for only a moment, and then leans down to my ear, his empty eye socket grazing my skin.

"I like the sound of your screams," he growls quietly. "But there are other people here, so…"

He grabs a large ball gag and shoves it into my mouth, chipping a tooth. I whimper, but it's barely audible around the gag.

"I thought we only needed the blood," Blackstone says—to me or to himself I'm not sure—as he walks over to a nearby stack of equipment. "But my master says that wasn't enough. The secret must be in the mind."

From the assortment of equipment, he brings out something that I buried so deep blocked it out. Something worse than needles. Worse than injector guns.

It's a scanner.

The strange device has a handle like an injector gun, but three flat discs on adjustable arms replace the injector barrel. I know what those metal discs will feel like. Cold and unyielding—like the walls of the lab. Like her eyes.

I'd forgotten. Forgotten the long hours my "mother" searched my brain, looking for… something. I didn't want to remember.

Blackstone walks back, and I shake my head furiously, my body trembling uncontrollably.

"No, no, no, no, no…" I mumble unintelligibly around the gag. I need to get away. Escape. I can't. I won't. This can't happen again. Never again. Never—

The bindings don't budge.

Tears sear my vision. Blackstone adjusts a few settings, face cold and unconcerned. Without ceremony, he presses the scanner to my head.

The discs are so cold—then the electricity comes.

Lightning frolics viciously through my skull. My muscles seize, arching me off the table. I black out, snap awake, then black out again.

This has to end, right? It's got to stop sometime.

Kill me. Please, just kill me. Don't do this anymore. Please, just…

Thoughts blur. Pain bleeds into pain.

After centuries, millennia, he stops. In steady, unhurried movements, he walks to a screen and studies the results.

"Yes," he says. "That will do nicely."

Blackstone glances over at me, considering. "I would love to kill you, you know? Just for the hell you put me through. But… the master says I should put you somewhere. Just in case."

I don't even have the strength to scream as he hauls me off the table and slings me over his shoulder. I hang like a corpse.

What's the point of fighting?

But wait… are we going to…

I shriek, clawing at his wings, his arms, his face. He holds me away from him. With little effort, he flings me into an empty cell. I slide across the floor and into the padded wall, my legs flipping over my head. I barely notice the pain in my neck.

I scramble upright in time to stare back in horror at the narrowing ray of light. With the faintest curling snarl, Blackstone slams the door closed.

I rush forward, collapsing against cold steel. My shuddering sobs echo in the empty cell.

The darkness presses in. Heavy. Suffocating.

Alone.

PART 5

THE BLACKSTONE JOB

i hate the dark
too crowded, too loud
in the silence
—*The Journal of Taylor Grey*

36

NEVER ALONE

Taylor

"What's wrong, my starflower?"

"It hurts, Momma. The scanner hurts."

My mother tuts softly. *"It's just a headache, dear. But it's important, remember? I need to do the scanner a little more. Then we can play the game."*

She's right. It's always better when I obey. When I'm a good girl. She gets so happy and smiles and makes it all better. She'll—

Stop. Stay in the now.

I rake my claws against the padded floor, and the burning pull against my nails snaps me out of the memory. Glaring down at the brown fabric meant to mimic soil, I see a minuscule tuft of white. The texture's wrong—soft but faintly greasy. Like it absorbed every touch, every tear, for years.

I dig at the tiny spot, flashing talons ripping and tearing through the thick cloth.

There's a satisfying wrench as I rip a huge gash in the russet surface. I yank out the soft padding in great clumps, heart racing. A way out. There has to be a way out below this—

I stop, staring blankly at the smooth steel subfloor. I bang on its unforgiving metal again and again and again with every ounce of my Enhanced strength. Shrieking into the emptiness, pain streaks up my arm. There's a wet pop deep in my wrist, and my vision whites out.

There's not even a dent.

I moan, clutching my wrist as I curl into a ball in the tiny divot. The cool steel is strangely comforting. I burrow myself into the nest I've made, finally still.

There's no point in crying. I've spilled a lifetime of tears on this floor, and none of them helped. Nothing and no one helped, but… I thought Eiran would have. Or Kairo.

At first, I had wild fantasies of them coming for me, saving me, but… no. No one's getting in here. And why would they try?

I'm trapped. Alone again. Where I belong.

"*I'm always with you, dear,*" my mother says, tucking my red curls behind my pointed ear. She runs a hand along its pointed edge, gazing lovingly into my young face. "*Where would I go? I'm your mother. I'm always here. Now, come on. Try one more time.*"

Okay, Momma.

Screaming, I send a burst of magic hurling outward, electricity arcing in every direction. Azure bolts scrape along the green padded walls. Lightning claws furrow into the false protection, revealing the steel cage beneath. Tufts of singed fluff float like raven feathers, covering the world in a soft blanket of stuffing and ash.

Coating me. Burying me.

The grave I deserve.

No. I'm not getting dragged down into this shit again.

"Breathe in the scent of the Luminar Essence. Exhale your contribution to the Aether."

Eiran will come for me. Even after what I said. Even after pushing him away. He'll come.

And if he doesn't? The thought crashes coldly through me like a wave, but I shake my head, gritting my teeth.

If he doesn't, I'll find my own damn way out of here.

Somehow.

37

FACING THE FIRING SQUAD

Eiran

"What the hell do you mean, you can't get her out?!"

I pace back and forth in the back room of Kairo's shop, the place dark and eerily quiet. The "Temporarily Closed" sign keeping would-be visitors away fits my mood.

"What do you expect me to do, Eiran?" Thorne asks, sounding exhausted. *"I warned you to be careful. Besides, it's over anyway. We have no use for her."* It's a good thing he's on Nuvaleheim. If he were on Vale, we'd be having this conversation in person, and I might be tempted to throttle the man who's been a mentor to me since my brother died.

I stop wearing a hole in the bookshop's expensive rug and glare at the comm unit, even though Thorne can't see me. I can feel Kairo's gaze burning into the side of my head, but I don't look at him. He shouldn't be listening to this, but I leave the conversation on speaker.

I throw up my hands in frustration. "What do I expect you to do? I expect you to get on the comm and call someone in that wide contact network of yours and tell them to let Taylor Grey go. That she doesn't belong there. That she isn't a criminal or a patient—"

"They have the records," Thorne says, as if repeating the news will help it make sense. Kairo lets out a quiet scoffing sound, and I glare at him, silently reminding him to keep quiet. *"She is, by all records, a criminal named*

Taylor Grey. She is a convicted felon, a delusional schizophrenic, and a patient in the medical ward of the prison. You created that record yourself."

"I created a record for Taylor's cover, but it didn't say anything about the medical ward! If the records say that, then Blackstone or Darrow faked them!" I insist again.

By the Aether. Is this all my fault? She should have stayed away from me. I should have made her.

"*Darrow's in a coma. Blackstone's in the wind. How do you expect to prove anything?*"

I let out an irritated groan. "Just tell them that Grey is an SRF asset and needs to be released."

"*But she's not an asset,*" Thorne replies, and I still. "*No one by that name has been registered, and you have no known CIs. You know our guidelines, Eiran.*"

"Well, yeah, because you said—"

"*And* furthermore. *If Grey were an SRF asset, then you were there on an SRF-sanctioned op.*"

Kairo's eyes are as wide as mine.

"It was a sanctioned op."

"*I have no record of that.*"

I can't believe this. The man is disavowing the op. The same man who put a warm hand on my shoulder at Kaelen's passing ceremony, telling me we'd get the bastards who did it. Who first invited me to become an agent.

"There are no records," I grind out, "because you said to keep it off the books."

"*I said that because I thought you were smarter than this!*" Thorne snaps. "*I told you to keep it quiet and clean. This is* your *fuck-up.*"

It's like he reached through the line and slapped me across the face. I feel like a petulant child, and that is *not* a fun feeling.

"*Eiran… there's an inquiry. You're officially suspended without pay. Your union rep will be in contact.*"

"I'm being *fired?*" I cry, slamming a fist on the counter near the comm and feeling the expensive wood crack. I can't bring myself to care. He said "inquiry," but I know what that means.

"*Just be glad Darrow didn't die. That saved you from prison.*" After a moment of hesitation, he adds, "*Eiran, I am sorry. For what it's worth.*"

"Save it," I snarl. I press a button, ending the call before hurtling the comm across the room. It shatters against a bookshelf, little pieces raining down among the books. "Fuck!" I shout into the empty space.

"So, what now?" Kairo asks stoically. His whole body is tense, and his unhidden wings rustle in barely contained rage.

We'd already had our shouting match. My ears are still ringing.

When I couldn't reach the service ward, I'd left to find Kairo. He'd laid into me so hard he nearly hit me. I'd have deserved it too.

It was the best we could do to keep it together as we changed into maintenance gear and drove the service truck to pick up the recycling—where Taylor, Gael, and Frank were supposed to be hiding. The plan was to cart them off right through the gates without anyone noticing.

When I opened the bins to find Gael alone, her face streaked with tears... I knew. Kairo nearly drove into a tree as he tried to help Gael restrain me from going back and getting her. He kept insisting, "She'll find another way out. She always does."

I did my bit of shouting about that later.

It took two days to figure out what had happened to her. They found Frank and Darrow, but not Taylor. That gave us hope, but... when we found out where she was? That the fucking cyborg trapped her in a cell? My fight with Kairo was one for the ages. And the worst part? He was right. This is my fault. I'm the one who got her into this mess.

"So now," I say slowly to Kairo, taking a deep breath, letting his repressed rage quiet me. "We get her the hell out of there."

"How?" Kairo asks, his tone sharp enough to disembowel me.

I pull out my blaster, checking the charge. "The old-fashioned way."

Kairo gives a wide, dreadful grin. "I like the way you think, Leaf Boy."

"Do you have Sylara's contact?" I ask, and Kairo's gaze snaps to me. "We have the relic now. If Corvane wants it back..."

Kairo growls. "You're really going to give it to them?"

I stare at the counter, jaw tight. The relic's been in my hands for barely a day. Handing it over sounds as appealing as sawing off my arm. But Taylor's in there. "If we have to."

Kairo surveys me then, respect and something more uncertain warring on his face. "I... may have another idea."

His tone sends my instincts into overdrive. "What?"

"The Rythmus Shard," he says, resigned. "I know where it is. And I'll tell her. If she helps."

The muscles in my neck go taut. "Where is it?"

"My father has it." His chagrined smile slowly morphs into a more vindictive one. "I didn't know what it was. But after some research, I'm sure. So, if she can actually take it from the bastard, more power to her."

"You'd do that?" I ask, knowing the answer.

"Hell yeah."

I grin back at him. "Then call her."

38
POINT OF NO RETURN

Eiran

I walk casually and confidently to the guard station, trying to resist the temptation to reach for my company-assigned blaster. "Hey, Faylen."

The guard on duty startles, looking for someone to bail him out. "Brennan? Weren't you—"

"How's it going this morning?"

"Good…" the guard says cautiously. "You're not supposed to be here."

I frown. "What do you mean?"

The guard's cheeks brown. "Well, umm… I mean, it's not my place to say this, but… you'll have to talk to someone at the central office. I don't know what's going on, but—"

"What is it?" I ask, raising an eyebrow at him.

The guard gathers himself, injecting some steel into his tone. "Your access has been revoked, so you'll need to vacate the premises. Call the front office and—"

Kairo drops out of the purple-pink sky, wings and illusion billowing over us simultaneously as he slams the butt of a blaster rifle into the guard's head, knocking him to the ground. Not giving him a second glance, he hands me the other rifle, his face grim.

Sylara walks up beside me, spine extended. Before the guard can so much as moan, she jabs her spine into his leg, holding it there for a moment before retracting it. "There," she says, appearing equally unconcerned as the guard twitches momentarily and then stills, as unmoving as the dead. "With Valen physiology, we have about an hour before the catatonia wears off. And he won't remember anything that has happened since he woke up this morning. Now where is the Rythmus Shard?"

"No way," Kairo hisses. "We get Taylor first."

Sylara shakes her head. "Information. And then I help."

Kairo and I both freeze. "And let you run off and leave us?"

She shrugs. "I won't."

Kairo scoffs. "Like we'd trust you."

The huntress steps into Kairo's space, scaly mouth a hard line. "If I say I'll do it, then I'll do it. Besides," Sylara glances to the horizon and then back. "I owe her."

Kairo watches her for a moment and then turns back to me. "You know what this means, right? You working with us on this?"

I grab the guard's badge. "What?"

Kairo stares at me seriously. "Doing this means you're a criminal. One of us."

I throw the rifle over my shoulder and give him the briefest flash of a grin before donning my black mask. Kairo copies me. "It's kind of fun. You got the cameras?"

"Knocking out building-wide."

We follow Sylara past the half-built cells to the door.

"Okay, remember," I say to them—but mostly to Sylara. "Incapacitate. Don't kill."

Sylara holds up her extended spine, hand gripped on one of her two blaster pistols. "I promise not to use my blaster to kill anyone." I roll my eyes but can't help but grin at the obvious loophole. "Your professor friend. She still has the money she was going to pay Corvane for the relic?" she asks.

I grin. "She does. Do this and you can have it."

"Very well."

I reach for the handle, and we move as one into the main prison.

The guards shout, spotting us at once. Kairo launches into the air, his rifle trained on the three guards manning the walkway. They go down in a series of precise blasts. Two fly into the row of cells, and a third flips over the railing onto the floor below. I wince as the shuddering thud of his body echoes over the alarms, a harsh counterpoint to the prisoners' rising shouts.

The guards nearest us lurch forward, and I pin them down with a row of fire as Sylara leaps forward, landing between two guards. She stabs one and blasts the other, leaping forward to the next set of guards before anyone can react. The stench of scorched cloth and ozone hits my nose, mixing with the acrid tang of fear.

There is open chaos in the prison now, alarms echoing as prisoners lumber to their seats, taking swings at the guards, us, and each other. With one hand still laying down fire to keep the pandemonium at bay, I reach up with the other, extending my magic to the planters above us. I connect with several of the plants, growing branches down to grab guards and prisoners alike.

Kairo covers us from above, firing to clear a path for Sylara and me. Sparks rain down with every shot, briefly painting his demonic silhouette in orange firelight. A moment later, he lands beside us, wings extending as he sends a rolling tide of white light. The crowd stumbles back, half-blinded. Sylara crouches to the stone floor as we walk, and walls of spikes rise up on each side, keeping everyone back.

The three remaining guards huddle around the entrance to the medical ward. Before they can raise their weapons, Sylara is upon them. Three swift stabs with her spine, and they're down, Kairo and I stepping impassively over their twitching bodies. The smell of blood mixes with the hot recycled air, clinging to my tongue. We push open the door, moving into the next room.

The laser grid room is every bit as intimidating as Gael promised—a thicket of searing red lines, each one humming with heat. I reach toward the Gruundlith button, but Kairo shakes his head.

He extends his hand, and the beams bend slowly, supple like the sway of branches in the wind. The air shimmers with heat as they scrape against the metal walls, scoring them with molten lines that hiss and spark. The scent of burned metal sears my nose, sharp and acrid.

In moments, a narrow archway opens in the deadly grove. We step through, alarms wailing at our backs, the heat nipping at our heels.

I walk over to the potted plant in the corner, grabbing it. Following Kairo and Sylara into the corridor, I set the plant down beside the door. I fall in step behind Sylara and Kairo as guards fold out around the corner. Kairo launches into the air, soaring across the space while Sylara runs alongside him, attacking from below.

I send branch after branch bursting from the plant, avoiding the guards' eyes even as Kairo sends blasts of light into them.

I think of Taylor. Alone in that cell. Waiting for me.

I have no other choice.

With a shout and a burst of magic, the guards not brought down by Sylara's blasters or spines are wrapped in thick vines that knock them out or bind them. The vines thrash like living ropes, their small thorns scraping thin bloody lines across the guards' uniforms. I blast the edges of the vines as we pass, breaking them off, leaving the guards struggling helplessly.

We make it down another corridor, this one empty. As we near the end, Sylara grabs Kairo and me, hauling us backwards. Her powerful antennae twitch, clearly sensing something we can't. Sylara holds up her fingers in a quick flash—ten, then ten again. Then she gestures sharply toward the hallway.

Shit. Twenty guards.

We're so close, and yet it feels so far away. Before I can spiral, Kairo raises a finger and then signals for me to close my eyes. I do, but the world still becomes a void of searing white, the brightness burning through my eyelids. There are shouts and wails from the hall beyond. After a count of three, we round the corner as one, me blinking and Sylara shaking her head to clear it.

Still blinded by Kairo's light, the guards don't see us coming. Kairo and I lay into them with the rifles as Sylara crouches below, both of her handguns discharging. For a moment, the hallway is filled with guttural cries and scorching blaster fire.

And then, silence.

It doesn't take long.

We walk ahead through the mound of stunned bodies, heading for a room at the end.

I run forward, eager, desperate. Then, I pull to a stop. For a second, I can't move. What if she's not—?

No.

I shove the thought down. She's there. She's safe.

She has to be.

With the stolen badge in hand, I scan it at the entrance, and the door responds with a beep, allowing me inside.

Light slowly filters into the nearly dark cell. There, half-buried in a cocoon of torn padding, is Taylor. She lifts her head slowly, and then her eyes go wide. "Eiran?" she breathes. Her voice is so faint, so rough. "Is that… are you real?"

I run to her then, lifting her up to her feet. She wobbles slightly, but I catch her, and she leans into me. I kiss her hair, needing her to feel me. Needing to feel her as well. To know she's really here, and she's alive.

"I'm real, baby," I say in her ear. She's crying now, her tears staining my shirt as she clings to me for dear life. "I'm here, Taylor. I'm here. I'm taking you home."

I scoop her into my arms, and she presses her face against my shoulder. It's incredible how tiny she is. She's so fiery, so capable and smart… I guess she always seems larger than life.

Her voice a faint whisper, she says, "You came. You rescued me."

I smile down into her beautiful eyes, and say, "Of course. I'll always come for you. But look at you. You're alright. You made it through that hell. I'm so damn proud of you."

Her lip trembles then, and I can barely hear the word she mumbles. "Fr… Frank—" She sobs, gasping. Desperate.

My heart breaks for her. I wish I could cleanse it all away. Take it away and make it okay. "I know. I'm sorry. I'm so sorry." The words are useless. Meaningless.

"I tried. I could… Blackstone. He just…"

I can't make out the rest of it.

I reach for her hand, but she winces. It's then that I notice the bad angle.

"Eiran, we've got to go," Kairo says, running up to us. "More guards are on the way."

"I know," I snap. "Hold on." I put a hand to Taylor's cheek, feeling the soft warmth there, wiping away the dirt and tears with a swipe of my thumb. I send out a tendril of magic. With a shout of pain, Taylor's wrist sets. That should alleviate the worst of it until we can get her back to Lirion.

If only I could heal her heart as easily.

"Eiran—" Kairo prompts.

I look into Taylor's beautiful cobalt eyes for one more moment.

"Gael told me everything. She told me all you did. You did so good, baby. You did everything you could. And… and look at Gael. She wouldn't have made it if not for you. You saved her life."

"I… I tracked him," she breathes, and even Kairo stops pacing. Taylor looks between us. "Blackstone. I tracked him. With the bug from Darrow's crate. I tracked him. He didn't even notice."

"No fucking way," Kairo mutters with a faint chuckle.

I stare in awe at this amazing woman, at a loss for words. "You're incredible. You know that?"

She manages a faint version of her signature smirk. "I know."

"Of course you do," I smirk back. "Now let's get you home."

"Yes," she says, and despite everything, her voice is stronger than I'd expect. "Let's go home… and get this bastard."

39

MENDING

Taylor

Eiran takes his time driving us back home—when did Silberwald start feeling like home?—my hand gripping his like a lifeline. My jumbled thoughts unspool and spool again as we skim along the grassy plain, and Eiran lets me work it out. He seems to understand that I need the silence, the time. He doesn't ask something stupid like, "How are you doing?" He just lets me work it out.

We're entering the now-familiar main drag when he turns to me and says, "Are you hungry?"

"I could eat." I give him a small smile, hoping that from it, he understands all the things I can't put into words. How grateful I am that he came. How sorry I am about Frank. Maybe it will even tell him how much I appreciate his kindness, his strength, his understanding of me at every turn. Even coming here, knowing I'll need a minute before I face the thunderstorm that is his family. Need the quiet and the familiar.

That seems a lot to ask from a smile, but it's what I can manage.

Eiran returns the grin, and I feel like somehow he understands everything I can't speak after all.

He pulls the stryder over in front of a quaint, touristy pastry shop that appears new. "I'll be back." He jumps out, running into the shop that is miraculously open in mid-afternoon. Moments later, he returns with a large white bag of what I am sure are donuts. I take a bite of one and sigh, the sweet warmth of it filling parts of me—a small step to making me whole again.

Eiran watches me, trying to remain calm, supportive. But I can see how worried he's been. It's in the lines around his eyes, the weariness and deferred terror. With an impressively normal tone, he asks, "Donuts? They're your favorite, right?"

My smile turns sad, but I nod. "There was… this guy. A human named Marcus. He introduced me to them. Couldn't believe I'd never had them before."

I laugh at the memory before the joy snuffs out again, a match burning short and bright.

"He… died. And it… I thought I had everything planned. All the details down. But…" The thin veil of calm I'd constructed minces into tatters, and I'm sobbing again.

I reach for him, and he pulls me close, drawing me over the nav stick and into his lap. I collapse into his arms, and he wraps me in them, the world closing down into just that space. Just us. Slowly, the tears subside, and we sit there. Holding each other.

He looks down at me, and I can't understand how he can appear so fascinated, how he can look at me like that when I look like this and he… I reach up and run a hand through his dark green hair, the smoothness of it silken beneath my touch. He closes his eyes and sighs, leaning into my hand like a cat being petted. I lean in to put my lips to his, but he puts a hand on my shoulder, stilling me.

Does he… does he not want me? I don't think I can take it if—

"I want to. Aether help me, do I want to," he says, reading my expression and the faint shaking of my hand. "You're amazing, and sexy, and… But you're also hurt and messed up and not thinking clearly. I won't—"

"I am thinking clearly," I say softly, urgently to him. "I'm… I'm messed up. I always have been. And likely always will be. But you see me. You see how messed up I am, and yet you're here. You… you make me stronger, Eiran. If it weren't for you, I would have broken in there. I doubt there'd be anything left to save. But I breathed, and I calmed, and I waited. Because I knew you'd come." My voice breaks as I laugh, but then I say, "I mean, I started to wonder there, but… you came."

Eiran's beautiful amethyst eyes burrow into mine, and I feel as if I'm being x-rayed, completely opened and on display for him. And for the first time, I'm okay with that. I grasp his neck, leaning forward again, and this time his mouth moves to meet mine.

His lips are soft and lingering, and I open my mouth for him, our lips and tongues exploring languidly, thoroughly. He places a palm on my cheek, his fingers intertwining with my hair as I deepen the kiss. I want more of him. All of him. His hand slides under my arm, thumb tracing the side of my breast as he lifts me slightly, pulling me closer to him.

I'm straddling him now, with all the most important parts of him pressing at all the places I want them. I kiss him again, my mouth tracing a line across his jaw to his ear. He shivers as I give it a tiny flick with my tongue, and I grin wickedly. With a small gasp, his hands tighten in my hair. He gently pulls my head to the side and plunders my neck.

"Has anyone ever told you how elves claim mates?" he says against my soft skin.

"N… no." I breathe, although from my conversation with Maelara, I have a good idea.

He runs a trail of kisses up to my jaw and back down again. Gods, he's so hard against me. "It's a bite."

Something goes through me like an electric shock. I expect the fear, the spiraling, after everything that's happened. But the idea sends a spark down to my depths.

"It's not something I would ask of you, of course, but they say beyond the pain, it feels really—"

Tap, tap, tap!

I nearly jump off Eiran as our heads snap to the window. Eiran's sister is there, grinning like a fiend. "Are you two planning to make out all day or what? Aunt Maelara has supper ready, and I'm starving."

Eiran rolls down the window, and I toss the bag of donuts at her. He rolls it back up over her shocked laugh, his mouth returning to mine even as the tension breaks.

This time, Wynn smacks the glass. "Hilarious. Now let's go before Lirion comes and gets all doctorly on you two. That is, if you can hold off on playing doctor yourselves long enough for us to hear what's going on."

Eiran groans as I roll off him. I pat his thigh. "We'll resume this later. Maybe not any neck biting, but… anyway, I should let Lirion check me out."

Eiran mumbles something too soft to catch, but sounding like something no brother should say about his sister. We drive off, leaving Elowynn cackling in the parking lot.

***

In the end, it's probably good that we left. *Everyone* is there when we arrive. Even so, I'm grateful for the distraction. Eiran must have understood I needed that, too. I'm not nearly as messed up as I thought I'd be, but I'm still fighting the spiraling thoughts. With Eiran's mouth on my neck, it makes it harder to worry about things.

I'm thankful that I had time to calm down and process, because as soon as we walk in the door, everyone launches themselves at me. "She doesn't want a billion questions. Everyone back off!" Eiran barks, and most of the chatter dies down.

I can tell from their looks, though, that they're all still worried, so I say, "I'm okay. I won't say I'm fine, because I'm not, but… I'm okay."

"Why don't you let me decide that?" Lirion says, crossing his arms and frowning. "We'll be back." He leads me into a bedroom that someone set up as an exam room. Eiran follows us in, and Lirion shakes his head. "Patient only."

Eiran crosses his arms and leans against the wall, daring Lirion to try to kick him out. "He can stay," I blurt. "I'd… I'd like him to stay." The corners of Lirion's mouth twitch slightly before he nods, his cool doctoral demeanor back in place.

Lirion does a quick but thorough workup, healing my wrist, checking everything and treating every cut. His eyes flick to Eiran before asking me to remove my shirt so he can treat the rest of my wounds. Wordlessly, I pull it over my head, sitting there in my bra as he examines me. Eiran's eyes smolder, his lips a tight line as he takes in the marks on my chest, my arms, my shoulders.

"I'll kill him," he breathes quietly enough that I suspect he doesn't realize he said it aloud.

Lirion's eyes raise to mine. "Me too."

I nod, grateful.

Lirion moves with excruciating care and precision, ensuring every wound is treated properly. After a while, Eiran steps up without prompting, assisting Lirion with the ministrations. They take a good hour or more to get everything. Eventually, they're done, Lirion's mix of healing magic and medicine taking care of the vast majority of my physical pain.

If only they could treat the emotional trauma as easily.

Eiran walks beside me as we return to the living room, his hand resting reassuringly on the small of my back. As soon as we enter, Gael comes running toward me, shocking me as she wraps me in a hug, her long arms winding tightly around me. Startled, I take a second to respond, but I quickly put my arms around her as well.

"I'm so glad you made it out safe," I say quietly to her.

She pulls me back to stare desperately at me, tears streaking down her pretty olive face. "I should never have left you. If I hadn't... You saved my life. I never would have... I'm so, so sorry. I never should've left you there." She bawls, and I grasp her arms reassuringly, finding her eyes.

"If you'd stayed, I would've kicked your ass," I say with a stern look, and she lets out a sobbing chuckle. "You did the right thing. You got out. You got the relic out. And got the word out about me. I owe my life to you as much as to Eiran, Kairo, and Sylara."

"She *was* quite insistent we rescue you," Eiran says, his mouth tugging upward.

A question comes to mind, and I turn to Eiran, wishing I'd asked this in the car. "What about Frank?"

His face falls, but Kairo is the one to speak. "I was able to retrieve his body. We spun a story about him being part of the waste department that got lost. They blamed it on a patient. Apparently, some are pretty violent and—"

"We'll lay him to rest in the Quiblin way once this dies down," a soft voice says in my mind. I turn, astonished, and find Emma's slight form in the crowd. *"We'll need to make a trip to Schattenwald. It's the closest we can get to Hyoukō."*

"Oh, Emma!" I walk over to her, crouching to look the Quiblin in the eye. *"I'm so sorry. I did everything I could. Frank, he... he saved my life. He fought Blackstone single-handedly and—"*

"I have no doubt my brother fought bravely," Emma says, her usual stoic

expression cracking. *"I… I'm proud to call him my brother. I will grieve him as Quiblins do, when appropriate. But now… how can we help, Miss Grey?"*

"Emma, you don't—"

"It is what Frank would want. I don't know that I'm trained to go with you, but I would dishonor his memory if I didn't help you. And before you consider going after Blackstone alone, know everyone feels the same way." I glance around the room, and though no one can hear what Emma is saying to me, it seems from their firm gazes they can guess, or else they've discussed this beforehand. *"But if Frank won't be with you, we'll need to be sure you're trained in mental shielding. We have some* strenuous *lessons ahead."*

Nodding my thanks, but unsure how I feel about that, I turn to Eiran. "What was Darrow doing there? Surely it wasn't only a ruse to trap me."

"We don't know."

"What did they do to you?" Lirion asks. "I mean, physically I've seen, but—"

I shudder at the question, the ghostly memory of cold steel on my temples.

Kairo steps forward, looking worried. "Taylor, we don't have to—"

"I don't know what the proper term is," I say, steeling myself. "Dr. Grey always called it a scanner. I think it records brain patterns, or something like that. Blackstone said… he said that the blood he drew wasn't enough. That he needed to understand how my brain works."

Lirion's face hardens, but he nods. "I'm familiar with such devices. They're a dangerous and controversial bit of biotech. If he used that on you…" The lines at the corners of his mouth deepen.

It's probably time to change the subject. "I need to message Sylara and thank her. I didn't have time before we—"

"You're welcome," Sylara says from a corner somewhere. Astonished, I turn to see her sitting on a couch, her five-foot form hidden behind all the giant Valen.

"Oh! You… you're here. You stayed. I thought—"

"Thought I'd leave as soon as you were out?" Sylara asks.

I glance around the room at all the towering, too-tall Valen. "Can we talk in private?" She nods, and I excuse us and head to Eiran's bedroom. Once she closes the door, I start, "Look, Sylara—"

"Is this some sentimental human reunion?" Sylara crosses her arms, giving me the sort of cold look only she could pull off. "Dr.

Beutwinn is paying me the money she would have spent on the relic. It was business."

I frown at Sylara, conflicted as always by her strange dual nature, wishing I could trust her. "If you say so. But then, why are you still here?"

"I thought about it. Leaving. But I need Corvane dealt with. I don't enjoy looking over my shoulder. Besides, Eiran told me what was at stake. I don't leave things unfinished." She flicks her antennae, uncomfortable.

Whatever her reasons for staying, I'm grateful.

"Where are they with Blackstone?"

"We have him thanks to you," Kairo says from the doorway. His eyes are bright, appearing proud. "He's preparing to leave, we think. It's nearly impossible for him to travel unnoticed, looking the way he does. He's too recognizable. So, he's traveling aboard one of the smugglers heading back to the Union."

An idea brews slowly in my head. "What smuggler?"

"Not that one," Kairo says, raising a suspicious eyebrow.

I turn to Sylara, and she cocks her head at me. "You're thinking of doing something insane," she says mildly.

I consider a minute. Can I trust her? I trusted her once. We know how that went. But then, she helped get me out, and that was dangerous on several levels. "It'll be risky." She needs to understand. To be on board. "For you specifically."

She leans against Eiran's desk, raising her chin defiantly. "I saw you that day. With the Harmonix Crystal. You came back for me."

I cross my arms over my chest, self-conscious. "I… we were a team. I wasn't going to leave you."

"You thought about it," she persists, and I incline my head, conceding the point. "But you didn't. You had my back. I should have valued that more. You were right before. I do owe you for that."

I stare at her sternly, desperate for her to understand, to agree. "If you have my back, then I'll have yours. It's the only way this works."

"The only way *what* works?" Kairo asks, clearly exasperated.

I grin. "We need to get Blackstone on Corvane's ship."

Kairo gapes at me. "You're insane!"

Sylara laughs. "As I said."

40
ALL ABOARD THE CRAZY TRAIN

Taylor

For three days, the Valtir house has been alive with an infectious energy. My whole body is buzzing with the swarm of activity, and I feel better than I have in weeks.

Even if Elowynn's trying to kill me.

"Okay, one more position," she says eagerly.

"Wynn," I whine. "You've twisted me into every weird position possible. I think you're making things up at this point."

"Last one, I promise!" she insists, grinning widely from the mat next to me. We're lying in the lush back garden, staring up at the pinkish-blue sky, the last vestiges of the solar storm retreating.

The goal was to relieve stress, but so far, it's been *more* stressful. I remembered Eiran mentioning "eldertree alignment" and made the mistake of mentioning it to Wynn. She was *way* too eager to show me.

"Now this one is called the Budding Fork," she says, laying back on the soft woven mat. "I know, another dumb name, but trust me, it's great. First, pull your leg up like this." She pulls one knee up to her armpit, and I copy her. "Then do it with the other one." She drops that leg and pulls up the other.

"This isn't too hard," I sigh, raising my leg as well.

"Now do both at the same time. Then spread them like this."

Still lying on her back, she pulls up both legs. Grabbing the inside of her feet, she spreads her legs wide apart… and I burst out laughing.

"Okay, that's it. I'm done."

I stand, and Wynn struggles to follow me. "Wait! It's a real thing. It's a good way to open your—"

"I know exactly what it helps open. Thanks."

Wynn's cheeks go brown. "Hips! It opens up your hips and helps—"

"My hips are plenty open," I laugh, and she grabs my arm.

"Are they?" she asks. "Have you two—"

"Where have you been?" Gael snaps, appearing in the doorway, thank the gods.

Because the answer is a big, fat, no. We've been slammed from dawn well into the night. There has been no "hip opening," much less any "slamming" of the *fun* variety.

Gael glares at us, looking very much the annoyed professor. "We're on a timeline."

Wynn salutes, and I snigger. "Yes ma'am. Reporting for duty."

Gael rolls her eyes. "Just get in here. We need your help with this whiskey bottle."

Wynn waves to me, and I leave her in the kitchen with Maelara. They need to finish working on a very special bottle of rye whiskey destined for Liam Goran. As lead engineer, Goran has unrivaled access to Corvane's compound and his ship—making him a perfect target for a badge lift. Again.

Maelara gripes at Wynn in a friendly, motherly sort of way, and the usual pain doesn't come as strong. Instead, it's an ache that's mostly just… is this… joy?

I follow Gael back into a living room overtaken by excited overlapping conversations by the remaining Valtirs and extended family. The clamor is exacerbating the ever-present headache I've had since beginning psychic defense training with Emma, but it still makes me smile.

Her face serious, Gael points to Kairo, who's working with Roderic to modify a pair of powerseeds. "Those explosives coming along alright?"

"Yeah!" Kairo says. "You'd be surprised how much Roderic knows about blowing shit up."

The older Valen grins at Kairo, and that weird happy ache twists further. "I'm from the country. That's practically an official pastime."

Gael rolls her eyes again, but the corner of her mouth twitches. "Okay, good. Now, where are we with the other smugglers? Charles Coble is on his way back to Kagēkami to meet your dad. Or so he thinks."

Kairo laughs. "Man, he's going to be pissed when the Kuro Oni has no idea who he is. The idiot. Coble never had enough wind in his wings, if you know what I mean."

"Not really. No." Gael rolls her eyes and then turns to Eiran. He's still typing away at a small interface, ignoring the rest of us. Something about the sight is a steadying thread amid the tangled noise. "And the *Doomtreader*—"

"That's the dumbest name for a spaceship ever in the history of spaceships."

"Yes, Kairo, you've said. Several times. Eiran, the *Doomtreader* is also leaving early, already on its way back to Nosferalis. Apparently, returning to the Night Realm to face the Coven was better than getting arrested by Union intelligence. Thanks for helping with that."

Eiran shrugs, eyes still on his holo display. "No problem. A friend owed me a favor."

"So, then, with those options gone, Blackstone—" I glance at Emma.

"*In orbit on Corvane's ship*," she thinks to the group. With her guidance, I'm getting better at recognizing the difference in the mental timbre of a private comment and a public one. "*He still hasn't found the tracer you planted.*"

I sigh, relieved. Step one of the plan is set, at least. "Speaking of that…" Maelara walks in from the kitchen carrying a package. "This bottle of Saharan rye whiskey is ready to ship to… Golan?"

"Goran," I correct with a small grin. "Thanks. The tracker in there?"

Wynn holds up a comm. "It's pinging well. Lifespan should be around a week. Right, Eiran?"

He doesn't look up from the interface unit. "Yeah, that's right."

"Excellent," I grin. "What's the note say?"

Gael chuckles. "Thank you for a wonderful night. No signature."

"You think he'll buy that some random woman sent him a bottle of whiskey after a night of sex?"

I give her a look. "You didn't meet him. When I went to get the ID from him to get into Corvane's office, he was so busy talking about his past conquests he didn't even notice the theft. Trust me. He's arrogant enough. And now we can find Goran's location on the ship. That'll speed things up. We'll have such a narrow window once you arrive."

"Speaking of which, how's it going with Taylor's way on the ship?" Gael asks Eiran.

"Working on our in as we speak."

Gael gawks at him, exasperated. "Well, hurry. We need this done today."

"Keep your ears on," Eiran grumbles. "Phase one is happening tonight. According to my contact, the SRF is raiding his compound at midnight. He knows about it from a leak inside the organization, but he's thrown off. Sets up our 'in' perfectly. I just need to finalize with my friend in Customs. We'll be fine."

"But will you? Be fine?" Maelara picks at the edge of the box she's holding, looking unsure for the first time since I've met her. "I don't understand why you can't just let—"

"We're not letting the authorities take care of this," Eiran says kindly but firmly. "We need to make sure everything is recovered and then handled *properly.*"

In other words, destroy it and all records of it.

"What, and you don't trust the SRF to handle it properly?"

"No." Eiran's eyes burn in a way I haven't seen from him when talking about his former employer. He may once have trusted the SRF with the enhanced seeds. No more.

"There's one more thing," Lirion says, his tone somber.

"Is it time?" I ask, trying to sound as nonchalant as possible.

"It is," he confirms.

"I can do it," Eiran says for the umpteenth time, eyes burning intently. "If you're so intent on doing this fucking foolhardy thing, then I'll do it."

"No." I shake my head. "Lirion is trained, and I don't want you hovering over me, all paranoid and protective. Sylara needs this. The entire plan hinges on it. I'll be fine."

Lirion puts a hand on Eiran's shoulder. "I'll take good care of her. If not, you can kick my ass."

"I'll hold you to that," he grumbles.

Lirion leads me into the spare bedroom. Turning to me, he asks,

"You ready?" Tightening my fist until my knuckles go white, I nod. He pulls out a small scalpel, and tilting it slowly, he shows it to me. I breathe in and out as Lirion waits, giving my racing heart time to adjust.

I'm safe. I'm safe here with Lirion. Eiran is here. Kairo is here. Lirion is safe. It'll be okay.

Inching forward, he reaches the scalpel up and places it where my left index finger meets my knuckle.

"Don't watch," he advises, but I ignore him.

With his other hand, Lirion sends a tendril of magic into my hand, numbing it. The sensation is strange, like my skin doesn't belong to me. I watch with morbid fascination as he slowly, efficiently removes my finger before dropping it into a bag.

Blood pours from the wound, the soft white towel blooming red as it saves Maelara's good sheets. My breathing hitches and stutters, visions of the night Blackstone cut my hand off clawing their way back. I stare at my right hand—the black charred skin a permanent mark of the dark magic in the blade and the struggle the medics had to reattach it.

Then—a tickle. A phantom itch deep in the bone. A long white shard grows from the bloody knuckle like a branch bursting through soil. Tendons slither and muscles knit together, wrapping around the bone as the finger regrows before my eyes. A trickle of red blood flows from Lirion's nose.

Finally, he stops, a slightly too-pale digit twitching faintly where the old one once was.

Suddenly, Lirion collapses, and I catch him. "Easy," I say softly, righting him. "You shouldn't have pushed yourself."

"I didn't… go… into the prison," Lirion gasps, voice weak. "This is… my way… of helping. All I'm good for. Cleaning up after."

"No," I say, shaking his arm, making him look at me with bleary eyes. "You're coming this time. You're helping. I need someone to set off those charges to create a distraction for us. You'll do that for me, right?"

Lirion gives a tired grin, and I can tell he's glad to be included in my latest insanity, despite the risks. "Whatever you say, boss lady."

I should correct him, tell him that Eiran's in charge, but… something in Lirion's tone makes me proud.

I smile back. "Alright. Now let's get this fucker."

41

TOOLS, BOXES, &
OTHER INNUENDOS

Taylor

Eiran crouches next to me, barely able to fit in the back of the stolen box trellar. Beams of midmorning sunlight reflect strangely off the various metal tools and surfaces in the dim, tight work vehicle. The silhouette of some interstellar craft is blurry through the frosted rear windows, and a rolling tool chest looms between us in the six-foot-high space. The red metal box is large-*ish*—almost taller than I am—but not big enough. And it'll be home for the next several hours. Can I really do this?

"You ready?" Eiran asks, as if reading my mind.

"Yeah." My response is too quick, and he raises an eyebrow. "It's… small."

He laughs, and I don't blame him. "You crawl in tunnels all the time! You can't stand there and tell me you're claustrophobic!"

I punch him in the arm and try to frown, the trellar creaking with the movement. "Hey! Tunnels have openings! I don't mind tight spaces. I just… don't enjoy feeling trapped."

That sobers him. Shit. I shouldn't have brought it up. Didn't mean to trauma dump. Again.

Before I can laugh it off or make it a joke, he puts a hand on my shoulder. I look away from those understanding eyes, trying to center myself. "I get it," he says, his voice is a caress, as tender as the touch of his finger to my chin, pulling my gaze back to his. I lose myself in those amethyst eyes.

Maybe he gets it after all. He certainly doesn't seem to mind that I brought my shit into the moment. Again.

"Taylor, it's an honest question. You sure you want to do this? There's still time to adjust."

"I'm sorry. I'm not trying to make everything about me or my shit. The mission. Us. All of it. I'm always messing things up. Like at your apartment. That night was so perfect, and I—"

Eiran leans in closer, the scent of mint and elderwood, the scent of him, overwhelming every remaining defense. "You have nothing to apologize for. That's why we're here. Together. You don't have to do this. It's not always up to you. You have a team now. You have me."

My heart swells as those strong, tender eyes look unflinchingly back into mine, the amethyst brilliant despite the near dark. "I can do this *because* I have you."

His eyes crinkle adorably, and he looks down. A slight frown forms as he takes my hand in his. "What about the finger?"

I wince at the memory, wiggling the slightly paler forefinger. "It's fine. It doesn't even hurt anymore."

I don't say the rest. That somehow the regrown finger doesn't feel like mine. Different from when the doctor reattached my hand after Blackstone… no. Get it together, Taylor.

Eiran is still frowning as he plays with the tip of my regrown digit. "I'm still not convinced this finger stunt is necessary."

"Sylara will need it. Cutting it off sucked, but it was a moment of pain. Worth it to bring down these assholes."

My tone is fiery, but the heat of Eiran's gaze turns the fire into something… other. Molten. The heat settles lower as he runs a hand along my forehead, pushing back a stray strand of hair before cupping my cheek.

"I need to discuss something with you. After."

I frown, stepping away. "Why not now?"

"Don't freak out." He chuckles, and I'm tempted to hit him again. "It's a good thing." The fear morphs to panic, even as Eiran's mouth struggles not to curl in a laugh.

"If you try to bite me, Eiran Valtir, I swear to Hikario, or the Aether, or whoever I need to swear to, that I will kill you."

And now he *is* laughing.

I can't tell if I want to laugh too or run screaming. Particularly because he doesn't actually deny it. Instead, I opt for a smile. "You never explained that mating thing. If you tell me it's some mystical eternal bond that—"

He snorts. "Nothing that dramatic. It's just a claiming, and it's not even binding. Hasn't been for centuries. It means that two people are attached, bound. Like I said before, it's a bit old-fashioned. And patriarchal. Most city elves don't do claiming anymore. But in places like Silberwald, you see it pretty often. Maelara has a mating mark on her wrist. Have you never noticed?"

I haven't forgotten Maelara's ring of teeth marks… or the loving gleam she got in her eye when she talked about it. What if Eiran did that to me? His teeth against my skin… I shudder. Eiran raises an eyebrow, noticing the reaction. "Would my biting you be so bad?"

I look away, and Eiran seems to realize what the idea of biting, of sinking his teeth into me, would mean. "Oh shit. I'm so sorry. You know I'd never do that to you. I know how much it—"

I raise a hand to stop his babbling, because somehow… I realize he's wrong. Not here. Not with him. "No, it's not that. You're fine, Eiran. I talked about it briefly with Maelara, but then she changed the topic. Started asking about why I'm a thief."

"I should have known she'd pull something like that," he mutters.

"It was fine. We had to discuss it at some point. And I mean, yeah. In theory, biting should bother me. But… it doesn't."

Proving the truth of this, the molten heat blazes at the idea.

Well, damn. Maybe I'm a freak in more ways than I realized.

In a quieter tone, I explain, "What I'm saying is… it was a good shudder. The biting part, I mean." Eiran's eyes sharpen then, and I feel my smile become positively deadly. I step forward, placing a hand on his chest, leaning close to his ear. "Maybe we should try it sometime…" I give that earlobe a flick of the tongue.

His body trembles as he groans out, "You'd be into that?"

I run a finger along his chest, tracing down to curl underneath a pec. "Maybe. I mean, we could work up to—"

He pulls me to him, cutting my words off. My heart pounds as he runs a thumb along my neck before leaning down to kiss the hollow there. His teeth graze along it, and I let out a tiny gasp.

"Maybe I should take you right here," he murmurs into my hair. My chest is heavy and body aflame as I try to get closer, to grind into him. He spins me, grabbing my hip hard and making me gasp again. "Keep teasing me like that, and our first time will be in the back of a dirty cargo trellar."

"Promise?" I arch into him again, pressing my ass almost painfully against his growing hardness.

"Aether, save me," he groans. He runs a hand up my side and along my stomach before taking my breast in his hand. He plays with a sensitive peak, making me whimper. Then he pulls his hand away. "Not here. This isn't—"

I elbow him in the ribs, and he doubles over slightly. Not this shit again. I spin in his arms, slamming him against a metal wall, tools clanking. His length is impossibly stiff as I pin him there. My hand wraps around his throat, and I let the faintest hint of claw poke against his skin.

Gods, he's so hard.

"You listen to me, Eiran Valtir. You've been coming up with excuses to stay away from me since we met. I have too. But honestly, I'm tired of them. They're all bullshit, and we both know it. Could we have done this days ago in a comfy bed? Sure. But we don't do things the normal way, do we? I want this. Here and now. With what we're about to do, I'm not wasting another moment. So, it's your choice. Now or never."

I've never been this open with anyone before. This blunt about something so personal. But I want it. Want him right now. He seems to understand, his body relaxing slightly as the air goes taut between us. There's one more moment of pause, then he lurches forward, and we collide in the small space.

With searching fingers, he reaches under my shirt. His claws extend, tracing faintly up my back as we slide together to the floor. Our lips touch, and I breathe into him, ragged and desperate. I want more of him, all of him.

I clamber into his lap, and I pull off his shirt as he tugs on mine. They pile on the floor in a tangled heap, his tree tattoo on lurid display in the half-light. He traces another line of kisses down my neck, continuing along my shoulder blade. One hand holds me upright as I arch back, the other working deftly at my bra.

Eiran's lips find my peak, and he makes a home there. He worships me for long minutes, tongue and teeth swirling, sucking, biting. I'm on edge, nearly there just from this. I grind against him, hating the cloth between us but seeking the friction of him against me. Long fingers play with a peak as I find the right angle. I writhe against him, and it doesn't take much before I shatter apart against him.

When I still, my eyes find his, and we exchange a look of fiery understanding and need. Together we reach for each other's waists, sliding clothing down, kicking them off awkwardly. Neither of us cares. I need him. Here. Now. I need to be closer. And I can tell he feels the same way.

With one final, frantic kick, the pants are off. I sit back on his thighs, in awe of him, of the curves and ridges. Words well up inside me. Words I've never said to anyone. Not like this. But my twisting, aching heart tells me this is the most real thing I've lived through. "Eiran, I—"

"I love you," he says, his eyes firm. Determined. "I have for a while. I didn't want to freak you out, but… I mean, I couldn't let you say it first, right?"

My insides break, crumble, and reform with agonizing joy as I give a watery laugh. "I love you, too."

I crawl forward, and he trembles as I wrap my fingers around him, marveling at the contrast. I lower myself onto him in slow inches that destroy and remake me. My eyes remain on his, watching the silver flecks in his purple eyes as they rove over me. We gasp together as I reach the base, and we stay like that for a long moment.

I lean in, kissing him as I begin to move.

Eiran grips me, hands on my hips as I ride him, raising me up so I can then plunge back down. His hips rise to meet me, the tension in me building and building as his long fingers find my most sensitive core, moving in time. He takes a peak into his mouth again as I move, his tongue flicking. That's all it takes, and I'm breaking apart again, clenching against him. My pleasure crests, and then I finally slow.

His fingertips run along my back as he remains inside me. He looks at me in awe, like I'm more valuable than any treasure we could steal. Like I'm the most precious thing in the galaxy. "By the Aether. You're beautiful."

Reaching up, he uses a firm, gentle hand to pull me off him, turning me. Guiding me on all fours, he moves behind me. There's a pause, and

I can tell he's watching me. I wiggle my ass, because he needs to hurry the fuck up. Literally.

He chuckles faintly. With powerful hands gripping my hips again, he slides me back onto him. I let out a small moan as he lands home. And then he's moving inside me in long strokes. A steady, relentless pace. Unhurried as my fingers dig into the rubber floor of the trellar. His thumbs dig into my ass like a brand. A claiming all our own. I arch my back, slamming back to meet him, claiming him as well.

Oh gods. How can I be reaching the edge *again*? This isn't possible. This has never… but it's building. Impossibly, undeniably.

"Eiran…" I breathe.

And somehow I'm shattering once again, Eiran moving and helping me ride the wave before he pauses behind me.

"I want to see you," he says.

He turns me, my back now against the hard rubber floor. It's dirty and a tad gross, but I couldn't care less as he moves between my legs. I reach up and grasp his strong shoulders, looking deeply into his eyes, and he moves into me again. This time his pace is strong, furious. I'm already too sensitive. The exquisite pain is almost too much, but my body tenses again.

I'm lost in those amethyst spheres as, for the fourth time, I build. And this time. Eiran is building with me. It's not long before we release together. My scream rattles the metal walls before he clamps a hand on my mouth.

With slow, heaving breaths, we finally come down. His arms are firm as he hovers above me, his eyes still alight with amazement. "You're incredible."

I grin. "Back at you."

His eyes turn reluctant. "I hate to say this, but… we probably need to get you ready. They'll be here soon."

I whine, but he's right. There's so much I want to say, but later.

There *will be* a later.

Eiran helps me dress, and then I sulk over to the rolling tool chest. He opens the top, revealing the empty cavity inside. Still frowning, I raise my arms, and he lifts me up, placing me inside.

I look up at him, and I feel tiny inside the large box. His mouth turns down, a finger tracing reluctantly across the lid. "Are you sure you'll be okay?"

I reach up and cup his cheek, running a thumb across the faint stubble. "I'll be fine. I promise."

"Okay," he says, kissing my forehead. "See you soon, I guess."

"See you soon," I echo a tad ironically as he closes the lid on me.

Just before the line of light narrows to darkness, he says, "I love you, Taylor. Be careful."

"I love you too."

42

DROP-OFF

Eiran

My head is spinning as I roll Taylor's chest along a stony pathway toward the large frigate tucked into the open-air hangar. I glance around the grassy expanse marking the launch area, not really taking anything in.

I don't know what's harder to process: the mind-blowing sex or the fact that I actually told Taylor I loved her. And meant it.

Maybe it's both.

Doing that was reckless, crazy even. But leaving things unfinished… as Taylor made clear, we aren't promised tomorrow. Anything could happen on this mission—no. Not a mission. A job. A heist. We're going in without cover. Without backup. We need to live in the moment. It may be the only one we get.

"Are you ready to load up?" I turn toward the sound of the voice, where a burly man in a brown work tunic and slacks is walking up to me, a pointy grin visible amidst his bushy green beard.

"Hey Daelric!" I say, grinning. "I owe you one for this."

Vale's customs inspector general waves me off. "If this goes the way you promise, I'll owe you." He hands me a stack of clothes that match his own. "These are for you. I'm borrowing it from one of my guys' lockers, so try not to get blood on it if you can help it."

I shake my head. "Not this time, Daelric. It's a simple in and out. Just got to drop something off."

I pat the metal case, but Daelric holds up his hands. "I don't want to know. I've told Captain Arminas that you'll be joining her team, and not to ask questions. You'll be fine with her. This isn't her first time."

"Thanks again. I appreciate it. And I *do* owe you one." I didn't tell Daelric that this isn't SRF business. I wonder if he'd care.

"To be owed a favor by Eiran Valtir? I won't be turning that chance down twice. Good luck to you." He pats me on the shoulder and then walks off.

I step inside the sun-drenched hangar and don the coverall uniform. According to my name badge, I'm "Eldwyn" for the day. A torrent of chatter swells, and I look up to find the customs inspection team approaching. With a polite smile, I introduce myself to the captain, a female with a severe bun and a "take no shit" air.

Arminas nods swiftly. "Eldwyn? Good to have you. Stay out of my way, do your job, and don't get lost or break anything. Manage that, and we'll get along fine. Sound good?"

I'm a little taken aback. "Yeah, uh, yes ma'am. Sounds perfect."

"Excellent. Get your gear stowed. We're leaving in ten." I kind of like her.

I walk over to the toolbox and rap it quietly on the side. There are two almost inaudible taps in response, Taylor telling me she's okay. "Alright, let's get you loaded up." No one around notices that I'm talking to my toolbox, which is as I expected. I get Taylor loaded and strapped down, and then find my seat, several of the crew giving me curious looks.

My ass has barely touched the surface before the frigate, a Galathir-class ship called *Skälthur*, takes off, pulling away from the Valen surface. A minute later, the ship enters orbit, pulling up alongside the *Obsidian*, Corvane's massive cruiser. Captain Arminas presses a button on her large chair and says in clipped tones, "This is the *VSS Skälthur* hailing the *Obsidian*. Come in, please."

An annoyed voice comes on the line. "*This is the* Obsidian. *What is it now?*"

"This is Captain Falir Arminas of the Valen Republic Department of Customs. This is a routine inspection. Prepare to be boarded."

"*Routine my ass.*"

Arminas doesn't respond to this, seeming unsurprised by the surliness.

"*Bay Alpha.*"

The *Skälthur* flies smoothly over to the large bay, and when it lands, I line up with the rest of the team, walking with my toolbox down the ramp and onto the ship.

I'm struck again by how different the human-built ship is from elvish design. Fingerprints and grease spots mar the walls. Large holographic projections display everything from technical updates to ads for onboard gambling, vid halls, and ultra-processed rations. The smell is sharp and heady, the acrid scent of burning circuits overriding everything. Add in the harsh lighting, and it only takes moments to develop a headache.

A tall, wiry human officer is standing to "greet" us, his long arms crossed and his scowl so deep I'm surprised he can see past his down-turned eyebrows. The garish blue and purple lights split his face. "Can you frogmen finish so we can leave?"

"It takes as long as it takes," Arminas says, breezing past him.

"Now hold on! You need an escort to…" His voice is lost as he chases Arminas's team through the door and into the rest of the ship, leaving me alone.

Hoping this tech Emma gave me works as well as she promised, I press a button on my watch. That should kill all cameras within a thirty-foot radius for the next minute. I quickly lift the toolbox lid, finding Taylor scrunched up inside.

"Oh, thank the gods," she mutters, reaching up to me as I pull her out. I set her on the floor of the bay, and she wraps me in a quick hug. With a peck on the cheek, she says, "See you soon," echoing my words from earlier. With a final grin, she scrambles off, disappearing into a vent and taking a bit of my heart with her.

Reluctantly, I close the box and rush back to the team to complete the inspection. Because the faster I get home, the faster we can help Taylor. And Aether knows she's going to need it.

Whether or not she wants to admit it.

43

REUNION

Eiran

There is an intense sense of déjà vu as we approach the *Obsidian* again, although this time we're in open space and approaching in Sylara's sleek bird-shaped Hitari ship, which she's renamed *Basix*. Lirion, Gael, Kairo, and I huddle awkwardly behind the Zeridian huntress, barely enough space to stand, much less sit in the small stolen craft. The wooden corner of a cabinet digs into my hip, and the prismatic swirling patterns of the kōjyotsu steel walls make me nauseous, but at least the glamour tech allows us to come right up next to the ship unseen.

Sylara presses a button, and I can tell that the enchantments that power the glamour have lifted because we get an immediate, panicked hail from Corvane's ship.

"Unidentified vessel! Name yourself and your intentions, or we'll blast you out of the sky."

"I'd like to see you try, Gregg," Sylara says in a bored tone. "What bay?"

"Oh, uh… Sylara. I didn't… Gamma."

"Tell Corvane I'm here." Sylara clicks off, and we cram into an out-of-the-way corner, Kairo using his magic to hide us from sight. Kairo's huge wings are everywhere. Gael backs into them, and he gives a tiny involuntary shudder. Hidden behind the glamour, we watch Sylara lower the ramp of the ship and exit. The scent of rust and oil wafting in from the bay is a sharp reminder that we're not on Vale anymore.

"Sylara, darling. Such an unexpected surprise!"

"*Corvane*," Kairo mouths, and I nod.

"Well, I'm not sure why it's so surprising, Ryland. You said to kill Taylor Grey. I'm here to collect."

Corvane lets out a surprised little chuckle. "Is that so?" Something about his tone sets my nerves on edge. I grab Gael and Lirion's arms in warning, trying to exude calm.

"It is," Sylara asserts. "I have her finger here as proof. Check the prints. DNA. Whatever you'd like."

"That's impressive. Very impressive." Corvane's tone is all wrong, and I'm a live wire. Kairo grasps my shoulder, subtly holding me back. Clearly he's heard it too. "It's particularly impressive since my guests tell me that Grey is very much alive. So, I'm wondering how you managed to accomplish it."

There's a loud rustling of struggling men, but it's short-lived. Sylara didn't put up much of a fight. "I always knew you were a paranoid bastard, Ryland," she says instead. "I didn't peg you for a foolish one, though." Her purring tone promises the death and destruction she's more than capable of delivering.

"She calls me foolish, but she's the one who comes on my ship selling me lies. Can you believe this… uhh… woman?"

"Who are these 'guests' of yours that claim I am lying? I'm interested in learning how they claim to know more about Grey than I do when I'm the one that has her finger in a container. Where, I wonder, did I get it if not from her?"

"That's an excellent question, Sylara. Where did you get it?" Corvane laughs again. "Ah, you sure are a clever little bug, aren't you? Come along. Let's figure out what to do with you."

The sound of their footsteps recedes, and we wait for what seems like hours before I decide it's safe to move. "Let's go."

"Will she be alright?" Gael asks as she clambers down the corrugated metal ramp, looking strangely concerned for the deadly huntress.

I shrug as I join her on the cold steel floor of the massive vessel, the air tasting of metal and coolant. There's a faint hum rattling my teeth, the light above buzzing like it's on its last legs. "You haven't read her file. Trust me. She'll be fine. Let's focus on the plan. Lirion? You know what to do. Mischief and mayhem, but not until it's time. We don't want to create more problems for ourselves."

Lirion nods. "Got it."

"I'll come find you in a bit," Kairo adds.

I turn to Gael. "We need to get access to the ship systems as quickly as possible. So be safe, but be fast. And keep an ear out for the keyword in case we need something dramatic. It's *buffoon*."

Kairo scoffs. "Good luck finding a natural way of saying 'buffoon' in an emergency."

"Don't underestimate me."

Gael rolls her eyes at us and leads Lirion out of the bay, where they split in opposite directions.

"Taylor?" I ask over comms, half-expecting her to materialize out of nowhere. Which, let's be honest, she totally might.

"*Hey sexy.*"

Kairo lets out a gagging sound. "Ugh, gross. This is an open channel, you two."

"*I can't believe I'm saying this,*" Gael mutters, "*but I agree with Kairo.*"

"*Same,*" Lirion chimes in.

Taylor laughs. "*Prudes. All of you. I'm in a maintenance closet right now. I'll send my location.*"

We navigate a maze of empty corridors and maintenance shafts to the hallway Taylor's tracker shows. When we near where she's hiding, Kairo motions for me to stop, a devious look on his face. Curious, I let him take the lead. Slowly, we creep up to the closet door and then swing it wide.

Taylor comes bursting through the door, wielding a mop at Kairo's head. He jumps back, and I grab her, putting my hand over her mouth. Taylor struggles to regain her breath as she glares at us, and we try our best to contain our laughter. "You are both children," she hisses, though I see the way her knuckles whiten around the handle.

"At least you were prepared," Kairo chuckles. "You would have really mopped the floor with whoever'd found you." I burst out laughing again, trying to keep it down.

"You're lucky I didn't come out with my blaster," she grumbles.

I grin, shaking my head. "So, did you find him?"

"I did. That ingestible tracer works well. He's in his stateroom now. Let's go get him. Gael?" She leads us to one of the many nondescript doors on the long hallway.

"*I'm here,*" Gael says in a whisper. "*We now have access to all ship systems. Emma's virus worked. Anyway, I'm in some sort of conference room. Opening door… now.*"

The door slides open, and we walk into a medium-sized stateroom glowing with sickly pink strip lighting. The space is large enough for a separate dining space, small desk, and a bedroom area, and is sparsely adorned, some sort of badly done spray paint art on one wall and a small, neglected plant sitting half-dead on top of a mostly empty bookcase. A stringed instrument of some variety is collecting dust in one corner.

Goran is sitting on the couch watching a vid on the large screen. He leaps up in surprise, and I stun him with my blaster, sending him flying halfway across the space.

"You didn't need to stun him at such a high setting," Taylor murmurs.

Kairo chuckles. He picks up the large man and places him on his bed before taking his badge. Taylor looks quickly away as he draws blood from him for the biometric sensors. He pats the unconscious Goran on the shoulder and says, "Thanks again, man! Always great seeing you."

"*Hide! Now!*" Gael hisses over comms. I notice a faint shimmer as Kairo throws a glamour on the three of us. "*Sorry. They must have taken control of the cameras from me without my noticing.*"

I barely register this before Blackstone darkens the doorframe, a second cybernetic eye now joining the first. He clomps into the room, looming large enough that I almost miss the man behind him.

Dr. Alexander Kane.

The one who first carved Blackstone into something unrecognizable. The surgeon, the visionary, the butcher. My ghost. My mistake. My first kill. I was so sure he was dead. Because he *had* to be.

Yet here he stands, breathing recycled air, smiling like the years between us never happened. Blackstone at his side, proof that Kane never stopped building monsters. Proof that I wasn't enough to stop him.

The pieces crash together: the experiments, the ethics burned to ash, the girl treated like a lab rat. Helix didn't just carry Kane's signature—it was Kane, all along.

"Taylor Grey," Kane says smoothly, looking around the space as though he could actually see us. "I heard Sylara is on board, so I know you're here with that Hitari fence. And Eiran Valtir as well. Show yourselves." When none of us moves, he adds, "Don't be children. I can have Adrian here shoot up Goran's bedroom, but why get messy? Come on now."

The SRF officer in me wants to lunge, but I know better. The boy I used to be—the one Kane manipulated without ever meeting—just wants to scream.

"*Hold on,*" Lirion says. "*I'm heading your way.*"

"*No, Lirion,*" Gael cuts in thankfully. "*Get the charges set. We may need a distraction sooner than later.*" I can't argue with that.

Kane? How could Kane be here, alive? It all makes sense now. Who else would have founded an organization dedicated to pushing humans to their limit, to blowing past ethical boundaries to give humans abilities they don't have naturally? Who else would treat a little girl like a lab rat in the name of more power? Hadn't he done that for years with Blackstone?

Of course, it's Kane.

Kane is the leader of Helix.

44

RAISING KANE

Taylor

My eyes remain on Blackstone's imposing figure as the glamour falls from us in an icy trickle, leaving us raw and exposed in the harsh neon light. I push back the tide of fear as that red eye flicks to me, and then smoothly past. As if nothing happened the last time we met.

Bastard.

Eiran steps forward, his usual dimpled grin becoming something dangerous, his pointed teeth put to full effect. "Dr. Kane." His tone is light, but underneath, it's jagged. Barbed. Meant to cut.

I take in the older, slightly pudgy man in the crisp suit. This is Dr. Kane? The architect who made Blackstone a monster? He's the one who healed him after the explosion! Has worked on him ever since. If he's here…

"Valtir," Kane replies, beaming. "A pleasure to see you. It's been a long time."

"Yes." Eiran cocks his head. "I thought you were dead."

Kane chuckles. "In a way, I was. After what you did, I went into hiding. Lost my friends, my partners, my research, my funding… I couldn't work in the light anymore, you see. I had to work in the shadows."

"Oh, you've always worked in the shadows, Kane."

Kane tuts. "Such animosity. You know, I'm surprised at you, frankly. I thought your experience in the field would have made you less idealistic since our last meeting. You were such a wide-eyed college boy. The SRF should've taught you that the world isn't so black and white. And yet, here you are. Mad at me when you're the one who ruined *my* life."

Eiran gives a lifeless corpse of a laugh. "Is that so? Poor Alexander. Forced to leave his cushy job to… what? Head one of the galaxy's most dangerous terrorist organizations? An organization you'd already founded years before."

Kane spreads his arms wide and bows his head. "Well done. Took you long enough. You worked on this for… how long?"

"Ever since you killed my brother," Eiran growls. His claws extend, and his shoulders hunch like a predator about to pounce. He looks practically lupine.

What does it say about me that I find it kind of hot?

Kane leans away from Eiran, deep lines forming in his eyebrows. "Your… brother? Dear boy, I don't have the foggiest idea what you're talking about."

Eiran scoffs. "Kaelen Valtir. They found him eviscerated. Disemboweled like the rest of your sick experiments."

Kane cocks his head. "This was… several years ago, right? I remember this now. Yes, that caused quite a stir early on because we had no idea who'd done it. Still don't, frankly. That was your brother?" Kane lets out a truly boisterous laugh now.

"*Bastard,*" Lirion mutters. "*Kick his ass, Eiran.*" Eiran snarls like an animal, and I take a breath, willing Lirion to shut the hell up.

"Is that why you've been such a thorn in my side? Because you thought we killed your brother? Oh, that's hilarious."

Eiran shakes his head like a grazehorn batting away flies. His eyes blink furiously as he tries to make the words make sense. "No. No, I'm not letting you play with my head. I know—"

Kane laughs again. "You know nothing. I had nothing to do with your brother. Why would I? We performed experiments at the beginning. I won't deny that. Sacrifices must be made in the name of science. We took remarkable magical people to find out what made them that way. Find out how we could better ourselves. Your brother, Eiran, was not remarkable."

Eiran stumbles back as if struck, but Kane turns to me, his aloof grin turning more feral. "Now you, my dear, are exceptional."

He steps forward, his eyes bright with greed. "And why wouldn't you be? Your mother told us what she'd done, but… she said the plans had failed. That the Vale Effect was nothing but a dream. She said she had destroyed the experiment. Didn't want it—you—in our hands. Even when we asked her… forcefully. All the way to her end, she insisted. And when we looked for you, we couldn't find anything to contradict her story. Why wouldn't we believe her?"

My world warps and spins. "You… are you saying that you…" I couldn't make it fit. It couldn't be true. It just couldn't. The Lorathar Initiative killed my mom. That's what I always… no.

"I was convinced. Even Adrian was convinced. No one lies under the treatment we put her through. And we couldn't find a trace of you either. Yet, to my surprise, we find you alive after all, in Vaeloria City of all places. Working as a thief. How remarkable… and utterly convenient."

"That's… that's why you wanted me to steal the seeds." I feel hollow. Wrung out. An empty exoskeleton standing here, ready to topple over at the slightest push. "Why you didn't have the Eclipse Consortium do it?" Something snaps me back at the thought. "It was what? A test?"

"Exactly," Kane says, his eyes blazing eagerly like a dragon stalking its horde. "You were protected by the son of the Kuro Oni."

For the briefest moment, his eyes slide to Kairo before returning inescapably to me.

"They appeared estranged, but it was too much to risk. So we came up with—to use your word—a test. The task was almost impossible. Definitely too much for a human girl to achieve, even an Enhanced. Even one as well trained as you. And yet you succeeded. You proved my suspicions—that you could be the key we were missing. So, I sent Adrian here to collect your blood along with my seeds." He waves at Blackstone. "He was, unfortunately… overeager."

Blackstone doesn't move or react, looking like a shut-down robot. Kane pats him on the shoulder, but he still doesn't move. "He tried, but…" Kane wags an annoyed finger at Eiran. "You were there. Turning up yet again to foil things. Then come to find out—"

"It didn't work without a brain scan," I supply, trying to keep him talking.

"Exactly," Kane says eagerly. "I'm glad you're paying attention. Yes, we were missing something. I needed you. Or your brain, anyway. Of course, by then I'd realized I couldn't come to you. I needed you to come to me. So, I reached out to Ms. Darrow." He holds his hands up, and I know what he means. The prison. It was all a ruse.

Kairo crosses his thick arms, the tattoo standing out as his muscles clench, the only sign of his restrained fury—other than that smile of his. It's not sleek and cocky like Eiran's. It's wilder. Unkempt. A cresting tsunami. "But Taylor was just a side mission. Wasn't she, Kane?"

Kane inclines his head, conceding the point. "The seeds. They were the key. Your mother figured it out years ago."

The word "mother" feels like a knife to the ribs, but Kane keeps talking, eyes a half-crazed inferno. "If we had the original luminar essence from the Eldralume Relic and the essence the Lorathar Initiative enhanced… they're the connection to understanding the Aether. The secret of how magic works, at least on Vale. If we can capture that connection, discover the secret to how they made them better, then we could truly understand the secret of how magic works. And if we also had you…" He shakes his head in wonder.

I glance at Eiran, and he growls, "So what do you want now, Kane? You have everything you need. You lost the Eldralume Relic, but I imagine you had enough time to learn what you wanted to know." Eiran shakes his head in disgust at the violation. "So what now, Kane? Why are you here?"

The terrorist considers me before responding, "Well, Eiran, I wasn't going to bother with trying to take Miss Grey with me. Too much hassle and red tape to risk it. But since she's here—"

With a swoosh, the stateroom door opens. Sylara strolls into the increasingly cramped space, and behind her, looking positively apoplectic, is Ryland Corvane.

45

PREDATOR

Eiran

Corvane enters the room like a thunderstorm, his finger a lightning bolt pointing from Taylor to Kane. Two imposing Zeridian guards march behind him, and I quickly glance at Kairo. Thank the Aether he's keeping a straight face.

"I knew it! She was right. I'm sorry I ever doubted you, Sylara."

Sylara crosses her arms and cocks her head at Taylor. "No problem, Ryland. She fooled me too."

The lines on Kane's haggard face deepen. "I don't… what's going on here, Corvane?"

Corvane gives him a snarling grin. "What's going on is that Sylara here's told me everything. How this girl stole my relic… for you."

Kane goes very, very still, while Blackstone crouches slightly, a silberwolf ready to spring. Taylor wilts, and she glares desperately at Sylara, tears glistening in her eyes. "I trusted you! And you pull this shit? Again?"

Sylara raises a single shoulder. "I got a better offer—my life. And the bounty I was originally owed."

"Your life?!" Taylor spits, grabbing the neck of Goran's guitar and taking a step toward Sylara, wielding it like an axe. "Better watch your back after this. I can't believe you told Corvane that Kane and I were working together! I promised you a third of the take, plus more jobs down the road. And you want to give that up, give up working for a proper organization like Helix for a slimy smuggler like this asshat?"

Corvane growls, taking a half-step forward. "Watch your mouth, you bitch."

Kane holds out his hands between them, his large, crazed brain looking like it's about to explode.

It's fucking hilarious.

"Now, now. Hold on a minute." He motions to Sylara. "I don't know what this scorp bitch has been telling you, but—"

Quick as a flash, Sylara's stinger is at Kane's throat. The nearest Zeridian guard steps forward too, bypassing Corvane in a rare moment of insubordination. His stinger also goes to Kane's throat. Sylara's antennae twitch. "Call me a scorp again. I dare you."

Blackstone lumbers forward then, his wing-mounted blaster aimed at Sylara's head. She doesn't flinch, but she does pull the stinger away, chuckling darkly as the guard retreats behind Corvane.

"As I was saying, I don't know what she's been telling you, but Taylor Grey does not work for me."

"She didn't steal my relic on your behalf?"

"Technically, she stole it on Isra Darrow's behalf," Kairo chimes in, seeming to be thoroughly enjoying himself. "But Darrow worked for Kane. I helped set up the contact."

"I should have known you would have been involved in this, Kairo," Corvane mutters.

The fence shrugs, unconcerned. "You know how it works, Corvane. I don't ask about origins. I set up the buys. Just like I've done for you. Don't like it? Find someone else next time you come to Vale."

Looking slightly worried at this suggestion, Corvane waves Kairo off. "Whatever. I don't even care about the relic. What I care about is—"

"The weapons you have on this ship?" Taylor guesses. The bluff is so smooth and believable. She's a fucking natural at this. "Why do you think we're on this ship? Stealing them from you is so much easier than buying them."

Corvane goes a dangerous maroon color. Taylor seems to have confirmed his deepest suspicion. "So, you admit it, then?"

"Why deny it?" I grin. "When you're enough of a *buffoon* to make it so easy—"

Kane's eyes go wide. "I still don't—" but he doesn't have time to finish speaking. The lights go out, Gael's reaction perfectly timed to my keyword.

I knew I could work "buffoon" into a sentence.

There's a loud thump as Corvane dives for Kane. While neither man is exactly in shape, Corvane has about ten years and fifty pounds on Kane, and the groan of pain confirms he's tackled him to the ground. There's a rush of air beside me as the two guards tackle Blackstone in a coordinated attack, shoving him to the wall.

I grab Taylor and yank her toward the door as a horrible wrenching sound fills the air. Blackstone screams, and there are two squishy, floppy thunks on the ground. I can only guess they're the cyborg's wings. As I rush behind Taylor toward the door, there's a scream and a hideous crunch, and I'm abruptly hit by something heavy and unyielding. The force sends me sprawling to the grungy metal floor, as the large whatever-it-is oozes and trickles rancid-smelling gunk all over me.

It's a guard. Or half of one, anyway.

Shuddering, I sling the corpse off me, only to see a glowing red eye blazing in the darkness. How the fuck is he this strong? No Enhanced, not even a cyborg, should survive this. We've thrown everything at him, and yet he's still going. Kairo blasts Blackstone with light, trying to disrupt his sensors.

There's a streak from the cyborg's blaster, and Kairo crumples.

Oh shit.

Taylor screams, and I say, "He's fine! Run!" Desperately hoping that's true, I turn to Blackstone and reach out to the tiny plant on the bookshelf. Come on, little guy. Please have enough life for this. I send branch after branch, growing and thickening to surround Blackstone. I wrap him again and again and again, trying to slow him down.

Sylara is next to me, and she reaches to the floor as Blackstone flexes, sending bits of root soaring out in all directions. The concrete rumbles underneath us at the dwarf's touch. I know her magic is less effective on artificial stone, but soon tiny bits of rock fly up from the ground. It's like a miniature meteor shower wrenching metal from flesh and flesh from bone.

There's another scream, and Corvane tackles us both from the left. "You were working with them the whole time, you traitorous little—"

Taylor appears out of nowhere, swinging Goran's guitar at Corvane's head. He goes down, only to have the remaining guard pull her off. He throws her across the room, where she bangs into the doorway.

Corvane stands, wiping blood from his brow. In a flash, Blackstone's metal fist rains down on him, sending him down for the count. The cyborg looks ghastly in the half-light from the hallway, the white bone of his dwarven/human arm visible beneath the missing chunks of flesh. His metal bits move jerkily, the ear-piercing screech noisy over the din. An orangey substance trickles down his emaciated side, glowing faintly.

It's his blood.

Something's wrong. Blackstone's too strong. Kane's done something new to him. And from the looks of the unmoving lump in the corner, he won't be telling us what it was anytime soon. I glance back at Blackstone. The way his blood glows like that. The strange orangey color. It's the luminar essence.

Kane injected him with it.

"Gael! Lights!" I yell, and the lights blare back on.

Blackstone is momentarily disoriented, providing me with the perfect opportunity. I leap at him, tackling him to the ground. "GO!" I yell at the others.

Sylara grabs Taylor, forcing her toward the door. Taylor screams, eyes locked on me. I look away, but feeling them on me is still somehow grounding.

There's a rustling in the corner, where Kairo stumbles to his feet, crimson staining his side as he lumbers to help Sylara drag Taylor toward the door. Extending my claws, I tear into the human side of Blackstone, tearing and ripping at everything I can.

Blackstone throws me off, slamming me into a wall. I hear a loud crash and look up in time to see Taylor tearing toward Blackstone, Sylara and Kairo in a heap by the door. Taylor stretches out a hand as she runs, and the little plant goes flying toward her. I bound off the wall, surging at breakneck speed and leaping onto Blackstone's back as Taylor grabs the plant, sending tendrils, too small to hold him, to wrap around his shoulder and chest. Making the most of Blackstone's distraction, I sink my claws into him again.

"Kairo! Sylara! Get the seeds!" I glare at Kairo, who looks mutinous at the idea of leaving Taylor here, but Sylara pushes him through the door, forcing him off. "Gael!" I call through the comms. "Go in my place. We'll meet you there in a minute."

Gael's voice crackles on the comm. *"Eiran, what are you—"*

"Just go!" Taylor yells, leaping out of the way of a burst from Blackstone's blaster. My vision hazes red at the near miss, a feral roar releasing involuntarily. My grip slips a second, and the cyborg flips me over his shoulder. I wrench away flesh as I move, the bloody mess covering me as I collapse on the ground.

I grin at the warm comfort of it.

No. Taylor. Remember Taylor. Keep your head.

Above me, there's a hideous grinding, followed by an inhuman scream. More gore sprays, and when I hear the loud clanging crash, I realize what she's done. Taylor used the tiny strands from the plant to slide into the joint where mechanics and flesh meet. And then she used them to rip his mechanical arm off.

The sights, the smells. They're too much. I feel myself slipping. I can't fight the calling anymore. Maybe I don't want to.

I leap once again, jamming my hand into his side as Blackstone's hand wraps around my throat like a vise. Taylor's tendrils continue to pull at his mechanical pieces, and he lets out a strange wheezing growl as I gurgle, thrusting my claws deeper, pushing past bone.

The claws of one hand scrape against his Zeridian exoskeleton while I sink my other hand deeper, deeper. My vision dims until there's a loud crack, and Blackstone's grasp slackens, the arm falling away under Taylor's savage blow.

With a final savage roar, I sink my fangs into his exposed neck.

Something about it feels like home. This is what I am.

Without hesitation, I rip out his throat with a crunch. The metallic tang coats my mouth as the wetness of his failing heart flutters under my fingertips. Pulling it out along with my hand, I whirl at a sound behind me. Three more dwarven guards have come to see what's happened. I shouldn't feel so happy to see them.

No, push it back. Give them a choice.

They reach for their blasters as I grin at them, Blackstone's blood trailing down my chin, his heart in my hand. "Your boss is alive. And you will be too… if you leave now." Not needing to be told twice, the Zeridians, the fiercest warriors in the galaxy, flee.

Shame, but I'm not surprised. The Zeridians know. They've heard stories of the Valen. They know what we really are. There's a reason our nations have a tenuous peace. They remember. The humans always seem to forget… except Taylor. She never forgot.

I know if I look at her, I'll see it. The fear. But then, she should be afraid. Because she's right.

At our heart, Valen are predators.

I think of the three guards, and a wild, evil grin spreads on my blood-soaked face.

Fuck it.

I leap through the door after them.

46

KILLER FLOWERS STRIKE BACK

Kairo

I hurry down the long hallway, Sylara close behind me. I'm warring with myself while also ignoring the fire lancing down my side.

I should go back. I can't leave Taylor there with that… monster.

Eiran is with her. That should make me feel better. But the look in his eyes before I left…

Gael comes running up to join us, those warm brown eyes wide with frayed nerves. "What happened to Eiran? And where's Taylor?"

The question snaps me back. I ruffle my wings, irritated by her asking about the agent who was once her boyfriend… fiancé… whatever.

I turn away, pushing down the strange feeling, while also zipping my jacket to hide the red patch on my shirt. "They're fighting Blackstone."

"You left them there to fight that freak?" Gael gasps, stopping to gape at me. I avoid her gaze, hating the guilt that trickles at her words.

Or maybe that's just the blood.

Lirion groans. "*Oh, fuck no. I'm heading there now.*"

"Get the charges planted, Lirion, or we're all going to be stuck here!" Gael snaps.

"We severely injured him before we left," Sylara says. "They'll be fine. We need to get these powerseeds before more security arrives.

Otherwise, we'll have bigger problems than Blackstone."

We slow at the door, pausing for a second. She looks at me, and we exchange a nod. Gripping my blaster tighter, I badge the door and enter the engine room area. The room flickers with badly phased lighting and weird electrical bolts that occasionally crackle out from the poorly shielded wiring. The three engineers on duty look up in surprise. In a blur, Sylara is through the door. She has a spine in the neck of a worker before he can register our presence. The other two fare little better. There's no time to respond before Sylara and I stun them.

The quick action sends another lance of pain to my wound, but I can't let it bother me. Not now. I know pain. I learned about it long ago. I learned from the master. I can ignore it.

Gael looks aghast at the fallen men even as the dwarven huntress and I walk straight over them. I spare her the briefest of looks, flashing a smirk to annoy her into action. "Let's go, Doc. We don't got all day."

Gathering herself, the good doctor hurries forward to catch up with us at the door to the main engine shaft. I badge the door again, and we enter a large cylindrical column of metal that's nearly 100 feet wide, a cyclonic breeze swirling up from giant fans far below. Spiraling metal pipes surround a towering engine core, a soft rumbling drone barely audible past the thrumming fans. The scent of ozone is heavy, giving a tingling in my brain like I need to sneeze. Gael's eyes travel up the giant interstellar engine, her lovely face turning strange colors in the blue lighting.

"Where—" she stammers.

"Where it says forty-two." I point to a number far up on the wall.

She frowns. "That's a metal plate."

Sylara pats a plasma cutter on her belt. "Not a problem."

Cutting through the wall isn't exactly ideal. It's slow and noisy, but like the rest of this plan, it'll work. And that has to be good enough. Beyond that wall is the secure storage floor.

The one place on the ship Goran's badge doesn't give us access to.

Gael is still tilting her head in confusion. "Okay, but... how do we get up there?"

Sylara's scaly mouth twitches in what I suppose is her version of a smirk, her faceted eyes glittering in the strange bluish light. Then, she leaps thirty feet into the passage, landing on one of the slick metal pipes with ease. With a scraping and skittering, she clambers up without a downward glance.

Gael mutes her comms briefly, and I copy her. She bites her lip, and I hate how much my eyes are drawn to the motion. "You think they'll be okay fighting that... thing?"

"They'll be okay," I say, and surprisingly, I mean it. But then, my head swims, and I force myself to push past the pride and add, "I'm not sure *I* will be, though." My voice sounds weak even to me, and I can feel my jacket getting wet. I must be bleeding worse than I thought.

Eyes widening, Gael lurches forward. I unzip my jacket, and she quickly lifts the front of my shirt. Her cheeks go brown as she eyes my bare torso, but I don't have the strength to even make a smartass comment about it.

"You're okay," she says, her voice sounding... relieved? Annoyed? I can't tell. "It's mostly a graze, but... oooh, yeah, this is bleeding a fair bit. Hold on." She places a hand to my side, and my skin blazes where she touches me, right above the wound. Though whether it's from her healing magic or something else, my brain is too fuzzy to untangle.

"Didn't know you cared, Doc," I manage instead.

"I don't," she replies, the twitching corner of her mouth betraying her. Eyes still on the gash as she knits it together with magic, she says, "So Eiran's okay? He sounded off."

Again with the fucking Eiran questions.

"Yeah," I grumble, pulling away from her as soon as the pain subsides. "Honestly, he looked a little... crazed when we left."

Gael's eyes widen further in alarm. "Oh, no." She presses a hand to her comm, unmuting it. "Lirion, I think Eiran's gone over the edge."

"*Fuck*," Lirion spits. "*Is he alone?*"

Gael looks at me, eyes wary. Apologetic. "Taylor's with him."

"*Shit.*"

"What?" I ask, fear spiking because I already know the answer. I've heard people talk about it, seen the effects of it. Seen what happens when elves go feral. It's never pretty.

Fuck, I left Taylor alone with that?!

"*The Rökkurgrimm,*" Lirion says, giving voice to my worst fears. "*Valen predatory instinct. When it kicks in, it can make us... well, feral.*"

Dread sinks into my stomach at the words. "Shit. *Shit!* Lirion, you need to—"

"*Eiran's fine,*" Taylor's voice says over the comms, making me sag in relief. *"I have him. We had a bit of an… incident, but we're okay. Heading up to you now. Tackle the first room the best you can, and we'll join ASAP."*

"Fucking hell," I mutter, and Gael looks at me quizzically. She wasn't supposed to be with us for this part. I don't think she's ready. But I can't say that.

"Come here, Doc," I say, my skin prickling with the proximity as I move into her space. With a single motion, I pick her up, the wound in my side barely a twitch now. Thank the gods for elvish healing abilities.

Her chocolate eyes are glued to mine as I walk to the edge of the engine column, furrow my wings, and jump into the corridor. I breathe in the honeysuckle scent of her as we climb, my wing beats a steady backdrop to our ascent. Sparks from Sylara's plasma cutter sparkle in the distance, falling like glittering stars and framing Gael's face. Sylara's gleaming exoskeleton reflects the cutter's glow, the whole thing creating an absurd, yet beautiful backdrop.

"Kairo," Gael says hesitantly, barely audible over the cacophony. "What are we doing?" She blinks, and then adds, "I mean, what's the plan? I wasn't in the discussion for this part. I'm not supposed to be here."

"No, you weren't," I agree, hating that she's here. That she's in danger like this.

But if she's here, she needs to know. Needs to be on guard. "We don't exactly know what we're about to face. That's why it was Eiran, Taylor, Sylara, and me going. We're used to that. From the intel we gathered, there are two outer rooms before the main room. Given what we know about Corvane, there will probably be different security measures in each chamber. Top-notch enchantments from across the galaxy."

"But… you're ready for it, right? We'll be able to break in."

I avoid her gaze, focused on the passing engine core and Sylara working with the cutter. "Of course. We just need to be prepared for anything."

I don't let my tone betray the truth. There's a reason Taylor only took the Eldralume job once we knew it wasn't on Corvane's ship. When we thought it was in the ship vault, she almost turned it down.

And for Taylor, that's saying something.

There's a loud crash as the bulkhead falls away, the brightly painted number forty-two flashing intermittently as it bangs off walls on the way down the large open cavern.

"Are you… prepared for that?" Gael asks.

At her odd tone, I follow her gaze through the hole in the wall. When I realize what lies beyond the small elevator lobby we've carved into… I freeze in horror. "Oh, shit."

The room is dangerously unassuming. The ceiling of the ten-by-ten-foot cube glows strangely with greenhouse lights, and a straight, very human-designed path cuts across the otherwise Valen space, allowing Corvane and other non-intruders to pass through without delay. But somehow I doubt we'll have such luck, because covering the floor is the largest concentration of Gruundlith-enhanced plants I've ever seen.

"This is going to suck," Gael says, watching Sylara scramble through the scorched hole into the elevator lobby, the scraping whine of keratin on metal making my teeth ache. I lower Gael through the hole, careful to avoid the still-searing edges. I hover there and examine the too-small gap, unsure how to proceed.

With a small scoff, Gael steps forward, holding out a hand. After a brief hesitation, Sylara does too, and the ladies haul me through the gap into the tiny lobby.

I turn to Gael and explain, "So the plants are—"

"Security grid," she says flatly. "I get it. I'm not an idiot."

"Never said you were, doc."

She doesn't reply. Just points at a large tree in the center of the space. "There. That's the biggest plant here. If I can control that, then I can deal with the rest."

Kairo shakes his head. "Not possible. Even an elf can't override a security enchantment."

Gael rolls her eyes in exasperation. "You can if you know the underlying spellwork. They're old magic. Trust me. I can do it." She bites her lip as she looks back at the tree. "Assuming I can reach it."

"Are you sure you can do that?" Sylara asks, her voice cold. Calculating.

"No way you're getting over there," I say with a shake of my head.

"Then you'd better cover me." Gael gives me an admirable attempt at a cocky grin before stepping onto the pathway.

She immediately ducks to the ground, narrowly avoiding a long, thorny branch aiming for her head.

Fuck.

I leap into the air, but the ceiling's too low to give me much advantage. My hip gives a sudden, searing lurch, and I let out a pained cry. I look down to see multiple vines, damp and earthy, have reached out and grabbed my feet. I flap wildly, but branches continue to coil up my leg, squeezing me and pulling me back.

While I combat the vines, Sylara slides forward, ducking under me to stab a crimson-petaled emberblossom before it can spray us. The last thing we need is to be tripping our asses off in here.

I'm jerked back to the ground, and my hand flies to my vest, retrieving a VerdantBoost capsule Taylor gave me. I toss it wildly, where it shatters in a burst of green liquid. Moments later, the vine on my leg stops moving, and I regain a couple of feet of altitude even as more branches reach for me.

This would be so much easier if we had Eiran's ability.

"Clear me a path!" Gael says, and my heart lurches into my throat as she launches forward toward a large plant in the middle of the space.

I reach for my vest again, trying to fly over to follow her, but a branch wraps around my waist and chest, the spines digging into me. My remaining canisters burst, withering the offending vine. I shove it off me, and I notice distantly that my pants are soaked in a mix of green enhancer and red blood. Another branch reaches for me, wrapping around my ribs. A thorn scrapes along my sensitive wing, and I scream in pain as it squeezes. Sylara leaps up, severing the branch with an extended spine. The branch wrenches back, withering from her poison as if burned.

Another branch reaches for me, and, absent my canisters, I blast the plants to clear a path in this overcrowded death garden, Sylara fighting alongside me with both spines and blasters. We're in a losing battle, the plants regrowing as quickly as we can shatter them, even as more vines try to strangle us to death.

Gael finally reaches the largest plant, a squat bush with thick branches and purple leaves. One branch swings for her, and she dives to the ground, wrapping her arms around the wide trunk. The bush shakes and shimmies but doesn't attack her.

The other plants do, though. She doesn't seem to notice as thorns tear at her flesh, sending rivulets of blood streaking down her thighs. With a scream, I continue blasting vines away from her as best as I can, trying to ensure none of us dies from vindictive shrubbery.

A large root suddenly wraps around my throat, squeezing tightly. The corners of my vision dim, and I just make out Sylara's blaster flying across the room as she's knocked to the ground. I'm slammed to the earth as well, my wings, torso, and throat covered in roots, pulling me under.

My breathing is so heavy now.

Dirt covers my face, stinging my eyes and falling into my mouth.

I push. Thrash. Kick. Or try to. But I can't move.

The roots are pulling me under.

We're not going to make it.

I'd never considered that we might not make it.

Strange. I'm less accepting of it than I'd thought I'd be. I want to live. I didn't think I would when it came down to it. Not after all I've been through. Kind of a shitty time to realize it.

I push with all of my might, but my body refuses to respond.

Holy shit. I'm actually going to die.

I pray I've bought Gael enough time.

As my world fades to darkness, I hear a loud, rending crash.

I barely make out Gael's whimpering cries next to me before all is black.

47

A HEART OF GLASS

Taylor

It takes me a second to register the image of Eiran leaping through the doorway.

I run after him, only to find the hallway empty. Where the hell did he go?! He was just here!

I try to calm my roiling thoughts. Even with my enhanced speed, I never have a prayer of outrunning an elf, particularly one who…

Something's very wrong with Eiran.

The Rökkurgrimm. It must be. I remember the Valen boy from the park so many weeks ago. The blood on that human's face. The way it took both parents to haul the elvish boy off the playground.

I have to find him.

As I run from hallway to grease-stained hallway, I allow myself a few moments to process the rest of what happened.

My mom… elves didn't kill her. It was Helix. Kane had admitted as much. Dr. Grey… my mom had been a mole for Helix. Then she took me to the Hitari embassy, told Helix I was dead, and then… they'd killed her.

And what about Kane? Is he dead? Just injured? What if I never hear the rest, hear whatever else Kane had to tell me about my mom? Instead, I'm tracking down Eiran, leaving Kairo and Gael to face the challenges Eiran and I prepared for. While I track down a crazed elfin spy who—

I round another corner in this rusted maze of a ship before stopping in my tracks. Eiran is standing, shoulders hunched and panting. At his feet is a body, one of Corvane's goons. Blood pools from a huge gash in the human's neck, large claw marks marring his chest. Crimson drips from Eiran's clawed hand, and he's staring down at the corpse, unmoving other than his gasping breaths.

"Eiran?"

He rounds on me, and I can't comprehend what I'm seeing. It's like a vision from my worst imaginings. This is the Valen I always feared. The nightmare that stole sleep for years. Red blood slicks his mouth, glistening on the row of serrated teeth he bares at me. His claws drip with dwarven green ooze, drips falling in a line along the hallway. The holo ads set his face aglow in a magenta tint, and he lets out a deep, guttural growl. Snarling, he hulks toward me, and I step forward too, as if pulled by a string.

Eiran. This is Eiran.

Eiran snarls and bends, a panther preparing to leap.

"Eiran." I lower my head, trying to be nonthreatening, even as I meet his eyes.

He snarls again but doesn't move forward. I take a step, and then another. He's watching me, purple irises mere halos around large, dilated pupils. His snarling has turned into a low, consistent growl, a rumbling that's barely audible.

"Eiran, it's okay." I try not to let my voice break, to show the fear that's turning my insides to mush. He's a predator… but beneath that, he's still Eiran. He's still mine.

Mine.

I know what to do.

Adrenaline surges in my chest, my heart roaring. I can't deny the pull—half fear, half desire—toward him.

I take another step forward, and he's close enough to touch now. He still hasn't attacked. I reach out slowly and place my hand on his chest. I can feel his heavy breathing as the low rumble subsides. Still looking him in the eye, I incline my head, revealing my neck to him.

I turn my eyes up to him, and his pupils contract a bit. He blinks once, and they seem to clear somewhat. "It's me." He scents me, nose tracing along my neck, those teeth so close to my skin. I want him to do it. I've wanted him to do it for a while, I realize. On some level, at least. Even before I heard the term.

He inhales another long breath and pulls back. His eyes are clear again. "Taylor?"

"Hey," I say with a shaky laugh, relief washing over me. "Welcome back."

He lets out a soft keen. "It happened. I never thought... Taylor, I... I killed Blackstone. I ripped out his throat. It was—"

The comms crackle to life. "*Lirion, I think Eiran's gone over the edge.*"

Eiran winces at the words, and I draw his eyes back to me, muting my mic. "I know, Eiran. I was there. I was with you all the way."

"*Fuck. Is he alone?*"

Eiran's eyes widen as my words and Lirion's blur together. "You were there?" He shakes his head to clear it. "But I could have... I wasn't sure if that was real or—"

"*Taylor's with him.*"

"*Shit.*"

I put a hand on Eiran's cheek, and he stills finally. "Eiran, you're okay. You're good. And I'm glad you put that son of a bitch down."

"*What?*"

Kairo. That's Kairo's voice. Tension I didn't know I was holding leeches out. They're all okay.

"*The Rökkurgrimm. Valen predatory instinct. When it kicks in, it can make us... well, feral.*"

Eiran's breathing is heavy, and he barely makes out, "You're not... scared of me? Even though I... sort of freaked out?"

I smile, a memory coming back to me. "You said you'd freak out later. It was your turn."

"But I... I almost bit you."

"*Shit. Shit! Lirion, you need to—*"

"Eiran's fine," I say, unmuting the comms. "I have him. We had a bit of an... incident, but we're okay. Heading up to you now. Tackle the first room the best you can, and we'll join ASAP."

Clicking the mic back on mute, I turn to Eiran again. "As for the biting... would that have been so bad?" Another echo of his earlier words.

Eiran gasps. "Taylor... what are you saying?"

I gaze at him for a second, and then admit, "Eiran, over the past few months, you've saved my life how many times? You've fought for me, fought with me, challenged me, cared for me in ways no one has ever done in my life. You're smart, you're funny, and you're sexy as hell. Is it crazy? Of course, it's crazy. But life is short in this business. I could die tomorrow. So fuck it. Let's do it."

"You mean that." It isn't a question. He sounds amazed. And pleased.

I shrug, tossing my red curls over my shoulder. "I mean, maybe not *now*, because our friends are like, risking their lives and shit, but yeah. I mean it, Eiran."

He laughs, those amethyst eyes glinting. "Alright. Let's go."

I wink back. "Lead the way, Leaf Boy."

***

I stare up at the massive engine room, wondering how they got up there without the grappling hooks I'm carrying… until I remember we're dealing with a dwarf who can climb walls and a winged Hitari.

I hand the second grappler to Eiran, trying to resist the temptation to ask if he's alright. After exchanging a nod, we fire the electronically guided grapplers through the maze of piping, navigating a safe course to the gaping hole in the wall I assume must be floor forty-two.

"You okay?" I ask, unable to help myself.

Eiran, predictably, rolls his eyes. "I'm fine. Let's go."

"If you say so," I mutter, and not looking back, I press the retract button and zoom up to the floor, the whizzing sound behind me assuring me that Eiran is following.

As we near the door, though, a thunderous discordance of creaking, crashing, and screaming overwhelms the hum of our grapplers.

When I reach the edge of the wall and can see through the cooling metal gash, my blood freezes, fear like icy shards prickling my veins.

The room, a massive Gruundlith grid denser than I've ever seen, is in shambles, fauna and broken lighting panels hanging at odd angles from the ceiling, rotten plants and splintered branches strewn everywhere, and amidst it all, three vine-covered mounds that must be our friends. The large tree-like bush in the center is thrashing about, rearing to smash the largest mound.

Kairo.

In a flash, Eiran is through the door, arms spread wide. The giant bush halts its advance in the face of Eiran's magic, shaking with effort as it tries to push forward. Tries to ignore the strength of his will.

No Valen should be able to do this. You don't countermand the enchantment on a Gruundlith grid. You just survive it.

The tree bows, bending back under the force of Eiran's onslaught. He screams, arms trembling, but he never stops his advance.

Eiran crosses the threshold into the grid, but rather than attack, the shrubs and thorns seem to shy away, as if trying to run from him despite being planted. The room is filled with the overwhelming tide of creaking wood until…

Silence.

The room is motionless for a long moment.

Then, the place comes alive again. The smaller plants attack him, coiling to strike. Eiran doesn't react.

There's a shuddering noise as the big bush aims not at Eiran, but at the other plants. With his hands still wide, Eiran traces the bush's large branches along the ground, uprooting the plants in long, sweeping arcs. Finally, everything stills for good.

Eiran and I run forward then, pulling the vines and roots away from our friends. With a crash, Kairo manages to sit up, gasping a heaping lungful of air. "What is it… with these fucking… murder rooms… that kill anyone… who isn't on the approved list? Who came up with this shit?"

"Anton… Palmer…" Gael says, rising from where Eiran and Sylara have freed her. "Half-elf… security genius… from about a hundred and fifty years ago. Came up with the concept of rooms… tied to the auras of specific—"

"I don't think he was actually asking," I tell her, smirking.

She looks at me blearily. "Well then, he shouldn't have asked. Took you two long enough."

"Yeah," Kairo agrees. "I was starting to get the tiniest bit worried there. Just for a second."

Sylara shakes her head, muttering something about "stupid alien bastards" as she leads the way into the next room.

I step forward and wrap an arm around Kairo, letting the relief flood through me even as I push back the unspoken tide of today's revelations. I won't think of Mom right now. Of Helix, or Kaelen, or The Initiative. Of Eiran or what could have happened to Kairo, Gael, and Sylara.

I can worry about all of *that* shit later.

The huntress suddenly stops in the entryway, throwing out an arm to halt us (and, thankfully, my spiraling thoughts).

The large room is as lifeless as the last was verdant. The walls and floor are covered in slate, a chill emanating from the smooth gray stone. In the center of the floor is a large circular pit surrounded by four stone pillars, each with a light purple crystal in the center that flickers with an orange light. To reach the other end, we'll need to cross a long stone walkway.

Unfortunately, the path is blocked by a colossal statue.

The slate gray body is roughly humanoid, but without detail. Just rectangles for the body, arms, and legs, with no discernible way for them to attach beyond magic. The face of the statue is a large diamond-shaped crystal that's glowing with the same flickering orange light.

Kairo lets out a shaky little laugh. "Uh… what are those?"

"Golems," Sylara whispers. "Sentries. They guard the space between those columns. Only their master can cross the path safely."

"So, if we walk past one—"

"They'll come to life and try to kill us," Eiran finishes, mouth a thin line.

"Exactly," Gael agrees. "It's old dwarven magic, right? I haven't read about anyone making golems in a *long* time."

"Centuries," Sylara agrees. "The magic is sacred. Using them like this is a disgrace to the ancestors. Who would… I'm sorry. It's not the time for these questions. To destroy them, you need to shatter the crystals in their faces. But first—"

Kairo swiftly pulls out his blaster and fires three tight shots at the golem's face. The round head snaps back at the force, but then turns slowly back forward. The web-like cracks in the crystalline face weave back together like retreating vines. The fire-like glow flickers angrily on its face as it makes one ground-shaking step forward, the light in the crystal of one column brightening briefly in reciprocation.

Sylara flicks her antennae at Kairo as if to say, "Idiot!" She then leaps onto the nearest column. "But first…" She jumps to the next column as the golem lurches forward, giant stone fist aiming for her head. "…you must destroy…" She leaps to the next column as the place she was crouched goes up in a cloud of stone shards and dust. "…the support column before it heals it."

She finally reaches the column that lit up earlier, scrambling down to its crystal heart. The golem leaps across the open pit toward her, and I dive to meet it midair, sending the statue into another pillar. The pillar topples, and we roll across the sharp corner of the rectangular column and crash into the nearby wall.

With an ear-splitting scrape, the pieces of the column slide back into place, reforming it. My world spins in a gut-wrenching spiral as the golem flips me onto my back, looming over me. A thick branch winds around the golem's middle as Eiran pulls in plant life from the other room to help us.

The branches only slow it for a second, but it's enough. With all of my enhanced strength, I deck the ember-like face. The crystal shatters, only to reform a second later.

But the golem freezes while the crystal reforms.

That'll work.

My fingers ache with pain, but I punch again and again, skin splitting and bones cracking as the crystal in the face continues to mend itself. A shadow looms over me as another golem nears, but Eiran jumps on this one, following my lead and shattering the crystal repeatedly to keep it frozen.

Certain I've broken several bones by now, I slam my fist into the crystal one last time. The orange glow in the lavender stone sputters, and then dies, the stone freezing above me.

I look up to where Sylara stands, hands on either side of the dark, now-cracked crystal. With a heavy breath, I say, "You were right, Eiran. That did suck."

Eiran smirks until the golem grabs him by his feet and throws him across the room. He lands on the edge of the pit, scrambling for purchase as he hangs perilously on the edge.

Sylara leaps across the space, landing near Eiran and pulling him back up. As he stands, she holds up a hand, quieting him while her compound eyes rove the room. I quickly crawl out from underneath the inert golem, whimpering at the pain in my wrist before I notice Sylara's twitching antennae. Standing, I follow her gaze.

The second golem isn't attacking.

And there are *three* more glowing columns.

Sylara pushes Eiran to the side, and with a boom that rattles my bones, the remaining two golems slam down from hidden spots in the ceiling, one of them landing right where Eiran was standing. "Aww, shit," Kairo mutters as they crouch, preparing to leap toward us. He fires a shot at one, noting which column lights up as it heals.

With a flash of light, a replica of him appears beside a golem next to the column in question. It trundles toward the illusion, passing through the fake Kairo to topple it. Sylara leaps toward it, putting a hand to the crystal in a shower of purple slivers. The shot golem prepares to jump toward us, only to lurch to a stop halfway as I shoot it with my blaster.

Fuck, my hand hurts.

With a dizzying spin, the golem plunges into the pit, bouncing with a loud crunch against the stone walls on its forty-foot fall, exploding into broken shards at the bottom.

"Sylara!" Gael yells as she spins, examining the room with a keen gaze. "You need to destroy the columns."

"I do not take orders from an elf," Sylara spits back.

"Just fucking do it," Eiran hollers, not bothering to see if she'll obey or not as he turns to me. "Taylor, stand at that end of the walkway. Get one of their attention as you go, but hurry! Gael, you too."

I nod, not questioning his plan. I sprint for the end of the walkway, firing potshots at a golem's head. It thunders after me, just as Gael lures the other golem to the opposite end of the narrow stone walkway.

While he fires, Eiran shouts, "Kairo! Illusion! Middle of the walkway on my mark. Do it… now!"

With a flash, illusions of Gael and me appear in the middle of the walkway, shining fake blaster shots flying over the golems' heads. The column crystal shatters with a resounding crash, the sound echoing through the room as a golem falters for a moment, its heavy footfalls slowing slightly before resuming its measured, relentless advance toward me.

 They're not taking the bait.

"You need to get out of their line-of-sight!" Kairo yells, increasing his fake blaster fire.

Gael nods at me, but I yell, "Duck!" She crouches before the golem can take off her head. With a push of her Valen might, she shoves the golem several feet backward, enough to break its eye contact while she leaps into the pit. Sylara hurtles across the pit in a massive aerial, staying out of sight of the golem's gem gaze. Following her lead, I send a massive wall of air toward my own pursuing golem, spinning it against the wall with a crunch, one of its stone arms lying limp on the floor.

While it seems to stare in disbelief at its lost limb, I jump into the pit, using air to slow my fall. Turning to Gael, I'm concerned about her making the drop until I hear the rhythmic scrape of her claws against the stone as she carefully descends, landing safely.

We exchange weary glances before a thunderous crash causes our heads to snap up. The two remaining golems crash together as they pass through the illusion, and a gravelly rain falls on our heads. The room suddenly falls into an eerie silence, broken by the crunch of stone as Eiran lands next to me.

"Are you alright?" he asks, lifting my chin so I meet his gaze. I nod shakily, then wince. He puts a hand on my forearm, and I wince at the pain of my healing bones.

I flex my fingers, grimacing at the rushed healing. At least I can use my hand.

"Okay," I breathe. "So, that was Zeridian magic?" Sylara nods. "And obviously, the first room was elvish. Kai, you're sure there's only three rooms?"

"Absolutely. The final room guards the vault door."

Eiran pauses. "So, will the magic be Quiblin or Hitari? Or one of the other races?"

"Most likely it will be both Quiblin *and* Hitari," Sylara says. "More types of magic make it harder for any single person or crew to bypass all the enchantments."

"So what should we expect?" I ask.

Kairo shakes his head. "No telling. But if someone has mixed our illusion magic with Quiblin psychic magic? Buckle up."

Gael scoffs nervously. "What does that mean, 'Buckle up'? That's not a plan."

"The plan is for you to go back," Eiran says firmly.

Her eyes widen. "What? No! I'm not leaving you guys again!"

"We need you on comms," I insist. "Get back to the computers. Monitor the guards' movements, or we'll be flying blind on the out."

"But I left you," she says, eyes watery. "You nearly died and—"

I push back memories of the prison. Of the crowded cell.

"You got out," I say instead. "You got help. And now we need help again. We can't do it without you, Gael. You did great. Now go."

She hesitates another second, but after a nod from Kairo, she turns and heads back.

"So, the plan?" Eiran asks, muting his mic.

"The plan is to stick together," I say firmly. "Whatever this is, it will try to fuck with our heads. We don't let it. I'm your anchor, and you're mine."

"If you have my back, then I'll have yours," Sylara says with the closest I've ever seen to a smile. "It's the only way this'll work."

"Alright then," Kairo says with a nod. "Let's do this."

With a final determined look at each other, we cross as one into Corvane's vault entrance.

48

MIND FIELD

Taylor

The white, featureless room materializes, instantly giving me a headache. My brain tries to latch onto something for a point of reference, but there are no doors, walls, or ceiling. And worse: no people. I'm alone.

"Eiran! Kai!" No one responds. They're probably trapped in the same illusion as I am.

"*Hello, little Starflower.*"

I'm shaking before my mind can place the voice. I turn slowly, swallowing the scream as I come face-to-face with my mother. She opens her arms wide to me, and my heart aches. Some small part of me, the lingering child, wants to run to her, for her to pat my hair and tell me everything will be alright.

That part is stupid.

I step back. "You're… you're not real."

Mom smiles. "*Oh sweetie. Of course I'm real.*" Like paint sliding down a canvas, the laboratory materializes into view.

"No. This isn't… you're not…"

Abruptly, I'm six years old again. My tiny hands tremble as the cold metal of the lab presses in.

Mom steps forward, brandishing a syringe like a sword. "*It's time to*

335

play the game."

There's a clank to my left. I jerk my head and find Blackstone standing there wearing a lab coat. *"I have some new assistants today,"* my mother says with a smile of glittering teeth and cold, dead eyes. *"Adrian, Phina. I think we're ready to begin."* Blackstone holds up a scanner, light glinting off the three flat plates. Phina, the Valen bully from my childhood, holds an injector gun dripping with blood, her pointed teeth stained crimson.

"No," I say firmly. "You're not real. This isn't real." The illusions step forward, and I charge at them.

I attempt to barrel through the illusion but bounce off, collapsing to the floor. No, this can't be. Blackstone presses down on my shoulders, and Phina grabs my legs. *"Stop squirming, you geneblight bitch."*

I flinch at the cold prick against my neck—no. It's *not* real. It's psychophysical. Hitari and Quiblin magic. I can beat this.

I close my eyes for a moment, and I can finally sense the attack. Using the skills Emma taught me, I form a shield in my mind, pushing back against the onslaught of mental images. I open my eyes again, keeping that shield in place. Even as the foreign tide tells me that the needle is pushing farther into my neck, I push the torrent of images back, building a cocoon around my mind. I sit up, and my mother's hand passes through me like smoke.

Without the Quiblin magic telling me otherwise, it's just a Hitari light trick. Just an illusion.

I stand shakily and walk right through Blackstone. The world flashes white, burning with intensity.

Suddenly, everything darkens again, and I run smack into the hard frame of Sylara. We collide with a crack, but she doesn't say anything, doesn't move. Her entire body is quaking, and she's cradling her arm as if it's broken.

Sylara's back is plastered against the rust-colored wall of a rocky tunnel, the crumbly stone yielding slightly, leaving an almost imperceptible imprint. I'm standing next to her in the small alcove, her features barely visible in the faint glow of purple lichen. The air is rank with the stench of dirt, stale air, and something faintly acidic. Sylara doesn't move, her scaly red mouth opening and closing. At her feet is a dwarven male, and he's… oh gods.

The exoskeleton on the dwarf's chest has cracked open in a huge, ragged gash that's leaking a putrid green ooze. And from Sylara's trembling, this can only be one person. Her mate.

Ankáriel.

His throat shakes with a violent cough, and more green ooze trickles from his mouth as he struggles to speak. *"You. You did this. You let this happen."*

"No!" Sylara whines, voice trembling as much as the rest of her. It's so quiet. I don't know how I've intruded on Sylara's private vision. I shouldn't be here.

I grab her shoulders and shake violently, feeling her exoskeleton under my fingers. "Sylara, wake up! It's not real."

"Ankáriel… please…" My heart breaks at the vulnerability in the tone. I've never heard Sylara sound like this. Her legs buckle, and she clutches at the apparition as though it were real. As though he were still breathing.

Reaching out with my mind, I touch her consciousness. *"Sylara."*

The dwarf stills. She shakes her head as if to clear it, her antennae stilling. "How are you here?"

"I'm not. You're not. It's a dream. It's not real. Hold on." I reach out again with my mind, sensing the onslaught against her mind. Extending my shield as best as I can, I cover her as well, though it's like an umbrella against a thunderstorm.

Shit, I wish Frank were here.

When the noise dulls somewhat, I turn to Sylara. "We need to find the others. Stay close." She doesn't react, large eyes still fixed on her lost mate. "Sylara!" Finally, she nods, stepping carefully over Ankáriel's illusion as if it were real. When we reach the rocky wall of the tunnel, Sylara presses her hand against it. It doesn't move.

I try again to extend my shield further, to block out more of the psychic attack that's telling Sylara the wall is real. It's hard, like stretching clothes shrunk in the wash. Finally, I pass through the wall, dragging Sylara with me. She screams as we move, as though she's being torn apart.

The dim light of the tunnel washes away with another waterfall of searing white light.

Still blinking, we're thrust into yet another vision. We're deep in the edge of Silberwald Forest, the broad vine-covered trees branching out overhead. The dappled gloom hangs overhead, a dense fog bracing the clearing in sinister shadow. The scent of earthy decay fills the air, and the leaf-strewn ground crunches as two hunched shapes circle each other.

Two crouching monsters.

Two Eirans.

One Eiran, who I assume is the real one, is still wearing the same dark clothes he boarded the ship in, now stained green with dwarven blood. The other? He's like someone out of my worst nightmare.

His face is a gnarled, evil version of the man I love, a sinister little smile mangling his face. He bares his teeth at the real Eiran, and the teeth are long, jagged points. A nightmarish warping of reality. Eight-inch claws drip crimson pools onto the forest floor.

And behind him, is a mangled heap. A body.

My body.

I battle back violent tremors. It's not the blood. It's not even my brutalized corpse. It's the way my heart shatters for this man.

The room shows us what we truly fear. And for Eiran… that's himself.

The Evil Eiran steps forward, a low, gnarled chuckle trickling out of his mouth. "Look at what you did, Eiran."

"No…" he says, so quiet I barely hear it. He takes a stumbling step back, eyes on the motionless mound behind his doppelgänger.

I run to him, trying to pull him away, trying to draw his focus. "Hey! Eiran, it's okay. I'm okay."

He won't move. Doesn't react. Just trembles as the twisted vision of himself moves inexorably forward.

With another mental stretch, I touch his mind… and find him screaming. The wailing inside his head is like a wildfire, consuming everything it touches, growing bigger and bigger. The onslaught of the psychic attack uses his fear like fuel, scorching his consciousness.

And as the fire grows, so too does the evilness of the vision, his face twisting, his fangs and claws lengthening to impossible proportions.

"You've got to fight, Eiran!" I shout into his mind. *"Fight back!"*

Evil Eiran leaps forward, and the real one finally moves. Screaming, he rips into his counterpart, tearing off an ear and spitting it out, where it lands at my feet with a vile splat.

The Evil Eiran laughs in earnest. "See? You're a monster. You know you're a monster."

"NO!" Eiran screams, and the surrounding space flickers white. But then the vision returns.

I need to help him.

I try to stretch my mental wall further, but I whimper. My mind hurts. The protection can only grow so big. I don't have the practice. If I stretch further, I won't have anything left, and I know this only gets worse. I can't—

"I'm okay," Sylara says with a grimace. "I've trained against Quiblin attacks, now that I know to expect them. Protect the elf."

With a heave of mental effort, I remove the shield from Sylara and wrap it around Eiran. He sags under the weight of relief, even as Sylara sags under whatever voices are attacking her head. I reach in to touch his shoulder, and he startles. "I... I..."

"It's alright," I say, pushing past a lump in my throat. "You're not a monster, Eiran. You're the most amazing man I've ever known. You could never hurt me. I've never felt as safe with anyone as I do with you."

I run a thumb along his sage-colored cheek, catching a stray tear as it falls. "I love you, Eiran. You're safe. But we need to go."

He takes a deep breath and gives a tiny nod. "Okay. Okay. Let's... let's go find Kairo." I take his hand, and the three of us walk into Kairo's memory.

This time we're in the office of a sprawling manor house, its walls paneled in light, polished wood. Silvery inlays of Kōjyotsu steel give an aethereal glow to the space, the light refracting in prismatic patterns. The large window is is framed by cloth hangings in deep garnet, and the view from the window is of rolling blue hills and floating islands drifting through the mist. It must be Kagēkami, the Hitari homeworld.

Kairo doesn't look much younger than he is now, though that means little. His wings are spread, held in place between two bookshelves by large steel clips. Standing in front of him is Akio, his father.

The Kuro Oni is surveying Kairo, tapping a long, wicked-looking ceremonial knife to his chin in contemplation. There's a narrow crescent etched into the shimmering Kōjyotsu blade, the same symbol I saw branded on the skin of his followers.

The mark of the Eclipse Consortium.

"*Via Yamiyo'n kageshuku, Hikario shin prakaar,*" the Kuro Oni chants in Hitari. "*Peetosh vi peedami, Kagekari tsulama varanai.*"

"What's he saying?" Eiran whispers, but I don't reply.

There's no way I could explain that he'd chanted, *"Only through Yamiyo and the blessing of her shadows can Hikario bring his light. Only through pain can Kagekari bring their balance."*

I shiver as Akio runs the large blade against the thick, sensitive skin of Kairo's wing. In a low tone, Akio continues in Hitari, *"Your actions today prove you have forgotten your destiny. I think you need another lesson."* Without warning, the vision of Akio stabs the knife through the wing, tearing a huge gash.

Kairo screams. Vision or not, the pain is real.

Oh, gods. I have to stop this.

Screaming aloud along with Kairo, I force back the onslaught against him with every ounce of effort. My head pounds, sweat stinging my eyes. I'm like a girl on a beach trying to stand against an oncoming tsunami.

Wordlessly, Sylara steps forward and smacks Kairo hard across the side of the head. "Sylara!" I yelp, but Kairo looks around in a daze as the vision snuffs out like a candle. The hit somehow broke the contact, and now we're back in the white, endless room. There's a pause, as if the room doesn't know how to attack us.

Kairo starts some sort of muffled chant or prayer in Hitari before trailing off, his eyes clearing. "What? What happened?" Kairo runs a hand through his mop of hair, his voice muffled in confusion.

I look past his face to his wings and breathe, "Kai?"

Hikario save us. His wings. They're covered in scars. Absolutely covered in them, giving the wings a tattered texture, rip upon repaired rip marring every inch.

And prominent in the center of each wing is a giant carved scar in the shape of a thin crescent.

Kairo glances exhaustedly at his wings, and the scars vanish.

"Where's the fucking safe?"

I want to ask about Akio's talk of "destiny," but there's no time.

"It'll be hidden in this room somewhere. Behind the illusions," I tell him instead. "We need to use our magic together. You try to push past these visions, while I try to block—"

"Starflower. It's time for a game."

I give the vision of my mother the briefest of glances. "...that."

"Don't you dare move, son," says a vision of Akio.

Kairo vaporizes his phantom father with a radiant blast. He stares at the place where his father's illusion disappeared for a long moment, but then walks forward with forced determination. Sending more light bursts here and there, he rips apart the visual illusions as he searches for the door. It appears that without the illusion, the mental attacks don't work.

Still, the room repairs them just as quickly as Kairo can banish them. Eiran and Sylara spread out, trying to find a wall or other physical surface beneath the illusion.

"You were never really my daughter, you know?"

That's it. I turn and stare down this evil approximation of my mother. She scowls back at me. Behind her shoulder, Blackstone materializes from the white nothingness, huge and imposing. I reach out with my mind, feeling for a connection the way Emma taught me over the past few weeks, like I'm trying to talk to the enchanted machine behind this hell. It takes a moment, but then… there. A tiny… something. It's not a consciousness, but rather an enchantment, likely tied to artificial intelligence.

It senses me, and the enchantment attacks me directly, a spike of psychic energy driving straight through my brain. *"Filthy geneblight freak!"* Phina, Blackstone, my mother, and Akio all holler as one, their voices rising along with the tsunami of magic.

I scream, but then I push back, imagining my thoughts as a dagger and stabbing right at the heart of the enchantment. It dodges my attack, coming at my thoughts from a point I don't expect. I'm more prepared this time, and I quickly build a mental wall to deflect it.

"Let's play a game, son," Akio says in my mother's voice.

"It's getting confused!" I shout as I continue to attack and counterattack, keeping the enchantment busy.

"Here, Kairo!" Eiran shouts, feeling along the nothingness and clearly detecting something hidden by a glamour. Kairo blasts it with a concentrated beam of light, revealing a small interface screen.

I sense the attack on my mind lessening, like the enchantment is turning its focus on something else. Kairo. He groans in pain, grabbing his head. I strike out with more mental force than I've ever used before, flooding my love for Kairo into the beam. How dare this *thing* hurt my friend, the closest thing to a father I ever had?

I sense the tether between us. I feel along it, tracing back to a small box high above us. There, hidden by enchantments, is a small box. I try grabbing it with my magic, but it slides off. I keep pouring my energy into the mental attack.

I can't do this alone.

Pointing to where the device lies hidden, I say, "Sylara! There!"

Not stopping to question how I know, she fires three blaster shots in that direction, but they bounce harmlessly off. Damn it. It's shielded.

"You won't best me that easily, you bastard," Sylara hisses and then leaps to where the box is. With her spine extended, she thrusts right through the shielding, a burst of sparks flying as she punctures the box. The room darkens into a gray steel cube, empty save for a single door with a small screen.

Kairo hands me Goran's card. "I think you deserve the honors." Grinning, I badge the door to the safe along with a small sampling of Goran's blood. The door slides open, revealing a room the size of a large walk-in closet with several rows of shelves. On the shelves glitter jewels and artifacts, piles of precious metals in neat bars, and, surprisingly, several old books.

I glance at Kairo for the tiniest of moments, and his grin widens.

Finally, on a shelf tucked into a corner, I find my bag. I grab it, opening it to reveal the powerseeds. I grab the bag and throw it over my shoulder as the entire ship rocks from a gigantic explosion.

The SRF is right on time, for better or worse.

"Gael, you set?" Eiran calls over the comms, stepping back into the darkened room and not noticing Kairo slip into the safe behind him.

"*I've got a path for you,*" she calls back. "*Assuming Emma's counter-security program works as intended. Sending the path to your units now.*"

"*Starting the explosions… now,*" Lirion confirms.

"Great," I say. "Excellent work. Now, you two get going. Meet us at the *Basix.*"

With our timeline shrinking, the four of us run back through the destroyed murder rooms to the elevators. Following the route Gael laid out, we do our best to navigate back to our ship—without being blown up. The little explosions are Lirion's calculated blasts, designed to block off corridors and separate us from the bulk of Corvane's men. The big explosions, though? That's the SRF—someone not exactly read into our plans.

An unpredictable elvish raid aside, I'm happy for all the chaos.

Between the Valen attacking from outside and Lirion keeping the ship busy from the inside, no one is in the halls we're hurrying down. A small boom echoes from a few floors below us, proving my point.

As we run toward Bay Gamma, a loud voice comes over the speakers. *"Commercial Vessel. This is the Stelrion Reikonhach Fulast of the Valen Republic. You are being detained on suspicion of violating intergalactic weapons trade regulations. Prepare to be boarded. Any person found impeding our investigation will be arrested. Our officers will use deadly force against anyone who attempts to harm our team."*

Lirion and Gael come running up to us, and Gael calls, "Kai! You alright?"

"Time to go, Doc!" Kairo calls as we near the doors to the hangar where Sylara waits for us. Explosions marking time as surely as a clock, the six of us quickly clamber up the gangway onto the ship.

"Stop!" calls a voice behind us. We turn to see Ryland Corvane, head bloodied, lumbering clumsily toward us, baring a large blaster rifle.

Just as Corvane raises the rifle, Lirion says, "Oh, wait. I forgot." With the tap of a button, the hangar door explodes, sending Ryland flying into a wall. A shaky hand emerges from beneath the rubble as the door closes.

"Kairo!" Gael gasps in shock.

He smirks. "I think I like Kai better."

I grin, not commenting that this is the first time he's ever let anyone but me call him Kai. "Sylara, let's get the hell out of here."

She gives me a small smile—a gods-damned smile!—and glamours the craft as we fly out of the hangar, passing two large Valen ships.

"Did you get the seeds?" Lirion asks, glancing at us.

I pat the bag, and then glance at Kairo, who looks, ever so briefly, at his own pack. It's our turn to share a knowing little smile. Suppressing a laugh, I turn to Eiran and reach up, pulling his face down to me. Kissing him on the cheek, I say, "Let's go home."

49

ONCE BITTEN, TWICE SPY

Taylor

"Where are we going this time?" I ask for about the tenth time. It's been a week since we've returned to Vale from Corvane's ship, and every day this week, Eiran's had some new adventure or experience he's been desperate to show me. We've also gone out every night, either by ourselves or with some mix of family and friends. And at night… well, let's just say I haven't slept much.

I've loved this week, even if Eiran's been like a man on a mission trying to show me all the great things on Vale. All the many reasons I should stay.

I haven't told him I've already decided.

"You are so untrusting," Eiran admonishes, stepping over a gnarled root. "You know that?"

I laugh incredulously, swatting at him as we trudge past yet more trees. "I'm a thief! Of course I am! Besides, are you really going to criticize *me* for being untrusting?"

Eiran chuckles, pushing a branch out of the way, sending a small shower of leaves fluttering into his emerald hair. "Fair point," he concedes.

He holds the branch for me, and I slide past him, the temptation to touch him like the pull of a magnet. "I mean… aren't we supposed to be meeting your aunt and uncle for lunch? If we're not back for this grilled corn dish that Maelara made special for me, she may actually murder us."

"We'll be back for lunch. I promise." Eiran grins, and those dimples do me in as always.

"Okay, so where are we going? Where's this 'great site' you had to show me? You said we were going for a walk, not a hike."

Eiran raises an eyebrow. "It's only been an hour."

"Exactly, Leaf Boy. An *hour*. Where are we going?"

The man has the audacity to shake his head in exasperation. "It's right up here," he insists, turning.

A few minutes later, he pushes past another set of trees, and we step into a beautiful clearing on the edge of a large lake. The water is smooth and clear, like fine Zeridian crystal. Starflowers line the lake's edge, their distinctive purple and yellow blooms blanketing the area. Intermixed among them, tall and white against the sea of purple, are lorathar blossoms.

Eiran notices them at the same time I do, his brilliant grin falling at the sight. "Taylor, I'm… I'm sorry. I—"

"It's beautiful, Eiran." I take his hands in mine, breathing in the scent of the fresh air and the quithra trees and yes—even the lorathar.

It's like Maelara said. You can't escape bad memories. You just replace them with good memories and good people.

"Thank you for bringing me here, Eiran. It's amazing." I try to inject every ounce of joy and gratitude I can into the words. Every ounce of sincerity I have, so he knows I mean it.

"You are what's amazing," Eiran says, squeezing my hands. "Taylor, you're the most incredible girl I've ever met. I could live a Zeridian's lifetime and never meet anyone like you. You infuriate me and exasperate me and—"

"Wow!" I laugh, cutting him off. "You really aren't great at this."

He groans. "Will you please shut up? I've practiced this for a week."

Something about those words makes the hairs on my neck prickle. My leg shakes in nervous anticipation.

Eiran runs a thumb along my hand, reassuring me. "You make me laugh. You make me see things in a new way. Brought light and truth into my life in a way I didn't think possible after Kaelen. You're beautiful and talented and sexy and kind. I don't know what your plans are. What you want to do. But I… Taylor, will you be my mate?"

My heart shatters and reforms, expands and wrenches at his words. Mate? Bound to him. Sworn to him. A mutual devotion.

"You… you would want that? With me?"

Eiran puts his hands on either side of my face, looking deeply into my eyes. "Yes, Taylor. A thousand times, yes. No matter where you want to go, I'm with you. I'll follow you to the end of the galaxy."

I hesitate. "What if… what if I wanted to stay here? In Silberwald, I mean. It's the first place… the first place that's ever felt like home."

Those dimples are like brilliant stars, blinding and beautiful. "I'd love that."

"Well then," I say, and the breathiness undermines my attempt at bravado. "What are you waiting for?"

I tilt my head, exposing my neck to him.

He stands there for a moment, taking me in. "Beautiful," he mutters in amazement.

"Come on, Leaf Boy. Or are you too scared to—"

Eiran lunges forward, toppling me to the ground. We roll amidst the grass and flowers, laughing slightly before his teeth claim my throat, his lips a greedy caress on my neck.

Despite the violence of the motion, the bite barely breaks the skin. The sweet pain of it sends tendrils of feeling down my stomach and lower. His lips are claiming, a brand. A tongue quickly replaces his teeth, swiping against the cuts and lapping up my blood. I wrap my legs around him, and his growl becomes a groan against my neck.

With a single arm under my ass, he adjusts the angle, his length pressing against my core as he feasts. Pain and pleasure continue to swim and swirl around each other, tension rising. I want to be a puddle, to trickle into the mountain lake and be one with the Silberwald.

I grasp him, wrapping my legs around him as I hold on. He continues to lap at my neck, his fingers sliding beneath my waistband to find my wetness. His fingers and tongue work in tandem as the tightness builds and builds in an impossible crescendo.

Finally, when I can't take it any longer, I break apart, crying out loud enough to send birds flying. With one final, luxurious swipe of his tongue, there's a slight tingling sensation, and the pain in my neck eases.

Eiran pulls away, panting as his eyes scour me. I continue to stare in awe at him as I place a hand on my neck. He stopped the bleeding, but the wound is still there, two curved ridges under my fingertips. His mark claiming me as his.

I reach for him, but he pulls back, offering his hand to pull me up. "As much as I'd love to stay here and do all manner of unaetheric things to you, Maelara will probably kill us if we miss lunch. So if you want to shower before we eat…"

I groan, but accept his help up, grinning like an idiot. "So… later then?"

His grin is feral, sending my blood racing. "Definitely. So you're staying?" I nod. "What are you going to do then?"

I consider him. "I'm not entirely sure. But I have an idea."

Eiran chuckles. "You have that 'I have a crazy plan' look in your eyes again."

I shrug coyly. "Maybe…"

He laughs loudly, kissing me on the forehead. "Great. You can tell me all about it on the way back."

***

Laughter and the delicious smell of burning meat waft through the open window, beckoning me to join the party outside. The warm caress of the early summer sun brushes my skin. It's another call to the outside, but I wait one more minute. Pen hovering over the page, I put the last touches on the poem that's taken me almost three months to write.

The words are still raw, but they're beautiful. Because they're me. And being seen is all I can really ask for.

Speaking of which, I stand and adjust my outfit in the mirror, as if anyone will care. The cut of the shorts is sure to drive Eiran insane, and the thin strap of the sleeveless top does nothing to hide the curved lines of his bite. His mark on me. I pull my hair back into a ponytail to further show it off.

There's a knock at the door. "Come in," I say, still looking at my mate-mark in the mirror. I trace a finger along it as Eiran enters, my eyes flicking to his in the reflection.

"Hey, the steaks are about…" He trails off and his eyes darken as he watches the path of that finger. "Having second thoughts?" he asks, and despite the confident dimple beginning to hollow in his cheek, I can see the honesty behind the question in those gorgeous amethyst eyes of his.

"Never." A tiny part of me still twists at the loss of that dream. But even the pang of not moving off-world is slight. Because if I have to pick, I'll pick here with him every time. In fact, I almost ask how long we have to date before it becomes seemly enough to tell people we're mates.

Eiran walks up behind me, putting his warm hands on my shoulders. "You know my aunt will freak out about this."

"I'm not ashamed of it," I say, reaching up to hold his hands. "I'll hide the mark around the rest of town if it'll avoid whispers or whatever, but not around your family."

"*Our* family," he corrects mildly. "And I don't care if anyone knows. I'm not ashamed either. Just be prepared for how Maelara will react."

"And how's that?" A bit of worry creeps into my gut, cutting through the warm glow. "Do you think she won't approve?"

Eiran traces a claw along my chin, making me shiver. "No, she adores you. She'll just say that I'm rushing into things as usual." The claw traces down from my ear to my throat, moving on to my neck before he pulls it gingerly away. "But she can say whatever she wants." He places a kiss below my ear. "I chose you, and…" He traces a line of kisses lower, down to the mark. "…I still choose you."

His teeth plunge into my neck again, barely breaking the skin this time, but I still let out a gasping moan. I wrap an arm around his back, working it under his button-down. I let my claws extend, tracing them lightly across the smooth curves of his back. He gasps before leaning down again, tracing that glorious tongue lazily along the line of my neck. I run my fingers through his hair as he sucks and licks and bites.

With two final languid passes, I feel the tickling at my neck as he reseals my wound. I trace my hand from his head to his cheek, getting lost again in those eyes. "I love you." I lean in and kiss him, opening myself to him as our tongues intertwine for a moment. Pulling away, I let my hand go back to his hair.

With a light tug, I pull his head to the side. A grin plays at the corner of his mouth again, and he yields his neck to me. I trace my own line of kisses along his firm jaw, flicking his ear with my tongue and pulling a chuckle from him. I nip at his neck once, twice, and he lets out tiny gasps. "If only I had fangs…"

His eyes smoldering, he says, "Lock the door."

"I thought you said Maelara would kill us if—"

"She can wait." The man has a point.

Slowly, my hands trembling slightly, I click the door to lock. A warm hand softly touches my shoulder, and I calm. The rightness of that touch centers me, and I exhale the last of my jitters. When I turn, his eyes, as dark and rich as the deepest wine, meet mine, anchoring me to the spot. With a shaky hand of his own, he reaches out and cups my cheek. "I love you."

I hurtle into him, and he leans to meet me, his mouth capturing mine. Reaching an arm under my ass, he lifts me up to him. I wrap my legs around his chest as he deepens the kiss, exploring as he carries me across the room. After a long moment, he pulls away, winking before throwing me onto the bed. I let out a gasp of a laugh as I bounce once, then settle.

The light sends glistening emerald highlights through his green hair as he stares down, his lips falling open in a tiny "oh."

My heart wrenches. How can he look at *me* with such… awe?

With infuriating slowness, he unbuttons each button of his shirt, exposing that immaculate chest, the quithra tree tattoo revealing like a gift.

I sit up, reaching to slide the shirt off his powerful arms, reveling in the smoothness and firmness of him. He lets the shirt fall before reaching down to grab the hem of mine, pulling it slowly over my head. He stares for a long moment, mouth slightly wide until, with a groan, he leans down, claiming my throat again as a hand grasps my breast, a thumb playing with the edge of my bra. I sigh, running a hand through his hair as the other grabs that incredible ass of his. With a small mental flick, I unclasp my bra with magic, letting it fall.

Eiran lets the bra slide the rest of the way off as he stares at me, appearing somehow in amazement. I don't understand how he can gaze at me with such rapture, but I will forever hold on to that memory, as it belongs only to me. He belongs only to me.

Leaning forward, Eiran claims a peak with his mouth, teasing the other with his fingers. Tiny sparks of electricity burst down to my core, and I slam my mouth shut before I moan too loudly. He worships me for a long moment, fingers keeping pace with the swirling flicks of his tongue.

Finally, he moves away, and I grumble a protest before my breath catches again as I realize the direction his mouth is heading. His kisses travel lower, down the curve of my stomach to the edge of my shorts. With slow care, he unbuttons them, sliding them down off me. I allow myself a satisfied smirk as his eyes widen in surprise.

"No panties?" he says as I open my legs, displaying all of myself to him. "Naughty girl."

"You have no idea," I smirk. His grin widens, those predatory teeth glinting with memory, with promise. I almost shiver as a tongue snakes briefly along them.

"I want to show you something, but it will mean using my magic on you. Is that okay?"

Normally, I'd at least consider the question if I didn't just say no instantly. But now? I flex my fingers in frustration. "Baby, you can do whatever you want. Just fucking do it." He chuckles, and then leans forward, tracing kisses along my inner thighs. As his tongue teases and licks and flicks and does other things I didn't think a tongue could do, I feel a new sensation building at my core, a glowing flame of electric heat.

It's Eiran's magic.

Before the initial shock can turn into fear, the sparking flame in my core ignites into an inferno, engulfing every inch of me in blazing pleasure. Suddenly, the sensitivity of every nerve ending is heightened to a thousand percent. Every trailing touch is charged as a finger joins pace with his magic and his glorious tongue. "Oh, gods," I gasp, and he clasps a hand on my mouth before I can scream. I shatter once, twice at his ministrations before he leans back.

I stare up at him bleary-eyed and mumble, "Are you trying to kill me?"

"I love the taste of you."

He wipes the back of a hand slowly, obscenely across his face before his fingers lower to his pants. Wrung out and exhausted, I watch in lazy fascination as he removes his slacks. The bulge there sends my heart into my throat. He lowers his pants, revealing his hardness, the roots of the tree tattoo reaching down to mid-thigh like a frame. I gasp, amazed yet again at him.

He crawls forward, halting to plant a light kiss on my lips before continuing his trek upward. Finally, I can feel him against my entrance, and I whimper as he slides home. And that's what this is with him. It's home.

Soon, we find a rhythm, our bodies moving as one. "I love you," I moan softly.

"And I you," he murmurs in a raspy pant. "Always. Forever."

My claws sink into his skin as I near my peak, and he growls, pounding harder and harder. The world ceases to exist, and all that remains is the bond between us stretching across the vastness of the universe.

Leaning down, he bites my neck again, a glorious, painful pleasure, and the two of us find our release together. The world comes apart, tiny pieces of me breaking and reforming as peace settles on us both.

With another languid lap of his tongue, my neck heals. Concentrating, I run fingers along the slight cuts my claws left. I feel the skin knit together, but I'm not sure I did it right. "Those might scar."

He shrugs. "Nail marks on my back? I'll take them." I laugh as he climbs off me, plopping down beside me, pulling my head onto his shoulder.

"Can we just stay? Do more of that? Who needs grilled corn anyway?" I unabashedly eye his gorgeous naked form next to me, marveling at the lines and curves, and excited to explore and re-explore every one. And I have time. All the time in the world.

"I wish," Eiran replies with a rakish grin, patting me on the thigh. "But everyone's waiting for us, so they'll probably come knocking if we don't hurry."

Five hurried minutes of cleanup later, we wander our way down to the rest of the group. I may have "just fucked" hair, but honestly, I don't care.

"About time," Kairo mutters, handing me a plate. "What took you two so long?"

"Oh, Kairo, if you have to ask that, I'm going to worry about you, dear boy," Maelara says, and I have to choke down a laugh. I can tell my cheeks are flaming as she turns. She smiles, but then her eyes fall to my neck and where the now even brighter mark lies exposed. "Taylor Grey, what is that on your neck?"

"Umm…."

"What the hell is that?!" Kairo exclaims.

"Holy shit," Lirion chuckles. "He actually did it."

"Did someone bite you?" From his tone, it sounds like Kairo can't decide if he's baffled or upset.

"He did," Gael says, pointing to Eiran while fighting a laugh at Kairo's expression.

Lirion rambles, "I can't say I'm entirely surprised, but… do you know what that…" I nod, blushing. "Well. Um… congrats, I guess."

"Congrats on what?" Kairo asks, still sounding thoroughly confused.

"They're mated," Gael explains.

"What?!" he shouts. "You're mated? Like, married?"

I laugh. "We're not married."

"You are," Maelara corrects firmly.

"Aunt Mae," Eiran says. "Don't you start—"

"It's not a complaint. It's about time, actually." We both gape at her, but she shrugs. "What? As soon as you brought the girl home, I knew she was special. We didn't actually take bets on how long it would take—"

"But we should have," Lirion finishes.

"Am I the only one surprised by this?" Kairo asks.

"Yes, dear," Maelara confirms, patting him on the shoulder.

Kairo shakes his head in wonder, like we're both insane. Eiran and I share a knowing grin. Is it madness? Sure. Do we care? Not in the slightest.

"Are you disappointed?" I ask, biting my lip. Kairo raised me to be independent. And getting mated… married… whatever at twenty-two to someone you met just months ago is impulsive to say the least.

"I'm not saying I'm not happy about it," Kairo says quickly. "I am. Leaf Boy's alright, and you two are lucky to have found each other. It's just… Taylor, I thought you were going to leave." My stomach plummets at the question. "Don't get me wrong. I don't *want* you to go anywhere. But I decided some time ago that if you want to leave Vale, I would support you. Of course, now you're mated to this guy. How is that going to work?"

Everyone stares warily at Eiran, but his eyes are only for me. He grins widely. "I don't have a job. I'll go wherever she does." His eyes sparkle with such love, and I know he means it. Something lifts in me, and for one last moment, I picture us moving together, traveling, and settling far from Vale. From Kairo. From Silberwald and this new family that has accepted me—

"I'm not going anywhere," I say to him, and his eyebrows raise. A challenge. Letting me pitch it. "In fact, we have a suggestion."

"What's that?" Kairo asks dubiously.

"Okay, look. Eiran doesn't have a job, like he said. And he doesn't want his old one back either, right?"

"Not in the slightest," Eiran says. "Not that they would give it to me." I don't comment on that bit. I know he still has questions. Questions about his brother, about the SRF, and about what's going on. But he's right. They're not offering his job back. We'll hope a lead arises to help us find out more outside the system. But then, working outside this system is exactly what my idea is all about.

"And Gael," I say, turning to her. "You don't seem to teach much."

"I'm more of a researcher," she admits.

"Is the pay good?" I ask.

"It's shit."

"What's this about?" Wynn asks, appearing confused but excited.

I glance around the deck, wondering if they're all going to say I'm crazy. "What if we formed a guild? A thief's guild. Here. Kairo still has the bookstore. He can make connections. We'll do the jobs."

"I don't want my nephew being a thief," Maelara says, and Roderic grunts in agreement.

Eiran grins in victory, and I roll my eyes before motioning with my hand. Offering him the floor.

"Well, Taylor and I disagree on the terminology a bit. She calls it a thief. To me, it's… independent intelligence. Taylor's idea is—"

"It's more like… item recovery," I cut in, and he sticks his tongue out at me.

Really mature.

I stick mine out in return.

"Call us thieves. Call us spies… hell, call us whatever you want. The point is: people have items they need returned. Items that would be difficult to recover through… normal channels. Good people with stuff in the hands of bad people. They pay us a fee, and we get the item back for them."

"Like the Eldralume Relic," Gael says, a grin breaking across her face.

"Exactly," I nod.

She shrugs. "Well then, I'm in."

Eiran frowns. "My only concern at this stage is the money. We'll need significant capital to start and operate. I'm not convinced we have enough, even with what you've saved up."

My stomach twists at this. I left this bit out earlier. I glance at Kairo, and he nods, telling me it's okay to offer it. "Well… Kairo and I just made quite a bit of money."

"What?" Eiran asks, shocked.

"The books in the vault," Kairo explains with a broad smile. "I mean, it's not like Corvane needed them."

Eiran gawks at me, somewhere between exasperated and amused. I pat his cheek. "If you're stealing from someone like Corvane, is it really even stealing?"

"I'll drink to that!" Lirion says, taking a big swig of anthalas before reaching for the grill. "Now that's settled, can we eat?"

Eiran grins at me, showing off that impressive row of teeth. "You're a bad influence."

"Always," I say.

He leans over and whispers into my hair, "Let's get through this party, and then I can punish you for being such a bad girl." He nips my earlobe, and I squeak.

I glance around nervously, but everyone is focused on getting supper—or at least pretending to be. I still marvel that I'm here. I once dreamed of other worlds, but now I dream of this. Of bonfires and bickering and warm nights full of laughter.

Sighing, I lean into the man that showed me I could find a whole new world right where I am. "You know what?"

He smiles. "What?"

"It's nice to be home."

AFTER

THE PRISON AGAIN

Akio

I walk along the barren steel hall beside the Grand Operative, the subtle whisperings and sinister chuckling a fitting backdrop for my mood. This meeting could go either way. Everything hinges on the Grand Operative's verdict. On this contract. It is Yamiyo's will.

I've declared it so.

"The girl?" the Grand Operative asks as we near the lab.

"Alive. Staying on Vale, from the looks of it."

"And Corvane?"

I can't help but chuckle. "Arrested. Whatever evidence they planted on him must have been convincing, because my spies tell me he won't be getting out ever again."

"Excellent." And excellent for me as well. The Consortium is already moving to take over his business. Hikario always sheds his light on the right path—for those strong enough to walk it.

Choosing my words carefully, I ask, "And what did you want done with—"

"He's exactly where I need him. For now." The tone allows for no further discussion. The Grand Operative sighs. "Well done, Kuro Oni. We'll need the Consortium again soon."

Something loosens in my chest. I am rarely intimidated by anyone, but this man? Even with my resources, it would be difficult—likely impossible—to stop him if he were to turn on us. Not that I would admit that to my followers. "What would you like done with Helix? Blackstone's death and Kane's arrest have crippled them and left them in disarray, but several of the leaders are still in play. We have their locations with operatives in-system. I could deploy my assassins and have them destroyed within the week."

The Grand Operative considers and then shakes his head. "No. We still have use for them. Leave them be for now."

"Very well," I shrug.

"The rumors?"

"Going well. People are scared and distrustful. The VerdantBoost disaster moved the efforts along nicely. I think we are about ready. Speaking of which… what about the doctor? I recovered him for you."

Though I smile, I grimace internally. The doctor was key to this contract's success. If I'd failed to bring him, the compact would have fallen apart. Though I fear without him in my possession, all Yamiyo's plans—of my plans—will be for naught.

Balance must be restored. Gifts unworthily taken must be recovered.

Arriving at the lab, we both gaze at the transparent cage in the corner. Helix's Valen doctor is hunched over, white lab coat in tatters, long-dried blood littering the wrists. A garish wound is still visible on his leg from where the infected sage hare bit it. The gashes are badly healed, with tendrils of black snaking away from them. The dark lines shimmer with a faint orange glow, the scorched color of dying embers.

The doctor hears our entrance and lurches toward us, his jagged claws scraping noisily along the glass. Gray spittle drips from his bared teeth as he growls at us, slamming against the surface again and again.

"He's progressing nicely," the Grand Operative says. "I want regular updates. But you're right. Everything is in place. Phase Two can begin soon."

9 798218 827151